Walt's Last Year

F.T. Vanliew

Author: F.T. Vanliew
Editor: Julia Van Liew
Cover design: Paul Tarbox

Contact: ftvanliew@gmail.com

Library of Congress Control Number: 2020905573

ISBN, print: 9798627165028

Printed in the United States of America

DEDICATION

To my mother and the mothers of families.

CONTENTS

This is what you shall do. Love the earth and sun and the animals, despise riches, give alms to everyone that asks, stand up for the stupid and crazy, devote your income and labor to others, hate tyrants, argue not concerning God, have patience and indulgence toward the people, take off your hat to nothing known or unknown or to any man or number of men, go freely with powerful uneducated persons and with the young and with the mothers of families, read these leaves in the open air every season of every year of your life, re-examine all you have been told at school or church or in any book, dismiss whatever insults your own soul, and your very flesh shall be a great poem and have the richest fluency not only in its words but in the silent lines of its lips and face and between the lashes of your eyes and in every motion and joint of your body.

- Excerpt from the Preface of the1855 Edition of *Leaves of Grass*

THE AGREEMENT

March 26, 1892

328 Mickle Street
Camden, NJ

Entry from the journal of Horace Traubel:

It was after this that I came in, at 6:07. Hearing the front door open, Harned came from W.'s room and met me in the hallway. "Walt is dying," he said, "it is nearly over." It struck my heart, yet it was the hourly fear at last fulfilled. I hastened into the room and up to the bed. His face was looking toward the windows and his eyes were closed. Dr. McAlister sat at the head of the bed—Warrie and Mrs. Davis were on the other side—Tom strolled in at the foot. McAlister accosted me in quite positive tones, which seemed for an instant to arrest W., whose eyes fluttered open as he struggled to get his right hand out from under the bedclothing, as if to grasp my own (as so often in days gone)—but the effort died of its own weight and the eyes closed wearily. Once, he moaned. McAlister remarked, "This will not last long, unless he rallies—and he can hardly do that." I took W.'s right hand and from this moment to the end held it, as if it was my last touch of his life. He breathed on, more lightly, more quickly—the mouth open, now and then twitching—his color all gone and death's white upon him. Again the Doctor said, "See, it grows fainter." And Warrie leaning forward, ears and eyes intent (as ours, too), exclaimed, "Did you see—he skipped a breath or two," as indeed was the case. This phenomenon growing more marked and the breath becoming very irregular—the mouth working again and several times the brows contracting as if from the difficulty of breathing. "What we expected in December is happening now?" "Yes." I asked, "And still there's no hope?" "None—he will go." "And rapidly?" "Very soon."

At 6:25 he emitted a marked "Oh!" and seemed to stop breathing.

Then . . .

Walt. It's Emerson.
Who?
Emerson. Ralph Emerson.
Oh!
Walt, I'm sorry about your situation. It appears you won't make it through the night. Few are ready when the time comes. Their hearts too heavy. I suspect yours is as well.
Emerson, it's been years. Why are you here?
Old fellow, we've been talking it over. We want you to have more time.
I'm miserable. Why would I want more time?
We can take away your pain.
I'm curious.
You'll learn soon after you pass that there are no new experiences. What is new comes from those recently deceased. We rely on them to keep us interested.
What do you want from me?
We can give you one more year, provided it's in the 21st century. We're concerned with what's happening to America and believe you can give us a detailed accounting. If you agree, you'll have twelve months of good health. And food will taste good again.
What must I do in return?
A year from now you'll share with us what you've learned. In the meantime, you'll need to take good notes.
That's all?
It's a lot Walt. Things have changed. Well beyond your imagination. It will be overwhelming at first. But we think you'll adjust.
How will I get by?
You'll be provided comfortable accommodations and a modest income. Friends of ours will keep an eye on you. Your first contact will be Thomas. We think you'll like him.
What if I say no?
Then you'll be with us in a few minutes.
You drive a hard bargain Emerson. When do I start?
When you wake, it will be March 27th, in the year 2019. You will spend two days in Camden then meet Thomas.
Will I see you again?
I'll visit from time to time, as will others.
I'm a bit apprehensive.
You'll be fine, Walt. By the way, no one in the future will recognize

you.   You'll be just another old man.   One last thing, you'll need to change   your   name.

FIRST MONTH

March 27, 2019

It was a long night. I never woke. I don't believe I ever moved, though I dreamt throughout. When I first opened my eyes, I was leaning against the front door of my house, a satchel at my side and an envelope in my hand, a letter from Emerson inside:

Dear Walt,

I apologize for the brevity of last night's conversation. There wasn't much time. The window of opportunity for transport on any given day is brief. In the bag are a few essentials—a comb, a brush for your teeth, a piece of soap. Most important is a pocketbook with modern currency. You will appreciate the five-dollar bills with the portrait of President Lincoln. The money will have to suffice until you meet Thomas. There is also a map of present-day Camden, a receipt for lodging at the City Hotel where you will stay the next two nights, and a notebook with pencils. Finally, there is a small time piece that you should strap to your wrist. Remember, I will check on you from time to time.
Best wishes,
R.W.E.

The contents of the satchel were as Emerson described. After completing the inventory, I gathered my feet. It was easier than expected. No pain in my hips or chest. I breathed easily and felt younger. Leaning over the railing, I saw my reflection in the window. I was still Walt Whitman, but my hair and beard had been trimmed. My shirt, trousers, and shoes were new. In a corner of the window was a small sign, identifying the dwelling as the "Walt Whitman House"—hours 10 AM - 12 noon and 1 PM - 4 PM. It was just past noon on my timepiece. A gentleman approached, slight in stature and holding a bottle of beer. Introducing himself as Billy, he asked if I'd read Walt Whitman. I told him I had. He wondered if there might be Whitman books in the local library. I replied that I hoped so. He said he's also a poet, having published "From Prison to Poetry—My Story in Verse." I inquired of his family. His wife of thirty-eight years passed not long ago, survived by their two children. His son lives a short distance away. His daughter is across the street in the County Jail, serving time for a petty offense. A second man approached and unlocked the door. He said admission is by appointment only but, if I liked, I could join a small tour at three. In the meantime, I might want to walk north to the college campus where I would find a statue of Whitman. Setting off, I drew alongside two young women and inquired if they might direct me to the Whitman statue. Neither knew of it but suggested I follow them to a statue they pass nearly every day. Perhaps it's the one I'm in search of. A short distance further and there I was, life-size and cast in bronze.

March 28

I spent the morning acquainting myself with my surroundings. With directions from a bunk mate, I made my way to the "Men's" room where chamber pots have been replaced by "toilets." I know something of them. On his visit to Camden, Oscar Wilde told me of their growing use in England. He was certain they'd make their way to America. I'm not sure when they arrived, but they're a significant improvement over pots. After finishing my business, including a body cleansing under streaming hot water, I dressed and made my way to the lobby and the front entrance. For the next few hours I wandered about, in search of what Camden had been just two days before. There was little to be found of it. The homes of my neighbors no longer exist. The Mickle Street of my last years was quiet and tree-lined. A well-maintained roadway frequented by strollers and horse drawn carriages. The dirt is gone now, replaced by hard pavement. The width of the traveled portion is three times its original. Four-wheeled machines whiz by, their operators intent on getting somewhere in a hurry. Signs now advertise "Dr. Martin Luther King Blvd." I had misgivings about the bargain I struck with Emerson. Better to be dead, perhaps, than inhabit this strange land. But my mood lightened thanks to the kindness of strangers. A police officer asked if I needed assistance. A woman directing traffic halted a vehicle so I could pass. A young black man gave me directions. A Persian man served me at "the best coffee house in Camden." The guide at the Whitman House shared his knowledge and love for the "Good Gray Poet."

March 29

Another long night. But much different than my deathbed journey. Throughout, there was a persistent whisper, akin to the howl of wind in distance trees. Soothing in the way of a rocking cradle. It carried me

along to wherever it is I am now. I woke to daylight. The window
covering was drawn, but I could see a table next to my bed. Hanging
from a chair was the satchel given me by Emerson. There was a note on
the table.

Dear Mr. Whitman,
Welcome. Regretfully, I'm not able to greet you in person. I had every
intention to do so, but I was called away on business and won't return
until late tomorrow. Nevertheless, it is an honor to have you as my
guest. My home is yours to use freely. I imagine you slept late. Travel
can be difficult, particularly in the manner and mode that brought you
here. I hope you enjoy the quiet time of the next two days. By way of
direction, you are in a guest bedroom on the lowest level of the house.
Outside your room, and to the left, is a bathroom with toilet, sink, and
shower. I trust you will find everything you need. The stairway to the
right of your room leads to the main level, including the kitchen. There
are appliances you will not recognize. I had hoped to acquaint you with
each and will do so when we meet. However, explore to the extent you
are comfortable. Of primary interest may be the refrigerator, or what
you likely call the "icebox." It's stocked with milk, cheese, eggs and
produce. There is more to share, but perhaps it's best to wait until we
meet. We've found over time that travelers such as you require an
incremental orientation.
Yours truly,
Thomas

Thomas appears to be an agreeable fellow. Following his directions, I
made good use of the bathroom before exploring the kitchen. I'm certain
the refrigerator will become my favorite appliance.

March 30
I spent the day in front of the fire, I'd nearly forgotten such quiet.
Mickle Street, business matters, the burdensome correspondence and
stream of visitors, Horace stopping by nearly every day, most days more
than once. Near the end—Mrs. Davis, Warrie, McAlister, Harned. All
well-intentioned. Each essential in some respects. But all that busyness,
curiosity, attentiveness—it takes something from a man. What fed my
soul in the beginning could not compete with the crowd. I see how
necessary those early years were. The freedom of travel and beholding
to no one. Seeds planted in the rich soil of anonymity. Perhaps death
and its accompanying silence is the great gift. Emerson stopped by in the
night. "Just passing through," he said. He was curious as to my

adjustment. Emerson resides in a rarefied air. Always has. As a young man, I found him to be kindhearted and sincere, but too proper for my tastes. I regret how I sometimes treated him. Perhaps someday I'll tell him so. He sensed my melancholy and offered encouragement, reminding me that few are given notice of their final year. He cautioned me to be judicious in my disclosure of intimate thoughts with others. What I take note of is not to be shared with strangers. What I observe, experience, and reflect on is for those who have passed over. I need to be about the task of choosing a new name. Emerson's given me permission to retain "Walt" if I like, but not Whitman. Perhaps I'll take after my brother and go by Walt George or follow mother and become a Van Velsor. How often do we have the opportunity to choose a name of our own liking?

March 31
I woke to the familiar. The smell of eggs frying in bacon fat over a flame. It must be Thomas. I started the day with only minor aches to remind me of my age, unlike the past year, when no position could be tolerated for long. I appreciated my friends' willingness to turn me from side to side but did not thank them enough. I hope they know how much I loved them. Taking the steps up, I was ready to make a new acquaintance. Deep in thought, Thomas was bent over an iron skillet, turning the bacon and adjusting the eggs. He sensed my presence and smiled. Any trepidation I had was gone. His arms opened wide and he grabbed my shoulders, pulling me in. I don't know what Emerson told him, but I felt accepted. Thomas encouraged me to take a seat, serving me as if I was a favored guest at a fine restaurant. We commenced to get acquainted. He's much like Horace, though twice his age. Attentive, deferential, quick-witted. A newspaper man for many years, he saw the best and worst of what life doles out, taking it in with an abundance of curiosity. He recognizes that each of us is dealt cards only to be played once. Like Mr. Twain, he would have been at home on a Mississippi riverboat, most likely a dealer of blackjack or poker. His keen eye would have spotted a cheat in a second, while his good nature would offer condolences to a man down on his luck. Today will be a "stay at home day," Thomas said after breakfast. "There are chores to be done." He then inquired of my ability and interest in helping out. I welcomed the opportunity to be active and told him so, adding that I always enjoyed working with my hands before the infirmities set in. He gently probed as to what my limitations. I offered that Emerson had remedied most. What remained was nothing out of the ordinary for a man my age. An ache in my shoulder, a toe that throbbed at times, knees that have seen

better days. Nothing that would prevent me from doing my share. He excused himself, returning shortly with a bottle. "Aspirin," he said. "Two of these may help. They're not a cure-all, but they should take the edge off." I thanked him and fifteen minutes into sweeping the kitchen I was moving about easily. Next were the dishes, piled up in a deep basin over which hovered a faucet dispensing water controlled by a lever. Thomas explained that, depending on positioning, the water could be hot, cold, or somewhere in-between. He placed a stopper in the sink, adding "dish soap" which quickly produced the most delightful bubbles. Handing me a washcloth, he gave me permission to do as I liked. It was pleasurable - tending to each plate, cup, bowl, utensil, pot and pan. Washing, rinsing, and drying them, and discovering their proper home. The kitchen work completed, Thomas gave me a coat, cap, and gloves. It being a sunny day, he suggested we work in the yard. Over dinner, Thomas explained that there are matters to be dealt with in the coming weeks - a physician's exam, shopping for proper clothes and personal items, acquiring identification papers so I might move about legally and without threat of exposure.

April 1
Another day of firsts. I rode with Thomas in his four-wheeled machine; what he calls an "automobile" or "car." My excitement was tempered by dread. Unreasonable as my fears might have been, something could go wrong. I trusted Thomas, but with so many on the road how could collisions not occur? I expressed my concerns and he took them seriously, assuring me that though accidents happen, in all his years he'd never been a party to one. We headed out, Thomas behind the wheel, me holding on as tight as possible. It wasn't long before I loosened up. I could see that Thomas is adept at motoring, paying heed to the many signs and signals, all the while checking his place on the road in relation to others. The car is certainly an efficient means of getting from one point to another. The windows down, it was as delightful as skimming Long Island Sound at the helm of my boyhood skiff.

April 2
I'd been waiting for the right moment, for a time when Thomas and I had nothing to do and nowhere to go. Over lunch the time presented itself. Thomas had previously shared some details of his life, but they didn't answer the questions - who was he; where did he come from; how does he know Emerson? I blurted them out as they'd been perched on the tip of my tongue, ready to spring forward when impulse met opportunity. Thomas was imperturbable, replying that he wondered when I would get

around to it. As a toddler, he nearly drowned in the bath. Face down, in a few inches of water, he was snatched up. In an instant, he was on the lap of someone reminiscent of his great-grandfather. There were others. Advanced in age as well. He can't recall all the details, but he understood most of what was said. There seemed to be a debate going on. Whether to take him in or send him back. There were good arguments in favor of each. If he stayed, he would have an eternity without pain, but his destiny would be denied. There the argument turned. They knew that Thomas' soul guide, before he was ever conceived, had chosen for Thomas a life in which he would also be a guide. He wasn't destined to be a scientist, a scholar, or a great leader. He would not be a renowned artist or athlete. Instead, he would assist others returned by the Wise Ones. To deny him the opportunity to fulfill his destiny was a fate worse than death. The vote was unanimous. As quickly as he left, he returned, retrieved from the waters by his eldest sister. For years he served as an apprentice - observing, reflecting, gaining in wisdom and understanding. But he wasn't ready. The last hurdle was the greatest - to learn compassion. He must come to know, with his third eye, that all is in balance, as it had been from the very beginning. At his late age, Thomas says he's still learning. But the Wise Ones trust him now. He's been given the task to guide me through my last year.

April 3

Thomas left early this morning, leaving a note of apology with a promise to be home for dinner. There was also a list of suggestions as to how I might pass the time, and a package.

Dear Walt,
Enclosed is a gift I thought you might appreciate. Open at your leisure.
Thomas

I unwrapped it immediately. To my delight, I was greeted with the 2016 edition of the *Merriam-Webster Dictionary*. In my time, *Webster* was an essential resource. I always carried the most recent. Noah Webster was a frequent and faithful companion. Without him and his life's work, my work would not have been possible. Words have been more than the tools of my trade. They've been a lifeblood, carriers of history and culture, communicators of the past and present. It was never my task to invent new words, but to position those in existence in such a way that a new language might be born. I came into the world to do that. I appreciated Thomas' suggestions for the day, but there was only one thing to do to pass the time. After a breakfast of eggs, bacon, and toasted bread - I've mastered the electric toaster - I sat close to the fire, coffee in hand and Mr. Webster on my lap. Starting with the As, I sounded each word and syllable, noting its origin, recognizing or not the present form and usage, imagining how I might put to use the most recent creations. I held with reverence the forward march of the English-speaking world.

April 4

I walked alone to the market, Thomas sending me with directions, a list, a bag, and sufficient money. Taking my time, I wandered the neighborhood, admiring houses large and small. Nearly every dwelling had a car parked on the street in front. Spring has arrived. The grass is green and lush. The trees full with buds or young leaves. Flowers lift their faces to bask in the sun. Perhaps the muse will return, and I'll sing again of wonder. The market offered its own bounty. Fruits and vegetables as fresh as any harvested the day before. Nuts and grains, domestic and exotic. Products canned, boxed, and bottled—some from as far away as China, Thailand, and Chile. Coffee, tea, sugar and flour, milk, butter, cheeses, fish and meats, bottled drinks of juice and flavored water. I found nothing lacking. The people of this time are blessed. Placing my selections on a counter, a young woman identified the price of each item, recording its cost by pushing squares on a pane of glass. Somehow, the individual numbers were added up and she announced what I owed. I counted the bills, handing them to her. In return I received a few dollars and some coins, as well as a piece of paper memorializing the transaction. I left the market, loaded like a pack animal on the Silk Road. The return home was a slow one, but I was in no hurry. There is so much to see.

April 5

Thomas invited a friend over for lunch. A lawyer considering a run for public office. He wants to be the county prosecutor and has ideas he thinks will turn things around. We sat at the kitchen table to bowls of beef and vegetable soup that Thomas spent the morning preparing. After small talk, Matt started in. He doesn't like how the current prosecutor and his staff handle cases. He says they don't consider the circumstances of those brought to their attention. Most are considered criminals with little promise of contributing to society. Most are poor, black, or immigrants. Matt wants to reverse the trend and says he'd do things differently. He'd find out what was going on in a person's life when the crime was committed. Whether or not they were drunk or using drugs, had a job or not; how far they advanced in school; what it was like for them as a child. He's convinced the only way to decrease crime is to make life better for the accused. Times haven't changed much. Walking the streets of Brooklyn and Manhattan as a young journalist, I witnessed the poor and colored mistreated by the police. I sat in courtrooms, observing the administration of justice. How the "haves" were rarely punished and the "have-nots" were punished regularly. I wrote in the *Brooklyn Eagle* about the disparity, hoping the average man and woman would take notice of the system's treatment of their brothers and sisters. Some stood up and called for reform. But their voices were too few to rally the many. The politicians fed the fear of those who elected them, proclaiming that the law-abiding would be safe only if the trash was swept away. I had hoped that this age would be more enlightened. It appears it's not. Thomas must travel to Maine and asked if I'd accompany him. We leave tonight.

April 6
I'm growing accustomed to the nighttime travel. Falling asleep at the usual hour and then at some point I'm on my way. I don't know how long it takes; whether the time in transit is dependent on the passage of years, the distance to the destination, or both. I dream and then I'm awake. This morning I was in a bed, in the house of friends of Thomas. They're on a trip and asked Thomas to watch over things in their absence. After breakfast we walked. I was reminded of the Long Island of my early years. Buildings dating to the time of my parents and grandparents, and earlier. Narrow houses with wood siding, nearly all painted white. Small grass patches in front. Porches ideal for a summer evening. It felt good to stretch my legs and take in the seaside breeze. We passed a church with a stream of visitors entering. "There must be a funeral," I thought. But a notice said a conversation about race would begin at ten. We decided to listen in. I learned some things. That black people are no longer called black, or negro. They are African Americans. A name I need to practice and get accustomed to. That slavery is still prohibited but continues to exist in subtle ways. That white people struggle with talking about race and the privileges that come with the color. That women are more sensitive to prejudice than men. Having considered myself the poet of slaves, having witnessed their sale and harbored the fugitive, I wanted to speak but restrained myself.

April 7

Thomas left me to my curiosity to wander about Portland. It took little time to see that the young are attracted to this port city. They were out in large numbers, walking Congress and Commercial Streets and the narrower streets between. This is a city of tolerance. Women walk hand in hand with women. Men with men. Whites and African Americans, too. My great desire was that this land someday embrace Democracy in its largest sense. The War shattered that hope. I didn't think I'd ever see the day the races could share affection in public spaces. Or that lovers of the same sex would walk about, proud and unafraid. My private life was so often the subject of rumor, but I dared not speak outside the bounds of my verse about intimate feelings. I wonder if Portland is unique among the cities. Will I find such openness elsewhere? How did it happen? What were the struggles along the way? Were there casualties? Were bodies piled high during a great war for equality? Portland isn't perfect. There are homeless, sitting in the sun barely off the walkways. A few have lost their minds, shouting to no one in particular the rants of their inner demons. I stopped for a while in front of a church on the corner of Cumberland and Chapel. Adjacent the small white structure, a crowd had gathered. Fifty or more, with boxes and bags to be filled with produce from an unknown source. It was a peaceable gathering. No pushing or jostling. Most appeared to have arrived in the recent past from a Latin country or the dark continent.

April 8

I'd been hearing about it but hadn't a clue as to its meaning. "March Madness." I thought it might be a disease. Cyclical in nature, like influenza in October and November. My mother told me stories of the winters of 1825 and 1826 when so many died. I mentioned my theory to Thomas. He chuckled. "March Madness is a kind of disease," he said, "afflicting young and old, mostly men, but not exclusively." Then he educated me about basketball, a sport played with a ball roughly 30" in circumference. Scoring happens when someone on one of two teams shoots the ball into a basket. It can be played outside, but mostly in a gymnasium. There is a floor, or court, with a basket at each end. Each team is assigned one of the baskets. A memory was jarred. It might have been Horace who told me about a similar game, newly invented less than a year ago - in 1891. I've always been fond of games. Horace knew that. One afternoon in late January, Horace mentioned an article he'd read about a teacher in Massachusetts struggling to deal with a rowdy class. The students had a case of cabin fever. Routine exercise insufficient to assuage their edginess. The teacher mounted a peach basket at each end of the gymnasium, dividing the boys into teams of nine. They weren't allowed to run with the ball, only pass it to a teammate close enough to attempt a shot. Thomas chuckled again. "The teacher was James Naismith," he said, "the inventor of basketball." Thomas said basketball is played all over the world. A regulation game has five players on a side but oftentimes there are "pickup games"—one against one, or two against two. Adults play too. A few make a very good income doing so. "March Madness," Thomas said, is a tournament held every year in which college teams, men and women, play to see which is the best in the country. The final two women's teams played each other last night. Baylor University got the best of Notre Dame. Tonight, the University of Virginia men are favored to beat a team from Texas called the Red Raiders. Thomas said he always cheers for the underdog.

April 9

I've been anxious to visit a library. When I was still able to get about, I'd take the ferry to Philadelphia on a sunny day, crossing the Delaware to spend hours at the library Ben Franklin and his friends started a century before I was born. It was a treasure - novels, poetry, plays, history, travel, science. There were evenings when they had to kick me out. I would have rented an overnight cot if one had been available. I woke this morning wondering how libraries have changed. They must be modern in the way so many other things are. As repositories of human knowledge and progress, they must tell the story of how far we've come. I asked Thomas if there might be one nearby. He said there is, apologizing for not thinking of it himself. Unfortunately, he had commitments most of the day, promising to take me soon. He asked if, in the meantime, I'd like to see his collection. He took me into his office, a small room in the far corner of the house. There was a chair, a desk with teapot and cup, a map of the ancient world hung on one wall and a print of a pastoral scene on another. On the opposite walls were shelves lined with books from floor to ceiling. Like the Franklin Library of my day, there were plays, poetry, history, and science. But most titles were unfamiliar, as were most authors. But interspersed, there were the great books - the Bible, the Iliad and the Odyssey, the Bhagavad Gita, the Divine Comedy, Paradise Lost. And the great writers and poets - Plato, Ovid, Shakespeare, Yeats, Blake, Byron, Austen, and Shelley. Even Irving, Thoreau, Emerson, and Poe. I told Thomas I was in no hurry to visit a library elsewhere.

April 10

All day I sat, a single book occupying my time. The *Road Atlas*. I've always loved maps. As a boy in Brooklyn, no longer attending school but visiting the museums on Saturdays, maps always captured my attention. They were windows to the world, before history and literature and everything else. I would travel the trade routes by ship and by caravan. Meander the streets of the great cities, navigate the great rivers, climb mountains, and cross deserts. Looking back, it must have been the maps that planted the seed of wanderlust. The open road has always been my companion. And now I find that innumerable roads crisscross the land. As often as I envisioned the future, I never imagined the network of highways that page after page of the atlas depicted. Each one a tentacle of commerce. And there are new states as well. Although I'm less surprised by this - there has always been the expansion west. In my last years, North and South Dakota, Montana, Washington, Idaho, and Wyoming were added. Now I find that Utah was admitted soon after, with Oklahoma early in the new century and New Mexico and Arizona in 1912. Had I been alive then, I would have thought that was the end of it. The continent was complete, from ocean to ocean, with Canada to the north and Mexico the south. Every square mile defined by statehood. How could I have known there would be an Alaska and Hawaii nearly fifty years later? That far up the Pacific coast, long after the states give way to Canada, there would be a new state, an appendage, that would dwarf half the states below and nearly touch Russia? Or that far to the west, rising up from the depths of the ocean, there are islands whose inhabitants would become our brothers and sisters?

April 11

Thomas said it was time I decide on a name. A friend would be coming to the house to prepare "papers" that would allow me access to public transportation, events and, eventually, to make purchases without the use of currency. Thus, the need for a new name to wear for the remainder of my time. I'd already decided to hold onto "Walt," but I struggled with an alternate surname. The Whitmans go way back. Thomas handed me a pen and pad of paper and we started in. Walt Grayman. Walt Whiteman. Walt Camden. Walt Washington. Walt Franklin. Walt Jefferson. Walt Lincoln. I nearly settled on Lincoln, my hero. Then I thought of my mother. I was always fond of her family name, Van Velsor, and its heritage going back to the Dutch of the Old World. While my passion comes from the Whitmans, my steadiness is derived from the Van Velsor bloodline. "Walt Van Velsor." Thomas liked it, too. And just in time, as a knock at the door announced the arrival of Thomas' friend, a young man he introduced as P.T. Clutching a black leather case, he explained that I need a "social security card" issued by the United States government. "It's foundational for all other forms of identification." He removed from the case a slim, silver container. Opening it exposed a window, similar to the one at the market. Thomas said the device is a "computer," promising that I would learn more about them another day. Today, I would be given a random number to go with my new name. P.T. went about his work, pressing various letters on his "laptop." He found a nine-digit number that had never been used and would be mine alone. He then pulled from his case a black box. "A portable printer," he said. Finally, he removed a sheet of blue and white paper with "Social Security" centered at the top and "USA" at the bottom. He adjusted the paper in the printer. In a minute, no more, the paper rose up, my new name and number affixed. He trimmed it and showed me where to sign. Thomas shook P.T.'s hand, slapped me on the back, and announced "Walt, you're legal now!" P.T. excused himself. He had a customer waiting but would return soon to photograph me for a state identification card.

April 12

Last night after dinner, Thomas informed me that I wouldn't have another meal until lunch today. We'd be visiting a doctor in the morning and I could only have water until after the exam. Blood would be taken, and it was essential I fast for the twelve hours leading up to that. Having some understanding of medicine, I know that what is eaten can have an effect on the elements of the blood. I followed Thomas' instructions. This morning, we set out shortly after ten. On the drive, I recalled the many physicians I'd had over the years. Some were quacks and did me no good. Truth be known, their methods may have brought me harm. But in the last years, particularly in the final months, I received the best of care. Warrie was a faithful nurse, always attending to my needs and strict when it was in my best interest. Dr. McAlister was faithful too, practicing in the modern way as he knew it. But Richard Bucke was most special, coming all the way from Canada when possible. His understanding of the human body and human mind was unparalleled. He shared his spirit with me as well, touching me deeply. That last visit, shortly after Christmas, felt like yesterday. Neither of us could stop the tears. If I'd had a different life, I could have had no better model than dear Dr. Bucke. Thomas woke me from my reverie. We'd arrived. He parked the car a short distance from a small brick house, nestled on three sides by thick pines. In a few minutes I'd meet Dr. Knight, Thomas' physician and a longtime friend. He'd been told enough about me to do what was necessary, with no questions to be asked beyond that. We were greeted at the door by a young woman in white who escorted us into a room with chairs and a bed of sorts in the middle. Before I could sit, Dr. Knight entered. Tall, with black hair and eyeglasses, he was nearly the age of Dr. Bucke when we were last together. Strangely, he had a similar air. He grasped my hand with warmth, offering assurance without speaking a word. And then he did speak, inquiring about how I was feeling, my sleep, my eating and exercise habits, any pain or concerns I might have. I answered as best I could, holding nothing back. He asked if he might examine me. Slowly, he surveyed me from head to toe, at various times using an instrument to probe my inner ears, my eyes and throat, finally pulling out a small rubber hammer and tapping my knees. Next, he asked if I might roll up a shirtsleeve so he could check my blood pressure. I recalled the many times McAlister had done the same, explaining that the result was an important indication of my health. Dr. Knight then wrapped a firm gray cloth around my left arm above the elbow, placing a round disk connected to earpieces at the point of flex. He listened intently, betraying no emotion. "Not bad, Walt," he said, "could be a little better, but a daily walk with a diet of fish, poultry, fruits and vegetables will take care of things." He excused himself, informing me that he would ask the nurse to draw a blood sample so laboratory tests could be run. He wanted to make certain there was nothing amiss. By noon, Thomas and I were on our way. In a few days we'd get a report on the health of my blood.

April 13

Thomas regularly visits a man at a nearby prison. At fourteen, he got into an argument with his best friend. They'd been drinking and got under each other's skin. Yelling led to a fist fight. A bat was grabbed. One swing and the boy's buddy was on the ground, never to breathe again. This morning we visited the boy turned man. Arriving in an April shower, we were greeted by a large complex enclosed by barbed fence. A brown and white sign pointed toward a small building where we emptied our pockets. We then walked through a narrow apparatus Thomas said detects firearms, knives, and other metal objects. Having passed the test, a guard dressed in gray with a gun at his side escorted us through a maze of bleak passageways. Along the way there were men of all ages dressed in blue shirts and trousers, performing tasks or loitering. I caught the eyes of several. Not one of them caused me concern. These are the men who carried the load in my time. In factories, on fishing boats and ferries, as hunters and trappers, construction workers, farmhands, and day laborers. We finally arrived at a large room with desks, chairs, and men quietly reading or writing. Thomas waved to a tall, lanky man who returned the greeting. The instructor said we could talk privately in her office. We sat with Thomas' friend for nearly an hour. With a stranger present, he was quiet at first. But then he became animated, sharing excitement for his studies. He said life behind bars means months and years of boredom, interrupted from time to time by violence. His studies keep him from going crazy. Scheduled to be released in a year, he's anxious, knowing the world is not the world he left behind. He's hopeful, though, that he'll find meaningful work and do some good. Thomas and I talked on the drive home about the wasted years and on how they might be different.

April 14

It was a lazy day. Thomas and I walked the neighborhood most of the morning, watching Sunday worshipers come and go. He shared that, as an adult, he's never been one for organized religion. I concurred, adding that I adhere to the practice of never arguing about God, believing any person's opinion about a deity is best kept private. I think it was Robert Louis Stevenson who said he had a new religion every year. Which makes sense, it being difficult enough to know from one day to the next who I am. My preference is to find God in a child's face, or a blade of grass, rather than between the covers of a book or under a summer revival tent. It's a relief to discover that Thomas and I have similar sentiments. This afternoon we worked in the garden, preparing it for spring planting. Just as we finished, the gentleman next door shouted at Thomas from over the fence, "Tiger did it. He won!" I hadn't a clue about the cause for his excitement, but Thomas did, celebrating the announcement. The two commenced to revel in the details. At dinner, Thomas explained that Tiger Woods is an American golfer, once the best in the world. Earlier in the day he outlasted a field of the game's finest in a tournament called the "Masters." I'd never heard of the Masters, knowing little of the game. I do recall that golf is a favorite of the British who often spend weekends knocking a small ball around a large field in an attempt to get it into a hole.

April 15

I never lived abroad, though I considered it more than once. The poor reception of *Leaves* left such a sting that domicile in a foreign land seemed an appropriate antidote. Later on, when I saw that the British were buying more copies than my own countrymen, a move to London or the English countryside appeared likely. In the end, I couldn't leave my family behind, particularly mother. With father gone and her health failing, it would not have been right. Still, the thought of starting over, living day to day without the burden of familiarity, had an allure. To walk the streets, oblivious to greed and corruption, would have been a welcome respite. But I suppose I would have tired of being an observer of the mere surface of things. The human condition being as complicated as it is, I eventually would have wanted it all. I shared my thoughts with Thomas. His suggestion was that I devote some attention to the daily news. He cautioned, however, that as the world is so connected, it could be overwhelming. "Global events are available in an instant," he said. "One can drown without a filter." He offered to resume his subscription to the *Register*. Delivered to the house every morning, I could acquaint myself with local issues and events, along with limited coverage of what was happening elsewhere. I told him I'd appreciate that.

April 16
Up before sunrise, I was excited to read the *Register*. Shortly before six there were steps on the porch. I was at the door in time to see a man, bag over his shoulder, walking away. At my feet was the newspaper. I was like the child at Christmas about to unwrap a gift of unknown delight. Bending over, I was greeted with horror, a half-page photograph of Notre Dame Cathedral engulfed in flames. My earliest recollection of Our Lady was Hugo's *Hunchback*. Later, I saw a photograph in a travel book. Men with their top hats and canes, horses pulling carts and wagons, vendors selling their wares - all dwarfed by the monument of medieval genius. Below the fold was the story. The fire started the evening before and was soon out of control. Neither the cause nor the extent of the damage was known. The French president wants it rebuilt within five years. Experts say it will take at least twenty, at a cost of a billion dollars. The great church was built on the backs of the poor. I imagine it will be rebuilt by the same. It's always the poor who bear the burden.

April 17
Thomas raises chickens. Not on a large scale. Just a few hens for morning eggs. I've taken on the chore of caring for them. They're very little trouble. Water and ground corn. Fresh bedding. Putting them out early and coaxing them in at night. Thomas lost one of the original five last summer. Probably to a raccoon. Securing them in the coop before nightfall is a must. I still recall the chickens mother kept. I liked helping, gathering eggs in the late afternoon, keeping the water clean and the feed ample. We ate a lot of eggs. For breakfast and in baked goods.

Mother made delicious breads, fruit pies when the season allowed, and cakes year-round. The move to Brooklyn changed that. When we could afford to buy them at the market, they were never as good. Thomas brought four chicks home today. No more than a week old. If they make it, we'll have eight laying hens by fall. For the next few weeks they'll be in a large box with miniature feed and water dispensers. Thomas rigged a heating lamp to keep warm them at ninety degrees. I'm always amazed how birds grow to maturity in such a short time. After they settled on, we sat with the catalogue, comparing photos of the young with their grown counterparts. We then assigned names - Dominique, Brahms, Lucy, Glory. Next March they'll be old-timers and the next generation will be ordered. It saddens me that I won't see them grow up.

April 18
We talked this morning about transportation and how I would get around. Thomas would like me to be more independent. "Freedom of travel," he says, "is a great gift, expanding our horizons in a way little else can." After we moved to the city, I walked to and from the schoolhouse. When I left school at the age of ten, my neighborhood increased considerably, expanding to the commercial and theater districts. Soon after, the streetcar arrived. "Horsecars," they called them. I remember the earliest, pulled by one or two horses, sometimes by mules. On a sunny day, and when a pair got along well, we would move at a good clip. I enjoyed the camaraderie of my fellow passengers. I learned a lot, listening to the small talk of friends and the sweet talk of lovers. There was much to see as well. New buildings going up. Newspapers being hawked. Prostitutes offering their services. Merchandise moving in all directions. I would not have become a poet but for the education of the street. Had I stayed in school, I most likely would have gone the way of my classmates - office worker, clerk, shopkeeper, streetcar operator. I can't say that I chose the poet's life as much as it chose me. That life is over, but I still have much to learn. I asked Thomas what I might do next. He suggested I become familiar with the public bus. There's a stop a five minute walk from the house. For $1.50 I could get to nearly any place I'd want. He promised I'd have a timetable and a handful of quarters by tomorrow.

April 19
After breakfast and chores, Thomas handed me an orange and white schedule for Local #14. From the nearest stop, a ride to the Central Station is less than thirty minutes. During commuter times, I can catch the 14 every half hour. By midday, that stretches to forty minutes.

Thomas cautioned that the local buses are nearly always on time. If I'm a minute late, I'll likely miss it. And I'll always need the exact fare as the driver won't make change. He then handed me a pouch of twenty-five cent pieces. When P.T. returns to make an identification card with my photograph and birthdate, I'll be able to ride for seventy-five cents, the "senior" fare. It was decided I'd take the 10:22, giving me time to prepare. Thomas compared my timepiece, he calls it a wristwatch, with his to make sure of its accuracy. I was out the door by 10:10, arriving at the stop with time to spare. It arrived as scheduled, a massive machine, with huge rubber wheels and windows on all sides. A door opened at the front with three steps up to the operator. I asked where to put my quarters. On his right, at knee level, was a large, upright box. He pointed to a narrow opening about three inches wide. I dropped them in, one by one. He then said I could sit anywhere. Toward the rear, were elevated chairs. I took one on the door side. There were a dozen passengers or so, most about my age. "Each has a story," I thought. It was a great pleasure to motor along, passing shops and houses, walkers and bicyclists, an occasional bus as well, along with cars of all colors and sizes. Without warning we pulled into the Station. In no particular hurry, I was the last to exit. Three hours later I was again on the 14, headed for home.

April 20

I've been thinking about Thomas' method. How he decides what to introduce me to and what to delay. Did he devise a plan, set in motion the day I arrived? He's intimated that he's done this before; been a guide for others. But he's yet to share any details. Emerson must be the architect. Having died a decade ago, he's had well over a century in his present role. He must know that someone can't be snatched from a different time and thrown into the sea to sink or swim. I'm beginning to appreciate the complexity of the task. I'm a stranger here. It would be impossible for me to make it on my own. Even with Thomas, it can be overwhelming. There must be an unfolding, slow and incremental. They must measure my steps, opening doors just wide enough, introducing me to the new and unimaginable in small packages. Has there been trial and error along the way? Have others become disoriented and gone mad? I had a dream last night. That a citizen from another world arrived in the dark, waking in an alien bed. He was competent in formal English, educated in the broad outlines of human history and culture, zoology, botany, cosmology, and other areas of scientific inquiry. But he knew nothing of our time. I was charged with the responsibility of guiding him, taking great care that no one discover his place of origin or learn of the motive for his existence among us. I woke with a renewed sense of trust in Thomas and an appreciation for the task he's been assigned.

April 21

Thomas keeps a calendar in the kitchen, making notations on appointments and upcoming events. I look at it every morning. It's nice to see a week in a glance, to be reminded of what's coming our way. It also marks the holidays. Just before sitting down to breakfast I discovered that this is Easter. Our family didn't celebrate it much, but I witnessed over the years its importance to others. I asked Thomas if it means anything to him. He informed me that he was raised Roman Catholic and attended schools in which religion was part of the education. At an early age he began to question much of what was taught by the priests and nuns. It didn't make sense. But he did find value in the Sunday mass. It was a time of mystery. Latin was the language of the mass when he was a boy. There was a beauty in Latin that he didn't understand but felt. When he was eleven and twelve, he was an altar boy, assisting the priest in the ritual. He enjoyed wearing the gown, lighting the candles, and ringing the bells at the prescribed times. There was a sense of otherworldliness, of a time before there were machines and other accoutrements of the modern age. He often imagined living a village life in a foreign land, much like Jesus of Nazareth. To this day, unnamed feelings rise up in him. The days leading to Easter especially. Although he rarely goes to church, he asked if I might like to attend Easter mass. Having never set foot in a Catholic church, I was curious, despite the irrationality of the notion that a man who'd been dead for three days came back to life only to leave again for a place called heaven. Thomas suggested we go to the cathedral in the center of the city. "There's something about the older churches," he observed. Soon we were inside and seated. The vaulted ceiling, stained glass windows, miniature altars on the side, and the grand altar ahead created a reverential space. Throughout the mass I reflected on the Christian belief in resurrection. I felt something in my chest open up. Near the end came a revelation. I've been resurrected. Transported in a manner I'll never understand, to a place beyond my comprehension and a time that hasn't happened. I am the man I was, and yet I'm not.

April 22

It's Earth Day. Thomas says for the past fifty years people have gathered on this date to protest man's abuse of the planet. The greed of the wealthy and big business is the major culprit, but everyone is culpable. According to Thomas, protests started in 1970. University students were awakening to the damaging effects of mass consumption. It was the beginning of what's now called the "Environmental Movement." Thomas explained that "dirty energy" - the burning of coal and oil - was, and continues to be, a significant cause. But other practices are killing the planet as well, including the use of pesticides to increase profits through large-scale crop production. Even before the first Earth Day, researchers were speaking out about the grim effects of pesticides on nature. Rachel Carson, a marine biologist, had led the way. Thomas recommends I read her book *Silent Spring*; that it's impossible to ignore the devastation after doing so. He's never forgotten her statement: "Knowing what I do, there would be no future peace for me if I kept silent." Thomas observed with a sense of sadness that technological progress is changing life on Earth forever.

April 23

I slept poorly, troubled by yesterday's conversation with Thomas. For years I believed human progress would win out. While there might be setbacks, the long-term trajectory of our species would be toward the better. I was wrong. The desire for comfort, security, the amelioration of pain of all kinds, has led to grasping for material things in the search for comfort and happiness. The monied interests feed into this, according to Thomas, enticing the populace with toys, diversions, food, alcohol and drugs. The results are pollution and waste on a scale that no one in my time could have foreseen. All around the world people are sick and dying from chemicals in their drinking water. Poisons are in the air they breathe. He believes a turning toward the sacred and a reverence for life is our only hope. Despite his fears, he's encouraged by the efforts of some. There are scientists and engineers devoting their lives to the development of clean energy to replace the burning of fossil fuels. Energy from the sun and wind is being captured. More and more cars are powered by electricity. People are walking, riding bicycles, and relying on public transportation. There's little I can do in my short time here. But I can be part of the "movement" Thomas talks about. I'll walk more, ride the bus, and maybe learn to ride a bike.

April 24

When I'm out, I see older people everywhere. With a partner or alone. Some with a cane, others pushing a device with small wheels. A few ride silently, seated on miniature cars, powered by something that can't be seen. They appear to enjoy the experience, taking in the sunshine and spring air, content in their wrinkled skin. Just weeks ago, I was moments from my last breath, awaiting the relief the dark would bring. Now I'm like them, a white-haired warrior, stretching my legs and filling my lungs. It's odd, being one of them, walking about anonymously, free of notoriety. I don't miss that, nor do I miss those who knocked at the door, without warning, in search of words of wisdom I didn't have. Perhaps I should have been more patient, accepting the role of elder, dispensing advice as best I could. I wonder if age is an attitude. Yeats wrote: "When you are old and gray and full of sleep, and nodding by the fire, take down this book, and slowly read, and dream of the soft look your eyes had once, and of their shadows deep . . ." Does it have to be that way? Should the last years be a mere looking back as Yeats suggested? Or should they be years of looking at the present? When I was footloose, I would spend hours doing nothing but enjoying everything. Shouldn't I be doing that now? There are no demands placed on me. No lectures to give or readers to please. Emerson gave me this year to observe. Perhaps I can visit a zoo. I'll ask Thomas at dinner if there is one accessible by bus.

April 25

A restless night, and for good reason. I could barely contain my excitement. I caught the 8:50 to Central Station. By 9:40 I was on the #7 southbound. There was much to see en route, but all I could think about was the strange and the exotic. A day at the zoo does wonders for the child inside. I'll never forget my first visit, the year after my stroke in January of '73. George had moved me to Camden to live with him and his wife. Mother fell ill shortly after and died that May. I fell into a dark depression. Gone was my good health and gone the one I loved more dearly than anyone else. For months life held nothing for me. I didn't write. I didn't care to entertain visitors. I wanted nothing but escape. It went on for over a year. Then, on a June afternoon, George burst into my room. The Philadelphia Zoo would finally open. Years in the planning, the War had gotten in the way. But on July 1, in less than a week, visitors would pass through its Victorian gates for the first time. George insisted we be there. And we were. For a mere 25 cents, we joined three thousand others to meander through the garden-like landscape, and be enthralled by mammals, birds, and reptiles from every continent. It was the first real zoo in the New World. My depression fled as quickly as it had descended. George and I visited several times after, until my health was such that I could no longer tolerate the journey. Today's adventure rivaled those to the Philly Zoo, if not in grandeur, certainly in stimulation. The great mammals were there - elephants, rhinos, giraffes, the big cats. Smaller ones too, but no less fascinating. There were birds I'd never seen or heard of. The kookaburra from

Australia stands out. And Barnaby, a tortoise of several hundred pounds and a decade older than me, manifested a wisdom that belied his reptilian heritage. But the highlight was the children. Their curiosity and amazement added to mine considerably.

April 26

With P.T. coming later in the day to take my photo, Thomas thought it best I get a trim. I could go to a shop down the street or walk a short distance further to Vince's. The nearest is a busy place, three or four hairdressers most days. Or I could try Vince, an "old school barber" who gives a good haircut for five dollars less. I chose the latter, thinking that older might be better. The added distance was well worth it, with flowering trees along the way. I recognized eastern redbuds, white dogwoods, and the southern magnolia. Others I don't know but will do my best to learn about. Following Thomas' directions, I arrived at Vince's, a half-dozen steps below street level with a small patio out front and a large window displaying everything inside. The lone barber's chair was unoccupied, as were all but one of the chairs for waiting customers. There sat an old man, legs crossed, reading the *Register*. It must be Vince. I introduced myself as a friend of Thomas' and asked if I might get a haircut and beard trim. "Of course," he said, "that's why I'm here." Thus, began a most stimulating hour. Vince has worked on thousands of heads over his fifty-plus years in business. He's heard stories he can never repeat and stories that will break a heart. He's been a confidant to more people than a parish priest and shared enough laughs for a lifetime. His 80th is coming up, an age when most have taken to a rocker. I asked Vince why he's still at it, although I already knew the answer. He paused, lowering the silver scissors to his side, and looked me in the eye: "You always have to have a place to go." What more could be said? A man needs his fishing hole, his cabin in the woods, his barber shop on a tree-lined street. I could have visited with Vince all day but for a dad and a boy waiting their turn. I handed him a ten for the trim and three ones for his time, promising that I'd return in two weeks.

MONTH TWO

April 27

All day it rained, continuing into the evening and through the night. I don't recall when I've slept better. I would say nothing disturbed me, and that would be correct. But I wasn't alone. There was a presence. It was vigilant, having the feel of a father keeping an eye on his child. There was no voice, or sound of any kind. Only watchfulness. I might call it God at another time, but it was more human than divine. Perhaps it was Emerson. I went to bed missing him, wondering when he might return. He's the lone link to my past. I knew him as flesh and blood. It was a complicated relationship. His ideas woke me from a slumber. I dare say, had I not discovered his essay "The Poet," I might not have become one. But it was imperative I break from him, as every son must from his father. I had to go my own way. Thoreau taught me that. His love for solitude validated mine. Yet it's Emerson who remains in my life. Why he cares for me, I can't say. I'm seventy-two and he's still in my head. I know I disappointed him at times, uncomfortable as he was with my poeticism of sexuality. It was there that we had our falling out. I see now that its source was his concern for how the public might perceive me. Emerson wanted me to succeed and reap the rewards he thought my efforts deserved. I regret I didn't acknowledge his good intentions. Perhaps this gift of a year has a purpose beyond the stated tasks of observation and reporting. It seems the making of amends is possible only while we are here. That the door shuts on that opportunity after we pass over. It could be that hell is reserved for those who carry their regrets with them. I want to speak with Thomas about taking a trip. I'd like to travel to Concord and visit Emerson's home. It would be a good place to have a talk.

April 28

This morning Thomas introduced me to a new device, a rectangular box about the size of a paperback book. Like the laptop, it has raised buttons. Above or below each are various labels. Volume, tuner, display, on, and off. There are symbols as well. A miniature bed, a clock, an ear. "It's a radio Walt. A descendant of the work of Heinrich Hertz in your time. You might remember that he experimented with transmitting electromagnetic waves through the air." I did remember. It was in the '80s, a time of great innovation. It seemed anything was possible. Thomas told me that waves of various lengths are transmitted all over the world now, and into space too. The box receives sound, primarily music and the human voice, sent from radio stations. Depending on the complexity of the box, signals can be received from stations hundreds, even thousands of miles away. Thomas said the radio is like the newspaper in that events of the day are gathered together in one place for the reader or listener to pick and choose at leisure. There are differences. A radio gives access to many transmitting stations, each offering varied content and, oftentimes, differing opinions. It's possible to listen to Bach or an opera, a Baptist preacher, a sporting event, even the president. But like the newspaper, there's the danger of being overwhelmed. He suggested I limit my listening time to an hour a day. With that, Thomas left me to explore. Within minutes I could navigate and distinguish one station from another. In the process, I learned of a horror. A young man in a California city entered a synagogue with a firearm, killing a woman and injuring three others. Broadcasters said the assailant was an "anti-Semite." Nearly every station was reporting the tragedy, several offering opinions on the need for federal legislation to limit access to guns.

April 29

On a shelf devoted to astronomy, geology, and biology, I happened upon *A Brief History of Time* by Stephen Hawking, a British physicist. I was intrigued. How is it that time has a history? Hasn't it always and everywhere been the same? On the back cover was a note that Hawking was born on the anniversary of Galileo's death. The editor's concluding comment was that Hawking ". . . is widely regarded as the most brilliant theoretical physicist since Einstein." I was never a student of mathematics, having left school before we'd progressed beyond basic numbers. But I often mused about our origin, not just in the way Darwin did, but well before, back to the beginning of everything. Without mathematics I couldn't go far, but I did my best to read and understand articles in various journals of popular science. I had great admiration for Copernicus and Galileo for breaking through the cosmological myths of the medieval church. Then Newton arrived, postulating laws of motion and gravity. Another century passed before Young's theories of light and kinetic energy and Dalton's theory of matter. Not long after, Ohm postulated on electrical resistance and Faraday on electromagnetic conduction. Each discovery seemed to lay the foundation for the next.

No one, though, tried to explain how it all started. I wonder who this Einstein fellow was, and what Hawking learned from him. I've only begun Hawking's brief history. But even in the opening pages he's asking the big questions: Where did the cosmos come from? Has it always been here? What is the smallest piece of matter? Why do we remember the past and not the future? It's as if I'm starting school all over again.

April 30

"Exhilarating" best describes my first time on a bicycle. Thomas cajoled me this morning into giving it a try. He said bicycling is a transcendent experience. As close as you get to flying without leaving the ground. He's been riding since he was seven, starting out on a little red bike with fat tires. He found it frightening at first. But after a couple of falls, he got the hang of it. Thomas is still an avid rider, getting out nearly every day if the weather allows. He's been wanting me to learn so I can ride with him. I couldn't say no, as supportive as he's been in all matters. Truth be known, I've always wanted to try. I remember the first bicycles after the War. I'd heard of a two-wheeler built by a Scottish blacksmith sometime in the '30s. But it wasn't until two Frenchmen added a crank drive with pedals that it became popular. They were called velocipedes back then. I'd see them on Sunday afternoons with their big front wheels, pedaled mostly by young men intent on demonstrating their prowess. Later in Camden, after I moved to Mickle Street, I'd sit on the front porch watching them compete with the horse and buggy. Admittedly, I was a bit envious. Had I been younger and healthier, I would have been out there with them. Thomas gave me a second chance. We walked his two bicycles a short distance to a paved area next to a church. Thomas demonstrated, straddling his bike, placing his left foot on the left pedal, and pushing off with his right. He glided a few feet, gaining his balance, then placed his right foot on the second pedal and took off. It looked easy as he made a wide turn and pedaled back. Then he repeated each step, making sure I understood. Returning, he suggested I try. I mounted the second bike, placing my left foot, just as he had, and pushed forward. Thomas supported me as I added my right. I was wobbly at first, but he stayed with me, making sure I was in control before setting me free. I did it! Having enjoyed much in my long life, I have a new pleasure.

May 1

Thomas and I traveled east last night, arriving in Maine sometime before dawn. I woke to a most sublime sunrise over Panther Pond. Strata of muted pinks, yellows, purples and blues rose up from distant pines and reflected off the still waters. There's a cabin on the south shore owned by friends of Thomas. Oftentimes he has the use of it when they're elsewhere. It will be ours for the next week. Thomas has business in the city most days, leaving me to explore. But that will have to wait until Friday. During our journey here, Emerson accompanied us. There was little opportunity for conversation, as the mode of transport makes it difficult. But he did inform me that tomorrow he'd be at his home in Concord. He returns there two or three times a year, for a few hours at the most. Any longer risks a rupture in the "space-time continuum." I'm not sure what that means, but it suggests something about how all of this works - traveling through the centuries, overnight jaunts across continents. I often mused about the relationship between past and future, here and there. But there wasn't the science to help me. Perhaps Hawking will, if not Emerson or Thomas. Tomorrow morning Thomas will put me on the 9:45 bus to Concord. A three-hour journey. Emerson said he'd arrive at the house promptly at one. If it's quiet, we'll have time to ourselves. He said he'd wait for me in the study. I was last there in September of '81. I had come out from Boston by steam, spending the good part of a Sunday at the Emerson home. Mrs. E. was there too, along with Ellen and Edward. Much of the conversation was about Thoreau, who'd been a guest on several occasions. I wonder how the house has changed, and Emerson.

May 2

I stepped off the bus, expecting a village I wouldn't recognize. Much had changed, but much remained the same. The half-mile walk to the Emerson's was not unlike before - the Concord Town House, the old cemetery, the Unitarian Church, the stretch of houses from the 1700s. Then, I was there. The "Home of Ralph Waldo Emerson." White siding, black shutters, twin chimneys. I pinched myself, not sure if I was dreaming. Just ahead, a woman knocked and was let in. I followed, noting the time - 12:58. To the left was a young man sitting behind a desk. To the right, Emerson's study. I stepped in. There was the red velvet sofa, the hundreds of shelved books, his oval writing table, and his rocker, vacant and still. So, I thought. As I approached it began to move, almost imperceptibly. Back and forth, as if breathing. A fine mist appeared, outlining a human form. I stopped and stood, waiting. Then he spoke for only my mind to hear. He said the house is open to the public now. There are days when no one visits, today not being one of them. He suggested we go for a walk. I exited the way I came in, Emerson following. We took a left at the sidewalk, in the direction of the town center. Emerson kept pace, whispering that a stroll out to the Old North Bridge might be nice. I agreed, recalling my last visit when I stood at the place where the shot "was heard 'round the world." Emerson then inquired about my journey south. Was the bus comfortable? How was the traffic? Were the people friendly? He was always gracious and concerned about others, preferring to listen rather than speak. We walked on, arriving at the bridge and crossing over. We stopped to pay tribute to the Minute Man, rendered in the finest detail by the young sculptor, Daniel Chester French. I nearly wept, standing in the shadow of the Concord farmer who left his plow and picked up his musket to defend land and liberty. I sensed a tear in Emerson's eye as well. We paid our respects, each in our own private way. Then Emerson spoke. He was sorry, but he had to leave. The time permitted him is always too brief. I was alone and sorry too.

May 3

I walked old Concord in the morning rain, a clerk at the Inn having loaned me an umbrella. My heart ached. Without Emerson at my side, my interest in the town's history had waned. On the bus coming down, I looked forward to seeing the Alcott House, the Wayside, Old Manse, the Thoreau Farm, and Walden Pond again. But today they didn't matter. Only the cemetery. All I cared about was visiting Authors' Ridge and Emerson's grave. To stand at the feet of what was once him. To bow, to kneel, to utter something of a prayer. How appropriate that his place of internment is named Sleepy Hollow. He surely planned it that way. I entered from the road, passing under the shady oaks and by the slender evergreens. Ascending the hill, I was quickly upon Emerson's gravesite, Lidian's and Ellen's on either side. A boulder of rose quartz supported the bronze plaque - *Ralph Waldo Emerson*. He was a rock of a man, unique among any I'd ever met. Below the dates of his birth and death, an epitaph read:

The passive master lent his hand
To the vast soul that oer him planned

Simply stated, even understated. Had I not read his essays, I doubt my own intellect would have been ignited. But ignited it was, learning from him before *Leaves* was even contemplated that ". . . poetry was all written before time was, and whenever we are so finely organized that we can penetrate into that region where the air is music, we hear those primal warblings, and attempt to write them down." I spent my years, from mid-life on, making that attempt, endeavoring to live up to his vision. Notwithstanding our disagreements, I hope I did.

May 4

Thomas left me to have lunch at a small restaurant near Monument Square. Nearly empty, I was seated at a table for two with a window view. Thomas has been goading me to consume more garden stuff, and less beef and bread. Half-heartedly, I ordered a salad of greens and diced vegetables. I'm not a happy convert, but I am a few pounds lighter. Working my way through the lettuce, spinach, and the rest, I found myself following a nearby conversation. Not English, French, or German. My guess was Hebrew. Whatever the language, I was certain it was an exchange between friends, or perhaps brothers. Timidly, I turned and introduced myself, offering how much I was enjoying their discussion, despite not understanding any of it. "We were speaking Farsi," the gentleman closest explained. "We're Persian, retired physicians up from Boston for the weekend." I told him I've long admired the Persian poets. "Aha, then you know Rumi." "Yes, of course. He's a favorite." He beamed, "Poetry is our national language. We learn it from the cradle." I would have liked to have compared poets, but the conversation shifted. "Most Americans are good people. But our president hates us. He hates all Muslims and encourages others to hate us too. We live in constant fear." I knew nothing of what he was saying and could only express sadness for their mistreatment. He then asked if I would take a seat. What followed was disturbing. Before today, I'd only heard the name "Trump." Nothing more. But what I learned is this president is an aberration. He's authoritarian; has tyrannical leanings; favors dictators; and is totally unfit for the job. He wants Muslims and others of color deported and wants asylum seekers from the Middle East and Latin countries denied entrance. White supremacists are emboldened by him. The wealthy support him because he does them favors. I didn't know what to say, except that it's a tragic state of affairs. As they rose to leave, I was handed a card and invited to visit. I accepted it, promising to contact them and make arrangements. Waiting for Thomas to return, I wondered if this Trump is why Emerson and his friends are so concerned with the present state of affairs in America.

May 5

I waited until breakfast to share yesterday's experience with Thomas. His usual lightheartedness vanished. "It was inevitable, Walt, that you would find out about this. I'd hoped it wouldn't be so soon. I wanted you to adjust before discovering the pall that hangs over the land. Those of us in opposition can see all too well the damage that's been done, and fear it will take years to be rectified." For the next hour, Thomas rendered with broad strokes the story of Donald Trump. It's almost unimaginable, except there have always been corrupt leaders, looking out only for themselves and their kind. In the years before Lincoln we had a string of them beginning in 1850: Fillmore, Pierce, Buchanan. I remember looking back on that decade, writing that "Never were publicly displayed more deformed, mediocre, sniveling, unreliable, false-hearted men." It was a discouraging time. How was it possible that the nation that produced Washington and Jefferson could empower the likes of those three imposters? How did the great Lincoln rise up in their wake? I shared this with Thomas. It was then I learned that before Trump, Americans had elected Barack Obama, a black man, as president. Brilliant and highly educated, he drew inspiration from Lincoln in great measure. Thomas reminded me that throughout our history the pendulum has swung back and forth, wildly at times, bringing to power the great, the mediocre, the incompetent, and the corrupt, each to play their part on the world stage. "It will always be that way," he predicted. "In the meantime, Walt, try not to have this presidency distract your attention from the greater task of living your life. You don't have much time."

May 6

Thomas had business in Damariscotta and asked if I'd like to ride along. Taking Highway One rather than the "the interstate," we passed through Yarmouth, Freeport, Brunswick, and Bath. The last of the "downeast" villages was Wiscasset, self-proclaimed "prettiest town in Maine." It's lovely. From atop a hill, we quickly descended, the main street with its shops and eating establishments giving way to a long, slender bridge spanning the Sheepscot. I asked Thomas to stop. I had some thinking to do. Promising to return by noon, he let me off at Sprague's Lobster, on the right bank of the tidal river. Unfortunately, it's yet to open for the season. I walked on in search of solitude, finding it at the end of an abandoned pier. Legs dangling above the outgoing tide, I retraced the last few days. It's finally hit me that I've been given a second chance. This isn't an extended holiday; a recess between life and death. It's serious business. I hadn't prepared for the end or, at least the end as we know it. I was merely sliding toward it as I lost interest in the delight of daily existence. Neither did I take up the challenge of envisioning the other side. There on Mickle Street, I engaged in small talk, complained some, ate little, and slept a lot. My behavior was not commensurate with the impending transition. Come next March, I'll again be presented with the opportunity to do it right. How do I live the hours and days between now and then? I'm obligated to Emerson and the others to take notice and report. It's hard work at my age to pay attention. But what else is there to do?

May 7

Just looking out the window, thinking. That's how I spent the morning. The first light brought with it a northeast breeze, picking up steam as the sun rose over Panther Pond. Small whitecaps danced across the blue - five, ten, twenty, hundreds. Too many to count. An endless procession of tiny warriors, intent on overwhelming the south shore. Little did they know a frontal attack would be their demise. And had they, I doubt it would have mattered. They had come into being for one purpose. That's what fate is about I suppose. It's easy for them. They don't ask questions or have doubts. They don't get highjacked by the demands of others or seduced by inconsequential enticements. They merely obey the imperative. Nothing can stop them. They have a finite beginning and a finite end, as we all do. But unlike the human condition, there are no sidetracks along the way. I could be envious. To be a tiny wave on the surface of the great unknown has its allure. But I was summoned into being for something else. Perhaps not better, but it has been an interesting journey. And it's not over, for which I'm grateful. My assault on the shore of nonbeing was delayed. Emerson provided an explanation. It made sense at the time. But I wasn't particularly lucid, waiting as I was for the hand of the reaper to grasp mine. Looking out the window, I can imagine alternative motives. This evening we're attending an event. Something called a "movie." Thomas is certain I'll be delighted.

May 8

There was talk about it. The possibility of moving photographs. After the War, a device called the zoetrope was making the rounds. I was fascinated by it, how it produced an illusion of motion by displaying a sequence of drawings showing progressive phases of that motion. A toy company picked up on it and many a child received one for Christmas. I imagined it wouldn't be long before photographs could be displayed, one after another like a moving train, telling stories with a beginning and an end. It never happened in my lifetime, but Thomas tells me it became a reality soon after. The "films" were short at first, a minute or two. But they developed over the years into what Thomas calls the "motion picture industry." I witnessed a later development of it last night in a building called a "movie theater." It wasn't unlike the opera houses I would frequent - rows of seats, one behind the other, facing a lighted stage with the spectators in the dark. As a young man, I fell under the spell of the masterpieces of Rossini, Bellini, Donizetti. During my New York years, before *Leaves*, I never missed a performance by Marietta Alboni. She roused whirlwinds of feeling within me. To this day, I don't think there's ever been a finer example of the human spirit. But last night I discovered her equal. A young woman by the name of Aretha Franklin. A black woman with a voice that soars up to the heavens but is so rooted in the lives of her people that it's impossible not to dance and sway and shout out in joy. It wasn't opera. It was Gospel music. I remember when Gospel songs became popular in the '70s. But they were nothing compared to those sung by this beautiful woman, call her angelic, for the benefit of a Baptist congregation in California. "Movie cameras" had recorded her performance on consecutive evenings in the summer of 1974. It was intended that a film be made. Something happened and it never came to be, until more than forty years later. Not since Marietta Alboni have my feelings been so roused. And the miracle is the film, called *Amazing Grace*, can be viewed over and over again, all around the world, for the benefit of rich and poor alike.

May 9
Breakfast this morning was at the "Other Side Diner." Eggs, bacon, and black coffee. There were other choices, but I'm a creature of habit. I should take a chance and try something else. Perhaps an omelet. They were a favorite of mother, a kind of pancake when she made them. Now they're made with an assortment of vegetables without the pancakes. My physician would likely endorse them. Three gentlemen about my age were seated at the table to my right. Each with that accent peculiar to the state. It's refreshing. No pretension or suggestion of class distinction. A reminder of the fierce independence of those with deep roots. It takes a while for the ear to adjust but, like the radio, once tuned in understanding follows. I had little trouble following the conversation, although there were terms for which I knew no meaning. I jotted them down as best I could, intending to consult *Webster* when back home. One of the men spoke with dismay about an impending increase on the tax assessed on realty. Reading an account from a local newspaper, he guessed the tax on his house would increase twenty percent in two years. All three agreed there's nothing to be done about it. Their talk shifted to the national economy, declining revenue, the ballooning debt, the widening gap between the wealthy and the ninety percent, free trade and the imposition of foreign tariffs. Each acknowledged that they would be okay, having adequately saved for the future. Their worry is for their

children, and their children's children. The quiet one of the three spoke up, opining that free market capitalism has lost its promise. That the good times are over. I've heard it before, but he may be right.

May 10

I woke thinking of Victoria Woodhull - brilliant, tenacious, ambitious. She and her sister were the first women to operate a brokerage firm on Wall Street, and among the first to start a newspaper. On May 10 of '74, the Equal Rights Party nominated her as its candidate for president. At 34, she was a year shy of the age required by the Constitution. But she wasn't deterred. Nor was she deterred by the fact that women didn't have the right to vote. In some ways we were kindred souls. She declared herself to be a free lover, with the inalienable and constitutional rights to love whomever she pleased. She didn't have a chance of winning and knew that. But she believed women had the right to try. She also knew that history would be on her side. I still recall her shouting out: "They cannot roll back the rising tide of reform. The world moves." I asked Thomas if he knew of her and if any women since had run for the office. He did, and yes, there was another woman. Three years ago, Hillary Clinton, a former senator and Secretary of State, was nominated by the Democratic Party as its candidate. She won the popular vote but lost the election to Donald Trump. The reasons why, Thomas said, will have to wait until we have more time. But her defeat hasn't dissuaded others. Of the twenty candidates for the next Democratic Party nomination, six are women, one an African American. Victoria was right. The tide continues to rise.

May 11

I learn something nearly every day about Thomas. It's not easy, as he rarely draws attention to himself. He's a quiet observer with no apparent agenda. Sometimes I think just being alive is enough for him. He rarely categorizes. His mind doesn't work that way. Everything and everyone he encounters is unique. I suppose he wouldn't make a good scientist. Hierarchies and classifications are antithetical to his nature. Race is an example. I don't believe he has a biased bone in his body. Skin color is merely a reminder of nature's diversity. Even in a world in which the wealthy have far more than they need, and the poor so little, he's not inclined to separate individuals by class. He despises riches but not the rich. Somewhere along the way he discovered that suffering isn't a respecter of privilege. While those with money have far more than their fair share, hardship often visits them in the guise of alcoholism, addiction, or insanity. I witnessed the same. The plight of the slave was deplorable. Nevertheless, the slave owner often had demons that pushed him to the brink. I always admired Emerson. Yet I begrudged his Harvard education, his travel abroad and his community of fellow Transcendentalists. I thought it unfair that he'd been touched with favor in a way I hadn't. His father was a respected minister. Mine a reckless businessman. Emerson had an Ivy League education. Mine ended in elementary school. He had a lovely wife and devoted children. I had neither. It wasn't until years later that I learned his father died of cancer when Emerson was just a boy. A younger brother died of tuberculosis when Emerson was thirty. A second brother of tuberculosis two years later. Most devastating was the death of his Ellen, just two years into their marriage. Friends said he mourned her loss all his life. I asked Thomas if he always sees the best in others. "Almost always," he said, "but there are exceptions. Try as I might, I've yet to find in Donald Trump any laudable traits. There must be something there, but it's buried so deep it's undiscoverable."

May 12

The journey was brief. No sooner had I fallen asleep at Panther Pond than I awoke to Thomas' footsteps across the floor above. It was good to be home, though I was in no hurry to start the day. The simple joy of staying in bed, distinguishing the song of one feathered creature from another, is one I rarely allow myself. This morning the sparrows and finches were in fierce competition. A lone oriole did its best to be heard as well. Adding to the chorus was a cardinal pair, oblivious to the others. They offer their spirits freely, without expectation of praise or desire for adulation. I'd be blessed to have the voice of any one of them. We consider their lives brief and accomplishments few, but our time is no more precious than theirs. I know little of the Hindu system of reincarnation, but I imagine at least one of its many sects honors the thrush, the robin, and the nightingale among the highest of life forms.

May 13

We went for a drive. Thomas said our destination was a surprise. Following the route of the #14, we crossed over a broad river swelled by recent rains. The road widened into a boulevard, flowers down the middle, shade trees on either side. Thomas had been quiet most of the way, then mentioned casually, "Walt, you have a birthday coming up." It hadn't occurred to me. "You're right. On the 31st. Although I wasn't expecting one this year." Then he queried, "Have you done the math?" I had not. "Walt, it will be your 200th." I'd never considered it as I'd turned seventy-two less than a year earlier. "Would you like to visit your birthplace?" I'd not thought it possible, but anything is possible these days. Without hesitation I said yes. He went on. "As a present, I want to give you a visit to New York City. After a few days, you could take the train to Long Island and spend your birthday where it all started." I retraced the years, back to when I was a toddler. My world was that small house and the little bit of land that surrounded it. Thomas woke me from my reverie. "Getting there will be different. You'll fly on what is called an airplane." He then provided a brief history, beginning with DaVinci's sketches, the Montgolfier brothers in France, the Wright brothers and the Kitty Hawk, all the way until the present and aircraft that carry as many as 800 passengers. Just as he finished, we turned off the road and by way of a long drive, approached the "terminal." "This is an airport. I want you to get acquainted with it. In two weeks, we'll return. You'll pass through security, board an airplane, and fly east. Four hours later you'll be on the ground and a taxi will take you into the city."

May 14

I struggle with my obsolescence. It was just weeks ago that Emerson interrupted my last night. It was a recruitment of sorts. He assured me I had a choice. Hesitant at first, ultimately, I couldn't turn it down - the opportunity to cheat death, or at least forestall it. Wouldn't everyone want a bonus year of sunrises and moon lit nights? With little time to decide, I could imagine no more than what I'd already experienced. When as a child, or young man, or even as a poet, I could never see much past my fingerprints. Whatever the future might hold, it would be similar, hopefully better. Poverty would abate. Lifespans increase. Wars subside. Justice would prevail and progress would favor everyone. But the increase in technological progress far exceeded my imagination. Of course, there was Jules Verne who envisioned journeys to the center of the earth, the bottom of the sea, even the plains of the moon. I delighted in the genre but appreciated the stories as delightful tales and nothing more. Now I know that fact has far exceeded fiction. What I learned from Thomas about airplanes and transcontinental travel has set me adrift. I'm unhinged, disconnected. Perhaps it's not meant for us to know too much. Our minds may be incapable of unlimited expansion. On the other hand, we're not far removed from our ancestors the apes. Darwin uncovered the secrets of evolution. He can't be faulted for not anticipating the pace of it when entrusted to human hands. I must see this through. It wouldn't be right of me to capitulate. And I have Thomas. It's his fate to guide me.

May 15

I set off midmorning astride a bicycle loaned by Thomas. My first solo
excursion. Assuring me I was up to it, he assigned me the tasks of
visiting the nearby library and obtaining a lending card. He then
sketched a map with possible routes. The most direct would take me on
roads likely to have automobiles. The second, more leisurely and with
less traffic. I chose the latter, believing it to be the safer of the two. The
journey was thoroughly enjoyable - pedaling, gliding, stopping when
required or just to rest. I rolled past women pushing infants in strollers,
children playing ball, and dogs of all kinds, secured behind fences and
yipping for reasons known only to them. Arriving with minimal effort, I
was greeted with a large sign at the entrance, *Franklin Public Library*.
Not everything has changed. Inside, however, modernity was the rule,
be it the lighting, the furniture, even the book covers. I inquired of a man
behind the desk about borrowing. He said I first needed proper
identification. Thomas had prepared me with a "driver's license" and a
billing statement for water and sewer with his address and my name.
P.T. had fabricated both. Soon enough I was handed a "Library Card"
with my assigned number and a line for my name. I proudly signed
"Walt Van Velsor." The man then gave me permission to browse and
borrow at my leisure. It was enough to walk up and down the rows.
Each identified with either numbers or letters and the genre printed
above: Mysteries, Fiction, Inspiration, Romance, Nonfiction, Science
Fiction, Memoirs, Biographies. I stopped at Biographies. Scanning the
shelves from left to right and top to bottom, I searched for the familiar.
Of the hundreds, there were several I recognized: Audubon, Franklin,
Grant, Benjamin Harrison, Jefferson, Samuel Johnson, Lincoln, Mozart,
John Muir, Shakespeare, Van Gogh. Then the W's. Washington, of
which there were four or five, John Wesley and Oscar Wilde. Between
the two, *Walt Whitman - Lives and Legacies*, published in 2005. On the
back cover, a quote: "This highly readable introduction to America's
greatest poet by one of his most knowledgeable and insightful
biographers." I held it, my hands trembling, trying to comprehend. This
was my life, as interpreted by another, and published in this century. I
had hoped in my younger days that I would be remembered centuries
hence. Privately, I was doubtful. But here was proof that I had survived,
at least in the mind of one interested writer. Returning to the man at the
counter, I handed him my library card and my story.

May 16

I was out early, foregoing breakfast to bicycle. It's such a simple
machine. No engine, a few moving parts, nothing superfluous. I'd not

imagined the freedom possible, pedaling so close to the pavement, unsheltered from the morning breeze. Thomas told me there are those who've crossed the continent with only their bike and bare essentials. A few courageous souls have circumnavigated the globe. I envy, with the best of intentions, the single-minded who set a course and follow it to the end. I honor those who plant a dream, as one would sow a seed, nourishing it over the months, sometimes years, until it matures into the only thing that matters. There are many who derive comfort from hearth and home, toiling to the brink of exhaustion to be ruler of a tiny kingdom. I have no quarrel with them. The world needs the stability such lives provide. Without them, I suppose, the wandering life would not be possible for others. In my youth, I too took to the open road. Healthy, free, the world before me, the long brown path leading wherever I chose. Those days still live within me. Each as valuable as a later year. Just as no man or woman can truly touch the soul of another, nor can anyone deprive a sojourner of the miles earned by sweat and will. They are as precious as any gem that might adorn the idle. More so, in my estimation. Give me memories of mountain vistas and rolling plains over any present day possession.

May 17

Adjacent to the library is a cemetery, stretching far beyond what can be seen. A solitary gate allows entrance with a wide path providing access. I saw a bicyclist in the distance, so I followed, every minute or so pausing at a tombstone. A few were recent, but most were dated decades past. Many as remote as my lifetime. It saddens me to see small stones memorializing the passing of infants. Some within days of birth, others in the first year. Childhood disease has always been a coldhearted thief. There's no ransom to be paid, even for the most innocent of hearts. Once I imagined myself with sons and daughters. But that privilege was denied me. In its place, however, was the blessing of never having to bury one. As I rode on, family plots gave way to row after row of military markers, miniature flags aside each. Reds, whites, and blues honored the fallen. I stopped again, resting my bike against a giant oak, imagining the collective valor. The markers were simple. Names, dates of birth and death, the war. I was laid low by what I learned. I'd thought that my War would be the end of it. I was in error. Our nation has sent the young to fight and die over and over again: World War I, World War II, Korea, Vietnam. The questions overwhelmed me. What were the causes? What were the outcomes? How many fatalities? Were we in the right? Is there a right? We've always glorified war. But just below the patriotic fervor, greed, avarice, and a thirst for power reside.

Nevertheless, the warrior should be honored, whether in victory or defeat. I knelt at the grave of a young man, a teenager when he fell in Vietnam. I was lost for words. An hour later I was home. Thomas was preparing dinner. He shared his day. We then talked of war. He said it goes on and on. The rich get richer and so many young never return. He suggested I visit a hospital for veterans. Survivors fill the beds. Some leave, still wounded and maimed. Others die in the night.

May 18

Emerson stopped in the night. "Making the rounds," he said. I nearly asked who else was on his list, but thought better of it. If it was my business, he would tell me. Whether or not I'm a priority does not matter. His presence and attention in the moment is enough. I rose to turn on a light. He said there was no need. He was comfortable in the chair adjacent the bed. Besides, there was nothing for me to see. Long I sang the wonders of the human form, but there's an intimacy between spirits I didn't know was possible. It occurred to me that flesh and blood might be an obstacle, a barrier to communication. Still, I'll greatly miss the ability to touch and taste. I was drifting and apologized for it. Emerson assured me that wherever I might be was fine. He had come as a reminder that I'm cared for. It wasn't necessary that we talk. Two souls in silence is its own pleasure. And so, we passed through the middle hours of the night. It was akin to a trance, but there was a clarity, not unlike the final step of a mountain summit, absent the exhaustion. It even resembled the moment of erotic bliss but without the separation. At the first hint of dawn, a tear came. I didn't want it to end. Inaudibly, I implored Emerson to take me, that I had no need to live out the remainder of the year. He placed his hand on my shoulder, promising the time would pass soon enough and I would be better off for it. The coo of a mourning dove broke the silence and I was alone.

May 19

Rain the last three nights. The radio said there'd be a break for two days, then showers the next ten. Already there is flooding. Families along rivers and streams have had to vacate their homes. Thomas says it's due to global warming. We have water in the basement. Fortunately, Thomas was prepared. He has a pump with a motor powerful enough to move the surface water through a hose, up a flight of stairs and to the outside, draining into the street. It seems to be a simple device, but the inner workings must have been years in the making, the labor of a succession of inventors and engineers. I'm afraid the garden will be lost. The spinach, peas, and radishes have just emerged and already are drowning. Much more rain and nothing will make it. I wonder how the farmers will fare. I couldn't have tolerated a farmer's uncertainty, always at the mercy of the elements and the markets. Even absent the uncertainty, I was unsuited for the task. My constitution required a freedom not possible for those who work the land. I admire their commitment. Without it, the majority of us would starve. It's a mystery how each of twenty children in a schoolroom mature to find their unique place in the world. There was nothing in those early years that suggested I would be a poet, or that my classmates would become ministers, bankers, or thieves. It's likely different, though, for the future farmer who works side by side with his father from an early age. Perhaps it's a balance of example and ancestry that determines the landing place of each of us.

May 20

I'm taking to heart Emerson's assurance that I'll be better for having lived this additional year. Little things suggest he's right. Witnessing the progress of Thomas' chicks, grown too large for their first home, living now with the older hens who will teach them their way. Visiting a woman he knows who raises puppies called labradoodles. The day before a two year old gave birth to a litter of six. Blind and barely able to move, they manage to find their way to their mother. Evenings on the front porch, spellbound by the ivory petals of the magnolia blossom and the perfume of the lilac. Were it only the wonders of nature, every day would be a delight, and an education of the highest order. Yet daily I learn of a new assault on mankind and the natural world. Unspeakable atrocities have occurred since my last night on Mickle Street. The wars are most prominent. Killing machines have been perfected. Millions died in the last century, soldiers and civilians alike. Cities were leveled and refugee camps filled. Many who survived the battlefield and civilian carnage died later from disease, mortal wounds, and insanity. Browsing the library, I see book after book about the wars. Authors penning histories glorifying the victors. I wonder how those untouched by bullet and bomb can live in hope of a better future, knowing of the recent past and the present day. The wars go on, Thomas said, in countries that did not exist in my lifetime. My Quaker friends say there are no just wars. I thought the war to free the slaves was an exception. But the price paid was exorbitant. Now I'm told that the atrocities go well beyond our own kind. There is a relentless destruction of habitats and species. Nature itself is at risk of annihilation. An organization called the "United Nations" has issued a report that a million species of plants and animals are threatened with extinction. Man, it seems, is a disease; the most

lethal the world has ever seen. Scientists warn that it may be too late.
That we've reached the point of no return. The Buddha taught that
everything conditions and is conditioned by everything else. His
followers remind us that we are in an inextricable relationship with
Mother Earth and our only chance is to heal that relationship.

May 21

Thomas commented at breakfast that I hadn't been myself the past few
days. He wondered if I might want to talk. I was reluctant, but if I can't
talk with Thomas, there's no one else, other than Emerson. And I never
know when he'll show up. So, it came out. I've been struggling.
Grieving even. Not for myself but for the next generation and the one
after. Actually, for all inheritors of the planet, not just humankind.
Those to come aren't responsible for what's happened but will,
nevertheless, pay the price. My generation must share in the guilt as
well. Power and greed were in great supply even then. Thomas sat
silent, then responded, "I understand. It's a daily struggle. The grief is
always present, just below the surface." He does his best to not let it
overwhelm him, seeking a balance. Grief and amazement. Grief and
wonder. Grief and joy. He's learned over the years to pay attention. To
events, certainly. But they're transitory. The headline on any given day
fades quickly, replaced by another and another. It's impossible to keep
abreast. And to what end? Thomas said paying attention means to
observe without judgment that which borders on the eternal. The cycles
of sun and moon, day and night. The passing of clouds across the sky.
The whisper that precedes dawn and accompanies dusk. The nocturnal
animals and insects. The seasons and the celestial bodies. And more
recently, he's come to immerse himself in the great questions, those
posed by the philosophers and, in our time, by theoretical scientists.
He's not interested in the minutia. It's the narrative told of our place in
the universe that offers meaning. "It's the witnessing of nature in the
moment, coupled with traveling to the farthest reaches of the universe,
that allows me to remain human and resist the degradation that attempts
to do otherwise." I recalled Blake, one of my spiritual forefathers, "To
see a world in a grain of sand, and a heaven in a wild flower. Hold
infinity in the palm of your hand, and eternity in an hour." Thomas
reminded me that I'll be leaving for New York City in a week, promising
when I return to help me find balance.

May 22

On a wall in Thomas' office is a photograph of a giraffe. Large, black
and white, framed, I've never seen anything like it. What I know of the

giraffe is from visits to the zoo or in those handsome sitting room portfolios with page after page of majestic beasts alert or afoot on the African savanna. But this giraffe is nothing like that. Its head is tipped, ears caught in mid-flutter, eyes wide and benevolent, a patterned neck supporting it all. There's something coquettish about it, as though a perfect pose will be rewarded in some way. It's a stunning portrait, reminiscent of the finest of the 19th century pioneers of the "new art." I came of age with photography, as it did with me. It influenced me greatly, teaching me to look closely at what was real, rather than at the painter's representation of reality. For nearly half a century photographers chronicled my aging. I was in my twenties when I was first photographed. The last time was just a year ago when I sat for Thomas Eakins. Horace and I would often look at one or more of the many frozen moments scattered about my room. I was fascinated that a singular invention could so accurately capture the history of a lifetime. There were some photographers I particularly enjoyed - the Americans' William Henry Jackson, Robert Cornelius, Matthew Brady, and the young Alfred Stieglitz who was coming into his own when I was last with Eakins. Nadar from France and Yoshinobu from Japan. The British produced several great ones - storyteller Lewis Carroll, Henry Fox Talbot, and John Thomson among others. My favorite was Julia Margaret Cameron. She was nearly fifty when she took it up, having received her first camera as a present. She threw herself into the details and her subjects, longing to "arrest all the beauty that came before me." Near the end of her relatively short career she reported that her longing had been satisfied. I can think of no better statement of the artist near the end of life who has abandoned all caution and pursued a form that allowed the soul to be seen. I did my best in that regard, though I still have misgivings from certain compromises I made. If I had it to do over again, I would have left much of my early poetry alone, allowing it to be judged more by later generations rather than by my contemporaries. That's the wonderful thing about photograph, they are what they were at the moment of inception.

May 23

We went to a ballgame yesterday. Thomas has a friend with a seven-year-old son. He plays "Little League." The game was much like baseball, with modifications to accommodate the youth of the players. There were three innings rather than nine, and each inning every player batted in either the top or the bottom half of the inning. A coach for each team pitched to his own players, maximizing the chance that a ball would be put in play. When a team was not batting it was in the field. Some players were attentive, moving appropriately in response to a hit ball, doing their best to catch and throw. Others threw rocks, played in the dirt, talked to a buddy or with a bird. Watching the boys have fun and begin to learn America's "great game" was a rich experience. I was much older when the sport came to my attention. About the time of the first publication of *Leaves* a baseball frenzy hit the city. New Yorkers were crazy about it and the local papers began to refer to baseball as the "national pastime." I'd go to a game whenever I could, marveling at the skill of the young men who played for the fun of it. The War interrupted that, and I didn't see another game until moving from Washington to Camden. By then, Philadelphia had become a mecca for some of the best players. On many a sunny day I'd take the ferry across the Delaware, spend the morning at the Franklin Library and the afternoon at Jefferson Park watching the Athletics take on all comers. I remember young "Cap" Anson. He could really hit. One year he averaged .415. Supporters came from all around to cheer him on. A few years later Cub Stricker arrived. About 5'2", he stroked the ball better than anyone I ever saw play the game. Five seasons he won the home run title and twice he batted over .400. Anson, Stricker, and a few others were great ambassadors. Their enthusiasm and prowess encouraged boys to middle-aged men to take up the sport. If I couldn't make it to Jefferson Park, I could watch it played almost any evening on streets throughout the city. Thomas told me that baseball is still widely popular and played at every level. New York City has two professional teams now, the Mets and the Yankees. Forty to fifty thousand fans pack their stadiums on a warm evening. Thomas said he'd try to get me a ticket.

May 24
Coffee has long been my favorite breakfast beverage. The same for Thomas. Every morning we begin with the preparation ritual. The rich earthy aroma follows soon after. We sip through the meal, clean up, then retire to our easy chairs with a second cup. The black brew primes our conversation. Coffee and conversations have been staples in my life since I was a young man. Writing for the *Brooklyn Eagle*, I would begin my daily rounds with coffee and eggs at a neighborhood eatery. Oftentimes I secured the kernel of a later story while listening in on nearby table talk. What friends and associates shared with each other frequently became the news of the day. The best of stories, those of human interest, were told by those living them. Thomas says that while baseball may still be the national pastime, the consumption of coffee is the national passion. Coffeehouses are as common as taverns in this age. Some, like Starbucks, are members of a worldwide enterprise. Others

are strictly local. There's one up the street I frequently walk or bicycle to. No matter the time of day, nearly every chair at every table is occupied. Discussions range from politics to fashion to sex, the black brew loosening the tongue as much as brandy or beer. This afternoon I set out on my bike in search of a new experience. I discovered Zanzibar's, an old brick store front, painted a pleasant beige with rust trim and an awning to match. Inside, tiny tables with two or three chairs each line the wall. I took the only table available. The opposite wall is mostly menu. Coffee beans from around the world are sold by the pound. The same coffee can be purchased by the cup. With so many choices I was unsure, finally taking a chance on the Jamaican Blue Mountain. In no hurry whatsoever, I hoped to learn about those nearby. Before I could get started, however, a young man asked if he might occupy the chair next to me. Following introductions and brief pleasantries, he shared the story of his uncertain marriage. I listened attentively.

May 25

Thomas thought it would be a good day for a drive. I agreed. So shortly after breakfast we were on our way, leaving behind the traffic and noise, neighborhoods, and buildings of commerce. The highway north gave way to two-lane roads dissecting fields a mile long and just as wide. This was farm country on a scale I hadn't known in my Long Island youth. Horse-drawn plows were nowhere to be seen, replaced by massive machines crisscrossing the landscape. Atop each, solitary figures surrounded by glass sat in easy chairs, controlling the green and yellow beasts beneath them. Thomas calls them tractors, the first of which arrived in the Plains states about the time of the automobile. Like nearly everything, they've evolved in the century since. What took a day with a horse and plow, and most of a day with its immediate successor, can now be accomplished in an hour. Thomas says even more modern tractors are being manufactured, roving the fields remotely, their handlers in a nearby farmhouse or an hour away. They sell for hundreds of thousands of dollars, requiring more and more land to be put into production. To make it work, corporations are replacing family farms. Absentee managers dictate the rules of agriculture, selecting the seeds to be sown, chemicals to be applied, prices to be paid at harvest, markets to be shipped to. Thomas says a bushel of corn is as likely to end up as fuel for automobiles or sweetener in cereals as feed for cattle, hogs, or chickens. The losses are many with the death of farm towns, school closings, and displaced families. And the health costs are in the millions from illnesses caused by poisoned streams and rivers that make their way into drinking water. I don't know what to think of all of this. It's not the progress I imagined.

May 26

I leave in two days. Even in Camden I never imagined I would walk the streets of Manhattan again or visit the home of my birth. Bedridden as I was most of that last year, I would not have been able to make the journey, let alone enjoy it. Now I walk and bicycle at a comfortable pace, covering a few miles a day, weather permitting. The difficulty won't be the effort required to make my way. I'm excited about that. It's the shock of change on a scale I've yet to experience. The city with its millions of inhabitants. Buildings towering over the pedestrians below. A diversity of color and culture unlike any other metropolis. Thomas assures me I'm ready. That the past several weeks have been adequate preparation. In many ways it's the future I dreamed of - rich, textured, democratic. His confidence is a great comfort, though not enough to allay all anxiety. And then there's the mode of travel. No preparation is sufficient for leaving the earth in a metal shell, remaining aloft for three hours at thirty thousand feet. Thomas says it will be one of the great experiences of my life. Looking down at a landscape without borders except those created by mountains and rivers. It gives me the shivers, not unlike the anticipation of a great opera or seeing Lincoln for the first time. I hope I can sleep these next two nights. I want to be well rested.

MONTH THREE

May 27

We pored over maps and schedules most of the day, considering possibilities and sharing stories. Thomas did most of the talking while I took notes. He's never lived in New York City, but frequent trips have given him a love for what he calls "the Big Apple." I'd never heard the expression and asked Thomas of its origin. He knew of course. A writer by the name of E.S. Martin wrote *The Wayfarer in New York* a few years before the start of World War I. Martin contended that folks out west are apt to see New York as a greedy metropolis and that "the Big Apple" gets a disproportionate share of the "national sap." Thomas said the label stuck and New Yorkers to this day are proud of it. I like it too, though I don't agree with Martin. I suppose I have a bias having lived there for nearly three decades. While visiting I'll proudly wear the label. Thomas told me recently that people often have a "bucket list," meaning a list of things they want to do before they die. I should have one too and will likely add to it a return to "the Big Apple." But foremost is the week to come. My first airplane trip. My first subway ride. My first Yankees game. My 200th birthday. I'm excited.

May 28

An amazing day. Mechanical stairs to the boarding level; security screening; the waiting area with nearly everyone glued to their devices; boarding by zone and seating by rows and numbers; attendants, male and female, offering assistance and providing instructions; the captain's welcome; the takeoff. I held my breath, grasping the hand of the young woman to my left. Just when I thought we'd go up and up forever, the plane leveled off at 35,000 feet. For most of two hours it remained there, hurtling through alternating patches of blue and gray. I dozed off and on, dreaming of the lazy days of summer. Then the announcement: "We are about to begin our initial descent. Please fasten your seat belts." And with good reason. The return to earth was a rocky one. We were buffeted by an unseen force, shaking our steel cocoon to the point where I feared it would split apart. Again, I held my breath, placing my faith in the pilots. There was no other choice. Finally, it was over. Once in the terminal I reviewed Thomas' instructions: "Go to ground transportation; hail a taxi for the Jackson Heights-Roosevelt Avenue subway; buy a one-way ticket for $2.50; take the F train to the Delaney and Essex station; exit onto Delaney Street; walk two blocks to Orchard; take a left; walk 100 feet; enter the Blue Moon Hotel; introduce yourself as Walt Van Velsor. They'll be expecting you." Arriving without incident, the desk clerk handed me a key to my room, the "Ella Fitzgerald," where I crawled onto my assigned bunk and rested. Later, after a pastrami on rye and a coca cola for dinner, I called it a day.

May 29

I met my roommates before heading out. Three young men. One from Atlanta, job-hunting after graduating from college a week ago. The second from China. I was unable to learn anything about him, but he smiled a lot and seemed to be enjoying his stay. The third, from Mexico, was taking a break from his studies in the Netherlands. I told him my mother's family was Dutch. He asked what it is I do. I said I was a poet once but, like him, I'm a student of the world now. He seemed pleased, commenting that I'm a "free spirit." After breakfast, I was out the door with the subway map Thomas had given me. He'd circled the Lafayette station where I'd catch an Uptown to Yankee stadium. Within minutes I was on the "D." It was a fascinating ride. Late morning and nearly every seat taken. All ages and every color of the ethnic rainbow. After stops at 145th and 155th, we were at 161st and the stadium. Following the crowd, I was there in minutes, the home of the "Bronx Bombers." It's a massive structure with nearly every seat taken. I don't know how many, but there must have been thousands. It was a celebration. Loud, rowdy, music playing; interrupted by an occasional announcement. At exactly 1:05 the anthem was played and then the first pitch thrown. Thomas had bought me a ticket behind center field. It was for "standing room only" patrons. I could see the entire playing area without obstruction. The Yankees, being the home team, played defense first. After three quick outs, they were up. Hitters one and two smashed home runs. I understand why they're called the "Bronx Bombers." The game moved quickly with the Yanks besting the "Padres" 7-0. It was a different experience from my days at Jackson Field. But it's the same game - bats, balls, bases, and home runs. I enjoyed every minute.

May 30

Walking is always the best way to know a place. As much as I enjoyed the ballgame and the novelty of the subterranean rail system, I've long held that a day afoot is a day well lived. I didn't have an agenda, though I hoped to rediscover something of the past. I last visited Manhattan in April of '87 to deliver my "Death of Lincoln" lecture at Madison Square Theater. It was attended by Andrew Carnegie, James Russell Lowell, John Burroughs, and Frances Burnett, to name a few. Wishing to find a few ghosts from that evening, I headed to 24th between 5th and 6th. Sadly, there were neither ghosts nor remnants of The Madison. An office building now stands where Prince Karl and Jim the Penman played to packed audiences. I then searched for one of the taverns that had occupied many an evening in the years before the war. I didn't find one. By midafternoon melancholy overtook me. But I was determined to make my way to the East River, believing it must still separate the island from the two boroughs. Retracing my steps, I followed Broadway to Wall Street, turning left in the direction of the waterfront. The river was broad as ever. And the Brooklyn Bridge still spanned it. I saw it just the one time in '87 and have never forgotten what a marvel of engineering it is. I would have liked to have walked the bridge to Brooklyn and back, but my feet weren't up to it. Instead, I strolled along South Street in search of a ferry. At Pier No. 11 I found it; more than one, in fact. I chose the Rockaway, as it stops at the Brooklyn Army Terminal on the first leg of the hour long journey. What a delight to sit back, passing ships and barges, Governors Island, and the Statue of Liberty, dedicated the year before my Lincoln lecture. She's as welcoming as when I first set eyes upon her.

May 31

I never expected a long life. The prospect of seeing eighty was unlikely given my health and family history. But when Thomas said my 200th was imminent, for the briefest moment I considered immortality a possibility. The notion was attractive, but fleeting. Nevertheless, I looked forward to saying, "I've lived for two centuries." But waking this morning I was faced with reality. This is my last birthday. I considered calling it off but didn't want to disappoint Thomas. Packing quietly, I was soon on the "M" to Penn Station. Once there, I boarded the train to Wyandanch, arriving an hour later. A younger Thomas drove me in his taxi to 246 Old Walt Whitman Road. I didn't know what to expect. All I'd been told was that the house was still standing. On arrival, I was greeted with a banner: "Whitman @ 200. Where it all began." Balloons lined a walkway leading to the entrance of an attractive structure. Large letters below the windows declared: "Walt Whitman Birthplace - State Historic Site." I'd been remembered, not just by academics but by the State of New York. Years ago, when I wrote of crossing on the

Brooklyn ferry, I spoke of others who would see the same islands, fifty and a hundred years hence. I imagined a few might read my poem, and their crossing might be the better because of it. But I never expected my birthplace to be honored. Inside, nearly a hundred listened as a gentleman spoke of my life and times. Behind those seated, exhibits with photographs lined the walls telling the story of my journey. Overhead were quotes from others, poets I assumed, who apparently knew of me as well. A most moving testimonial was among them, penned by a Mr. Langston Hughes:

Old Walt Whitman
Went finding and seeking,
Finding less than sought,
Seeking more than found,
Every detail minding
Of the seeking or the finding.
Pleasured equally
In seeking as in finding,
Each detail minding,
Old Walt went seeking and find.

Exiting through a side door, I walked onto a lawn with empty chairs, awaiting a later event I assumed. Just beyond was my home, where all first memories reside. It was much the same. The long, thin chimney; shingle siding faded brown; white trim and white shutters framing the many windows. I wondered if the ghosts of early childhood were still about. Peering into the distant past, a tale emerged of a child who went forth every day. How the first object he looked upon he became, and how it became part of him. That same child had a mother with mild words, and a father, strong, self-sufficient, manly, mean, angered, unjust. Wounds from those days remain.

June 1
The return home was an adventure, requiring a host of travel methods - taxi, train, subway, bus, and plane. I imagined a movie maker might weave the experience into a film of an old man's day. Near the end I was delayed two hours on the airport runway, the pilot waiting for traffic to subside. A businessman kept me company, telling stories of his athletic accomplishments as a boy and young man. He's a father now, and dreams of reading of his son's achievements in the local newspaper. "One can only hope," he said, after describing the prowess of his four-year-old and the hours of practice devoted to being the best. I wondered

if the boy is allowed to play alone and on his own time. Does he search on hands and knees for the little things others fail to see? Waiting for the return taxi yesterday, I found a resting place against a tree, thick grass all around. I ran my fingers through it as I would a lover's hair. As a boy I was curious about the origin of things. I wondered, "What is the grass; why is it green; how does it grow?" Does the young ball player wonder the same? Does he hold the slender blades with full hands and seek out a wise one in search of answers? Does his curiosity lead him from one question to another? It was finally our turn on the runway. The engines roared as we rushed headlong into the night, rising like a giant condor over the sprawling city. The businessman slept, dreaming of his son and leaving me to ponder old questions in this age of miracles.

June 2
Exhausted, I slept well into the morning. When the time was right, Thomas listened without interruption, as I elevated every detail to folklore. He's likely had similar experiences but honored each of mine as if one of a kind. Describing the gathering at my boyhood home, it struck me that he too may have had a 200th birthday, though he's offered no hint of it. Perhaps he'll tell me someday after the luster of my celebration has faded. After sharing everything, we talked about what was next. He said he'd spoken with Emerson while I was away. Although I'm free to chart my own course, Emerson thought it would be beneficial to meet and discuss possibilities. Emerson and the others are interested in recent discoveries on the big questions and hope I might be as well. If so, they can connect me with individuals who led the way in their own time. A few were prominent in my day. Most, however, were twentieth century pioneers who labored on the shores of the future. I told Thomas I'd like that and asked when I could start. He responded that the work could begin soon as the summer solstice is on the 21st. Communication with those on the other side is best on or near that date as climatological interference is less likely. Thomas said he'd notify Emerson so arrangements can be made. He then suggested I accompany him to Maine where I could enjoy the sea and sky. It would be a healthy respite. We depart midnight Tuesday, in the usual way. In the meantime, he said he'd teach me to drive his car.
June 3
Thomas drives a "Jeep." It's a box on wheels. Silver, with four doors and seating for six. It's not luxurious, but it's certainly more comfortable than the carriages I knew. On our drive this morning, he promised I'd be behind the wheel before long. I was apprehensive. I'd always been a passenger, whether on a carriage or omnibus, wagon or stagecoach,

locomotive or paddle steamer, preferring to own nothing that required maintenance. But the "plan" is that I incrementally gain greater freedom. Learning to drive is part of the plan. My education commenced at the county fairground. I'd observed Thomas enough to understand the importance of the key to get things started, the various gauges, the shifter for moving forward and in reverse, the use of the right foot to moderate the speed and to brake. I'd learned about the buttons and levers too. To signal right and left. Turn the lights on and off. Raise and lower the windows and operate the radio. Changing places, I coached myself that if I could learn to ride a bicycle, I could learn to drive. There were abrupt starts and stops for sure. Paying attention to what's ahead, the gauges in front, the mirrors right, left and above, looking side to side and to the back all took practice. But it came together, like many things that seemed overwhelming at first but eventually became second nature. By midafternoon I was weary but had gained confidence. Thomas suggested we call it a day and practice on the street tomorrow.

June 4
It didn't take long to realize that driving on a vacant lot is not the same as on a roadway. It's like tossing a ball in the air and trying to hit it, in contrast to batting in a game against the best of pitchers. I nearly froze, turning from a quiet street onto a busy thoroughfare. What appeared manageable from the passenger side seemed perilous behind the wheel. But Thomas coached me every step. "Keep both hands on the steering wheel. Stay in your lane. When changing lanes or turning, always signal, use the mirrors, and look to the side and back. If a car is ahead, keep a car's length for every ten miles an hour. Always know the speed limit and never exceed it. Pay extra attention to bicyclists and pedestrians." It's a lot all at once. But I slowly lost the sense that I was in a battle. It's a shared effort. If everyone plays their part, no one gets hurt. "Of course," Thomas reminded me, "people do get hurt. But the risk is minimized if you're at the top of your game." The first time I rode with Thomas he told me he'd never been in an accident. I have a greater appreciation of that now.

June 5
I woke shortly before midnight. Thomas said we'd be leaving soon. He asked what I thought of staying awake this trip. I hadn't considered it, assuming I'd sleep until morning. He said it's an experience to make the passage eyes wide open. Following Thomas to the reading room, I took a seat in one of the wingback chairs. The fire suddenly died out, but the mantel clock continued to tick. At first there was nothing, then pinpoints

of light emerged in the distance. How far off, I couldn't say. There was movement - slow at first, like a train leaving the station. Without windows, I couldn't judge my location, but I was certain I'd left the room, the house, the comfort of the earth's surface. The distant lights grew in size. I was moving toward them, or they toward me, or both. I continued to hear the tick of a clock, marking my progress along an invisible rail line. The lights began to take shape and sound. My speed increased, as collective voices separated into distinct beings. Languages emerged, none of which I understood. But there was a feeling, similar to what I experienced the night Emerson sat with me. I existed, unique and one of a kind, as did the light forms. Yet the barriers had fallen away. Perhaps they weren't human, or they were humans of an advanced state. It didn't matter. As beings in time, we shared a common ancestry and, I assumed, a common return. Wherever I was, I didn't want to leave. But as quickly as they arrived, they vanished, leaving only the starless night. I slept, waking to sunrise over Panther Pond.

June 6

Thomas has the use of a car while in Maine. It's a "Nitro." Similar to the Jeep, boxlike but longer. We had breakfast at a nearby cafe. I drove while Thomas tutored. Back at the house, he pronounced me fit to take it out on my own. We sat with a map of the state and considered possibilities. With a forecast of sunny skies, he suggested Popham Beach, near Bath. He penned instructions with supplementary notes and circles on the map. Like the best of teachers, he asked questions to test my understanding. Assured I was up to the task, he bid me farewell. Passing through forest and farmland, then skirting Casco Bay, I turned right just before the Kennebec. Phippsburg Peninsula was ahead with Popham Beach at its southern tip. Meandering along 209, I was in no rush. This was a land, neither mainland nor island, adrift in time. Approaching the town of Phippsburg, a sign was posted for the "Albert Totman Public Library." I followed the detour, intending to stop briefly. I should have known better. I've often been held hostage by a library for the good part of a day. Entering the small, white-sided building, I was greeted by a gentle woman reminiscent of mother. She inquired of my interests. "History and poetry," I said. Pointing toward the steps, she said poetry was in the 800s with history nearby. I thanked her and found myself alone, passing my fingers over Keats, Poe, Shelley, and Tennyson. I eventually chose a volume by Robert Frost, born shortly after I moved to Camden. I immersed myself, finding great pleasure in his language and images. I walked country lanes with him as I had in my own day. I searched for more. On the bottom shelf, next to Wordsworth, was a slim green volume, *Poems - Walt Whitman*, published in 1921. Slowly turning the fragile, yellowed pages, I scanned the Contents: *Inscriptions, Children of Adam, Calamus, Birds of Passage, Sea Drift, Drum Taps.* I wondered how they ever came to be. Was I merely a scrivener for an unseen poet? I returned to the Introduction by Carl Sandburg. He wrote some nice things. That *Leaves of Grass* "stands by itself and is the most noteworthy monument amid the work of American Literature." He spoke of its originality and that no other book can compete with it. That it's "an intensely personal book," with "the bravery of a first-rate autobiography." That I'm the best loved figure in American Literature, and the most damned. There was a light touch on my shoulder. "Sir, it's five o'clock. The library is closing." I thanked the kind lady and made my way out. Too late for the beach, I returned to Panther Pond.

June 7

Another sunny day, and another opportunity for the beach. I vowed to make it all the way, foregoing library stops and even an hour or two at the Maine Maritime Museum. Ignoring the turn onto Parker Head Road and the "Totman," I passed Town Hall, the grave of an 1812 War veteran, and Small Point Baptist Church. A short time after, I turned onto Popham Road in the direction of the sea. Rounding Spirit Pond and then Silver Lake, I was suddenly at the terminus of the Kennebec, gateway to the North Atlantic, Portugal, Morocco, and the Mediterranean. Nearby, and standing as protection for vessels large and small, was Sequin Lighthouse, commissioned by George Washington. Bringing the Nitro to rest, I looked upon the great blue body. I'd never been witness to it so far north. I imagined a life at sea, hunting the great whale as did Melville. I was land bound all my life and would choose that life again. But had I been given the lot of a mariner, seafarer, or sailor, I would have embraced it just the same. *Leaves* would not exist but perhaps *Waves* would have been its equal. A short distance from my stopping place was a path through tall grasses, leading to a rocky outcropping. I found a stone chair and sat with my thoughts. I observed other solitary figures walking the beach, napping on the sand, or fishing from the shore. Seagulls glided then swooped in search of a midday meal. Harbor seals popped up, looking about in every direction. A lone hawk grabbed hold of an updraft then leveled, surveying all below. Once, I encouraged others to stop with me, that they might possess the origin of all poems; the good of the earth and sun. It's the same now as it was then. On that rock, on the edge of a vast ocean, I was at the center of the universe from which all poems originate.

June 8

Thomas has a friend who has cancer. There's nothing that can be done about it. A year ago, doctors gave Kristen three months. Each month thereafter was to be her last. She continues to beat the odds and has a bucket list she's been whittling away at it. Nearly everything she wanted to see and do has a line through it. Sailing on the bay was one of the few remaining. Thomas has another friend who is a sailor. She has a thirty-two footer that once belonged to her father. He named it *Nightwatch* years ago because of his love for sailing by moonlight. The *Nightwatch* is Lizzie's now. She's every bit as capable as her father, sailing the bay and far up the coast when time permits. I met Thomas' friends today, invited to join Kristen on her first, and likely only, sail on the bay. She's a wisp of a woman with eyes for everything. Though any day may be her last, there's no sadness about her. After setting sail, she spoke of her morning ritual. At sunrise she gives thanks for all she's witnessed in a life that could have been longer but has been long enough. She has no regrets, having tended to them as she does the tiny garden behind her modest home. Kristen practices shamanism. For years she's journeyed to the lower, middle, and upper worlds in search of healers and teachers, and for aid in addressing the wounds of childhood. Having succeeded, she now teaches others to do the same. After a while we stopped talking, words less important than the sea breeze. I watched Kristen watch. Everything gave her delight. At the end of the day, stepping off the *Nightwatch* and onto the harbor launch, she gave thanks for the experience of a lifetime.

June 9

On my first visit with Thomas to Portland, we discovered Lois' Natural Marketplace at the intersection of Middle and India Streets. This morning I made my way back, ordering an egg and avocado sandwich. Taking a seat at the counter, a woman and her infant were close enough to touch but for the window ahead. Her little one slept in his cradle on wheels as she lifted his cap, adjusting it away from the sun. For a long time, she looked at him, shooing a fly with her hand. Beyond, a few hundred feet or so, open tents lined either side of the street. Soon enough I was amidst the crowd, which had gathered for the "Old Port Festival." There was a menagerie of food carts offering ice cream, hot dogs, french fries, soda, fresh juices, and ethnic foods. Sold for more than their worth, but sought after nevertheless. At the Market Street Park, shade trees offered refuge from the midday sun. Near the center of the festival, children were giving their full attention to a young woman in a white, knee-length coat. Wearing dark glasses with white rims and waving a container with an unknown liquid, she introduced herself as "The Mad Scientist." She probed the kids with questions about gases and solids, catalysts, chemical transformations, and flashpoints. Had I a teacher who cared that I understand the material world as much, I might have stayed in school. Nearby, a gentleman in a yellow jacket emptied a refuse container. I sought his company. He said he's come to the festival for nearly thirty years. The first time was shortly after arriving from Vietnam. His father was an American soldier and mother a village girl. He only knew his mother, who died when he was a boy. The war took much from her and she never recovered. He still grieves. He then told me this is the last day ever for the festival. City leaders fear it's no longer a safe place. Earlier in the week, he and other workers removed all the metal trash cans as a precaution against terrorists who might hide explosives in them. Having fled his homeland to escape the violence, he's considering a return with his wife and children.

June 10

I took the "workboat" this morning. A three-hour circuit making scheduled stops to deliver freight and mail to Little Diamond, Great Diamond, Long, Cliff, and Chebeague Islands. We shared the bay with sea taxis, lobster boats, ferries, yachts, and day sailors. A gentleman about my age boarded at Little Diamond, taking the seat next mine. He looked every bit a local. Long white hair tied back, denim shirt and weathered jeans, hands and face rough and wrinkled from years in the sun. He told me he'd fished most of his life in the nearby waters, raising a family during good times and bad. He fishes for himself now; his wife deceased, and children grown. Having sold the house and purchased a small cabin on the island, his needs are minimal. He doesn't get out every day. When the fishing is good, two or three days a week is enough. On other days, he works with driftwood cast ashore by violent storms. He uses the knife given to him by his father when he was a boy. It's been years since he'd sharpened it, allowing the grain to guide it as much as his own hands. He spoke of the hidden shapes revealed when he's patient. And patience he has in abundance now. Evenings when he sets the knife aside, he reads books on seafaring and marine life. For generations back, the men in his family took to the sea, gone for months, sometimes years at a time. He nearly followed, but fell in love before the first voyage, choosing family over adventure. Nevertheless, it's in his bones. I could have listened for hours to his tales of the islands, hidden rocks, shipwrecks, and lost sailors. But he had business at the Cliff Island Store and Cafe, leaving me with thoughts of a life I never knew.

June 11

The Good Life Market is a little place on the edge of town, catering to
locals most of the year. But by early June, the tourists have arrived.
Thomas says Panther Pond is left alone, but the much larger Sebago
Lake becomes the Cape Cod of Maine. We try to stay off the highway
that follows the eastern edge and passes by the Market, taking back roads
to and from Portland and other points along the Midcoast. Sometimes,
though, a meal at the Good Life makes it worth the effort. We took a
chance late yesterday, showing up an hour after the dinner crowd had
come and gone. Thomas encouraged me to try one of their salads. "It's
a meal in itself," he said. We sat in the small dining room, sharing it
with a young couple oblivious but to each other's company. It's said that
love is perennial. The boy and the girl bore witness to that. On the wall
above their table was a poem, framed and at eye level with no identified
source. It's a prescription, a suggestion on how one's life might be lived:

*Go placidly amid the noise and the haste and remember what peace
there may be in silence. As far as possible, without surrender, be on
good terms with all persons. Speak your truth quietly and clearly; and
listen to others, even to the dull and the ignorant; they too have their
story . . .*

I was a young man when *Leaves* was published. It grew over the years,
new and revised poems added with each edition. But I'm still most fond
of that slim first edition. Even the Preface is a reminder of the
enthusiasm with which I looked upon the world. Tucked midway
through was my youthful imperative on what we should do:

*Love the earth and sun and the animals, despise riches, give alms to
every one that asks, stand up for the stupid and crazy, devote your
income and labor to others, hate tyrants, argue not concerning God . . .*

June 12

"The alewives are running." I'd heard it four or five times since arriving.
I finally asked a store clerk what the talk was about. He was well versed.
"In late May when the waters warm, the alewife migrate from Casco
Bay, up the Presumpscot River to Highland Lake where they spawn. The
best place to see them is after the Presumpscot narrows to Mill Brook
where they congregate in a shallow pool." There, one by one, they
attempt the steep climb up a waterfall. Sketching a map, he said the best
access is a trail off Methodist Road. By noon I was on the trail,

following the Brook through lush woodlands. Twenty minutes in, I heard the cascading water. From the edge of the falls, I could see them. Hundreds, if not thousands, swimming in unison. As if on cue, every few seconds a lone alewife would break off to begin the ascent. Most were unsuccessful on the first try, sliding back into the pool to catch their breath and try again. Navigating the rocks, I made my way to the waterside and sat, mesmerized by the dance. Individually, each was a dark, slender arrow darting about. Collectively, they were a force of nature. At some point I fell into a deep sleep. Perhaps I was in a hypnotic state. A voice woke me sometime later. Seated beside me was a woman a few years older, but younger in appearance. She asked if I was alright. I assured her I was and had just drifted off. She wondered what I knew of the alewife. "Very little," I told her, relating my conversation with the clerk. She then shared her fascination for its mysterious inner clock and compass, and its tenacity. Every year she returns to the pool to better understand. The adults that succeed by making it up the falls and to Highland Lake spawn for two weeks before returning to the sea. A few months after hatching, the juveniles begin their own downstream migration, growing to full size in the estuaries of Casco Bay. As young adults they return to the sea as well, staying for three or four years before beginning the long journey and their first spawning. I listened on, enchanted by the story and the storyteller, until falling asleep again, waking alone but for the alewife and the evening songbirds.

June 13

If his schedule permits, Thomas meets with Kristen at least once each visit to Maine. He believes there's something of value in the practice of shamanism. Connections are made to certain areas of the psyche otherwise inaccessible by more traditional practices. "There's a place for it," he says, "in the task of coming to know ourselves." Intrigued, and with Thomas' encouragement, I met with Kristen yesterday. Knowing I was coming, she journeyed on her own the day before to discern whether or not I would be a good candidate. She was assured I would be. Arriving at ten, I was offered a cup of matcha, used for centuries by Zen monks in Japan and China in preparation for meditation. Sipping in the prescribed manner, I experienced a subtle shift from restlessness to calm alertness. After a few minutes, I was ready. Led to a small room on the lower level, comfortable chairs were waiting with candles lighted, creating an oasis in the near dark. Kristen explained that we would journey in the hope of discovering my "power animal," a spirit guide in animal form best suited to my personality and history. We turned the chairs toward each other and sat. Depressing a button on a small box, she released the sound of a drum then called upon a shamanic guide to assist her. Soon, she and her guide were standing on the shore of a great ocean. A dozen or more large white birds approached from a distance, landing a few feet away. They were albatross from the southern seas. After some communication, one separated from the others and stepped forward. Its manner and bearing suggested it was the leader. Through her guide, Kristen was able to communicate with it. Intimating that certain traits of mine made for a compatible match, he spoke of his willingness to serve as my spirit guide. "If you call upon me, I'll come." He then stressed the need for regular contact, joined his companions, and disappeared. The drumming ceased and Kristen returned. She asked if I accepted the albatross as my guide. Earlier in the day I wouldn't have imagined that a white bird from the south would come into my life. It seems reasonable now, even natural. I dreamt of Thomas, Emerson, and the albatross. Up at five, streaks of orange and yellow hovering above Panther Pond, I mused on the oddity of my situation and wondered what might be next.

June 14
As much as I enjoy traveling Emerson's way, there are tradeoffs. Yesterday I was to travel in the usual manner. But sunshine was in the forecast and Thomas was kind enough to purchase me a last minute ticket. Seated by the window, I imagined I was the albatross. Mile after mile I looked down on cities and towns, great lakes and rivers, dense forests and open fields, roads straight without compromise or winding through ancient mountains. Occasionally we passed through rolling white clouds. There was a comfort in the soft, billowy mass pressed against my window. The three hours passed in the space of a breath. Setting down on the narrow strip of concrete, I was at peace.

June 15
I'm fascinated by the albatross. Since journeying with Kristen, I've sensed its presence - intelligent and kind; neither human nor spirit. It seems to have an understanding of nature's ways and the unseen forces that influence the world. I asked Thomas what he knows about the great white bird - its lifespan, eating and mating habits, its ability to stay weeks at sea, never touching earth. "Very little," he said, suggesting we explore together. Excusing himself, he returned with a device similar to the laptop used by P.T. Raising the lid, he typed "albatross" into a narrow box at the top of the page. Instantly, a list of entries appeared. They're "articles," he explained, some by academics. He chose one from

the *Encyclopedia Britannica*. Entering a world I didn't know existed, a vast library was at our fingertips. Moving through text and photographs, appreciation for my new acquaintance was enhanced. There are more than a dozen species of the seabird, the largest having a twelve foot wingspan. They learn to fly within months of birth. Nevertheless, they're slow to mature, spending five years or more at sea before mating on land. In stormy weather they can stay aloft for hours, never once flapping their wings. Consulting additional sources, we discovered more about its wing structure, simple diet, monogamous ways, and long life. I hope to stay in contact with my feathered guide.

June 16

It was a hot day yesterday, making for an uncomfortable night. For the first time, I turned on the overhead fan. It helped, moving the air enough so I could fall asleep. But shortly after midnight I was awakened by a ticking sound. I thought it must be a clock. Then I recalled there isn't one in the room, except the timepiece Emerson gave me. I listened intently. It was coming from above; from the fan. The sound was more of a tap than a tick, repeating itself regularly, but slightly more rapidly than a clock. It was as if time was accelerating. I tried to ignore it, but it was insistent. I covered my head with a pillow, but to no avail. It persisted. I gave in, as it seemed to be conveying a message. I returned to the evening in Camden, the conversation with Emerson, his offer, and my decision to accept it. Nearly three months have passed. Soon it will be summer, then autumn, then my final winter. Closing my eyes, an hourglass appeared. I counted the grains of sand filling the bottom one by one. Time is running out. I know the day and hour the last grain will fall. I've learned much since I've been here, though I still feel adrift. This is a foreign land. I know not the language, nor do I have a road map. I meet with Thomas and Emerson later in the week. Perhaps the albatross will be there as well.

June 17

For the first time in awhile, Thomas and I took a morning walk. With the advent of summer, the neighborhood is changing. April and May were months of anticipation. A looking forward to longer days. Now they're here, as dawn calls for an early rise and daylight bumps up against bedtime. Green is in its season. Lawns are lush with it. Trees hold it so close the sun can barely break through. School is out and the children play hopscotch and hide-and-go-seek. Elders and teenage boys push their mowers through grass, ankle high and more. Women tend to their gardens and flowers. Men reshape their landscapes with brick and stone. Thomas appreciates it all, greeting everyone by name when possible. I've missed his regular company. In the early weeks, a day didn't pass that we didn't have a quiet hour together. Lately, though, our routine has been disrupted. It's no one's fault. I've had opportunities for travel and exploration. He has responsibilities. The absences have me thinking about what it takes to maintain a friendship. So many thoughts have passed through my mind that I've not shared with him. If they're not written down, they're lost forever. I miss our conversations. I miss Horace as well. He was faithful beyond measure. Four years of daily visits with rarely an absence. The efforts all his. Even at the end he was at my bedside, encouraging and cajoling. If I'd had a son, I would not have had a better one. I wonder what thoughts Horace has of me now. Does he feel the loss as much as I do? Emerson said I'll have the opportunity for visits from some who've passed. It would please me greatly to be with Horace one last time.

June 18

Thomas repaired the fan. The tapping is gone. Even so, I woke early. I'm not sure why. I'm not troubled with anything, nor do I have pain that would disturb my sleep. I have been thinking about the meeting. Thomas confirmed it would be this Friday, the summer solstice. "Midsummer" as we called it. The solstice will be late morning, but Emerson wants to meet at sunrise, before the heavy traffic. In Emerson's world, the conditions will be ideal for space-time travel. He prefers to stay put but is making an exception due the urgency he feels about my situation. I'm flattered by the attention, as I'm otherwise unseen here. But I'm anxious about what may be asked of me. I'm as fit as I've been in quite some time. Nevertheless, my energy is no more than the average septuagenarian. Always an afternoon napper, I begin to slide without one. I hope Emerson understands. He should, given his health in his later years. I wonder what he recalls of his temporal existence. If his state of lightness has immunized him from what was painful? There's much I'd like to ask, though Friday is not likely the best time. I've taken copious notes in anticipation of their questions. Surely, I'm entitled to questions of my own.

June 19

I've been thinking about the big questions again. The ones from which all others follow. When did it begin? And how? Was there a first cause or was it spontaneous? Was there anything before the start of it all? Thomas anticipates these are questions Emerson and the others will want to be briefed on. They've moved beyond the cosmological myths of the early religions, understanding that there was no science to inform the early theorists. They're aware of the progress that's been made since the 19th century but haven't been updated for several years. Thomas says their questions don't arise out of mere curiosity. The brightest among them believe that knowledge on the beginning of time may provide clues on how it ends. While some cling to the notion of eternity, most have a sense that it's a myth as well. I asked Thomas how I should commence an inquiry. Do I begin with the most recent discoveries or trace the questions back to the earliest answers? His response, like that of any good journalist, is I should start at whatever point makes sense. He then handed me a slim volume reputedly authored by Lao Tzu, an ancient Chinese wise man. The *Tao Te Ching*, according to Thomas, is an example of how one man, unfettered by belief or dogma, considered the great questions.

June 20

I spent the afternoon in Thomas' library with the *Tao Te Ching*. It's a masterpiece, written by a sage comfortable with his own counsel. As much as I admire Emerson and the depth of his thought, he would have done well to have studied Lao Tzu. The old master set forth in eighty-one brief chapters what took Emerson volumes. Even then, Emerson fell short. But I wasn't seeking to compare the two. I was searching for evidence of how a Wise One approached the great questions. Lao Tzu postulated that all that can be named originated from the nameless, and that source is darkness. He speaks of the "Tao" as elusive, intangible, and without essence; born before heaven and earth in the silence and the void. He doesn't purport to know who or what gave birth to the Tao but says it's older than God in whom he doesn't attribute the act of creation. Lao Tzu's cosmology is one of unfolding rather than of making. Matter came into being. The hand of a supreme designer nowhere to be found. I wonder where the science of today is on these matters. Does it lend credence to the existence of a Christian God, or did Lao Tzu better intuit the essence of our origin?

June 21

The day of the meeting. Thomas and I took a seat on the porch to enjoy the early morning rain. No sooner did it stop than a diffuse, orange glow burst through the gray horizon. Inexplicably, it erupted in my chest as well, rising up through my neck and face, and taking residence in my mind. A voice, not quite human, introduced itself. It was the albatross. I inquired of his name. He responded with a word I couldn't repeat, suggesting I call him Lao, in honor of a Wise One revered by his ancestors. It felt right. Emerson then joined us, apologizing for his tardiness. He said atmospheric turbulence had delayed him. Then he began. "Walt, you have six months to complete your primary education, beginning today and ending on the Winter Solstice. After that, your time should be spent preparing for death." I was taken aback by Emerson's directness, though he was never one for subtlety, always speaking with the utmost candor. He continued, "You should devote time daily to study and exploration. It's important you retrace the steps from the beginning, leading to the present day." Thomas waited for Emerson to pause, and then interjected. "Walt, I concur with Emerson. But you should also study the people of this time. They won't be here long but are just as important as those who have gone before." Lao spoke. "I agree with all that's been said. However, as your spirit guide, I believe it's important that you immerse yourself in the world of plants and animals, sea and sky. Existence may not be eternal, nevertheless, nature will persist long after the extinction of your species." More conversation ensued. There was give and take, and an agreement. I'd do my best to honor the advice of each, giving equal weight to past, present, and future. Having made the promise, Thomas and I were alone, and the rain came down.

June 22

I have my own computer now. Thomas insisted. It's a "MacBook Air," manufactured by the "Apple" company. They make handheld telephones too, which I see everywhere. Thomas said he was initially hesitant to give me the laptop, fearing it would occupy too much of my time. But after yesterday's meeting, he realizes it's a necessary tool if I'm to accomplish the tasks of the next six months, especially those Emerson insisted on. He then spoke of Lao, and how pleased he is that Lao has entered my life. "The virtual world of the computer is enticing, even addictive to some. The best antidote to its seduction is immersion in nature, every day if possible." He encouraged me to call upon Lao often. "I have no doubt he will be a great aid in helping you balance the various expectations." Thomas then asked if I'd be interested in accompanying him on a trip to Michigan. He's speaking at a conference and I'd have time to explore on my own. We'd be staying on an island known for its beauty. I could take the laptop and explore its world as well. As always, I agreed. Thomas said we'd travel by airplane, as the conference organizers wouldn't understand if he made the trip otherwise.

June 23

It was a long day of travel. The flight to Detroit. An hour wait for the flight to Pellston. An hour on the runway before it was decided the plane wasn't safe to fly. Then a long walk to a distant terminal and gate. Another hour wait. An hour flight. Thirty minutes on a tiny bus to Mackinaw City. One last wait, then twenty minutes on the ferry to Mackinac Island, the best part. The passage was rough and blustery across the narrow strait separating Lake Michigan from Lake Huron. On the lower deck, large windows protected us from the spray that leapt ten or more feet high. We could see Bois Blanc Island on the right and the magnificent Mackinac Straits Bridge on the left. I would have spent the remainder of the day going back and forth, never getting off. And would have enjoyed visiting with the captain and crew, learning the history of the Lakes, the sailors and the cargo lost in storms. But Thomas said dinner would be served soon, reminding me that I'd gone without lunch. So, I willingly followed, stepping off the ferry and onto an open carriage drawn by two brown beasts with a knowledge of the island so keen they needed neither direction nor prodding. They strode with a sure and easy gait, picking their way through pedestrians and bicyclists who crowded the narrow roadway. The village and traffic behind, we passed lovely, century-old homes, flanked by lilac bushes in full bloom. Leaving them behind as well, we ascended the long, steep hill to the hotel, perched on a hillside overlooking the great blue lake.

June 24

All day it rained. Without an umbrella I was free to wander the old hotel, exploring its shops, dining areas and library, conversing with staff well-disciplined in congeniality and polite manners. I particularly enjoyed those of foreign birth, for they seemed most genuine. When I wasn't exploring or conversing, I sat in a corner chair, observing the guests, the new arrivals and those already at home in their temporary residence. There were couples older than me, on their annual pilgrimage from points unknown. Newlyweds anticipated their first night together and children raced about, ignoring the pleas of parents to slow down. After lunch I napped, serenaded by the unremitting rainfall. Late in the day Thomas knocked on my door, reminding me of dinner. It was a banquet, honoring several judges recently elevated from their law practices to a seat on the bench. The principal speaker was a blind man, a longtime lawyer, now a justice on the state's Supreme Court. His theme was a simple one, that life can change in an instant. Matter-of-factly and without self-promotion, he told the story of a day in the park. A long-distance runner, he was walking on a Sunday morning, conserving energy for an upcoming race. Without warning, he was struck from behind by an out-of-control bicyclist traveling at a high rate of speed. Severely injured, he endured surgeries to repair his spinal cord and other broken parts. For months he knew only his bed, hospital staff, and visitors. One day he walked out, sightless but on his own, anxious to start his new life. It was a slow start. Day after day of rehabilitation and pain. Years later, the pain remains a constant companion. But he's a runner again, having completed a dozen marathons since that Sunday morning. He renders opinions on the most serious of cases. He's steeped in the Jewish tradition and a scholar of the Talmud. He concluded his remarks with the story of Jacob, his long night of wrestling with the angel, the injury he sustained, and his new life as the father of Israel.

June 25

Yesterday's rain left me restless, the sun's return pushing me out the door. It didn't take long to find the trail separating woodlands from shoreline. Most of the morning I was alone and without the disturbance of trucks or cars. I could hear everything. The lake bumping up against the rocks. The gulls squawking as they do for no apparent reason. The inland birds singing with intention and joy. I sat on the beach, following the zigzag of a northern duck unperturbed by my presence. Taking to the trail again, I followed at a respectful distance a lone seagull which, for the moment, thought it better to walk than fly. Wildflowers of pink, lavender, and white were in abundance. Occasional clusters of evergreens provided shade and cover for any creature in need. Overlooking it all were the cliffs, dignified and silent, content to observe without intrusion. Near the turning-back point, I happened upon a man emerging from the woods. Dark-skinned, with jet black hair pulled back and knotted, he steadied himself with a walking stick, grasped by fingers brown and weathered like his face. We exchanged greetings. I inquired whether he resides on the island. He said he's a mainlander but often visits to walk with his ancestors who made their home here for generations. They were one of the tribes of the Anishinaabegs - "beings made out of nothing." It's the belief of his people that they were created by a divine breath. He added that the island is special among the many places his people settled, created at the beginning of the world and populated with spirits that bestowed gifts and knowledge on his ancestors after their arrival. I would have liked to have learned more, but I sensed I'd interrupted his private time. Wishing me a good day, he walked to the shore hoping to catch a glimpse of his people, skimming the waters in their open canoes.

June 26

It's taken me time to adjust. Longer than I anticipated. Some would say that jumping ahead a century would be an adjustment for anyone. Perhaps. Yet as a young man, I could grasp the new the first time around. My memory was like flypaper. Nothing escaped it. But somewhere along the way I lost that facility. At first, I thought it was the War. I encountered so much pain and horror that my mind suffered as a result. It didn't move as quickly after that. I began to forget names, or the direction to a friend's house. I misplaced things, only to find them later, right under my nose. I'd read a few pages in a book, needing two or three times to gain a simple understanding. What was new remained new until I'd been around it long enough. It's possible that it was merely the inevitable decline that comes with the advance toward old age. Whatever the cause, I've yet to recover from it. The same is true here. My health is better. My step quicker. I've regained an appreciation for little things that once brought me pleasure. But in some ways, my mind is in a fog, unable to grasp what's going on around me. Today is an example. It was my fourth day of air travel. The flights to New York City and back. The flights to Detroit and Pellston and today's flights home. It was only this morning that I began to see the madhouse that an airport can be. How monstrous its size and diverse its clientele. There's the preoccupation with security and safety I've seen nowhere else. I'd walked through the detectors and had my bags checked on the previous occasions. Today I began to understand that an industry is devoted to scrutinizing those wanting to fly elsewhere. I spoke with Thomas about this. He said it was much simpler before. But everything changed on what's now called "9/11." He explained it's shorthand for September 11, 2001, when terrorists attacked the United States with commercial airplanes, killing nearly three thousand, injuring twice as many, and causing billions of dollars in damage. Those responsible boarded planes like other travelers. Everything changed after that. Thomas said the changes were necessary but have contributed to a general sense of insecurity. He suggested I devote some time to 9/11 and the events leading up to it. He suspects I'll discover that it's a complicated history.

MONTH FOUR

June 27

I approached Thomas this morning for help after attempting on my own to make sense of the MacBook. It's a technology foreign to everything in my life's experience. When Thomas first explained its function, I believed I could manage it. Though unusual in appearance, it was simple in design. Among its many uses, he said it has the capability of producing documents of all kinds, including full-length manuscripts and books. This delighted me, given the years I devoted to publishing long before I imagined *Leaves*. After my stint as a schoolteacher, I bought a used press and a case of types and went into business as editor and publisher of the *Long Islander*. I'd just turned nineteen when the first weekly came out. Though later a full-time journalist, I always considered myself a competent typesetter. Handed the laptop, I assumed it to be the modern equivalent to the printing press. I was in error. After the day with Thomas, I realized I possess one of the most powerful machines ever invented. I've been thrust into a world within our world. A world just as vast as the one we wake up to. An answer can be found for nearly any question. "Streaming" films can be watched day or night. Photographs of the mundane and the exotic appear on the screen just by depressing letters on the keyboard. Live "video chats" with others halfway around the world commence in seconds. Thomas introduced me to "Google," "Wikipedia," "Facebook," "NPR," "ESPN," and "Pandora." He demonstrated how to do a "Search" on any topic or subject. He showed me how to save what I find accessing it again at will. Then came his warning. My computer is a tool. It can be used for good for evil. For activities and pursuits serving no meaningful purpose. Unlike a book, whose message or story is fixed, the MacBook is a portal to innumerable worlds. It's up to me to use it as an aid in fulfilling the tasks ahead.

June 28

Other than my early walk and breakfast, my favorite morning activity is listening to the radio. I've tried several stations, each with its own character and emphasis. I particularly enjoy those offering classical music. Recently, however, I've developed a fondness for "Rock." I've learned about Bob Dylan, Simon and Garfunkel, the Beatles and the Rolling Stones. According to Thomas, they got their start in the 60s, creating a worldwide craze. He said they came on the scene at the right time for millions of young people disillusioned by the assassination of President John Kennedy, and the later assassination of a black minister, Martin Luther King, Jr. Creating the greatest tumult, though, was an unpopular war in Vietnam. This morning I listened to the public radio station. Though the musical offerings are limited, it digs deeper into events than other stations. This morning there was a story about the "Stonewall riots" of fifty years ago. Violence erupted following a police raid at the Stonewall Inn in Greenwich Village. Targeted were "homosexuals" or "gays," individuals sexually attracted to others of the same sex. The newscaster clarified that the Stonewall Inn was not an inn at all, but a tavern frequented by "gay" people. At the time, it was illegal for gays to dance together in public or even be served alcohol. Despite the riots, or perhaps because of them, a "gay rights movement" emerged. On the first anniversary of the riots, "gay marches" were held in New York, Los Angeles, San Francisco, and Chicago. Fifty years later, gay couples have a constitutional right to marry. Gay men and women run companies and hold public office. There is even a gay married man running for president, unthinkable when I was young. I once wrote a series of poems telling the love story of two men. Titled "Live Oak, with Moss," I never published it. Sadly, I cut the poems up, later rearranging and hiding them in "Calamus." Of my many regrets, perhaps the greatest is not having the courage to do the right thing for fear of public criticism. These days, there are countless gay men and women who have the courage to do the right thing. Given the opportunity, I would proudly march arm and arm with them.

June 29

There's a cluster of evergreens that separates Thomas' property from his neighbor's. Thomas says the three tallest were planted by the original owner nearly a century ago. The two others planted decades later. Together, they create a cathedral like canopy. Beneath is a circular area, thick with pinecones and needles. I've coveted the space as the days have lengthened. Yesterday, Thomas gave me permission to clean it up and make whatever use of it I wished. This afternoon I did just that, removing branches and limbs, broken brick and pieces of concrete. I raked the surface free of the remaining debris and placed a chair in the center. With the passing of twilight, I surveyed my tiny kingdom and made myself at home. At first, the only light that penetrated was from a streetlamp three houses down. But slowly my nocturnal vision emerged, and with it the ancient light of distant suns. Only a few at first, then more with each passing minute. Through the thick branches, shimmering pinheads of white managed to exploit the narrowest of openings. The old questions of origin surfaced. Were the stars created at the beginning of time or eons later? Are their numbers fixed or increasing? Do they have planetary systems like ours? If so, do they support life? I'm excited to find out.

June 30

Thomas was in the mood for a country drive and breakfast at Lou's Diner. "It's a greasy spoon," he said, serving portions few can finish. Every couple of months he gets up that way, as much for the patrons as for the food. Off the beaten track, outsiders rarely show up. It's farmers in the morning, workers from town over the lunch hour, teenagers in late afternoon, and anyone with an empty stomach in the evening. An hour after leaving home, we arrived. Had it not been surrounded by cars, I would have thought it abandoned. From the look of things, there'd been no repairs for years. Stepping inside, the interior was the same. In the center were open griddles with eggs, sausages, bacon, ham, and pancakes. An L-shaped counter was occupied by farmers deep in conversation or noses buried in the Sunday newspaper. On the walls were black and white photos of a bygone age. Antique tractors and automobiles; youthful heroes likely deceased; women of stunning beauty who'd long lost that for which they were coveted. We were fortunate to find a vacant booth along the perimeter. A young waitress handed us menus, returning with cups of black coffee. Thomas suggested we order "the farmers' favorite," warning it might be a while given the crowd. Turning my attention to nearby talk, I learned more about President Trump. How tariffs he's imposed on China are hurting the farm economy. The possibility that he might declare war on Iran. Of his fondness for the Russian leader and the North Korean dictator. A few acknowledged that perhaps a mistake had been made in electing the New York businessman who'd promised to "drain the swamp."

July 1

Summer's barely here and yet the temperature's been hovering around 90. Mother used to call these the "dog days," some years extending well into September. It was miserable starting school. Maybe that's why I stopped going. Earning pocket change as an office boy was better than sitting in an oppressive classroom. I never tolerated the heat well. Being Dutch, we were better suited to the cold. I could bundle up and stay warm even in the dead of winter. But in this heat, there's nothing I can wear sufficient to keep me comfortable. If I don't get my walk in before breakfast, it doesn't happen. So, it's with amazement that I watch the men on the roof two houses to the west. They started on Saturday, removing the worn shingles in the heat of the day. From morning to late afternoon, they never take a break. Bare from the waist-up, their muscled torsos are brown, glistening with sweat. Thomas says it's likely they're from Mexico or one of the countries further south. The work is difficult, dangerous at times, and the pay adequate at best. According to Thomas, it's rare to see a white roofer, or a black one. Only "Latinos" will do the work. It's true of other labor as well. Latinos work the fields and the orchards, care for the lawns and gardens of the wealthy, clean hotel rooms, and care for the elderly. Many don't have the necessary papers to be here. President Trump and many of his supporters cry for their deportation and the building of a border wall to keep them out. And yet, says Thomas, they're good citizens in the broadest sense - supporting their families, paying their bills, and generally causing little trouble. There's a big divide in the country over how best to treat those who come here to escape violence and oppression. Thomas doesn't foresee a resolution anytime soon.

July 2

"I loafe and invite my soul." I still remember the day I wrote the line. Thirty-seven years old and in perfect health, I vowed to begin, "hoping to cease not till death." I made a good attempt at it, but youth passed, and life came along. The War was enough to break even the strongest, the most resolute. There were times I was certain the muse had fled, and with her the poetic impulse. Day after day, working as a low-grade clerk and caring for the survivors of battle, there was little left in me to sing or celebrate. Everything ends though, as did the War. But it took its toll. Thousands died and many more were injured and maimed. The loss of soul was just as great, leaving much of the populace angry, hollow, or adrift. I did write again, poems not as fine as the early ones but sufficient enough that my work still sold. It was the stroke of '73 that finally robbed me of that inexplicable creative force. From that day forward, the decline was slow but inevitable. Those years of loafing at my ease, intent on observation, even of a simple spear of summer grass, were long past. Yet now, seventy-three years old, though not in perfect health, I'm healthy enough to loafe again. It's been three months since my temporary reprieve. Though death is not far off, I'm at ease with the certain outcome. It's late in the day, but tomorrow I'll begin early, inquiring of Google whether, as I once surmised, every atom belonging to me belongs to another just as much.

July 3

I woke with the feeling one has about to depart on a great journey. I never tired of it, standing at the threshold, boots laced, knapsack properly fitted and with the bare necessities. Always I carried a journal, my safeguard against inattention. A reminder that seeing is incomplete without the recording of observations. This morning I embarked on a "Google Journey." Seated at my writing table, the MacBook silent and beckoning, I paused to imagine what I might discover. Would I be disappointed? Overwhelmed? Confused? Amazed? I pressed the power button. The dark screen came alive. Introduced to Google by Thomas, I found the small white square with the rainbow colored "G." Moving the "mouse," I hovered over the "G" and clicked. The new age portal to human knowledge appeared. Near the top of the page was a vacant rectangle. I typed "atom," took a breath and then clicked "Google Search." Results flooded in. Nearly 3 billion according to the Google counter. I remembered Thomas' admonition, "consider well what you're searching for." And his instruction to choose my words carefully. I started over, narrowing my search to "the structure of the atom." A fraction of a second yielded 612,000,000 results. I had to do better. I tried "what is inside an atom?" Closer, but 165,000,000 was still too many. Then I recalled Thomas' further advice that search results on the first page are oftentimes the most accurate. He was right. Over the next few hours I read. I'll sleep on what I found and try to make sense of it in the morning.

July 5

If Google taught me anything yesterday, it's that I'm poorly educated; nearly illiterate when it comes to the world of science. What I believed most of my life about atoms was the stuff of childhood dreams. With eyes shut, I saw them as tiny, unseen dots, connected to innumerable others to create the diversity of matter. I was correct that they're small, but they're far smaller than I imagined. About a ten-billionth of a meter. I now know that to understand the complex wonder of atoms, one must be a physicist, a chemist, a mathematician. Sadly, I lack the most rudimentary knowledge. When I report to Emerson and the others, it will be impossible to give the atom its due. All I will have is a school boy's interpretation of the present state of understanding. What I can tell them is that atoms are the smallest unit of what scientists call "ordinary matter" - matter having the properties of a chemical element. Every atom has a nucleus made up of one or more protons and a similar number of neutrons. Nearly all of an atom's mass is in the nucleus. There are also electrons; not in the nucleus, but bound to it somehow. The electrons have a negative electrical charge, the protons a positive one, and the neutrons no charge at all. When the number of protons and electrons in an atom are equal, the atom is electrically neutral. If it has more or fewer electrons than protons, it has a negative or positive charge and is what scientists call an "ion." Electrons are attracted to protons in the nucleus by an "electromagnetic force." Whereas protons and neutrons are attracted to each other by a "nuclear force" which repels protons from one another. The number of protons in a nucleus determines what chemical it is, while the number of electrons determines an atom's magnetic properties. As small as atoms are, there are smaller "elementary particles" called quarks which make up protons and neutrons. As innumerable as atoms are, they're only 4% of the density of the universe. Yet our world is rich with them, almost all coming from a cloud of gas and dust that formed our solar system long ago. Whether my atoms belong as much to another, I'm still not sure. But they could have been my grandmother's or those of a Cayuga Indian or a great ape from long ago.

July 5

Memory is a fickle thing. I can recall a summer day from my boyhood as if it was yesterday. Or an evening with a friend by the fire though my friend has long passed. But ask me to plan for an event a month in the future and it's likely I'll forget it as though I never knew of it. So it was, a few weeks ago when Thomas said we'd be flying to California for the wedding of a friend's daughter. I was excited at the time, having never visited the Golden State. But yesterday when Thomas asked if I was packed, I was clueless as to what for. Fortunately, I travel light and we were out the door and at the airport an hour before our scheduled departure. In the air shortly after one, we landed an hour and a half later, taking into account the two time zones. Our ride to Long Beach was courtesy of "Lyft," a service Thomas prefers over the usual taxi. The price is reasonable, and Thomas likes that the vehicle is owned by the driver. He used a similar service for our lodging. Called "Airbnb," it matches guests with homeowners who have a spare room or two. Our hosts are wonderful. Delightful young men who've been a couple for years and hope to marry soon. Of the two, Jonathan is the more affable.

His father Chinese and mother El Salvadoran, he's a world travel with tales a man twice his age would envy. Among his interests is a fondness for the albatross, which he satisfies with frequent visits to the Hawaiian island of Oahu. Near his beach bungalow is the Ka'ena Point Natural Reserve. At its northernmost tip, jutting into the Pacific, is a sanctuary for hundreds of laysan albatross. They mate and raise their families on rocky outcroppings above the shoreline. When on the island, Jonathan makes the long hike to their secluded home, never tiring of observing the remarkable birds. I told him about Lao and my newfound appreciation for his kind.

July 6

The wedding was memorable. One of a kind. It was an evening affair in the heart of a Japanese garden. We arrived shortly before sunset, with time to wander the rock paths, feed ancient koi fish, peek into the ceremonial Tea House, and sit quietly on stone benches at the edge of a Zen garden. The service started an hour late, but no one minded. Beer, wine, and small food bites occupied the guests who, collectively, created a human tapestry. I wasn't able to speak to everyone, as over a hundred were in attendance. But I learned a little something from guests with roots in China, Vietnam, the Philippines, Pakistan, Italy, Morocco, Seattle, Chicago, Brooklyn, and the Bronx. The beautiful bride, a lawyer born in the Midwest, has lived all over the world. After completing her university studies, Kate volunteered for two years with the "Peace Corps," a government program that sends Americans to far-flung lands. She served in a remote African village, becoming adept at bringing water to small communities with little. Her husband, John, is Egyptian and works "undercover" for the Los Angeles Police Department fighting what he calls "the drug scourge." His parents came to this country as young adults. Brothers and sisters followed over the years. There was an Egyptian theme throughout the night as belly dancers entertained under the stars to traditional music. The young women were a sight to behold. As fit as I was at their age, I never had the flexibility they demonstrated. It was beautiful to observe their gentle athleticism. Later there were speeches, toasts and storytelling. We returned to our Airbnb well after midnight, greeted by Jonathan and his partner with a bedtime snack.

July 7

Thomas rented a car so we could explore. Everywhere the earth is covered. With houses, office buildings, parking garages, warehouses, shopping complexes, businesses of all kinds. Where it's not, there's concrete for the cars, trucks, motorcycles, scooters, bicycles, strollers, and push carts. Too many to count. Thomas calls it "urban sprawl." It goes on for miles in every direction, halted only by an ocean that's drawn a line in the sand. He said it's been growing uncontrollably for years. Not just here, but across the continent. Musicians and poets bemoan it. Thomas recited a few lines, penned years ago by a young woman:

"Don't it always seem to go, that you don't know what you've got till it's gone. They paved paradise and put up a parking lot."

Yet there's a vibrancy, unlike anywhere I've been the past few months. The Mediterranean climate must contribute to it - and the always present sea. The people are unique as well. Wanderers, transplants, dreamers, outcasts even. There's not the stodginess of the old cities. And much of the wealth here is new wealth. Nabil, the father of the groom, was an immigrant and poor when he arrived. He asserts that anything is possible in California if one has ambition and imagination. Thomas doesn't disagree but says there are exceptions. Thousands have crossed the southern border only to find more hardship. Some transcend their poverty. A few join the wealthy. Most labor in jobs no one else wants. Yet, at least for now, Thomas believes America is still the land of possibility - for most but not all.

July 8
The afternoon free, we found a beach near the airport. Californians throng to the ocean side like New Yorkers to Long Island beaches. Along with the walkers and joggers on concrete paths, others whizzed by on conveyances related to the bicycle as a child is to a grandparent. Some flew handmade airplanes while others operated motorized ones. There were surfers and hang gliders too, riding the waves and air currents with astonishing ease. But I felt most at home with the fishermen, separated from one another by a lengthy distance, masters of rods and reels designed for the open water. I approached a gentleman who'd established himself as far from the action as possible. He was standing between two long poles, their thin lines terminating well beyond the incoming waves. With sand crabs as enticement, he was on the hunt for the "cobia." Sleek and strong, it averages twenty to thirty pounds but can weigh over a hundred. I liked this man. Quiet and focused, he was doing what he loved to do. Careful not to intrude, I eventually learned that he arrived in California from Vietnam. He was one of thousands of "boat people" fleeing the "communists" shortly after the end of the war. He said it was worth risking his life rather than live under a regime

without freedom. On the night he stepped onto the small boat, he had no idea where he'd end up. After a week at sea, he and a dozen others landed on the shore of Indonesia. Shortly after, he was in a sprawling refugee camp. For months he waited to learn of his final destination. One day they came and informed him he was being sent to Los Angeles. That was forty years ago. Like Nabil, he says anything is possible in California if you put your mind to it. I wanted to learn more of his life, but the pole to his left was suddenly alive and bent toward the sand. He took hold of it gingerly, slowly reeling in something of significance. After a few minutes, a footlong beauty emerged. I asked if it was a cobia. He shook his head no. "It's a yellow fin croaker." Not a prize catch, but a tasty meal he'd take home to his wife.

July 9

We took a late flight to Nashville to visit friends before flying to Maine. The heat and humidity of the southern city was oppressive. So much that we were forced to take refuge indoors. Air conditioning must be a gift from the gods, bathing the body with its cool touch. Americans have a level of comfort even the affluent of my day didn't. Blessing that it is, I imagine it contributes considerably to global warming. I wonder about the tradeoffs. Greater productivity but more pollution. We spent the evening with Thomas' young friends. Zac is a computer specialist. Sarah a psychiatrist in training. The couple is expecting their first child. It was a pleasure listening to them talk of their shared dreams and expectations. Early risers, they were in bed by nine, leaving Thomas and me to watch the "home run derby" that precedes baseball's All Star game. I'd never seen anything quite like it. The games' best power hitters crushing pitch after pitch into the furthest reaches of the stadium.

July 10

We took the bus from the Boston airport to Portland. It's a pleasant ride. Water and pretzels were provided free of charge. Televisions as well. Each passenger was given a small coil of plastic covered wire. On one end a thin chrome rod to be inserted into its female mate so sound could travel from the television to the listener. On the opposite were tiny "buds," one for each ear, allowing the sound to be received. Thomas says the movies are usually a fantasy of some kind. But today's was a documentary. "Free Solo" is about Alex Honnold, a young rock climber considered to be one of the best in the world. What he accomplished two years ago had never been attempted. Climbing *El Capitan*, a vertical rock formation, three thousand feet from base to summit, bordered on the miraculous. The best climbers, utilizing ropes and other aids, have been challenged to their limit by the granite face. Alex ascended it without assistance, using only his hands and feet, wits and courage. I've often wondered what drives an individual to attempt the never before done. The great explorers come to mind, those who crossed uncharted oceans or mapped the mountains and rivers of a southern continent. I'd assumed that modern technology had brought to an end the days of discovering something new on our planet. It's reassuring to learn that new explorers continue to push the limits.

July 11
I met an old friend of Thomas' today. The three of us had lunch at the Green Elephant. According to the menu, it's vegetarian and "Asian Inspired." I ordered the Thai Curry soup. Delicious! It's unlikely I'll ever travel to Asia, but should I return at another time, Thailand would be on my list. Thomas' friend is an "analyst," trained in the "Jungian" school. She and her colleagues sometimes refer to themselves as "Doctors of the Soul." Suffering as I do with melancholia, Thomas thought it would be good that I get acquainted with Anna. As I know nothing of analysis, she explained that Jungian therapy endeavors to bring the conscious and unconscious parts of a patient's mind together. "This can lead to a more balanced life," she said, adding that dreams are a big help. "Coming to an understanding of their meaning is an important part of the work." Thomas interjected that everything I share with Anna is confidential. He then asked if I might want to speak of my past life, and of Emerson and Lao. I was hesitant, concerned I might appear delusional. But there was something about her that invited disclosure. So it all came out. Anna said nothing until I finished. Then responded that she wasn't surprised. "The universe is imbued with mystery," she said. "Without it there's no meaning." We continued until Anna had to excuse herself, suggesting as she was leaving that I contact her whenever I have the need.

July 12
Beautiful weather today. Mainers say it's these days that make the six-month winter a distant memory, until the next returns. Old town Portland was teeming with visitors from here and abroad. I walked by a group of tourists from Estonia and a second group from Japan. The atmosphere was festive, notwithstanding the anxiety that afflicts those sensitive to the daily craziness coming out of the Capitol. This morning, another one of President Trump's inner circle resigned under fire. Maine

Public Radio reported that in a previous position as a government prosecutor, the now-departed Secretary of Labor entered into a secret deal allowing a wealthy businessman to escape a long prison sentence. The pedophile is now being prosecuted in another jurisdiction for similar crimes. Following Thomas' advice, I try to limit my exposure to Trump and his associates to small doses. The radio a few minutes a day; the newspaper three or four times a week. Still, I read and hear enough to understand why so many people are on edge. There seems to be no end to the senseless and dangerous antics of the president. Some have told me that Trump is a pawn of the Russian government and was elected with the help of Russian meddlers. Others minimize the possibility, arguing that unemployment is low, the economy robust, and that anything else is inconsequential - even the crimes of past and present government officials he's appointed. I lived through corrupt and incompetent presidencies, particularly those leading up to the War. But Thomas and his friends argue that the stakes are much higher now. That the world these days is a bomb with a short fuse and Trump holds the match.

July 13

Daylight comes early to coastal Maine in midsummer, close as it is to the Atlantic time zone. Like roosters in the countryside, seagulls herald the dawn. Lying in bed, one would think they're the first to rise. But I was out with them and found the streets as busy as yesterday. It was a different scene though. Hours before the arrival of tourists, those without a bed had already begun the day. Like Southern California, Portland attracts the homeless. I've been told they're treated relatively well here. Left alone by the police unless they're causing trouble, they're easily seen resting on doorsteps or at bus stops, or still sleeping on a bench or under a tree. Beyond the waterfront and Congress, they congregate on less traveled roads. On Preble Street there's a shelter where warm meals and a clean cot can be had. Out front, anytime of the day or evening, they mingle. It's not what the average citizen might expect. There are certainly those whom life has beaten down. The addict and alcoholic among them. But amidst them are the young, male and female, yet to find their place in a world that oftentimes cares little for them or their potential. There are mothers too, who have lost their children to the system following eviction, a run-in with the courts, or a crisis too overwhelming to overcome. In the late afternoon, I sometimes listen to "Marketplace" on NPR. Always there's talk about the New York Stock Exchange and how it performed throughout the day. The commentator often suggests that the numbers are a reflection of how the economy is doing. Trump and his people suggest the same, intimating that if the numbers are high, all else can be forgiven. It makes little sense to me. There's no relationship, that I can see, between the giant corporations and the "have-nots" struggling to survive. There have been revolutions in the past when the divide between rich and poor had widened so much that violent overthrow was the only recourse. I remember reading about the July day in 1789 when an angry mob stormed the Bastille in Paris, taking over the prison. What looked like a riot at the time, came to be seen as the start of the French Revolution. I wonder where America is headed.

July 14

For the second time this week, I had a conversation about "tribalism." Not in a sectarian sense, which I've heard much about lately. But in an expansive, inclusive sense. On the flight from Nashville to Boston, the young woman seated next to me spoke about her "tribe." I was taken aback at first, until she explained that her "circle" or "tribe" has no boundaries. She's just as likely to meet someone for coffee the age of her grandparents as with a twenty-something. Or go for a hike or bike ride with an African American, a Buddhist, a Muslim, a gay man or lesbian, or an atheist. Race, gender, sexual preference, wealth or the lack of it, do not prescribe or limit those with whom she finds common ground. She said it's not always been that way, having grown up in a small, predominately Christian community, raised by parents having what she now sees to be narrow and conservative values. She spoke with pride of the sense of freedom she now has in making choices as she sees fit, without pressure or intrusion from family or anyone else. It's the same with the woman I had lunch with today. Sixty-five and recently divorced, she's free of the yoke that restricted her for nearly forty years. Similar to the young woman, her "tribe" is an eclectic one, far more diverse than earlier relationships defined by marriage, church, and social status. Her eyes sparkled when describing her new life. She's a practitioner of yoga and meditation, dates freely, and travels widely. She no longer fears a spouse who cut her off in mid-sentence if she attempted to express her own opinion. Now she interacts with those who allow her to finish, and distances herself from those who don't. It seems like I'm on a roller coaster ride these days. Discouraged by much that I learn of the larger world. Encouraged by those who push back and refuse to give in to despair.

July 15

I've recently learned about "tweets." It's my understanding they're something people read or do on their mobile telephones. Thomas previously told me about "texts." Tweets are like them, but can be sent to and read by thousands. On one hand they seem harmless, although I suppose they might consume more time and attention than they're worth. But Thomas believes, likely nearly everything in the virtual world, there's the potential for danger. President Trump, he says, is the greatest abuser. He has his own "twitter" account, dispatching multiple tweets a day to millions of "followers." Often, they appear to be the ravings of a lunatic, a pathological liar, or both. Thoughtful commentators fear the impact of the barrage of misinformation, contending that Trump's unfiltered dispatches are divisive, and sow hate and discontent. Many are blatantly racist, pandering to white supremacists and those privately leaning in that direction. I read in this morning's newspaper about yesterday's tweet suggesting that certain female members of Congress go back to the countries they came from, even though all but one is American born. There was also a report that the Trump administration was about to initiate a mass roundup of immigrants alleged to be living in the country illegally. Last week he had a meeting at the White House, welcoming several internet personalities with racist leanings. I'm saddened by the decline of the American presidency. And amazed that this country, having elected a black president in 2008, replaced him with the opposite.

July 16

What Trump is doing has me on edge. Sleep is difficult. I was restless until midnight, then abandoned the effort and went outside. The moon was full, shedding her gown of white upon the water. The image so vivid it was difficult to distinguish reality from illusion. Leaning back in the rocker, my burdens dissipated. I was reminded once again that peace is to be found in the presence of stillness. Slowly, my soul left this age to wander among the bodies of the night. For how long, I don't know. But as the moon floated just about the horizon, I realized I was not alone. There was a gentle rocking by my side, its cadence slowing my breath even further. Almost imperceptibly there was the clearing of a voice I believed to be Emerson's. I took a chance. "Emerson, is it you?" A moment passed. "Yes, it is Walt. I don't mean to intrude but thought you might like some company." We rocked in unison until Emerson spoke again. "These are challenging times Walt. I apologize that you're a witness to them, but it must be." He went on. "You need a break. Every life has an obligation to withdraw, on occasion, from the tumult." He then informed me I'd be traveling later in the night, waking at sunrise in a small room overlooking the ocean. For two days I could hike, boat if I liked, and reflect on the weeks passed and yet to come. If I'm of the right mind, I can call for Lao and he'll join me. I need but find a private place near the water and wait. We rocked on, the silence broken only by the call of a loon.

July 17

It happened as promised. After hours of deep sleep, I woke in a room of white, the crash of waves below. I had no urge to move, or even discern my whereabouts. Having come to trust Emerson, I was certain no harm would befall me. I could remain at rest or move about. It made no difference. After some time, though, my stomach caught up with my senses and I was aware of the need to break my fast. Next to the bed were clean clothes, my favorite shoes, and my walking stick. On the desk was a note, informing that the dining room provided service until nine. I dressed and within minutes was seated, a late before me with eggs as I prefer them, country potatoes and homemade toast. I wondered if I was in a liminal place, somewhere between my temporary residence and permanent one. But slowly, voices from nearby tables drifted my way. I was still in Maine. Well-fed, I walked out and followed a path to the beach. A young man inquired if I would like to rent a kayak. I'd read of their use by the indigenous peoples of the north. Of bone or wood construction and covered with animal skins, they allowed the Intuits and Aleuts to travel far and wide, hunting and trading for needed goods. But these were made of plastic, like many things I now encounter. Noticing my hesitancy, the young man assured me that his kayaks are stable and easily maneuvered. I relented and after a brief lesson was on the water, navigating between the fishing boats moored at high tide. Satisfied that I was up to the task, I left the confines of the harbor, paddling in the direction of a nearby island. About the size of my boyhood home, it was covered with gulls, eider ducks, and cormorants. White, brown, and black, they appeared to live in harmony, no matter the color of their neighbor. I paddled on, maintaining a close distance to the shoreline, nearly every rock of consequence hosting a white gull. Among them, I thought I might find Lao. But to no avail. I then recalled Emerson's directive that I must first find a private place and wait. With rain beginning to fall, I returned to the harbor with the intention that I would find such a place tomorrow.

July 18

I inquired of the man at the front desk where I might find a secluded spot to observe the sea. He said there are many and gave me a map. Of the several trails, he suggested I follow Cliff #1 in the direction of Christmas Cove, Norton's Ledge, and Gull Rock. He drew a circle, noting the best place to start, adding x's where I could sit alone and undisturbed. I stood on the front steps studying it, realizing for the first time that I was on an island, fewer than two miles long and half as wide. Christmas Cove is near the southeastern point. Only the deep blue separates it from Nova Scotia. I set off, arriving at the trailhead in good time. The going was difficult from there, and I was glad to have my trusted staff in hand. After several steep climbs and descents, I found it. A bare precipice overlooking a community of gulls at the edge of the breaking surf. It took all my effort to scramble to the top, but the reward was a perch I was certain Lao would appreciate. The sun high overhead, I sat and waited. I've come to know that time is relative, dependent on the setting and one's frame of mind. On the rock I could judge its passage only by the lengthening shadows and my growing anticipation. It often happens that by midafternoon I'm weary and nap an hour or more when possible. This afternoon was the same. In my slumber, I was startled by a voice not my own. I woke and wasn't disappointed. He was as I imagined. White head and white breast, giving way to gray feathers then black. A yellow beak with a blush of pink at the tip, a balance to the mass of his torso. Black eyes, benevolent and penetrating. Windows to a primal wisdom. "Walt, thank you for waiting. It was fateful that the shamaness brought us together." I believed the same, though I was clueless as to what lay ahead. "I'm grateful that you've come Lao. Tell me, when we communicate, should I speak or are my thoughts enough?" The voice inside again. "We find it best to share without sound. There is no confusion when doing so. You are a poet and will soon master our way." Lao then informed me that he can only appear in bodily form if we meet near the sea. Should I need him at other times, it's enough that I close my eyes and imagine. He then encouraged me to seek the wild and untamed whenever possible. As he departed, he suggested I return to the mainland by way of the water. Thomas would be awaiting my arrival.

July 19

I booked passage on the ten o'clock ferry. Weather permitting, the twelve mile crossing would take little more than an hour. There is a custom on the island that when friends and relatives depart, leaving like kind behind, they are given a spray of wild flowers. As the mooring lines are cast off and the journey begins, the flowers are tossed into the sea. Simultaneously, young and old jump from the pier into the frigid water twenty feet below. This morning, six boys and girls took the plunge, along with a gentleman old enough to be their grandfather. Each emerged unharmed, but quick to scamper up the ladder to loved ones with blankets and towels. I was heartened by the scene, the display of affection a testament to our species. There was much to consider as I sat alone on the upper deck. My meeting with Lao foremost. But my short time on the island had made a lasting impression in other ways as well. With no paved roads and few vehicles, I was reminded of simpler times. Though summers are brief and winters harsh, the permanent residents are steadfast in their commitment to a way of life the dominant culture has abandoned. I overheard several visitors speak of this with a longing that bordered on sadness. I was troubled too at the thought of what they were returning to. Perhaps their brush with paradise would prompt an inner transformation. They might even reimagine what their lives could be, and slowly reclaim an integrity buried by the marketers and moneychangers who feed off their pocketbooks. I was awakened to the present by the call of the captain over the loudspeaker, announcing our arrival at New Harbor. Looking down on the waiting crowd, I saw Thomas waving for my attention. There was much to share with him.

July 20

All week I've been hearing of the accomplishments of American explorers Neil Armstrong and Buzz Aldrin, the first humans to walk on the moon. They were members of a crew named Apollo 11, shot into space by a rocket that reached the moon's orbit after a three-day journey. For twenty-four hours and thirty revolutions, they looked down on the great white rock before leaving the mother ship in a tiny craft and descending to the surface. Their lunar walk was fifty years ago today. The black and white images I've seen are astounding. As is the recording of Armstrong's words as he stepped onto the barren landscape. Centuries from now, I imagine historians will consider their feat, and the efforts of all who aided them, as one of the great achievements of humankind. I've been reading poetry lately. Most written in the last century and the early years of the present. Much of what I've read I like. Earthy and succinct; self-contained, like a pocket story. This morning I discovered the English poet Stephen Spender. There's a poem of his particularly appropriate for today. In it, he writes of how he thinks continually of those who were truly great. He must have had Homer in mind, and Virgil, Copernicus, Galileo, Newton, and Darwin. Composed years before Aldrin and Armstrong's moment in the sun, Spender surely would have included them in his list "of those who in their lives fought for life, who wore at their hearts the fire's center. Born of the sun, they traveled a short while toward the sun and left the vivid air winged with their honour."

July 21

I was wide awake at three, still excited by the events culminating in yesterday's anniversary. I couldn't put to rest Armstrong's words: "That's one small step for man, one giant leap for mankind." They're humble and brash. Understated and provocative. But there was nothing small about that first step, made possible by centuries of scientific and mathematical discoveries and developments. And monumental as the moment was, equally compelling is the vision Armstrong offered for our future. Not a roadmap, but an assertion that anything is possible. Watching archival footage of the human family's reaction, how could one not think that we had finally turned the corner. That sectarian rivalries and patriotic wars would soon come to an end with survival becoming our universal purpose. But I've seen no evidence of that. On the contrary, the family is as dysfunctional as ever. And the window of time for reunification is closing at an accelerating rate. Unable to sleep, I walked out back and sat in the swing. The moon, in waning gibbous, was nearly at its zenith. What my poet's eye saw was an orb, a few days past its fullness, enclosed by a halo of sepia permeating the night sky. My father used to say that the moon is made of green cheese. The ancient Chinese said a rabbit lives there, forever mixing the elixir of immortality. Ages and ages hence, when all records of July 20, 1969, have been lost, perhaps the myth that will excite those still alive is that men and women once dreamed so vividly that it was possible to walk on the great white rock in the sky.

July 22

Thomas has a television but rarely turns it on. Preferring to keep up with current events by radio or newspaper, he limits TV time to an occasional movie or documentary. There's an exception, the Sunday evening program called *60 Minutes*. He watched the first broadcast in 1968 and has since watched every episode when at home. When away, he has the ability to record shows, viewing them on his return. Last night I joined him for the June 30 replay. There was a story about the nationwide opioid epidemic that takes thousands of lives every year. A team of lawyers is suing the pharmaceutical companies that manufacture the addictive drugs and the companies that transport them. A second was story about Ben Ferencz, a 99-year-old lawyer who was one of the lead prosecutors in what historians have called the "biggest murder trial ever." I learned about the atrocities committed by Germany during World War II. A few months ago, I found out there'd been such a war, but not until last night did, I discover that, of the millions of lives lost, six million were Jews who'd been murdered. Most were killed while held in "concentration camps," but more than a million died in or near their homes. I was sickened by the images broadcast of the nearly dead, liberated from the camps in the days and weeks after the war's end. The killing was orchestrated by the "Nazis" and their leader Adolf Hitler, who espoused a doctrine of racial purity and cast the German people as a master race. Jews in Germany and elsewhere in Europe were exterminated to preserve the race. The trials were held in Nuremberg in the months following Germany's surrender. The argument Ferencz and other prosecutors made was that Germany had committed "crimes against humanity," and Nazi leaders and senior officers must be held accountable. Watching the interview, I concluded that the war crimes were so horrific that similar brutalities would never happen again. But near the end, Ferencz said the accused men would not have been murderers were it not for the war. Particularly chilling was his observation that "war makes murderers out of otherwise decent people." It frightens me to consider what those who support President Trump's ongoing racist war might do if called to action.

July 23

At breakfast I mentioned to Thomas that I've been feeling lightheaded, especially upon standing. He nodded, responding that he's noticed my face has been reddish lately. We agreed a doctor's visit was in order. Within the hour I was in an exam room. Thomas' friend entered, looked me over, and commented how fit I look, with the exception of my flushed complexion. He then wrapped the cuff around my arm and placed the listening device at the bend. After a few seconds, he winced. "Walt, your blood pressure is up considerably from your last visit. What's going on?" I told him I'm eating well, perhaps better than at any time in my life. With some pride, I described my routine of walking, bicycling, and sitting quietly. He then inquired about my emotional health. Whether I have new troubles or concerns. I knew where he was going and couldn't deny it. Unsure of his politics, I nevertheless told him that the words and actions of President Trump have brought on an anxiety I struggle to control. He opined how that could well be the cause. That over the last two years he's been treating more patients for high blood pressure, even though most eat well and exercise regularly. Among them are young people who appear to be in excellent health but are distressed by the uncertain times. He concluded that, given my age, a simple medicine is in order. One that relaxes the vessels so the blood passing through them exerts less pressure. He said the one to try initially is a small pink one, taken every day before breakfast. He called the pharmacist in my presence and said I could pick up the prescription within the hour. He then assured me I'd be fine but, nevertheless, wanted to see me again in two weeks. About to leave the room, he took my hand. "Walt, you're doing nearly everything right. The pill will help, too. But I suggest you spend less time following the news and more time smelling the roses."

July 24

Thomas had an early appointment. Before leaving, he made arrangements for an Uber to take me to the pharmacy. I've had good luck with the rideshares and nearly always enjoy the conversation. If I had my own car, and years rather than months to live, I think I'd be a driver. This morning I met Richard. Just turned ninety, for a long time he owned a nursing home. But the "feds" came in and shut him down. For the past three decades he's been working on his bucket list. Driving an Uber wasn't on it at the beginning, but he took it up two years ago, bored and in need of the extra money. Richard has had tough times. His first wife died in childbirth before she was thirty. All through diapers, kids' sports, and school, he raised their two sons on his own. The second love of his life came along when he was experiencing what he called his "midlife crisis." She helped get the boys out of the house and stuck with him through the tough financial times, a heart attack, a stroke, and three battles with cancer. Richard was certain she'd outlive him, but five years ago cancer took her away. He was close to taking his own life, deciding against it after realizing he was still needed. He has a teenage grandson, diagnosed with "autism." The boy has trouble making friends, mostly because of his fear of being around people. Richard stepped in. The two spend hours together, watching old movies, eating popcorn, and playing chess. Try as he might, Richard has yet to win a game. I asked what's left on his bucket list. He said he's always had an anger problem. He wants to be better, for himself and the boy, and sees a counselor every week. He's making progress, but his old nemesis still speaks its mind, particularly during rush hour traffic when his grandson is waiting for him.

July 25

Things have changed in the house. Thomas has a new puppy. For sixteen years Harley kept him company. Named for a motorcycle Thomas rode across the country as a young man, Harley went with him everywhere. Even in his old age, he accommodated Thomas' need for a daily walk. When Harley died two winters ago, Thomas was certain he'd never have another dog. His best friend was irreplaceable. But not long ago, he met a woman who raises a breed called "labradoodles." Wilma, one of her favorites, was pregnant. Thomas took a liking to Wilma. She was as smart as Harley and just as gentle. He saw a photo of Wilma's mate and was convinced that any offspring of the two would be a good companion. After a two-month wait, he now has Molly. I had a puppy as a boy. He was my best friend. But early one morning my father's mare stepped on him in the dark. I thought I'd never get over it. I can still feel the pang of grief. Ever since, I've kept my distance from dogs, not wanting to be hurt again. But Molly is a sweetheart and will long outlive me. When Thomas leaves for the day, Molly and I walk to the nearby park. It takes a while, given her short legs. And everyone who sees her has to stop and say hello. Thomas says Molly is as much mine as his and so I beam with pride. At the park, she gnaws on sticks, plays with her toy monkey, and naps at my feet as I record my daily entry for Emerson. Later in the morning the children arrive and make her acquaintance. She treats young and old alike with equanimity. I wonder what this world be like if the Mollys were masters and us two-leggeds walked alongside?

July 26

I never cared much for calendars. When I paid attention to them, I focused too much on what I'd planned and failed to accomplish. Or I'd long for a future event and neglect the day at hand. Last night before bed I laid the year out before me, knowing that at the stroke of midnight four months will have passed from the evening Emerson lifted me from my deathbed. And in eight months more there I'll return, and the dark will close in on me for eternity. Setting the months aside, I was filled with both regret and dread. I'd accomplished little worth sharing with Emerson and the others. And I imagined that the rest of my time would offer little more. So it was that I took to my pillow an ache. But somehow, I slept without disturbance, save one. It was Emerson, passing through the night, on his way to others to whom he tends. When I was still young enough to sit on her lap, mother whispered that the Sandman would visit to help me sleep. She promised that, as I slumbered, he would sprinkle magic sand onto my eyes to bring good dreams. At the sound of his whisper, I imagined Emerson to be that Sandman, sprinkling his magic. But he offered no promises. Merely a simple gift I intend to hold close to my heart: "Walt, my dear friend, what lies behind us and what lies before us are small matters compared to what lies within us."

MONTH FIVE

July 27

Molly and I have a routine now. Up at five and outside shortly after so she can relieve herself. Breakfast follows. Puppy food for her. Two eggs over easy for me. Then a walk to the park. The route is always the same. A right at the end of the drive. Another right at the stop sign. A left at the first intersection. A few minutes later we're at the edge of the woods where we descend to the level of the creek, cross the footbridge, and climb up the other side to the ball field. Free from her leash, she romps as only a puppy does, never straying far from where I sit on the bench. This morning we witnessed the sun's rise as it cleared the tops of eastern hardwoods, shining down on the two of us. Molly finally wearied and we retraced our steps. As we crossed the footbridge, a young doe jumped the creek just ahead, then darted into thick cover. I recall attending a lecture as a young journalist in Brooklyn. The distinguished gentleman was a Brit, recently returned from an expedition to the Dark Continent. He recounted his time with an isolated tribe deep in the jungle, becoming well acquainted with their habits. He observed that the terrors of the night gave rise to a fear that daylight might never return. At the break of dawn, they'd emerge from their huts. Every man, woman, and child would then follow a path to an exposed overlook where they'd wait anxiously for the sun's rise. "For the first time," the explorer confided, "I understood at the deepest level the great myth of death, descent into hell, and resurrection."

July 28

I've long been fascinated by the sky, no matter the time of day. I studied it as I lay on my back on the bank above the river, and thought I knew much about it. That there are millions of suns, bright ones to be seen and dark ones unseen. Those with moons and those without. I was right in many ways, but missed the mark on the extent of it. Where I imagined millions, there are billions. Even billions upon billions. Today's astronomers report that our sun is one of 400 billion that make up a "galaxy" called the Milky Way. A few, perhaps a thousand or more, are what we see at night if we're away from the city. But as big as the Milky Way is, it's just average. There are spiral galaxies with a trillion stars and giant elliptical galaxies with 100 trillion. Just as mind-boggling is the number of galaxies. More than 170 billion as estimated by those who consider such things. Adding to the complexity is that not every star is the same. Many, like ours, are "main sequence stars" that convert hydrogen to helium, releasing a tremendous amount of energy in the process. There are red giant stars too, blue super giants, white, brown and red dwarfs, neutron stars, and others. There are things called "black holes" that scientists conjecture come into being when certain stars die and collapse upon themselves. The result is gravity so strong light can't escape. These are the dark ones that can't be seen. And there are just as many moons as stars. 170 in our solar system. 1.7 septillion in the universe. I looked up septillion. It's a number starting with 1 and followed by 24 zeroes. The universe must be infinite to contain so many celestial bodies. The ancient Chinese said that before anything, even before light, there was darkness within darkness. I wonder if the scientists have found that to be true.

July 29

I searched all morning for the book on Time but couldn't find it. Perhaps Thomas has it. I did recall the author. Stephen Hawking, the physicist who asked himself big questions even when he was little. As a schoolboy, Hawking argued with friends about the origin of the universe and whether God was required to get it going. On Thomas' shelf there's a book that references Hawking. I learned that, like me, he was apathetic when it came to formal education. An apathy that continued even while a student at Oxford. Then he had a life event. He was diagnosed with having a "motor neuron disease." A disease that rarely afflicts young people but is almost always fatal. The doctors said he'd likely have an early death. But with the diagnosis came an epiphany. There were things he needed to accomplish before his life was over. From that moment he resolved to take the big questions seriously and live to answer them. Oddly, his disease gave him an unexpected gift. As it progressed, he lost nearly all motor movement, becoming a prisoner in his own body. The loss of freedom liberated his mind to wander the galaxies. As a result, he gained insights that led to discoveries few of his colleagues thought possible. Scientists came from all over the world to learn from him. Believing most people can gain a basic understanding of the laws of the universe, he expanded his classroom to the general public. His premise was that the ideas be presented clearly and without equations, and one be curious.

July 30
I bicycled to the library to learn more about Hawking. *A Brief History of Time* was there. And a simpler, more recent book, *A Briefer History of Time*. And a third book, *Brief Answers to the Big Questions*. Pieces of his life stood out. On a trip to Switzerland he became so ill his doctors recommended his breathing machine be turned off, ending his life. His wife refused. Thirty years later he still wandered the universe, developing ideas and communicating them through his computer. Technology kept pace with his needs, allowing him to "speak" by controlling a sensor in his eyeglasses with his cheek muscles. Hawking died last year, having reached the conclusion long before that there is no God. Or at least not a personal God. His belief was that no one created the universe. Nor does anyone direct our fate. "Belief in heaven is wishful thinking." He concluded that when we die, we return to dust. He did, however, have an oversized belief in life, and with it the opportunity to appreciate the grand design of the universe. I have to admit that reading about Hawking has given me a greater sense of urgency about my remaining time. I'd like to share in his curiosity and try to make sense of what I see. Like Hawking, I want to wonder about the universe and what makes it exist.

July 31
On whether or not there was a beginning to the universe, I find it easier to grasp earlier opinions than the present understanding of scientists. Aristotle taught that the universe always existed, believing that something eternal is more perfect than something created. He wasn't alone in advocating for an eternal universe that didn't need a creator. Contrary to Aristotle, most religions have argued for a universe with God as its first cause. Ironically, the prevailing scientific view is that the universe did have a beginning, but the hand of God was absent. I'm learning that most astronomers and physicists believe the universe is about 14 billion years old. That there was nothing at its inception. Out of nowhere, a single, incredibly small point appeared, into which the entire universe was crammed. After a fraction of a second there was a "Big Bang." At that moment, the density and temperature of the universe would have been infinite. A second later, the universe expanded so much that the temperature dropped to about ten billion degrees. All that existed, in addition to pure energy, were protons, neutrons, and electrons, along with things called photons and neutrinos. After another second, the temperature cooled to a mere billion degrees, while the radius of the universe expanded at a rate of a million million

million million million times. During the initial expansion some of the protons and neutrons combined to make helium and a few other elements. But within hours the production of elements stopped. A million years passed. The universe continued to expand, but little else happened. It all seems incomprehensible. But so did the childhood story that the heavens and the earth were created in six days.

August 1

Try as I might, there's little in the story of the early universe I can truly grasp given my limited education. Something from nothing. A single dot, then seconds later a universe so immense numbers can't adequately describe it. Infinite density. Infinite temperature dropping to ten billion degrees in the blink of an eye. All I can do is take it at face value. After this morning's walk, I started where I left off yesterday. A million years out from the explosion of that solitary point the universe continued to expand and cool. In some regions, temperatures dropped to a few thousand degrees, slowing the motion of electrons and nuclei enough that their attraction for each other allowed for the formation of atoms. This attraction slowed expansion enabling the formation of rotating galaxies. More time passed and the hydrogen and helium in those galaxies broke into small clouds, which eventually collapsed under their own gravity. The temperature of the gases then increased, becoming hot enough to start "nuclear fusion reactions," which scientists believe are necessary for stars to come into being. Knowing a little about stars now, I hope to discover why there are planets.

August 2

During the fiftieth anniversary week of the moon walk, an image of the earth was broadcast over and over. It was a photo taken the day of the walk by the Apollo 11 astronauts. I was stunned by it. The blues, browns, greens, and whites of it for sure. A nearly perfect marble wrapped in a thin veil of gas. But more than the shape and the colors was the realization that we live on a tiny, fragile rock, adrift in the cosmos. No manmade borders were to be seen. No monuments to conquerors or tyrants. No skyscrapers erected for the wealthy. I let my mind consider its beginning. Long after the Big Bang, nearly ten billion years after, what is now the sun and its planets was a dense cloud of dust and gas whirling in space. Gravity caused the cloud to grow immensely hot and heavy in the center, eventually forming the sun. Solar winds pushed matter on the periphery of the sun out into space. Gravity caused matter in certain areas to come together, forming "proto-planets." Earth, third closest to the sun, was one of them. For a long while, the earth was large molten and extremely hot. Dense, metallic liquid sunk deep into the center, forming a mostly iron core. Less dense liquids settled on top. Comets and meteors bombarded the infant, giving rise to volcanoes. They, in turn, contributed to the formation of the surface crust, and the thin, protective atmosphere. Water vapor slowly condensed, accumulating in the atmosphere and leading to the formation of oceans. In some respects, the King James version of those early years wasn't far off. The earth was without form, and there was darkness. And the Spirit of God, manifested by eons of time and intricate processes, moved upon the face of the waters.

August 3

Thomas called late yesterday, about the time I expected him home. He apologized immediately, explaining that the project he's working on is more complicated than expected, requiring his presence for another week. He paused, cleared his throat, then spoke. "Walt, I have a child. A beautiful young woman now. I should have said something sooner." The story followed. Following his university studies, he entered a monastery. Attracted to a life of solitude, he hoped to become a monk. After several months the abbot took him aside encouraging him to return to the world where a decision could be better made. Heeding the advice, he left the next morning with no destination in mind. For years he traveled, throughout North and South America, Europe, the Middle East, Japan, and finally China. Interested in Daoism, he eventually found a home in the village of Caohai among the Yi people. There, a family took him in and treated him as one of their own. He worked in their garden, fished in the nearby lake, and taught English when asked. One of his students was the daughter of his hosts. Not yet a woman, she was thirsty for knowledge of all things, and took readily to his instruction. For the better part of a year, they hiked the mountain paths. He learned her ways, and she his. As often happens, the teacher and pupil became equals and they fell in love. But theirs was a doomed love, as the Yi people forbid their girls to marry foreigners. Nevertheless, nature took its course and she conceived a child. For many weeks, the secret was theirs alone. But the girl's mother grew suspicious and the girl told the truth. In the past, she would have been put to death. But she and her unborn child were spared, and Thomas was banished. Years passed and a letter arrived. Thomas had a daughter, Ling, nearly a woman. With great difficulty, he returned to Caohai, only to learn that the only woman he ever loved had died. But there was Ling, identical in all ways to her mother. From then on, Thomas supported her, writing often and arranging for her to attend college in the United States. Her medical school education completed, she'll soon begin formal training in Boston to become a pediatrician. Thomas had planned to accompany her on the drive east. Unexpectedly delayed, he asked if I would take his place. Ling would arrive the next day. If all went well, we would meet Thomas Wednesday morning in Boston.

August 4

Ling arrived this morning. She's a lovely young woman, just as Thomas described. I'd prepared a large salad for lunch. Ling ate more than I thought her slight figure could handle. With an impish smile that delighted me greatly, she said growing up as a child of the village contributed to her appreciation of a good meal. By one o'clock we were driving east. Iowa, Illinois, Indiana, western Ohio. Multi-wheeled trucks. Speeding motorists. Gas stations. McDonald's restaurants. Tollbooths. There was little on the way that was noteworthy. It was a fascinating drive, nevertheless. Ling recalled learning about her father. As a child, she was puzzled by her green eyes, as those of her playmates were brown. One day, she asked her mother about them. It was then that she learned of Tom, a handsome young man who arrived unannounced in the village. He was different than any man she'd ever met; kind, thoughtful, inquisitive. Ling's mother knew from the beginning that he would be important in her life. After a time, she asked if he would teach her English. He agreed, provided she teach him the ways of her people. Their education went on for many months. Quietly, they fell in love, making plans to start a life elsewhere. In the most important of ways they were a couple, eventually conceiving a child. Sadly, her parents discovered the nature of the relationship. Tom was forced to leave, and Ling's mother was watched day and night until the villagers determined she was safe. In the spring of the following year, Ling was born. Prior to the discovery of the pregnancy, Tom and Ling's mother had devised a plan, hiding Tom's books in a mountain cave. If they were ever separated, Ling's mother would secretly educate the child. And she did.

August 5

We were on the road by nine. Listening to NPR, we learned that America's unique brand of violence had struck again. Twenty people had been killed in El Paso and just as many injured. Hours later, nine more were killed in Dayton and twenty-seven injured. The two shooters were young, white males. Difficult as it was, we listened for much of the drive. The massacres were the latest in a long string of them. One commentator said there are 300 million guns on the streets, and politicians do nothing while the populace grows increasingly fearful. After every shooting there's a debate about gun control. But the Republicans in Congress stymie any attempt to enact reasonable legislation. Apparently, they receive large sums of money from the National Rifle Association, rich with support from its five million members. Ling and I agreed that there's no end in sight as long as elected representatives fail to do the right thing. For the remainder of our drive we talked about the paradox of living in America. Freedoms unknown in China are accompanied by social ills that jeopardize those freedoms. Throughout her university and medical education, Ling assumed she would remain in the United States, establishing a career and later raising a family. She's uncertain now. It will take her four years to complete her residency. After that, she may return home. Though there would be limits on her personal freedom, they may be a reasonable tradeoff for the safety she needs for her future family.

August 6

We spent the night on the outskirts of Ithaca Falls, New York, in a lovely home built the year I turned ten. It's owned by a couple who purchased it from the bank after foreclosure. They'd always lived in the city but dreamt in their later years of a country life. Now they're living it, renting rooms to travelers. The old house sits high on a hill, surrounded by acres of timber and hay fields. On our arrival we were greeted by Hal and his spaniel, whose best days are behind him. They appeared to be inseparable comrades. Once inside, we met Hal's wife, Chandra. Of East Indian descent, she spent much of her life in Brooklyn. Then Hal came along. They're good partners, sharing equally the duties of their recently established bed and breakfast. I walked the grounds with Hal before breakfast, commenting that Ling and I had driven along Cayuga Lake just before arriving and wondered if any of the Cayuga people remain. He replied that they still have a significant presence in the area, owning much of the nearby land. "Sadly," he said, "they're treated poorly and are often victims of discrimination." Two years ago, leaders of the Cayuga Nation approached Hal, wanting him to manage several acres of adjacent farmland. He agreed and word got out. Many of his friends abandoned him. He even received death threats. Hal is disturbed by what's happening in his new neighborhood, and by the mistreatment of non-whites all across the country. Ling and I were sorry to leave, wishing we could have stayed another night. For the reminder of our journey, I felt the white man's guilt.

August 7

Thomas had made arrangements for Ling and me to spend the night at the Colonial Inn in Concord rather than navigate the afternoon traffic of Boston. He said he'd meet us there and we'd have the evening together. The timing was perfect. Thomas had been waiting just a few minutes when we arrived. I was moved by the embrace of father and daughter. Thomas is different in her presence. Although always a good listener, he hung on her every word, never interrupting. He was forthcoming as well, answering every question and describing in detail his recent travels and present work. Since her first arrival in America, they've visited often enough that the initial twenty years apart meant little. Observing them, it was easy to see the traits of each in the other. Green eyes. Gentle hands. Fine facial features. Quick to smile in response to delight. A genuine warmth easily shared. After a while, Thomas suggested I drop by Emerson's house, as it would be open for another hour. In the meantime, he and Ling would visit some shops if she was up to it. We could then meet in the Liberty Room at the Colonial for dinner. It was agreed, and I proceeded in the direction I knew would get me there quickly. It was quiet inside when I arrived. A lone volunteer in the room to the left. No one in the study on the right. But as before, I knew he was there. The slight rock of his chair. The nearly indiscernible outline of his figure. I approached slowly, placing my hand where I believed to be his shoulder. He spoke softly, but distinctly enough that my mind could hear everything. "Walt, thank you for coming. I've missed your presence. I imagine you've missed mine." The hour passed quickly and without disturbance, until the announcement that the doors would be locked in five minutes. I asked Emerson when we'd meet again. He responded that, if I wouldn't mind, he'd accompany me home tonight. I said I'd like that very much. Dinner was wonderful. I had the Cape Cod oysters and a bottle of Sam Adams. Genuinely satisfied, we agreed to retire for the night. Thomas informed Ling that I'd be taking a late flight from Boston. A room had been reserved for me so I might rest before taking an Uber to the airport. I thanked Thomas for his thoughtfulness and hugged Ling, telling her how much I'd enjoyed our time together. She smiled, promising we'd meet again.

August 8
After taking my leave from Thomas and Ling yesterday evening, I sat at the table in my room. My intention was to record impressions of the few hours in Concord. I had little success as sleep took hold. My last recollection was of Thomas' handshake and Ling's hug. From there, I'm unsure if I remained seated or made my way to the bed. I only know that I settled into a dream from long ago. On that occasion, I'd fallen asleep

as well, on the gather'd leaves with my dog and gun by my side. Other images followed. Of a husband asleep with his wife. He with his palm on her hip. She with her palm on his. Of a mother asleep with her child. Sisters side by side, asleep in their bed. The prisoner asleep in the prison and the runaway son asleep. Males and females alone and asleep, clutching unrequited loves. The sleep of the living and the sleep of the dead. I looked upon all and felt a great tenderness, shedding tears for the sad times in their lives. Emerson arrived and sat with me. He who knows only too well of sadness. Having borne times of grief without anger or malice, he never dismissed them. Instead, he wove them into the fabric of his life. I reached for his hand and he grasped mine, holding it in a manner I'd never known, but as a father should. We sat for the longest time. He withdrew his hand and placed it on my shoulder. "Walt, it's time to go." I woke alone in the quiet of my bed. The sun well along in its day.

August 9

A friend of Thomas' passed away on Tuesday. His heart could no longer carry the load. With Thomas still in Boston, I took his place at the funeral. Nearly every seat was taken. Thomas told me that Jim was known by many and loved by most. For more than thirty years he owned a local restaurant, quietly attending to the needs of friends and strangers alike. He was always ready with a story, but reveled equally in those of others. The funeral was held at a Roman Catholic church. Having not grown up in the faith, I'd never observed the Mass central to its tradition. My father told me more than once that Catholics are not to be trusted and I should keep my distance from them. But there was nothing in this morning's experience suggesting my father knew what he was talking about. It was a family gathering. One in which those present were on the best of terms. There was sadness for sure. But it was clear his memory lived on. The service was presided over by a priest who knew Jim well. He had stories. Funny. Endearing. Revelatory. In between each, questions were asked. How do you use your time? Is it used to pass on the gifts of life and joy? Do you pass on the gift of joy to others in need, as Jim did? There was a reading from the New Testament. A passage from Paul's letter to Timothy: "I have fought the good fight. I have finished the race. I have kept the faith." It was suggested that Paul had Jim in mind when he wrote it. As is my habit these days, I read from the *Tao Te Ching* this morning. The teaching was a simple one: "The Master knows he is going to die. He holds nothing back from life. He is, therefore, ready for death, as a man is ready for sleep after a good day's work." Lao Tzu could have been speaking of Jim as well. I think of our

94

universe still expanding. That all goes onward and outward and nothing collapses. And to die is different than anyone supposed.

August 10

A neighbor stopped over with a piece of cherry pie, the fruit picked earlier in the day. She was aware that Thomas is away and thought I might like something sweet. Her two-year-old, who has a fondness for Molly, tagged along. The four of us moved to the porch to pass the time. Mary is a nurse and works at a hospital on a unit where the possibility of death is imminent. She shared an experience from earlier in the week. A young man had been brought by ambulance to the emergency room. He was in a deep sleep and barely breathing. His parents arrived soon after and disclosed that their son was a heroin user. They'd found him at breakfast time, asleep on the floor in his bedroom. On the table next to him was a plastic bag of white powder and the needle used to inject it. Unable to wake him, they telephoned for help. Mary said the doctors and nurses worked feverishly to restore consciousness, but without success. Stabilized with the aid of oxygen and fluids, he was moved to Mary's unit. The next day various tests were administered, and the worst was discovered. Even though the young man's heart, lungs, and other organs were still functioning, his brain had effectively died. If the oxygen and various tubes were withdrawn, his vital functions would cease. On the third day the family met with the hospital chaplain. For hours the possibilities were explored - medical, emotional, spiritual. By evening, the parents had decided that their son would want to be let go. However, he would also want some good to come from the tragedy. After more tests, it was determined that his heart was healthy and could be removed and given to another. That night, in the hour before midnight, the family arrived on the unit. On either side of the corridor, hospital personnel had gathered. Moments later, the young man was brought from his room on a gurney and the family followed him down the long hall to where the organ recovery would take place. Mary said everyone present was moved to tears. It was over in an hour. His heart left the hospital packed on ice. By morning, in a different hospital in a different state, another young man was given a second chance.

August 11

After meeting with Thomas, Emerson, and Lao on the Summer Solstice, I understood that my preparation for death would begin in six months. The timeline seemed reasonable. I had much to learn and death could wait. But the last few days have taught me that life has its own agenda. Try as we might to ignore death and focus our attention on the tasks at hand, the inevitable is never far from view. Thomas shared a story recently about the Dalai Lama. Eighty-four now, he was asked on his fifty-eighth birthday what he wanted to accomplish in the coming year. He responded that he hoped to spend more time preparing to die. I've heard that Buddhists are more realistic about death than most westerners. Even without a God, they're comfortable with the notion that death is a return to a presence the mind has long forgotten. I've yet to form an opinion on whether or not life continues in a hereafter. The idea that our universe had a beginning without a creator is not easy to ignore. But no matter how science might inform us, there is nevertheless the thing we call our soul. That essence that longs for a return. I believed once that the smallest sprout shows there is really no death. And if there is, it leads forward to life. From what I can tell there's no evidence to affirm or deny an afterlife. These days, however, I'm wondering if it's best to bet on the former.

August 12

Thomas is home. It's been nice having these days to myself, but I was ready for his return. Near the end in Camden, I never had a moment alone. If it wasn't Horace, it was Mary Davis, Warry, or Harned to tease or complain to. Sometimes an acquaintance would visit, and we'd pass the time with small talk. I'd always thought of myself as a solitary character, but old age and infirmity changed that. It's easy, even natural, to keep one's own company on the open road. But silence isn't a comfort when confined to a small house, a room, and finally a bed. Thomas is no longer a mere acquaintance. I value his friendship in a way I have with few others. He has my best interests at heart, though I sometimes disagree with him. Even when I'm pigheaded he never calls me on it. It's as though he considers all existence to be transitory. He seems to view any problem or predicament from both a distance and up close. I'm clueless as to the source of his wisdom, which extends well beyond learning. How old he is I still don't know, though I believe I'm close to getting at the truth of it. At dinner Thomas suggested we drive out west for a few days. He has a break in his schedule and is in need of some wide open space. We'll leave at sunrise with Molly.

August 13

Having packed simply, we were on the road before the morning rush. Without an itinerary or need to accomplish anything, we had four days to travel where we liked. Thomas asked that I open the atlas and determine a route across Kansas, Nebraska, or South Dakota. I took the task seriously, following every highway large and small across each of the three states. Occasionally I had a question about a town, park, or historic site. In the far west of South Dakota, I noticed an area identified as a "national park" and a second, smaller area labelled a "national monument." I didn't know about such places. Thomas said that in the early years of the last century Teddy Roosevelt was elected president. A great lover of the outdoors, he spent as much time as possible in the wild. With the rise of the big corporations he feared that commerce would swallow up large areas of natural beauty. To preserve them, he advocated for a federally funded system that would protect them. Eventually, he cajoled Congress into passing legislation creating a National Park Service. One by one, national parks and other designated areas were created. There are four hundred now, two in South Dakota - Wind Cave National Park and Mount Rushmore National Monument. So, it was settled. We'd continue west toward Omaha, then follow the Missouri River north in the direction of Sioux City. Traveling west again, we'd cross the vast plains to Rapid City and the "Black Hills." Arriving an hour after sunset, we rented a small cabin in the mountains for the night.

August 14

Molly and I walked early. Two hawks circled overhead. Deer moved in the tall pines. A lone crane stood silent in the shallow waters of a stream-fed lake. We stood silent as well. On yesterday's drive, Thomas told the story of Black Elk, a Lakota medicine man who lived in the Black Hills more than a century ago. As a boy he fell sick. After days of high fever, he had a vision. A foretelling of the future of his people, it remained with him all his life. He grew to become a man of great compassion, teaching that at the center of the universe the Great Spirit dwells. And that center is everywhere, including within each of us. As the sun rose this morning, I experienced the same, wanting nothing more. But it was time for Molly to eat, and she was incessant. Her needs met, Thomas and I packed and were soon at Mount Rushmore. It's quite a site. Profiles of four presidents carved into a mountain side, Lincoln among them. How could the memorial not include the great man? The likenesses of Washington, Jefferson, and Teddy Roosevelt were rendered as well. Even more impressive is a second memorial a few miles away. In 1948, Korczak Ziolkowski began sculpting Crazy Horse, Black Elk's cousin. A work in progress, the massive carving is a monument to the spirit of the Lakota leader and his people. When completed, his left hand will gesture forward in response to a white man's question, "Where are your lands now?" Crazy Horse is said to have replied, "My lands are where my dead lie buried." I'm again reminded of the white man's atrocities.

August 15

From midmorning until late afternoon, we hiked in Custer State Park, the same Custer killed by Crazy Horse's warriors in the Battle of Little Big Horn. Thomas is in better physical condition than I am, but I kept up. Although I suspect he maintained a pace he thought I could manage. The protected scenery was stunning. Roosevelt would be pleased. Rock formations towered over forested valleys. Wildflowers flourished in the most unlikely of places. Elk and deer were numerous. At high points along the trail we could see all the way to Wyoming. Although I've never been in the Rockies, the Black Hills have given me a taste of the high country. I labored on occasion, but my lungs rejoiced. A few times I thought my legs would give way. But with the passing hours I experienced a strength I'd not known since my youth. I wonder what my life would have been like if I'd left Camden after mother's death and settled in these parts. The doctors suspected that I'd contracted tuberculous during the War. Perhaps the vigor of daily hikes would have extended my years. This evening, Thomas caught up on his letter writing, including a long description to Ling of our visit. I sat on the front steps, weary but refreshed, reveling in the emerging stars. We leave in the morning, never to return.

August 16

We drove south on 385 all the way to far western Nebraska and the intersection with Interstate 80. I'm amazed at the work of today's road builders. The highway through the mountains is broad and curves gently when necessary. Never a straight line if a way around was possible. After leaving the mountains, we saw prairie dogs popping their little heads up from innumerable holes. Buffalo grazed undisturbed. Ranches with fine riding horses found their niche, blending in as if they'd been neighbors for centuries. Northwest Nebraska had its own beauty. Rolling plains with few signs of human habitation. A child born in those parts would know solitude for life, no matter what later years might bring. I mused for many a mile on the role of place in the construction of the human soul. How different to be born and raised amidst smokestacks or skyscrapers. I wonder if there are poets or painters from the flatlands, informed by endless sky. Would my poetry have been different without the streets and alleys of Brooklyn? Though I learned much from the city's museums and libraries, the endless noise of the urban landscape intruded in ways that took years to overcome. Everything changed the further east we drove on 80. Cars and trucks hurtled along. Commerce everywhere, whether advertised or a long exit ramp away. I sensed Thomas' sadness. We spoke little the last few hours, respecting each other's need for privacy.

August 17
It's good to be home and engaged in household tasks. The hens were productive in our absence. Having provided a beautiful bounty, I replenished their feeder with ground corn and filled the waterer to the brim. A reward of fresh-cut kale was strewn in the four corners of their run. The young ones, yet to lay for the first time, prefer to eat apart from the older generation. Though nearly equal in size, there is nevertheless a defined pecking order. It's interesting to observe the deference. A heavy rain in our absence awakened the August lawn, adding two inches of growth. One of Thomas' few luxuries is a riding mower, which I enjoy greatly. Sitting on the big yellow seat and maneuvering the green machine is about as close as I've come to farming. There was a summer when I made extra money shoveling out a dairy barn, but it was more like factory work than anything else. In my travels, I often stopped to pay respect to the men and women who truly lived on the land. It was a pleasure watching a farmer plough a field or gather grain; his wife in the orchard or milking goats. I had a farmer friend, a tamer of oxen. They would bring him the three and four-year olds to break. He could take the wildest steer and tame him. There is a rhythm known by farmers. Time is kept by sun and moon and the four seasons. Clocks are redundant. After the mowing I pulled weeds from the flowerbeds and garden. I then harvested tomatoes, cucumbers, and peppers. They'll make a fine salad along with the kale and lettuce not given to the chickens. Thomas will be pleased.

August 18
Mother frequently preached that Sunday should be a day of rest. Thomas has said the same, although often it doesn't work out. Today, though, we made the commitment and stuck to it. We walked Molly to the park and back. Had a leisurely breakfast. Rode our bikes on the river trail. Grilled burgers and vegetables for lunch. Read, played checkers, and napped. Late in the afternoon we walked again. The subject of marriage came up. I shared with Thomas my conversation with Ling. How her mother confided that Thomas was the love of her life. She believed Thomas felt the same. He agreed. Their year together was a lifetime. Forced to leave the village, he became a seeker. Not in search of another love, but for a purpose. After some time, he made his way to

Switzerland in the hope of becoming an analyst. In Kusnacht he enrolled in the school established to teach the Jungian method. He met Anna there, becoming intimate friends in the Platonic sense. They spent hours together - studying, discussing cases, sailing on Lake Zurich. In many ways, Anna was more advanced than Thomas. She was a year ahead in her coursework and more experienced in the ways of the heart. Thomas said he still recalls the afternoon on the lake when Anna kindly suggested he never marry. She said he had a gift. His fate was to be a guide. Should he marry, his energy would be diverted from his life task. Thomas disagreed, but knew she was right. There was no choice in the matter. To deny it would be to deny his nature. I wondered if I'd hurt Thomas by inquiring about marriage. He assured me I had not. That he felt relief in sharing that chapter of his story.

August 19
Ling begins her training next week to become a pediatrician. On Thursday there's a celebration in Boston for Ling and her colleagues. Thomas would like to be there, but he's sensitive to my need for rest after so much travel. I insisted he make the trip and asked if I might accompany him. He was delighted. We fly tomorrow as he has meetings in Portland on Wednesday. The following morning we'll take the early bus to Boston in time for the event. Friday and Saturday Ling is free, and we'll explore the area. I'm sure Thomas will want to spend some time alone with her. If so, I hope to visit the waterfront on my own. Perhaps Lao will come. He did say that I only need to call. It's odd. I've only met him twice, yet it feels as if he's been nearby most of my life. I've come to believe that certain things are preordained. That somehow seeds are planted long before our birth. It could be that my acquaintance with Lao is one of those. Thomas' friend Anna has offered to take us sailing, so we'll return to Portland on Sunday. If the weather cooperates, we'll have two or three days on the water. It may be my last opportunity. I intend to learn as much as I can. Had I been raised in Maine, I might have taken to the sea as a young man. Melville's tale intrigued me greatly, but I was too far along in life when I read his account. There are days when I'm ready for this life to end. And others when I think that one life is not enough.

August 20
Thunderstorms over Detroit required the pilot to detour west to avoid the tail end of the weather system. I didn't mind the added hour of flight time. As much as I appreciate the night transit arranged by Emerson, I've come to enjoy travel by airplane. I never appreciated clouds in the

way I do now. Or the bird's perspective. Life is simpler looking down. Human interaction seems inconsequential at 30,000 feet. As do the demands of clock and calendar. Since learning of the moon landing, I've read of the astronaut's life. How circling the globe in a tiny capsule somehow rewires the brain. Patience as a virtue gives way to patience as the natural way of being in the world. Back on earth, the astronaut walks at a different pace. A stranger in a strange land, he cares less for things he previously thought essential. It seems that the space traveler is a creature unto itself. An evolved being. Perhaps the savior of the planet, should the world as we know it last long enough. I imagine the ancient seafarers were much the same. Odysseus was a different man upon returning home. Nor am I the same after these months in the future. Leaving home has always been a prerequisite for rebirth.

August 21
Rain was forecast. I don't think it was a difficult prediction, as the foul weather followed us east. Rather than spend the day inside, I accompanied Thomas to Portland. The library isn't far from the site of his meetings. On the drive in, we talked about accuracy; about the professionals who foretell when it's going to rain or snow, and how much. I've thought a lot about the weather. How often it's calm under the full moon. Warm when I've been in a boat, lifting the lobster pots from where they were sunk with heavy stones. Of the weather-beaten vessels returned from months at sea, and those ships that crossed the great oceans and survived the capes, only to be lost at night to deadly typhoons and hurricanes. Thomas said the government employs scientists specialized in atmospheric conditions. They take seriously their responsibility. He cautioned that I be wary of the local weathermen and women. Unlike the government experts, they're not highly trained. More concerning is that they place entertainment above reliability. He said TV weathermen rarely bother to make accurate forecasts because they figure the public won't believe them anyway. Some even skew their prophesies to improve viewer ratings. Looking down on Congress Street at the black umbrellas, I thought of mother's trusted adage: "Red sky at night, sailors' delight. Red sky at morning, sailors take warning."

August 22
It was an honor to spend the evening with Ling and her colleagues. Ten men and women, mostly young, with years of work and study still ahead of them. I wasn't aware until this evening of the training required to become a physician. With so little formal education, I wouldn't have survived in this age. Ling, like the others, has completed college and

medical school. Eight years for Ling. Some with more. One of the women was a teacher for a while. When her children were old enough and her husband well situated, she pursued her dream. The residencies for each will be demanding. Long hours with difficult responsibilities and little compensation. Ling said it's worth it. Growing up in a village with no doctors, she saw much suffering. Particularly that of children and the elderly. Her mother was an only child, having lost her brother when he was two. He had a stomach illness treated by a native healer. Had the right medicine been available, her brother most likely would have survived. Ling grew up with the memory of her family's loss, vowing to do something about it. Encouraged by her mother and educated with Thomas' books, Ling far surpassed her peers. As a teenager she instructed the younger ones and tutored their grandparents, teaching many to read and write. It was obvious that Ling wouldn't remain a village girl. When her letter reached Thomas, and he responded, her life changed forever. In four years, she'll be a pediatrician and the decision will have to be made; whether to remain in America or return to China and her people. Both countries have given her much. She'll repay the debt to one of them.

August 23

We walked from Ling's apartment to North Station and caught the train to Salem. A colleague of hers lives in the nearby city. His parents were hosting a luncheon for the residents and had invited their parents as well. Thomas said I was welcome, but I deferred, preferring to explore the Old Town on foot. I strolled the narrow streets, admiring the craftsmanship of the colonial builders. Dwellings date back two and three centuries. The cemetery is home to many of the earliest residents. Rounding the Commons, I could see the waterfront at the end of Briggs Street. A marker identified Collins Cove. Above the beach a vacant bench overlooked the incoming tide. A perfect place to call for Lao. I closed my eyes, following my breath as Thomas has taught me. An image of the great white bird appeared, gliding silently across my inner horizon. The breeze picked up, bringing with it moist, salty air from the open sea. Across the expanse, masted vessels were moored in deeper waters. Above them he appeared. Approaching swiftly and without effort, in a matter of seconds he landed on the sand a few feet away. The magnificent being had heeded my request. I had questions. From where had he come? How long was the flight? Whom did he leave behind? Lao greeted me first, then responded. For the last month he's been resting on a small island. His mate is there and their young one, recently born. It's a long journey by wing. But from time to time he travels as

Emerson does. The passage on this day was short. He then inquired of me, wondering how I'd spent my days since our last visit. I related everything as best I could. He asked what I'd been doing to feed my soul. I wondered too, confiding that I struggle to please both Emerson and Thomas. In doing so I sometimes neglect my soul. He smiled a knowing smile. "All beings have such struggles, Walt. It is the nature of things when the eternal meets the temporal." He then encouraged me to be kind to myself, that the outer trappings of flesh and bone would soon be gone. In the meantime, I have my senses to experience existence. "Do your best Walt, in the remaining days, to appreciate the gift of sense and its connection to what is deepest within you." He then wished me well, returning in the direction from which he came.

August 24
Ling suggested we walk to Jaho near the lighthouse. A friend recommended it as having the best coffee and sweet rolls in Salem. Arriving shortly after eight, a line for orders had already formed. No one was in a hurry, pleased to be alive on a sunny Saturday. Taking an outside table, two gentlemen next to us said they'd been coming since opening day fifteen years ago. One of the men has a cocker spaniel. Sammy's a favorite of the locals and a good start to a conversation. What we thought would be a short stop turned into much of the morning. We spent the afternoon at the beach, visiting mostly with dog owners. With all the division in the country, I've begun to wonder if dogs might be a place of common ground. I can imagine legislators, even world leaders, meeting in parks and on beaches with their canine pets. Civility might trump caustic exchange. Returning to Boston on the late afternoon train, we spent the evening with Ling in her apartment. She prepared a wonderful meal, a favorite of the Yi. The conversation turned to her childhood. After a glass or two of wine, she told a story passed down for millennia by her people. There's a belief that even before the Yi knew themselves, there was a rabbit born on the far side of the lake. He had a difficult birth and was slow to run. Unable to protect himself, he developed an uncanny ability to sit in silence and observe. His great-grandfather, the Wise One of the clan, kept watch over the boy, recognizing that the gift would allow the young one to live far longer than any of his kind. One day, shortly after the death of the Wise One, the young rabbit left the clan to learn all he could. "Legend has it," said Ling, "that he's alive to this day, a Wise One who has learned from and counseled great men and women from ancient times to the present." On the return to Portland, Thomas said he'd heard much of the legend during

his year in the village. I asked if he thought there was any truth to it. He responded simply that "anything is possible."

August 25

We arrived at the dock as Anna came along side. It was nice to see her again. She'd spent the night moored in the outer harbor and needed fuel and water before we departed. I enjoyed my earlier lunch with her in Portland. At the time, I had no idea she was a sailor, captain of her own boat. Looking back, I recall that she spoke little of herself. A discipline that must serve her well as an analyst. We completed the needed tasks and pushed off. At the helm, Anna asked if I'd like to take over. I appreciated her trust but declined, explaining it might be best if I observe for a while. Thomas, a skilled sailor as well, obliged while Anna opened a chart of Casco Bay. She said we could make it to Jewell Island by dinner time and anchor for the night. Soon the engine gave way to full sails, propelling us at five knots for long stretches. The mainland behind, the sea is a world unto itself. There's nothing like sailing under a full sky in the service of wind and current. Though I skippered small craft as a boy and young man, I was never accomplished, always staying close to shore. But my grandmother's father was a sailor, possessing that surly English pluck of which there are none tougher. Watching Thomas and Anna alternate at the helm, I returned to nights by the fire. Seated next to the old man, he'd spin yarns of which I never tired. Whether truth or fiction, it made no difference. Perhaps they were a bit of both, his life merging with all the sailors he'd known and ever heard of. What mattered were his descriptions of sailors at work in the rigging, or astride the spars. They still live within me. The sun low in the sky, we arrived at Jewell, dropping the anchor on the protected side. Down below and dinner finished, we sat by candlelight and the stories continued.

August 26

Just before bedtime, Anna grew concerned about the shift in the wind. We went up top. The anchor was where it had been dropped but we'd swung 180 degrees, moving us too close to the nearest vessel. Should it swing, there could be a collision. We had no choice but to pull the anchor, motor a safe distance away, and reset it deep enough to account for the keel and low tide. With Anna at the helm and Thomas at the bow, it was done, and we retired for the night. At about three we woke to loud voices a few hundred feet away. With the flood light, we could see a boat longer than ours aground and tipped on its side. Anna said the owner apparently failed to account for the wind and depth at the tide's lowest point. The crew, unable to right the vessel, could do nothing but wait for rising waters to rectify the situation. Shortly after sunrise, the boat motored alongside. Looking a bit haggard, the helmsman reported that there'd been no damage, and everything was fine. Wishing them well, we had the cove to ourselves for the remainder of the day.

MONTH SIX

August 27

It rained all afternoon, ending just before sunset. It was a glorious event, made extraordinary by the pouring in of the flood tide and falling back of the ebb tide. All the while our boat rose and fell in step with a universal rhythm. Any other evening, that would have been the end of it. But the colors of day gave way to the grays of dusk, then pinpoints of white against the darkest of blacks. Dinner finished and dishes washed and dried, the nocturnal world demanded our attention. We moved to the deck with pillows and blankets where the stars took center stage. The Milky Way, that carpet of silk, laid down its splendor across the length of the dome. Space and time quivered before us. Distant suns swelling, collapsing, ending, serving their longer and shorter use. I swear that all the stars in the sky are for religion's sake and no man has ever been half devout enough. Knowing something of the birth of the pulsating furnaces, I strained to see the threads connecting them. They must surely recall their common mother, that single, incomprehensible, infinitesimal dot. We were spellbound and mute for the longest time, returning to earth with the emergence of the thin ribbon of gray to the east.

August 28

I woke to the aroma of black coffee. Thomas and Anna were at the table, sipping on the rich brew, a chart of the bay spread before them. In the background, a clear, self-assured voice forecast a brisk southwest wind with seas up to eight feet. Anna looked up with delight. "Walt, we have a vigorous sail ahead." Returning to the chart, she pointed to Thomas the surest route home. Looking up again, she offered an explanation. "Walt, the wind will be on our nose all day. We'll be tacking most of the way back. Are you in the mood for a workout?" I nodded yes, knowing we'd be "coming about" time after time with little rest in between. As a young man I relished the challenge of such a sail, sure of my body and confident of my mate. But the distance between those years and this is most of a lifetime. I knew my biceps would be strained to their limit, and my hands, gripped about the lines, would question their strength and tenacity. Nevertheless, I shared Anna's excitement and volunteered to hoist the anchor and stow it. Completing the task, I took my place in the cockpit. With Cliff Island on our leeward side, we motored the first while. But the calm was short-lived. Rounding the point, we were in the open. Great Cheabeague, far to the west, offered no cover. Anna yelled, "Prepare to come about." I manned the port side wench and Thomas the starboard. The shift of sail from left to right wasn't as smooth as Anna would have liked, but she appreciated the effort, predicting we'd get better. And we did, making our way through the outer bay, skirting one island after another. All our senses engaged, muscles and tendons too, there was no letting down until the end. As quickly as the wind had risen hours before, it subsided. Just ahead, the harbor beckoned, offering the refuge known to every sailor. Once ashore, the ache set in, that delicious ache that follows a job well done.

August 29
A few days at sea changes one's perspective. Like the astronaut having circled the globe. A break from civilization is a welcome tonic. But this morning I was eager to get reacquainted with the world. I learned that while we were away, Greta Thunberg, a young activist from Sweden, had sailed into New York City, having completed a solo transatlantic journey. Sixteen years old, she made the voyage to spread awareness about the climate crisis. Accounts describe her as shy, though not afraid to talk about a disorder she lives with every day. She has a condition called "Asperger's," speaking only when she thinks it's necessary. "Now is one of those moments," she says. In photos, Greta is not particularly imposing. But her size belies a strength. A year ago, she demonstrated outside the Swedish parliament. Her activism prompting students in other countries to protest the damage done to the planet by older generations. She's on a bigger stage now and will soon speak before the United Nations. This afternoon Thomas and I went to the movie *Maiden*. It's the story of Tracy Edwards, a young British woman who skippered the first all-female crew in the "Whitbread Round the World Yacht Race." On the nine-month, 33,000-mile journey, Edwards and her mates prevailed over extreme conditions, sending a message to the male-dominated sailing world. Thirty years have passed and Edwards' perspective has changed. She's about to embark on another 'round the world voyage, advocating for girls living in male-dominated cultures. The journey will raise money so thousands can pursue educations presently denied them. I've been learning that women everywhere are succeeding in previously male dominated endeavors. Hillary Clinton nearly won the last presidential election, having more

than enough votes to do so. There's a chance a woman will win in 2020. Never have women been needed more.

August 30

I met a young man this afternoon. Ping is Chinese-American, his father born on the Chinese mainland. When the Communists took over, he escaped to Taiwan where he met and married a young woman. They'd heard of "The American Dream" and eventually left Taiwan for California at the dawn of the computer age. They worked hard, succeeding at a high level. Ping was born and later sent to the best schools. After years of study, he became an expert in an emerging discipline called "nanotechnology." Ping explained that the new science provided tools to manipulate atoms and molecules for the fabrication of products. Seven years ago, Ping was diagnosed with Hodgkin lymphoma, a form of cancer. After months of treatment, he was told it wasn't working. He'd likely die if the maximum does wasn't administered. His doctors warned, however, that his heart might not tolerate the high levels. The treatment would either kill him or cure him. Ping survived but the experience raised questions. It didn't make sense to him that there's so little certainty as to whether a drug will work or not until after it's tried. So Ping started a company that "pre-tests" medications to determine which are the most effective and least toxic. Today, his company employs nanotechnologists, biologists, and electrical engineers. Working as "cross-functional teams," they create "human organ microtissues" so new drugs can be considered without human trial-and-error testing. Much of what Ping shared was over my head. Still, I was in awe of his story and what he's accomplished. I'm beginning to understand what Thomas means when he says anything is possible.

August 31

It's a tradition of our neighbors to the east to have a party on the first Saturday of the college football season. Thomas and I were invited. The house was full, and we were the oldest by several years. It seemed to make no difference. Everyone was friendly. And the food delicious, though not what my doctor would like me to eat. But Thomas told me it's ok to "fall off the wagon" once in a while. So, I had my fill of burgers and chips, various snacks and sweets. Beer, too. There's so much variety these days. Not being a connoisseur, they all tasted good. I wandered about until I got to the room with the television. A game was already in progress, the teams playing in a stadium filled with thousands. The first time I heard about football was a few years after the War. Two teams from Ivy League schools met to play a game somewhat like rugby, but with variations. Within a few years, other schools took up the sport. Princeton was one of them and had a large following. I would attend with friends, observing the athleticism of the players and the exciting play. What I saw on the television wasn't much different than the football of my time. Except that today's players are larger, faster, and more skilled. I enjoyed watching, though I cringed whenever there was a violent tackle. Thomas said players are often injured, some so severely they never fully recover. People are beginning to question the safety of the sport and some parents are prohibiting their sons from participating. Thomas believes if football is around twenty years from now, it will look much different from today's game.

September 1
I had an odd dream. Except for Emerson's visits, it was the first related to my being here. All the others have been about before. Childhood fears. Strangers, real and imagined. My search for fame. Last night's dream was different. I wasn't my old self. Instead, I was firmly placed in this year, with no connection to another time. It was like those who live in a foreign country and dream in the language of their new home and not their native tongue. I'm not certain who I was though, unlike the others, I was disconnected from family and friends. Perhaps I'd outlived them. Twelve of us had been selected to participate in a secret government project. For two weeks we would live as if there'd been an apocalypse of biblical proportions. Essential services would be limited, and no one could be trusted. Our task was to find a safe refuge and start over. We were to attempt to reach a remote area in the north, with no assurance we'd survive. But we had to try. I'm unsure of the dream's meaning, though I've experienced enough these past few months to share the collective concerns. I'd like to speak with Anna as her understanding of dreams is considerable.

September 2
I was restless all day, unable to set aside the experience from the night before. I've had many dreams, dismissing most. Occasionally, they've been relevant to a present relationship or the day ahead. Relevant or not, they're always narrow in focus. Limited to my person and place. Once, however, in the third year of the War, I dreamt I saw a city invincible to the attacks of the rest of the earth. It was a new city. One of friends. Nothing was greater than the quality of robust love. It could be seen in the actions of the men and women, and in all their looks and words. My most recent dream was of that quality. Considering it now in my waking

hours, I see the possibility of something new. Something better than the past. I've been following the news, more than usual. My heart is aching for those in the Bahamas. The loss of homes and loved ones from the massive hurricane. It will soon fall upon Florida. Residents are preparing for the worst. In cities across the county, rising temperatures mean misery for many. The poor and elderly suffer the most. Every day there are reminders of the worsening climate. Scientists are predicting that the point of no return is near. Perhaps my dream was a prophetic one, set in the near future during the years of great loss. For humankind to survive, small bands must start over as self-contained communities, planting seeds for future generations. Friendship with the quality of robust love will be necessary to withstand attacks. If I could live for years rather than months, I'd gladly volunteer for such an experiment.

September 3
The hurricane has moved on, leaving the Bahamas devastated. Neighborhoods are in rubble. Houses crushed into splinters. Boats tossed into heaps like playthings. Most of Grand Bahama is under water, massive waves still pounding its shores. The sea has always been ferocious. Its placidness becoming a brooding scowl with little warning. I've looked upon it as possessing a vast heart, like a planet's, chained and chafing within its breakers. Great beasts unloosed within its depths. I'm told that these freaks of nature are getting worse. The frequency of the most severe has doubled over the last twenty years. Climate change appears to be the reason, though the media says little about it. Big business and the radical right deny it altogether. But the scientists, at least those not in the pockets of the corporations, tell the truth. They say global warming is intensifying. As a result, the number of devastating storms will continue to rise. I asked Thomas about the connection between the earth heating up and the increase in extreme weather. His understanding is that the oceans take in most of the excess energy created by warming, and there is a direct link between rising ocean temperatures and the intensification of hurricanes. Sea levels will rise by as much as four feet by the end of the century. Storm surges will penetrate further inland. "I'm not without hope," Thomas said. "But the future looks bleak for millions."

September 4
I snapped at Thomas this morning, and immediately apologized. He'd done nothing wrong. In fact, he was trying to help by giving me a break from the chickens. I have a particular way of tending to them, which I think they recognize. Thomas deviated from the routine by placing their

feeder in the coop rather than in the run, not recalling that they prefer fresh air when they eat. But it wasn't Thomas. It was me. I've been on edge since our return from sailing. At sea, I'm a free spirit. Imagining I'm Lao gliding high above, I touch the clouds with my wingtips. Back on land, I'm anxious. Preoccupied. My mind wanders, struggling to pay attention to what's in front of me. I was awake much of the night, trying to get to the bottom of it. It was easy enough to lay blame on current events. They shout out their news twenty-four hours a day. But the more I considered it, the more I realized the source is as important as the content. When I read the local newspaper, I get disturbed at times. But for the most part, I gain an understanding of how people are living their lives. Listening to public radio is not the same. The focus is more on the larger world. Nevertheless, after an hour of "Morning Edition," I walk away better educated. Then I recognized that it's television. I don't know what it was like in the early years, but it seems its primary purpose these days is to raise the viewer's blood pressure and then sell something to lower it. Coverage of the hurricane is the most recent example. The destruction was tragic enough. But the broadcasters did their best to escalate the tension. Over the last few evenings, I was glued to the screen for hours. And to what end? I'd learn just as much listening to the morning radio. I've noticed when Thomas and I watch together, he rarely sits longer than an hour, walking away with plenty of time to read before bedtime. When I asked him for advice, he suggested I talk with Anna. She has an expertise in "existential depression."

September 5

Thomas made the call to Anna and then left me alone. She had a break between clients and was listening to a recording of Beethoven. I apologized for disturbing her, but he assured me that no time is better than the present when one's psyche is weary or troubled. She then asked how I've been since we left each other's company. I thanked her for our three days at sea, then confided that, shortly after, I experienced a considerable decline in spirit. The hurricane that ravaged the Bahamas was the catalyst, triggering a preoccupation with global warming and the general state of the world. Anna disclosed that many of her clients present symptoms arising out of similar concerns. "Existential depression is not new," she said. "Our species has long struggled with the bigger questions of life, death, meaning, and meaninglessness. Depression often follows when one concludes that critical changes are impossible." She said these are particularly difficult times for those aware that our planet is dying. "Ultimately," Anna said, "we must care for our own souls and hope others do the same. A groundswell is

possible if enough individuals adopt an attitude of reverence for life."
She then told me of the approach Carl Jung took in his later years. Jung
was wary of technological advances, realizing how they can distance us
from our inner wisdom. He'd often retreat to Bollingen on Lake Zurich,
where he'd built a stone dwelling. With no electricity or running water,
he'd chop wood and carry water from the lake. Jung found that "simple
acts" make a man simple. He also surrounded himself with beauty, no
matter how primitive. Anna encouraged me to continue with what I'm
doing. Caring for Molly and the chickens. Working in the garden.
Walking every day. She added that I should listen to music more, watch
television less, and focus on the eternal. Our conversation ended with
that. The remainder of the day, I sat on the porch doing nothing.

September 6
Anna said I should focus on the eternal, but I neglected to ask for an
explanation. I don't think she meant "eternal" in the literal sense, as in
"everlasting" or "having an infinite duration." I assume she'd like me to
explore what's below the surface of things. Emerson suggested a similar
inquiry months ago. Hawking devoted his life to the big questions. A
simple question might be to ask, "how do things work?" Everything I
see, from the really big to the really small, must have an internal
mechanism. My gut tells me that what's on the surface is the end
product of millions of years of incremental change. But all my life, I
only considered what the Buddhists call "maya," the world of appearance
and form. I suppose everything, including the unseen, is "maya."
Nevertheless, it's exciting to think about what lies out of reach of our
senses. The greatest minds took on that task. I spent an hour in the
library once, paging through *On the Origin of Species*. I knew I was
holding something monumental, like Newton's *Principia Mathematica*,
but I had neither the time nor the patience to digest it. I have more
patience now, but less time. In a dozen lifetimes, I could never get to the
bottom of it all. Still, it would be fun to peck around, like the hens after I
spread their feed. A nice thing about knowing so little is I'm not an
expert on anything. There's a freedom in that. The first time I met
Anna, she said if I want to know the answer to something, I should ask
the right question just before going to sleep.

September 7
On our walk this morning, Molly found something on the street and took
it in whole. Being a puppy, she's not to be trusted. More than once,
Thomas has banned her from the house for chewing on something she
shouldn't. Even when she's outside, vigilance is required. Calling for

Molly to sit, I stooped to learn of her discovery, extracting an intact acorn. All wet and glistening, I held it in my palm, rolling it about from side to side. I've never really appreciated the perfect seed, with its protective cap. Yet I've thought about it and the mystery of it becoming a giant oak. But the "how" of it never crossed my mind. I stuck it in my pocket, leaving it to dry while we finished our walk. Once home, I began my research, learning that there's more mystery than what can be seen. Like the best of books, the cover tells little of the story. What I think of as the cap is actually the "cupule," which covers the top of the seed and either side until about halfway down. The seed itself has multiple layers. The "pericarp" is the outer wall, sometimes called the fruit wall. It's thin and protects everything beneath. Just as thin, and immediately below the pericarp, is the "testa" or seed coat, which surrounds the "cotyledons." Equal in size, the two cotyledons are "organs" which contain the stored food reserves of the seed. At the bottom of the line separating the cotyledons are the "plumule" and the "radicle," which together make up the "embryo." The plumule is the part of the embryo that develops into the shoot that pushes up through the soil, attempting to reach the light as quickly as possible. The radicle is the embryonic root of the seed and grows downward. From what I can tell, the shoot lives off the stored food reserves until the radicle establishes itself, drawing nutrients from the soil below. When the shoot breaks through the ground, sunlight must begin to play a major role. What that is, I don't know. And where in this thimble-sized seed is the oak tree to be found? One question leads to another, and another.

September 8

Not a single egg yesterday. It being the Sabbath, I joked with Thomas that the hens must be Jewish. He didn't seem to get it at first, but then chuckled. I hope I wasn't politically incorrect. Attempts at light humor are offensive to some these days. I must remember to be careful, having transgressed often enough in my own time. Anyway, there were four eggs this morning, appropriate for a Sunday. It rained until noon but, shortly after, the gray sky gave way to sun, making for a glorious invitation. Molly and I took up residence under the shade of the old oak tree. I never tire of its embrace, it being like a beloved great-uncle or aunt. My initial intention was to continue research on the life cycle of the acorn and its progeny, but those matters are best left to libraries and computers on "stay inside" days. This being the Christian day of rest, I chose to honor it by leaving the books and electronic devices in their proper places. Seated under the gentle giant with Molly at my feet, I had at my disposal the simple tools of fingers and eyes, and a magnifying glass loaned by Thomas. I had the raw materials, too, of fallen acorns and low hanging leaves. I suspect the earliest dendrologists had little more. Unable to separate the cupule from the seed, I left Molly unattended to retrieve a pocketknife. Returning in a minute, two at the most, I found she had already undertaken the task. In front of her, as slimy as yesterday's, the cap with its tiny raised bumps was in three pieces; the inner workings inches away. Laid bare, they were as described in the acorn treatise. The light brown pericarp protecting the eyelash-thin testa. The cotyledons held tight by Molly's ivory paws, with traces of tooth marks punctuating her effort to know. Taking one of the pair in hand, I hovered over it with the magnifier. What my naked eyes had seen as a small, brown smudge with a slim, beige tail hanging below were verified as the plumule and radicle. I was awestruck. That smudge was of the same kind that had given rise to the remarkable tree behind me and the broad green canopy overhead. And the tiny tail was a descendant of one many years back that had produced a network of roots providing sustenance for a century or more. If a world can be seen in Blake's "grain of sand," there is much more in the offspring of a great oak.

September 9
Rain again, and cool. Much like an October morning. It seems that the weather gods are preparing us for autumn. Emerson has his cohort - Thoreau, Hawthorne, Poe, and Blake perhaps. I wonder about the deities. Do they gather in anticipation of the seasonal change? Particularly those for whom wind and rain are a priority. Zeus would certainly have much to say. Jupiter, too. But they tend to misuse their powers, leaning toward wrath and vengeance rather than the needs of creatures. Tragically, they're making a comeback. I'd like to think there's strength in numbers and that the lesser known will prevail when survival is at issue. Together, Indra and Vayu have served the Indian subcontinent since antiquity. Seth, the Egyptian, and Haddad, the Mesopotamian, have a decent history too. More than any, though, the New World gods are needed most in this age of climate uncertainty. Tate, the Lakota god of the wind. The Hopi god Yaponcha, a god of the wind as well. Toneinilli, the "water sprinkler," rain god of the Navajo. Nerrivik, food provider of the Inuits. And the Abenaki god Gluskab, protector of humanity. Beneath the oak where Molly and I sat yesterday, the squirrels are already about their business - selecting, gathering, storing. Thomas says they have remarkable mental maps, allowing them to return to their hiding places in times of scarcity. As skilled as they are, however, an occasional acorn may be lost or forgotten. Or the furry

one may die before consuming all of its stores. In those instances, the little gatherer may have performed the equally important service of "seed dispersal agent," having moved the fallen fruit beyond the mother tree to more suitable areas for germination. The acorns that survive comprise the new generation of oaks. And the cycle begins again.

September 10
Molly was up in the night, concerned that the outside sounds might intrude. She's too young to know that thunder is more bark than bite. I slept as best I could, my feet hitting the floor an hour earlier than usual. First things first, we went for our walk. Believing the rain was over, I neglected to take an umbrella. Five minutes in there were sprinkles. Five minutes more and it was pouring. By the time we reached the creek, we would have been soaked but for the leaf cover. The oak out back is a stunning creature, but now I see many of its kind line the neighborhood streets and inhabit the hills and low places of the park. Nevertheless, each is sacred in its own right, beneficial to man and nature alike. The acorns for sure. In my youth, the Secatogues and Nesaquakes on the south shore made a hearty bread from the droppings on the forest floor and brewed a delicious coffee-like drink after soaking and roasting the nuts. The broad leaves, as thick as kernels on a cob, provide cover from sun and rain, then fall to the ground in late autumn to nourish the earth. The twigs and branches have kindled many a fire and the stout trunks provided lumber for both fine and commonplace furniture. But like much of our universe, it's the unseen that's invaluable. The oak has a root system superior to any manmade transit system. The taproot is first to come on the scene, having emerged from the enlarged radicle. But soon it relinquishes its prominence to numerous lateral roots that penetrate the soil five feet deep and fifty feet from side to side. From the laterals, the fine root system develops, forming a dense mass to a depth of thirty-six inches. These silky hairs capture moisture and nutrients from the soil, channeling them upward with a power that belies their diminutive stature. The rain ceased and Molly and I emerged from the shelter of the giants, each lost in thought unique to our interests.

September 11
Nearly every morning after watching the sun rise, Molly and I descend the hill to be greeted by Mr. Owl. Perhaps he's watched from the moment we enter the woods. But only after we've crossed the bridge the second time does he make himself known. His timing is impeccable. As we set foot firmly on the stone path he swoops from his perch, gliding in a low-slung arc and then rising high before dropping onto the topmost

branch of one of the great oaks. It's certain that he's a guardian. Most likely of the bridge itself. It may be, at the end of his days, he's to make an accounting of all who entered and left the sanctuary he calls home. When we first met, I was taken aback by his fearlessness; the resolute manner in which he asserted his authority. What I took as arrogance, even haughtiness, I've come to understand as duty. He's been assigned a particular role in the order of things, executing his function with absolute faithfulness. I marvel at the reliability of nature. Each creature, no matter its size or complexity, unfailingly carrying out those tasks determined long before its birth. I imagine Mr. Owl comes from a long line of guardians. That each cell in his body, perfected by innumerable ancestors, holds a key to the events and actions of his life. I wonder whether he sees Molly and me as friend or foe. We'd never wish him harm, but others of my kind may have shown less respect. As a creature of the night, he sees what others cannot. A wisdom must arise from that perspective. One suggesting caution and that trust must be earned. Lao having been assigned my spirit guide, I wish for no other. Nevertheless, there's something of the teacher in Mr. Owl. It's worth my time to observe him whenever possible, so I might better open my eyes and look into the shadows.

September 12
It's been a week since I've watched television or listened to the news. The first two or three days I struggled. My finger itched as it hovered above the "on" button, inches from succumbing to temptation. I've watched many a drunkard at the bar, his hand shaking as it neared the glass that would be the death of him. It's a pity to see the addict, no matter the drug. Thomas says computer addiction is taking control of countless lives, replacing old hobbies and ruining relationships. The fingers that say yes to the television and to the shot glass are the same ones that compulsively press the telephone screen, seeking instant responses. What is it about our species that requires such gratification? Why isn't the world enough in its native state? The miracles taught by the church fathers were not part of my upbringing. But miracles surrounded me once I opened my eyes to them. Early on I recognized that all the things of the universe are perfect miracles, each as profound as any. Seeing, hearing, feeling - these are miracles. Animals feeding in the field. Birds in the air. The honeybee busy around the hive. Wading with naked feet along the beach. The delicate thin curve of the new moon. The acorn left to germinate. These with the rest, one and all, are miracles. Even in my despair, one or two would always appear, halting my step before the oncoming train. What's to be done for the young

116

ones before it's too late? A boy or girl with a dog, and woodlands to explore, would be a place to start.

September 13
We lost a hen in the night. Most likely to a raccoon. I'd gone out after breakfast to check on them and found the screen on the door flapping in the breeze. It had rained again and the winds were considerable. I assumed a gust had done the damage. But something was amiss. I stepped in. The hens, young and old, were huddled in the far corner. There was fear in the air. Just inside the door, feathers were strewn, more than usual. I secured the exit to the run after making sure none were out, then did an accounting. All four of the ladies were present, but only three of the adolescents. Lucy was absent. I checked the roosting buckets and the floor beneath. I didn't want to know the truth and searched for a "reasonable" explanation. Perhaps the storm had startled her and, in a panic, she'd rushed against the screen. She must be in the yard, hiding in the garden or amongst the bushes. I searched for half an hour and then the neighborhood for just as long. Walking home, there was no choice but to acknowledge the truth of it. The reality sickened me. I'd grown fond of Lucy, as I have of all the hens young and old. Like Mr. Owl, they're faithful to their calling, never deviating from the natural order of things. I think they even like me, or at least appreciate my role in their lives. After I fill their feeder and set it in their preferred location, they always make eye contact before losing themselves in the delight of the golden grain. When I call them in for the night, they make a point to brush against my pant leg before retiring. I wonder what their lives will be like now. Lucy had been a favorite. Even the old ones were fond of her. Will they grieve? Will they, for the rest of their days, hold Lucy in their memories? When new ones are introduced, next spring or the spring after, will they be more tolerant? Will jealousy give way to appreciation for uniqueness? Will they appreciate each sunrise a little more, knowing it could be their last?

September 14
A friend of Thomas' had surgery on Wednesday. The worst of the recovery over, we spent the evening with her. On the drive there I recalled my many days and nights in hospitals. At mother's bedside in Camden. Holding her hand. Doing my best to comfort her. Waiting for the end of which there was no doubt. In my own bed, recovering from the stroke. The nurses attentive and thoughtful. The visitors well-intentioned, bringing their own lives to the bedside. I imagined my life to come, limited in mobility and strength. But no experience could

eclipse those of the War years. When not at my desk, I threaded my way through the hospitals, whether in tents or under roofs. All with their long rows of cots. Up and down each side I went. The hurt and wounded I pacified with soothing hand and sat beside the restless all the dark night. I was only forty-two when it started. New York had lost its allure. Self-doubt a regular companion. But the War, with all of its horror and misery, offered a purpose I'd not foreseen. I learned much in those days of ministering. Perhaps most was the value of lending an ear to a young soldier in need of a friend. So, Thomas and I spent the evening at the bedside of his friend, saying little. Listening to the story of her life retold. The rhetorical questions of why and what's next. The self-revelation that with cancer removed, there's opportunity for a new life, uncharted as it might be.

September 15

I arrived in this age at winter's end. The mornings crisp, even frigid. The days short, though lengthening. Spring followed and its balance of light and dark, warm and cool. Then the long days of summer, my energy waning before nightfall. Now the pendulum has swung again. There's no longer an early sun. Sleeping late is again an option. Underneath there is a quickening. An acceleration of time. My hourglass nears the midpoint. Within days that point have come and gone. In my bed on Mickle Street, I wanted little. Only small and relief from pain. It was a comfort to know that with each day, death grew nearer. Death is again on the horizon. I turn the calendar pages and easily find the end point. But I'm not ready. Though I've lived my last spring and summer, I want more. Perhaps it was meeting Thomas' friend. The surgery gave her a second chance. On the drive home, Thomas remarked that her newfound optimism is contagious. His spirits lifted, he plans to pursue interests long neglected. I'm pleased for Thomas and for his friend. Sad, as well. But there is much yet to see and do. This morning the moon set just as the sun rose. I wasn't alone. The young doe with her two babes paused in recognition. I pray Emerson is right. That what we experience here we take with us.

September 16

Over lunch we listened to the news. 50,000 employees walked off their factory jobs. Union leaders say the workers aren't paid enough. An air attack on a plant in Saudi Arabia threatens to disrupt global oil supplies. President Trump blamed Iran as oil prices jumped and stock prices dropped. A company that manufactures an addictive drug that's killed thousands is being sued. The family that owns it hid billion dollars to avoid responsibility. I struggle to comprehend it all. The speed with which news travels. The impact on the citizenry. My time had its share of world-shaping events. Frontiers and boundaries of the old aristocracies were broken. The landmarks of kings removed. Famines and wars spread their tentacles from nation to nation. Even then the network of steamships was broad and vast, interlinking all geography, all lands. Trains and telegraphs hastened the reporting. The earth grew restive. Common was the question of what would happen next. I inquired of friends if soon there would be but one heart to the globe. Having quit school, I'd visit the libraries to learn of foreign lands. I was fascinated by the march of armies and the shifting of authority. Often, I'd imagine a world without countries. One in which a single government oversaw all. I no longer favor that notion, preferring diversity over sameness. Many in this country who would have an America with whites only. Should it happen, the loss of culture would sound the death knell of the human spirit. It seems that humankind is at a tipping point.

September 17

Mother loved butterflies. I observed the pride she took in growing flowers that attracted the brightly colored winged creatures. I remember her sitting on summer evenings, her day's work completed. Free to relax, she'd watch with delight their fluttering flight. My father thought it a waste of time and told her so. She ignored his insults, slipping into a place of quiet. He couldn't touch her there. Thomas loves butterflies as well, though he was late in discovering their magic. Midway through the journey of his life, he found himself lost. He took to traveling again, then running and bicycling, miles on end. The emptiness never left. His body aging, he bought this small house and took up gardening. First vegetables, then berries. The essentials established, he explored the world of flowering plants, pleased that they exist for beauty's sake. Of course, he was wrong. The bees need them, and the butterflies. Now he gardens for the winged ones, realizing there's beauty enough to go around. This evening we sat out back, the sun high enough to illuminate the flowers and their guests. The monarchs were dining alone, while two little white ones shuffled between each other, ascending high in the air. Thomas said they're of the Pieridae family and can be a pest, as their caterpillar has a voracious appetite. Yet he's careful not to disturb them. It's said they're the souls of departed ones. Thomas says a prayer for Ling's mother whenever he sees one.

September 18

If I'm home long enough I fall into the usual habits. An early walk. Eggs with coffee or, more often these days, green tea. A few minutes of "Morning Edition" followed by light exercise. Thomas has introduced me to Qigong. Depending on my mood, and my body, I read or do chores. Whether I read or not, there's always the chickens. I often observe the neighbors. The windows on either side of the house look onto their backyards. To the east is a college professor. His schedule such that he's home in the afternoon. He has a casual manner, starting a project with earnest, then leaving it unattended, oftentimes for days. There's no urgency in his method or manner. No matter the task, he approaches it as a pastime. A small pleasure providing a break from the classroom. He and his wife have a young daughter always eager to help. Like her father, she enjoys the doing with no concern for the finished product. To the west is a retired man. An engineer in his prior life. I see him best from the first floor bathroom. He has a total commitment to whatever he does. Always wearing the proper clothing and wielding the appropriate tool. He never hurries, and never slows down. Ticking within him is a finely tuned clock, set each morning according to the day's agenda. Despite his fastidiousness, or perhaps because of it, he bears a precision found most often in the natural world. Never an action or movement wasted, he's like the butterfly or the bee, doing exactly what's needed, when it's needed. I make no judgment of either man. Each appears comfortable in his skin, grateful to be left alone to go about his backyard life. I admire them. I'm envious as well, never having had a backyard until now.

September 19

It was well before six when Molly and I started our walk. Thomas joined us as he's home for the week. The world before dawn is an enchanting place, with only streetlamps to show the way. Descending the steep path toward the creek, we left even the scant light behind. Crossing the footbridge, we entered a dreamscape. The trees, always welcoming, had become shadowy figures in a melodrama. Thomas inquired of my interest in dreams. He asked if I take them seriously, and whether I find wisdom in their messages. I responded that I've always been a creature of the day. Night is for rest and forgetting. In his gentle way, he chided me. "Dreams are communications from God," he said. "Attempts by our soul to be in relationship with us. If we fail to take notice of them, we can lose our way." He went on, explaining that what we're consciously aware of is like the tip of an iceberg. That our unconscious, that which lies below the surface, is vast without boundaries. It contains riches whose antecedents reach back to the time of our primate ancestors

- perhaps even before. On our return, Thomas suggested I take a few minutes before rising to recall what had transpired during the night. I'd do well to keep a journal, recording my recollections before anything else. After a few weeks I may want to talk with Anna. Well-versed in dream interpretation, she can help make sense of the images that long to be understood.

September 20

Greta Thunberg led a "climate strike" in New York City today. One of many organized by young people all over the world, angry that leaders continue to ignore global warming. Since arriving in America, she's appeared on television shows, met with Barack Obama, and addressed Congress. On Wednesday she told a House committee that climate change is, "an emergency, and not just any emergency. This is the biggest crisis humanity has faced." A Republican congressman from the south suggested China is to blame. Greta responded that the argument is the same in her country. "Why should we do anything? Just look at the U.S." It's an old story, politicians protecting corporate interests while the world moves toward rising temperatures, mass starvation, and social collapse. I hear how the privileged bankroll legislation that gives them millions. I've yet to hear of a law good for rich and poor alike. Men so often abandon their families. It's no wonder they don't consider how their actions will bring misery to their grandchildren and great-grandchildren. Often, I've felt ashamed for being a white man. Now more than ever. Had my father not held my mother down, she could have been a congresswoman or senator if the law allowed it. The presidential candidates for the Democratic Party are in town tomorrow to speak. In little over a year one of them will be on the ballot. Though I won't be here to vote, I intend in the meantime to support the woman best able to beat Trump. It's a matter of survival.

September 21

It was a wonderful event. Full of optimism and promise. Thousands were there. All ages and colors. Staged outside under threatening clouds, the rain held off until the end. Nearly everyone brought a portable chair or blanket. The massive gathering was not unlike a revival, but without the fire and brimstone. Although there were warnings enough about the dangerous times with Trump as president. Each of the candidates appeared authentic. Only a few, however, could I imagine as president. Seated next to me was a gentleman who'd traveled three hundred miles to attend. He's well-informed about politics, going back to when he was a law school student. Between speakers he offered a brief history of the presidents since 1960 and the election of a young Catholic man. Tragically, John F. Kennedy didn't finish his term, the victim of an assassin's bullet. I thought of President Lincoln, my Captain, similarly taken. How I mourned his loss. How we all did as his coffin passed through the streets - the torches lit, the procession long and winding, the silent sea of faces, and the unbared heads. Turning back to the gentleman, I saw that his shirt had the image of a bald, bespectacled man, almost saint-like. "A photo of Gandhi," he said, "the father of modern India and one of my heroes. Slain by an assassin's bullet." The man said he always wears the shirt on this day, it being International Peace Day. Beneath the photo was a quote: "Be the change you wish to see in the world."

September 22

We lost another hen last night. Dominique, the smallest, was an odd thing with the look of a Parisian show girl. I don't think the others understood her. Often, I'd find her at one end of the bar that spanned the length of the coop. The others tucked together as far away as possible. I'll never know if she chose the solitary life of her own volition, or if it was imposed upon her. Thomas said it was that way from the beginning. As chicks in their first box, the three would huddle in one corner and Dominique in the opposite. She was always alone, even at the feeder. I don't know if she was an introvert or if something else contributed to her isolation. Whatever the reason, she might not have been abducted had there been solidarity in the coop. Now we need to find the predator. Thomas is vacillating on whether it's a raccoon or a possum. We'll spend the afternoon better securing the coop and the run, then shop for a live trap. Thomas insists we catch and release whatever it is that's fond of the hens. He has experience with such matters, unless it's a rat. Intelligent and crafty, there's no easy solution for them. Thomas says where there's one rat, there are others. We may be on the verge of a war with no end in sight.

September 23

We made it to the feed and implement store yesterday just before closing. I would have liked to have spent the afternoon wandering, but there was no time. Thomas explained our situation to a gentleman at the door. Soon we were in aisle fifteen, an array of traps before us. Unsure of our prey, it was suggested we purchase the dual pack, one large and one medium. Simple to operate, with injury unlikely. Thomas inspected them closely, announcing they were similar to what he's used in the past and would meet our needs. Back home, we prepared the traps by laying stiff paper down and drizzling sardine juice the length of it. Toward the back, we placed the tins full of meat. We then set the spring-loaded doors, aligned the traps aside the run, confined the hens for the night, and walked away. I woke early and anxious. Daylight hadn't come soon enough. Leaving Molly in the house, Thomas and I went out to inspect. Both traps were inhabited. Not by raccoons, or by rats. But by possums. One large and the second about half the size. Possibly mother and child. They looked up, fearful and uncertain. Predators for sure, but nevertheless like every creature, trying to make it in the world. They deserved a chance at life, but somewhere else. Thomas said we should relocate them at least ten miles away, and on the opposite side of the river. Arriving within the hour, we walked with our prisoners a hundred yards into the woods. The traps on the ground and side by side, we opened the doors in unison. Together they scampered away to begin their new lives.

September 24
Speaker of the House Nancy Pelosi announced today that a formal impeachment inquiry of President Trump would begin. In a statement to the press, Pelosi said Trump betrayed his oath of office when he tried to enlist a foreign power for political gain. She said he violated the Constitution and "must be held accountable - no one is above the law." She alleged that Trump pressured the Ukranian president to initiate a corruption investigation against Joe Biden. Biden is a Democratic Party candidate many believe has a chance of winning his party's nomination and defeating Trump in the general election. After Pelosi's announcement, Trump sent one of his tweets, blasting Pelosi for "PRESIDENTIAL HARASSMENT!" He'd earlier ranted that she was engaged in a "witch hunt." It's odd that Trump would refer implicitly to the Salem persecutions given his disdain for women. Whatever the outcome, it's likely to be a painful experience for America. Trump probably deserves to be impeached, but I wonder if it's good for the country given the deep division. Even if the House votes for impeachment, it's unlikely the Republican-controlled Senate will convict him. When I was still in Washington, I remember well the Andrew Johnson ordeal. With President Lincoln gone and the War over soon after, it wasn't long before President Johnson was embroiled in conflict with Congress. There was a fight over whether he could replace a cabinet member without the consent of Congress. The "Tenure of Office Act" was enacted to prevent it. When Johnson replaced the Secretary of War without Congressional approval, the House initiated impeachment proceedings. Its inquiry completed, the matter was sent to the Senate for

trial, where Johnson was acquitted by a single vote. The whole thing was a mess and deepened the partisan divide at a time when the country was in great need of healing. Like many, I'd like to see Trump gone. But the cost might be too high.

September 25
Later tonight we'll travel. Thomas has several days of business and wants to attend a climate change event as well. He suggested I accompany him as I'd likely find the gathering of activists stimulating. I might also want to reach out to Lao. The autumnal equinox will be here soon, and Lao is often on the move during times of transition. It was an easy decision. As much as I enjoy the routine of home, my days of being near the sea are numbered. I'll miss its tempestuousness; its alien nature. The heartland has its beauty, providing ample opportunity for observation of the commonplace. But the sea is a mystery. No hour ever the same. If I could create my own eternity, I'd choose a tiny cottage near the crash of waves, the weather ever-changing pursuant to an unknown timekeeper. I'd live there alone, though a dog would be nice. Molly perhaps. I'd like a garden and laying hens too but would disdain electronic gadgets of every kind. A few books and an endless supply of paper and pencils would suffice. Thomas says that Emerson will be joining us on our journey. He wants to see how I'm doing with the second half about to begin.

September 26
It was nice to return to the early days. Before the airports and security checks. Before the delays and the waiting. Travel is a simple affair when aided by those on the other side. I've yet to learn how it's done, though I'll likely find out soon enough. It was business as usual. After a good meal I showered, put Molly to bed, and turned in. Sleep came quickly and with it a dream. I was in the hallway of an old building. Before me a freshly painted door. White but without a handle or doorknob. There was something on the other side. Alive, but not human in the usual sense. Without a word it bade me to enter, but I was helpless to do so. The dream went black and I dozed. When I woke, the door was open, the morning sun illuminating the furnishings through white curtains. There was a desk, open with a pen and writing paper. A couch and matching chair, reminiscent of 18th century Boston, lined the opposite wall. And, as I expected, Emerson. Not as I knew him in years past, but as I've come to know him. There was the depression in the cushion of the chair. The mist where I would expect his head to be. His always welcoming presence. The stillness. I stepped across the

threshold and took a seat on the couch nearest him. As is customary, he initiated the conversation. "Hello Walt. The months have passed quickly. I'm pleased you could join." He inquired of my health and how I was holding up. Acknowledged my doubts and trepidations. Demonstrated an understanding of the troubling times into which I've been thrust. Reminded me that six months to the day I'd be joining him and the others. He then asked if I needed anything. Whether I had any questions. I'd anticipated the moment and prepared a list. But I was suddenly mute in the moment, unable to respond. Finally, not wishing to appear rude, I asked what advice he might have as I move closer to the end. He smiled, took my hand, and said, "Walt, do your best to live more and worry less. The right thing, always, is whatever leads to joy."

MONTH SEVEN

September 27
I spoke with Thomas about the conversation with Emerson. Nothing I
shared surprised him. He was pleased it occurred in a dream while
traveling to the sea, noting that in every life there are encounters of
particular import. Some are recognized as such and some not, whether in
the light of day or under cover of darkness. Oftentimes those in a dream
are the most propitious. He commented on Emerson's simple and direct
reply to my request for advice. It suggested my unconscious is attuned to
the present situation. I was comfortable with Thomas' interpretation.
Nevertheless, I would have liked to have had specifics. A map perhaps,
or at least directions. Thomas said that's rarely the province of the
dream. "The task in coming to know ourselves is to work with the
material until the truth of it is self-evident." He added that it would be
best to consult with Anna. "Her familiarity with dreams and the
language of the soul is superior to mine. In the meantime, do your best
to write down everything you recall."

September 28
Until today, Thomas had never mentioned my poetry, even though three
editions of *Leaves* occupy space on his shelves. I've wondered about his
silence. It could be he didn't want to disturb distant memories. Or
perhaps he's aware that the muse departed in the last years, leaving me to
tinker and scribble nonsense. Whatever his motives, I'm certain they
were guided by concern. But this morning he spoke of "Song of Myself"
and of his fondness for it. He first read it as a university student and then
every few years thereafter. Each reading opening vistas unknown to
him. Over time he imagined himself to be a companion, walking beside
me as my world expanded. When Emerson approached Thomas with the
possibility of serving as my guide, there was no hesitation. He'd been in
training most of his life, whether aware of it or not. Since his return
from Switzerland and the Jung school, he's served others at Emerson's
request. Most of the assignments had been meaningful, though a few
ended poorly. But he couldn't turn down the offer to walk with me my

last year. As he spoke, emotion was displayed I'd never seen. I was deeply touched.

September 29
How big is the problem? What needs to be done? What can we do? Is it too late? Those were questions asked at this evening's Climate Crisis Conversation. Held at the Tinder Hearth Bakery, nearly a hundred gathered to better educate themselves and explore local initiatives. A dinner of homemade bread, soup, and garden salad was served free of charge by the proprietors, a young couple committed to finding solutions. Thomas and I sat at a table of ten discussing organic gardening and sustainable agriculture. Other groups shared their interest in green energy, recycling, community education, mobilization, and political activism. As the sun set and the temperature dropped, we moved into the barn for music, poetry, and readings - all related to our dying planet and the urgent need for action. Particularly compelling were the poems read by high school students. For their generation it's evident that time is running out. There was a shared sense of grief, and a cautious optimism. That it's better to engage in the fight than wallow in resignation. Afterward, Thomas and I drove to the home of friends a few miles away. Well into the night we talked about concrete actions that can be taken. I went to bed convinced that little things do matter.

September 30
It's Thomas' birthday. Though he politely declined to disclose his age, he acknowledged that he's had a long life with few regrets. Thomas' friend, Charles, suggested we celebrate with an afternoon sail on Smith Cove, the seasonal home for his Herreshoff 12 1/2. Designed in 1914 by Rhode Island boat builder Nathaniel Herreshoff, Charles captains one of the first produced. He's owned and sailed larger but describes his Herreshoff in endearing terms. "It's one of the finest small boats ever made." Wood with a black hull and white deck, it's trimmed in mahogany that's withstood a century of beating. Even my untrained eye could appreciate the craftsman's attention to detail. After lunch we set sail for Castine, the waterside village that hugs the far shore. It was a pleasure to observe Charles at the helm, deftly managing the tiller and main sheet as casually as if sipping a cup of tea. Along the way, Thomas and Charles exchanged stories told and retold over the course of their long friendship. It was little surprise that Charles captained his Yale sailing team and later served as crewman on a voyage from the east coast to the Mediterranean. A day or more from the Portuguese mainland, he and his mates survived the 45' seas of a summer hurricane. Not long

after, a storm east of Gibraltar knocked him unconscious and nearly capsized their vessel. If I were a young man, I would crew for a younger Charles in an instant should he cross the sea again. After a stroll through the village we headed back, the breeze light but favorable. A pair of porpoises followed at a safe distance. Harbor seals feasted on a school of mackerel. Jet black cormorants perched on bobbing moorings. A white-headed eagle soared high above, following our progress. I was pleased for Thomas and the day made special for him by his dear friend.

October 1
The equinox arrived on Sunday, bringing with it the crisp air and falling leaves that suggest a deep sleep. Before leaving for Portland, I sat in admiration of the feathered ones who eat their fill of what's provided, then flitter off in gratitude. They're communal creatures, taking only enough to satisfy the instant need. They don't hoard, nor do they deny their brothers and sisters a seat at the table. Observing their dining habits, I considered the carpenter's simple request of his Father: "Give us this day our daily bread." Why is it that man always wants more? Why do those who have the most continue to acquire? I, too, was vain, greedy, and shallow at times. Thankfully, whatever the impulse that gave rise to such behavior has passed. It doesn't seem that old age, alone, is enough to quell the miserly desire. Perhaps it's the certainty of death that tips the balance in favor of moderation and contentment. What does the sparrow know of his end? Is he constructed to think not of the coming year, likely it is that there will not be one? Thomas has told me that all living things have something called DNA. That it resides in every cell as a code that determines how the organism is built and maintained. Does the sparrow's DNA inform it not to worry; to live every day as its only day with no concern for tomorrow? Does its DNA lack the code for greed, as its presence would lead to suffering and death before its time? I've never considered myself a Christian, but I wonder if the carpenter was doing his best to implant a code to forestall man's extinction.

October 2
I rode the bus today, going nowhere in particular. To the driver, just barely a man, I gladly paid the seventy-five cent fare. He welcomed me aboard with a smile, accepting my coins as if his own. Settling into a seat near the front, I recalled the many hours on the omnibus, crisscrossing the city as I approached adulthood. It was the same then. The destination of little importance. The pleasure was in the journey, and the passengers. Whether solitary or in pairs, they brought their

histories to disclose, bit by bit, between stops. This morning, two schoolgirls sat behind me, speaking in confidence of the boys they admire and long to know better. The younger of the two has never kissed and sought instruction from her companion. She believes the day will come soon when she'll be put to the test. A young black boy, handsome and athletic, had taken the seat furthest back. He tossed a ball into the air, then caught it, over and over, his face expressionless as he took in everything. Nearest the driver, a blind woman spoke quietly with a gentleman nearly three times her size. He demonstrated the utmost respect and curiosity as she described her life in the dark. His sincere attention a great pleasure to her. A few seats away another woman, perhaps a university student, entertained herself with music from her device traveling up the wires to the earpieces that transported her. Eyes closed and unaware of her surroundings, she swayed back and forth in the arms of her lover. An elderly man occupied the seat next to me, clutching the bag of hard-earned cans he'll redeem for a simple meal. I would have spent the entire day in the presence of such nobility had I not promised to meet Thomas for lunch.

October 3

I learned today of a man who was ten years old when I lay on my deathbed. Destined to be a painter, he showed promise even as a boy. Born Newell Convers Wyeth, from a young age he was known simply as N.C. He died tragically, a decade younger than me. But his muse visited nearly every day for forty years. It's difficult to imagine that one man could create more than 3,000 paintings and illustrate over 100 books. Classics I read in school and after - *Treasure Island*, *Robinson Crusoe*, *Rip Van Winkle*, *The Last of the Mohicans* - brought to life with stunning images. An exhibition has opened at the museum on Congress Square, a fraction of his work but enough to leave me in awe of his talent. Moving slowly from canvas to canvas, I can't say one was better than another, for as soon as I found a favorite, another replaced it. *The Silent Burial*. *The Bloody Angle*. *The Wreck of the Covenant*. *Captain Nemo*. *Dark Harbor Fisherman*. *Island Funeral*. *The Lobsterman*. Rich with color and texture, each told a story, so much so that I could touch the water disturbed by the drifting canoe or sinking ship. I tried my best to create images with poetry, but nothing can surpass a master equipped with paint and brush.

October 4

I've not always been a good friend, though I valued friendship as an ideal. Often, I would make a promise. Pledge to meet at a place and time, only to have life get in the way. Later I'd feel guilt and aspire to repair the harm. But the follow-through was as weak as the original commitment. I sought counsel from wise men, only to be told that if I badly wanted something, it would happen. It was true in my work but not my relationships. I consider my father in this regard, so poor he was in keeping his word. From Thomas I've observed the opposite, how he stays in contact with those for whom he cares. I had hoped to do as much with Lao. Yet after a week and more I'd yet to call for him. Had Thomas not admonished me at breakfast, it wouldn't have happened. Good friend that he is, he insisted I accompany him to the shore where he'd leave me for the morning. I sulked at first, my feelings hurt I suppose. But sitting on the rocks, I was grateful, and told him so later. There was no better place to wait. The clouds meeting the sea, separated only by the thin line of a distant island. Gentle waves breaking at my feet offered a soothing refrain. No sooner did I close my eyes than he arrived, resplendent in his whiteness. As regal as any king or prince. Like Emerson, his greeting was gentle and reassuring. Sensing my guilt for lack of faithfulness, Lao reminded me that being human is not without its flaws. He then inquired of my well-being, aware that remnants of my previous life remained. "Your hurts and regrets will not die of their own accord Walt. Only the light of day can put them to rest. Emerson, Thomas, Anna, and I can be of some assistance, but there is hard work to be done and only you can do it." Lao then encouraged me to draft an inventory of relationships in need of mending. "There is time enough, but the days are passing quickly." Taking his leave, he promised to speak more clearly at our next meeting. "In the meantime, Walt, tend to the needs of your soul. You have no better friend."

October 5

It's good to be home, if only for a short while. I've come to realize that I'm somewhat like Lao. A long-distance traveler who always returns. Until my infirmity, life was often like that. Afoot on the open road for days. Yearning at night for a bed of my own. The pendulum of my emotions would swing. At sunrise I would suppose nothing could satisfy the soul except to walk free with no superior. With dusk, though, came envy for those settled and with family. The farm life challenged my roaming spirit the most. Not just the fresh air and smell of fields. Or the innocence of calf and lamb. The comradeship shared at the raising of a barn or at harvest, left me lonesome more than once. Such goodwill, expecting nothing in return, spoke to me of the gospel message. Today I had a taste of that. Thomas knows a couple of whom he's quite fond. Their first child weeks away, there's much to be done. With a hearty breakfast as fuel, we worked for hours under the autumn sun. Cleaning the eaves, mowing, raking, filling sacks with nature's waste. Particularly pleasurable was the afternoon project. The drive adjacent the house slopes steeply. Heavy rain finds its way through the broken gaps of the cement border. Enough that the basement is frequently wet. Thomas and I assessed the situation, visited the nearby lumberyard, and returned with bags of gravel, concrete, and soil. Broken chunks of cement were removed, and a base of gravel laid. The concrete was mixed in a large tub and scooped carefully into the voids. Gladly, I accepted the task of shaping it with a fine-edged trowel, matching the ridgeline as closely as possible. Within an hour, the new was as solid as the original. The space between drive and house was raked clean. Rich, black soil was deposited, creating a ready bed for spring flowers. The tools cleaned and stowed in their rightful place, the call for dinner came.

October 6

Thomas invited a friend to dinner. I'd met James at the presidential candidates' steak fry. He's well-versed on matters of politics and wanted to talk impeachment. James has watched hours of cable news. I imagine he knows as much as any outsider. A lifelong Democrat, he recently registered as an independent, explaining it's best to have options. Still, he thinks the Democrats are doing the right thing. Trump should be held accountable, at least in the eyes of public opinion. Hearing him describe how the presidential office is being used for personal gain sickened me. I thought of how many have given their lives for this country - on battlefields and as public servants. The War taught me a great lesson; of the price to be paid so all are free. To have a president curry the favor of authoritarians and despots seems treasonous. It's said he's a "narcissist" and has an exaggerated sense of himself. There must be a stronger word for it. Feeling my blood pressure rise, I excused myself. The doctor says getting worked up is detrimental to my health. Molly and I walked under the half moon, its detached presence comforting. Approaching the footbridge, we were greeted by Mr. Owl, detached and comforting as well. Crossing over, we climbed the hill to the bench and sat for the longest time.

October 7

I didn't sleep well. Short stretches here and there, interrupted by images of Trump and what might come next. I know I'm not alone. Millions feel the same. Even some Republicans, though they're reluctant to acknowledge the mistake that was made. I like Thomas' friend, but I can listen only so much, no matter how credible the source. One person's anger doesn't help another. I should have excused myself sooner, leaving Thomas and his friend to carry on. A walk before bedtime usually settles me, followed by chamomile tea. Last night they weren't enough. Waking grumpy, I made the mistake of listening to NPR. The reporter was telling of Trump's latest rant: "As I have stated strongly before, and just to reiterate, if Turkey does anything that I, in my great and unmatched wisdom, consider to be off limits, I will totally destroy and obliterate the Economy of Turkey (I've done before!)." I was beside myself. Fortunately, Thomas turned the radio off mid-story. Leading me outside, he said he wanted to introduce me to "walking meditation," a practice he engages in regularly. Describing it as "a simple method of cultivating wakeful presence," he promised it would open me to my surroundings "and minimize the Trump distraction." Turning onto a quiet side street, Thomas encouraged me to slow down; to walk with a sense of ease. He then instructed me to pay attention to my body. And with each step feel the sensation of lifting my foot off the ground and placing it back down. We experimented with the speed until I found a suitable pace. Coaching me gently, he brought my attention to my senses and what I was seeing, hearing, feeling. He asked that I notice my breathing - inhalation and exhalation. For the next twenty minutes we walked up and back, fifty or sixty steps each way. My attention wandered at times, but with Thomas' encouragement I returned to my breath and the mindful lift and return of my foot to the pavement. At the end Trump and his tweets had lost their energy and I was rejuvenated.

October 8
Twice I walked today in the manner Thomas taught me. How often I traveled, the coming and going of mind taking center stage. It wasn't always that way. In the early years, before and after *Leaves*, I did pay attention. My notes would attest to that. I recall a stroll in Alabama, where I saw the she-bird at rest. Beneath her a nest in the briers and her hatching brood. So many pastures and forests I saw, animals wild and tame, the countless herds of buffalo feeding on short curl grass. On daylong rambles, the wood drake and wood duck would circle around, and the jay would trill in the woods. Through the cool dusk the wild gander would fly ahead, leading his flock. I acknowledged all color then - the red, yellow, and white at play within me. And considered green and violet to be just as equal. What's the mechanism that prompts the chatter of the past to take hostage of the present senses? Some say it's the curse

of Adam. Others argue that memory is to blame. Preferring not to accuse my ancestor, I accept that evolution has its drawbacks. I need only observe Molly to appreciate the near at hand. Nose to the ground, she explores everything in her path, interrupted only by a child at play or the flash of a hare across the lawn. Thomas often reminds me that we have only the present. In the moment, I believe that to be true.

October 9

Looking out the office window I see the usual. The porch. The bushes just beyond. The evergreens. The magnolia. The neighbor's maple and the distant treetops, too far away to label. They are what they were the day I arrived. Sadly, I've taken them for granted. Today, though, they're alive, inhabited by spirit. A breeze passes through them and each responds in its own way. The bushy branches of the pine sway as the golden wheat just before harvest. The leaves of the magnolia lift upward in praise, and those of the maple pirouette in unison. On the horizon, the anonymous ones tremble with joy. Individually, their personalities are as singular as their design. Together, they form a community of wise ones. As a boy I marveled at the woody wonders, honoring them with a reverence reserved for the saints. Why is it that the awe of youth is lost, replaced by apathy with the passage of years? Is it that the more experience we accumulate, the less impression is made? I think of my childhood consciousness, intermittent as it was, no more than a puddle in the pavement. But each new sight, sound, taste, and touch fell as a drop, and the puddle grew into a pond, a lake, and finally a sea. As the volume of my experiential water increased, new drops lost their significance and the trees lost their mystery. There are exceptions, even late in life. A shooting star continues to excite, as does the first snow, the full moon, and the cry of a newborn. So, I'm grateful to Thomas for sharing his practice and slowing me down. Awareness is a great tonic. I once met a man, a fellow traveler. We camped on the bank of a river for nearly a week. He'd been married once, losing his wife to illness. Everything changed the day they laid her to rest. He vowed on that winter morning to forever disdain ambition. Instead, he would earn his day's keep and tend the fire of wonder, never allowing it to die. I see him now, careful in manner, deliberate in movement, counseling me that patience is the great virtue.

October 10

We set the traps again. With three possums to our credit, it's likely there are others. Though the fence is six feet high, there are stretches beneath with two to three inch gaps. The gate, with its vertical bars four inches apart, is also a point of entry. It's clear that we're not critter-proof. The hens will always be at risk if left out at night. Even when confined, it's not enough to cover the window with wire screen alone. We purchased a measure of security by affixing "plexiglass" over the opening. As before, we offered sardines as bait and retired for the evening. Sunrise came and the inspection. The small trap was just as we'd left it. But the door of the larger had sprung shut and the empty tin was a good yard away. Whatever it was - raccoon, possum or rat - had entered, retrieved the meat and container, and retreated unscathed, shutting the door behind. I was impressed. This was no ordinary predator. It was smart, experienced, a risk-taker. Instinct is a great teacher. Ambivalence argued against setting the large trap again. But the smaller of the two was still armed and we left it as is. First thing this morning I inspected it, with little expectation. To my surprise there'd been a capture. A full-grown raccoon stretched out from end to end. Sensing my presence, it looked up with soulful brown eyes, hoping against hope that it might live another day. I meant it no harm and told it so. It seemed to understand and caused no fuss as I carried it to the car. Together we drove to the woods where I sat, considering its life, present and future. Trusting that its inherited DNA would enable it to thrive, I opened the door. Without hesitation, it sauntered off, fearless and yet humbled by its good fortune.

October 11

Thomas has an easy way with most people. He's rarely rankled by another's disposition or demeanor. Whatever the politics or religious beliefs, he has a knack of discerning the deeper truth, even that which the individual is unaware of. I've not been good at that. Nor have I tried. The poet's eye, or at least mine, always stopped at the surface, taking in the dress, the color of hair and eye, the gait, the mood. For me the story was in the appearance of things. I spent years searching for language to describe and distinguish. As much as I contemplated the soul, that which inhabited the individual man or woman concerned me little. I was much like the painter of landscape in that respect, shapes and contours dictating my verse. I did at times attempt to express the ineffable. But there's a difference between soul in the universal sense and that which defines the essence of a neighbor or passerby. I spoke with Thomas about this. He was pleased with my insights. When I expressed regret for what I'd missed, he assured me that there's still time. "There's nothing magical about it, Walt. Like many things, it's merely a matter of paying attention. When it comes to our brothers and sisters, deep listening is what's required. Even the most recalcitrant respond when only understanding is sought." Thomas has opened a new door for me. I'll make an effort in the days ahead to step through it.

October 12
Molly and I deviated today, walking late rather than early. The route was the same but there were differences, daylight being the most significant. There's a house near the park, set back from the street and barely seen in the dark. But midafternoon is another story. With Halloween approaching, it's delightfully decorated for the occasion. Most noteworthy is a scarecrow with denim coveralls and a farmer's shirt. On top, a pumpkin bearing a straw hat. Of course, Molly didn't recognize it for what it is. Instead, she saw it as a threat to be kept at bay. Had I allowed it, she would have barked until her bark was gone. But after proving she's no pushover, we moved on. Taking the most direct path, we were soon across the bridge and up the hill. To our surprise, the bench was occupied. A gentleman about my age moved to the far end and asked that I take a seat. Recalling yesterday's conversation, I accepted and inquired of his day. He said he was in town for the wedding of a niece. There would be an evening ceremony at a nearby church. I asked of his family and whether he was married with children. He told me of his high school sweetheart. How they fell in love within a week of meeting and married midway through their college years. Their affection for each other never waned, raising five children, each with families of their own. Sadly, his wife was diagnosed with cancer. She battled it but couldn't beat it. That was twenty years ago. Every day he thinks of her, and every day he grieves. But she was a strong woman until the end and made him promise to marry again if a suitable mate came along. A decade passed before he fulfilled the promise. Now his second wife is the grandmother of his grandchildren. "Life is good," he said. A few years ago, he left the bank and bought a small farm. His days are spent caring for the fish and the birds and other animals that happen by. In the woods he's built a stone memorial for his first love, visiting without fail every afternoon. I don't know why, but I grasped his hand, offering my condolences. He thanked me, rubbing tears from his eyes. I hope to meet him again.

October 13
I woke with a small regret, having failed to learn the name of the gentleman at the park. It occurred to me he might still be in town. Perhaps if I returned in the afternoon, I'd meet him again. After lunch and a nap, we made our way there. From a distance I could see the bench occupied. But as we approached, a young woman was seated

where the gentleman had sat before. Beautiful, with a light complexion, she held a child on her lap. I inquired if she'd seen an older man. She had not. I then asked if I might take a seat and rest with my dog. She smiled and gestured for me to sit down. Her son took a liking to Molly, and she to him. The woman was pleased so I placed Molly on the bench between us. "My son is Omar," she said, "named for his father, a rebel fighter killed in Syria a month before our son's birth." I told her I didn't mean to pry but wondered how she'd made her way to America. "It was at the time of your black president, when refugees were still welcome. After a year in a Lebanese camp I was told there was a home in the United Sates for Omar and me if I wanted to make the journey." She agreed and is now settled in a small apartment nearby. Acquaintances from the mosque visit weekly, bringing food and other necessities. Every day she works with her son to read and write English. On Sunday afternoons they come to the park so he can play with the white children and learn their ways. "It's a difficult life," she said. "Alone in a strange country. My family in camps or dead." Nevertheless, she has hope for Omar and prays that Trump will be defeated so they can remain. Just then, a girl about Omar's age approached and asked if he could play. The woman stood and extended her hand, informing me that in her family she's known as Aamira. I told her my name is Walt and hoped we'd meet again. She smiled and walked with Omar and his new friend to the swings.

October 14

Rarely does it happen. Sunrise and moonset just minutes apart. We knew it was coming, predicted by the celestial calendar that informs our daily walks. Hoping to catch the moment, we arrived at the park by seven, settled onto the bench, and waited. The sun rose first, just before the half hour. Shortly after, the moon disappeared. It was as if they were tethered, two brilliant orbs at either of end of a rigid but invisible lever, a fulcrum at the midpoint. Of the two, the full moon appeared to have the greater weight. Nearing the horizon, she tugged at her brother, boosting him just enough to ascend slowly but steadily on his own. We weren't alone. From behind, a middle-aged gentleman approached. A brown friendly face beneath a red and blue ball cap, he wore the uniform of a city employee. I introduced myself and he reciprocated. Orlando Manuel Juarez. He was anticipating the moment just as we were, having learned from his father the habits of sun and moon. Every morning he arrives at the park to discharge his duties. He enjoys tending the flowerbeds and trails. Painting when necessary. Maintaining the pool during the season. Cleaning up after the deer. Even gathering the trash left by careless visitors. Orlando grew up in Cuernavaca, two hours south of the Mexican capital. As a child, his parents would take him and his brothers to the municipal parks on the weekends. He dreamed of being a caretaker when he grew up. When his father could no longer support the family, they made their way to America. Orlando was a teenager and recalls well the long nights of travel on foot and the close encounters with authority. When they arrived, they had nothing. Fortunately, his father's brother was a landscaper and supported the family until they could make it on their own. In addition to his forty hours per week with the city, Orlando employs his father in the family business. Maintaining the swimming pools of the well-to-do. Mowing their lawns and clearing their sidewalks in the winter season. I asked why he works so hard. He explained that his father can't get a job anywhere else. And his brothers are afraid to work for another employer because of Trump and his people. "Besides," he said, "I have two children. Straight A students. They'll be starting college in a few years." I was humbled, almost ashamed at how little I contributed in my lifetime. Then I wondered what would happen to America should all the Orlandos disappear, leaving only whites to carry on.

October 15
I'm not alone in proclaiming autumn as my favorite season. If I could choose, I would have it continue through December and well into January. More of it and less of winter would suit me fine. And if there was a day to repeat over and over, it would be this day. Sunny skies. Cool enough to need a sweater. A breeze that never let up, busy as it was chasing falling leaves. How often in October did I visit the cider mill and taste the sweets of the brown mash. Sucking the juice through a straw in search of the last drop. Or play a good game of baseball, followed by a picnic with sandwiches and beer. Just such a memory prompted me to pack a lunch and head for the park. Arriving at the usual place, a fellow with a similar idea had taken a seat, a box on his lap and thermos by his side. He encouraged me to join him, explaining that he was on his break and would be leaving soon. I opened my bag and we ate in silence. He then introduced himself as William and asked what I thought of the withdrawal of troops from Syria and the Democrats' efforts to impeach the president. I knew what he was talking about, but was reticent to say anything, knowing nothing of his politics. But this large, broad-shouldered man was forthcoming. He said he's a Trump supporter and would continue to be, even if some of Trump's decisions don't make sense. I was curious as to why he voted for Trump but recalled Thomas' advice that I never ask the question. When Thomas

first informed me of the 2016 election, he educated my on the extent to which the American electorate is polarized. It's his opinion that a conversation can be had with nearly anyone, as long as Trump isn't mentioned. Instead, I inquired of William as to what brought him to the park. He smiled and explained that he's a coppersmith and had driven from Missouri earlier in the week to work on a nearby house. Built in 1930, it's being renovated inside and out. His task is to remove the original flashing and replace it with new that he's fabricating in his mobile shop. He then volunteered that he's been working with copper for over thirty years, having apprenticed at the age of eighteen with his grandfather. He showed me his hands. Large, but oddly delicate. "They're my best friends," he said, "every day I work, they bring me joy."

October 16

My father would preach that a man is at his best when he's early to bed and early to rise. Or that the day is wasted if you're not up by the crack of dawn. As a boy I resented his platitudes, and his intolerance for my sleeping habits. Now I follow in his footsteps. Most often retiring before the evening's end, I'm no longer a night owl. And in the morning, I'm up with the earliest birds, intent on catching the world as she opens her eyes. This morning we were at the park by six, the moon in descent but still present. First light a good hour away. I expected the bench to be vacant, as it always is before daybreak. Careful not to stumble, we were nearly upon it when a voice uttered a hearty "Good morning." There in the shadows, I could make out a bearded figure, wrapped in a blanket with trousers for a pillow. I apologized for disturbing him. He assured me it was not a problem. He'd be up and on his way soon. I wished him well, but he asked that I stay a minute, as he rarely has a visitor. And so, I came to know Harvey, as well as one can know a man in an hour. He'd been a lawyer once but lost everything to a drug called methamphetamine. Never a user of substances, his obligations threatened to overwhelm him. An acquaintance suggested he try "speed." It worked for a while. He put in more hours and his income rose. But soon enough, the means had become the end, and nothing mattered but the high. Deceit covered his tracks in the early going but the inevitable collapse came, like a house of cards in the wind. His home was taken. His wife left him. The authorities revoked his license to practice law, then arrested him. Five years he spent in prison for the money he'd stolen and couldn't repay. Now he's a felon and on the street. Working odd jobs. Sleeping on a different bench each night. I asked why he didn't go to one of the shelters for the homeless. He pointed to the setting moon, leaving its last light spread across the treetops. "Look at the view, my friend. Look at the view." He then asked if I'd ever read Thoreau. I nodded. "Then you know his prescription for the good life. That we live deliberately and seek only life's essential facts." He went on. "Like Thoreau, I want to learn what life has to teach and not, when I come to die, discover I've failed to live." I agreed with all Harvey had said. On his way down the path, he looked back. "My friend, know life by experience. And, in the end, give a true account of it."

October 17

Since the start of school, I've seen them. The yellow buses with the children. Mornings and afternoons, with the exception of Saturday and Sunday. Two or three times each week I happen to be out when they stop at the corner nearest the park. The times differ, depending on the school name beneath the windows and stretched across the side. If it's 7:18, a lone child boards under the watchful eye of her mother. A beautiful girl, about ten years old. Like her mother, her skin is black, and she has a royal bearing. A kiss on the cheek, then the first step up. The woman stands motionless until the door shuts and the girl is safely seated. Without fail, they exchange smiles and a wave of the hand. Only after the bus is out of sight does the woman move, walking in the opposite direction. Several times I've witnessed the departure. Never until this morning have we exchanged words. It would not have happened had she not deviated from her routine. On this day, she walked toward the park, expressing interest in Molly and her name. I paused mid-street so they could get acquainted. She introduced herself as Alice. Her daughter, Michelle, is named after the former first lady. I offered my name as well and told her that Molly and I walk to the park nearly every day to sit on the bench. She told me she does the same, but generally in the afternoon when her shift is over and before the bus arrives. We walked on. It was clear she knew the way as well as I. Seated, with Molly between us, she seemed at ease, accustomed to conversing with an older man. I learned that she's a nurse, as were her mother and grandmother. Early in her career, she worked nights at the hospital. But when Michelle arrived, it was necessary to have hours that accommodated the school day. Now Alice works at a nearby nursing home. Her parents and grandparents deceased, she enjoys the company of old ones. They remind her of childhood, when life was simpler. She carries the burden now of being the mother of a child of color. As gifted as her daughter is, she knows that the way will be difficult, and life will often be unfair. Every day, she reminds herself to teach Michelle something. "Knowledge is power," she tells her, "as is hard work." And when she tucks Michelle in at night with a kiss and a hug, she whispers, "Never give in to fear."

October 18

Thomas has a favorite writer by the name of William Least Heat-Moon. Once an English professor, he lost his position at the college and took to the road. Certainly, my kind of fellow. Somewhere in his writings he remarked that if he'd gone looking for some particular place rather than any place, he would never have found the sycamore and the spring running beneath it. For me, the bench in the park is the sycamore, and the creek at the bottom of the hill the spring. I've rested upon it for parts of three seasons now. The gods willing, I will visit it often in my last. Most days it's been a solitary place for Molly and me. But lately I've been blessed with the company of gentle souls. Arriving at sunset, I discovered a man in an orange robe, cross-legged, eyes closed. His head and face without hair. I know the meditator and resolved to pass by undetected. But Molly announced her presence, unwilling to grant the gentleman his peace. His eyes slowly opened, and he reached down for the creature at his feet. Without a word, he lifted Molly onto his lap, and stroked her in the manner to which she has grown accustomed. I apologized for Molly's intrusion. He smiled and responded that there had not been one. He then offered his hand and slowly pronounced his name - Duc Lai. Duc explained that he's a follower of the Zen Master Thich Nhat Hanh and has resided at Plum Village in the south of France since leaving Vietnam nearly sixty years ago. A boy when he arrived, he was in search of healing and found a home. For many years the Village was all he knew. He's an elder now, and often travels to sit with those near the end of life. He said he's visiting a dying friend, a Christian man who often visited the Village. I asked if he would share something of what he says as the moment of death draws close. He replied that words are unnecessary for those accustomed to silence. For others, there is the gentle reminder to let go of the idea that we are our bodies, and that we're not limited by them. "We are," he said, "part of a stream of life of spiritual and blood ancestors that for thousands of years has been flowing into the present and flows on for thousands of years into the future." He asked if I believed the same, that we are each present everywhere on the earth, and in the past and the future as well. Sitting with him, I said "yes," and I meant it.

October 19

On my first walk in the neighborhood, I saw him. A proud man. Likely an athlete in his younger days. He was wearing a ball cap and a casual shirt that revealed his fitness. A woman walked at his side. Trim, fine-featured, with silver hair. They held hands but didn't speak. In the days that followed, I recognized them as regulars. Usually in the late afternoon. Always holding hands and silent. Then they stopped. It was late July or early August. Perhaps they'd gone on a trip. Or the heat might have been too much. A week ago, I saw him again, wearing the same ball cap. Hands thrust in his pockets, he walked alone. His gaze fixed on the sidewalk before him. It was the same the next day, and the next. This morning, Molly and I left on good time. The park was alive and everything in order. After crossing the bridge we could see the bench, occupied by the gentleman with the ball cap. He held a book with one hand. Black and open in the middle. In the other he clutched a handkerchief. For the first time in a week we moved on, respectful of the man lost in the past.

October 20

There's a lush stillness at certain times of the day. It helps that bedtime has yet to end for most. Humans have a way of disturbing the natural order of things. I envy the Vietnamese fellow Duc Lai. He seemed to carry his own stillness. Even at high noon, I imagine he's at peace. Lao has that quality, as does Thomas most of the time. Emerson, too, when he's not intent on making a point. I've been trying to cultivate it of late. The walking meditation is helpful. And the twilight hour, when it's easiest to follow the breath. I rose early this morning. Too early to rouse Molly. Alone I made my way in the dark, hoping to find the bench free. As much as I enjoyed the recent encounters, I was in need of my own company. There lingers in me the Sabbath call to rest, encouraged by mother long before I knew its importance. Seated undisturbed, the passage of water in the creek below was a soothing backdrop to the beat of my heart. But then, unannounced, he arrived. Perhaps the mere thought of him served as an invitation. He has his motives, of which I'm not privy. For me to question them might appear inhospitable. As is his habit, he refrained from speaking until the proper moment. I did as well, it not being my place to initiate. Of course, he did speak. Brief and to the point. "Walt, I'm pleased for you. Your recent conversations suggest much about your development. That you demonstrated sincere interest is heartening; refraining as you did from self-promotion." He then informed me of what he termed "the next phase." "With increasing frequency, you will have additional visitors. The time and place will depend on your availability. Each will be knowledgeable of world events. It's important that you have an understanding of the key moments that created today's world. No amount of reading can replace listening to those who lived through them." Before I could pose a question or seek clarification, he wished me a good day and was off.

October 21

Emerson spoke of "the next phase." Inferring that there have been others. His comment suggests a plan or template, to be filled in by the day. I wonder, now, whether chance has actually played a part in the unfolding of my life. Thomas asserts that the die is cast before conception. That we're each assigned a guide to keep us on task. Before Thomas, I was unaware of any unseen assistance. In fact, I would have rejected such a notion, adamant as I was in the primacy of free will. I may have been wrong. What if the DNA Thomas has spoken of is our guide, dictating not only our appearance but our propensities as well? Or perhaps it's not biological at all but resides in the realm of the supernatural. Lady Macbeth suggested as much: "Fate and metaphysical aid doth seem to have thee crown'd." And what of Emerson's motives? At the outset, he offered a quid pro quo. An additional year in exchange for an accounting. It could have been a ruse, a subterfuge. Maybe there's to be no accounting. Emerson has tipped his hand more than once, revealing that he knows far more than I could ever learn. He's employed Thomas as a guide for others. It's possible they were given a second chance to get it right as, it appears, I have been. The visitors in the park. Was it happenstance that brought them, or were they actors in some cosmic drama? It seemed straightforward in the beginning. Live the year, take notes along the way, then report. Like a school assignment. It seems there's more to Emerson than he's let on.

October 22

I woke with an ache in my foot. Sitting on the edge of the bed, I was reluctant to stand, fearing the pain that would come from my body's weight on the arch and heel. In that moment, I regretted I was not a thin man. Never one to pass on a sweet or slice of pie, I've not known the delight of treading lightly upon the earth. There was a time when I endeavored to be as fit as the athlete or woodcutter. But the effort was too much and diverted energy from pursuits I truly enjoyed. Yet, it would have been nice this morning to experience my limbs and torso as nimble and lithe. Even more so when I stood erect and took the first step. The pain was excruciating, leaving me to hobble across the floor and up the stairs. Thomas greeted me, observing soon enough my distress. He rose, took my arm, and led me to the table. The relief was immediate, and I was able to describe in some detail my waking and rising. Thomas was as surprised as I was by the experience. He noted that I've been walking faithfully with no hint of infirmity. I concurred, adding that my routine has been constant and without deviation. Recollecting the recent days, neither of us could trace my present condition to a physical cause. "It might be psychic in origin," Thomas said. "The body has a mind of its own and will oftentimes alert us to an emotional disturbance by manufacturing an ailment or disorder." I'd never heard of such a thing but saw no reason to dispute Thomas' conjecture. The depth of his knowledge in matters of the spirit and psyche lent credence to his supposition. He suggested I take it easy for a day or two, soaking my foot and elevating it. In addition, he proposed that I do an inventory of sorts, mindful of unresolved issues in need of attention. "None of us are immune from the consequences of neglect," he said. "Oftentimes it's not until late in life that we have the opportunity to honestly address early wounds."

October 23
I followed through with Thomas' suggestions. They helped. I still hobbled from bed to the kitchen this morning, but the pain was diminished. Replaced by a discomfort that was oddly soothing. Step by step, it was a reminder of my mortality. Like a miniature angel on my shoulder, whispering that my days are numbered. Exhorting me to live the essential and discard the trivial. I thought and wrote much about immortality. Numerous the mention of it in *Leaves*. On one occasion I swore that there's nothing but it. That the exquisite scheme is for it and all preparation is for it. I recall a night on the prairie, supper over and the fire on the ground burning low. Everyone asleep but me, like the carpenter in Gethsemane. I stood speechless and looked at the stars. Seeing them for the first time, I admired death and absorbed immortality. It was easy then to embrace death, so far off it was. Believing nothing can happen more beautiful than death. Often, I was accused of naiveté, for seeing life as I wished and not as it is. I resented the mockers, judging them dull and pedestrian as I sat in my poet's tower. But death is close at hand now and can no longer be denied. Emerson would have me believe that there is life after. But how do I know that he's nothing more than the workings of my mind. No different than the verse that sprang from nowhere and flowed from my pen onto the page. I doubt I will ever know, at least not until the day after. It surely is the dilemma for every man and woman, whether to believe or not. Of all questions, it is the greatest. The man on the bench searches his black book for the answer. The young mother, her lover taken in battle, searches in the eyes of their son. The aging farmer searches in the stones that memorialize

his first love and wife of many years. Neither Thomas nor Emerson can provide the answer. In this, I am alone.

October 24

I had a dream. One of those in which the images are indistinguishable from waking consciousness. It was this time of year. A brilliant, blue day. I was alone on a footpath that followed a watercourse. The trail meandered, reaching heights well above the water's surface. Further up were hilltops, rounded and shrouded in native hardwoods. The arborescent forms populating the forest in thick clusters, reaching to the river's edge. Clothed in every color of autumn, each a manifestation of the divine. Somewhere a stream erupted, having survived the long, hard push through the subterranean. Free from its confines, it made its way easily through roots and around rocks before losing its identity in the broad river which, soon enough, would lose its own self in the waiting sea. Time passed and I came upon an ancient bridge. Narrow, with planks that had weathered many winters. Beneath it flowed the same stream, its identity still intact. Stopping to rest I sat, having found that sycamore of which the writer spoke. Below were a series of cascades, the stream leaping and falling and leaping again, like a boy at play on castle steps. The time from first step to last, only a matter of seconds. But in that span, I witnessed an illimitable joy and the meaning of existence. There was no fret or fear of the imminent annihilation. No stepping back from the approaching precipice. Then, for the briefest moment I was in my bed, five months hence, the river and sea awaiting. Would I leap with joy come that last second?

October 25

It's early morning and I'm sitting at a desk. A small lamp is on. Manufactured, I'm guessing, early in the last century. The floor is of wood slats. Narrow and dull. Like many I saw in homes of my time. The bed low to the ground, supported by a metal frame and covered with a multicolored quilt that could have been of mother's hand. The ceiling is slanted, suggesting I'm on the upper floor. Hanging in the center is a circular fixture with three exposed bulbs, also of an earlier time. On one corner of the desk are books. *Comparative Zoology*, published in 1893. Page after page of exquisite drawings of fruits and fauna, fish and mammals. *Medicology—Volume One of Ten*, copyright 1895. Ten pounds in weight, at least, with chapters on arteries, bacteria, fractures, glands, and lymphatic vessels, to name a few. A beautiful book of da Vinci prints, its text in German. In the center, and toward the rear, a microscope. An original Charles A. Spencer. Brass, like the lamp, and nearly identical to Dr. McAlister's. I'd often peer through its eyepiece, beholding that other world. On the wall above the desk, a framed original in colored pencil, of life-sized insects. Six in all. Perhaps rendered by an entomologist. A Van Gogh print is on the opposite wall and near it a small charcoal of a hermit's cabin. A second bedroom is to the left. Unoccupied. On a stand next to the bed is a device, likely a successor of the gramophone introduced in my last years. There's a bath at the end of the hall with sink and toilet from the early days of modern plumbing. At the other end a shelf with books on boats and sailing and life on and near the sea. To its left a narrow staircase, leading to a door. I stand at the top, hesitant. My room is comfortable and inviting. The door below, ambiguous. I wake.

October 26
Midway through the night I'm again at the top of the stairs. Something, or someone, urges me to descend. At the last step, I discover to the right a second door. I grasp the knob and turn. There's no admittance. I try the door ahead. It opens easily onto a porch. Choosing the stairs to the left, I walk along the old house, following a stone path to a barn. There are doors on the side with windows. A light is on. Inside, a solitary figure. I knock but receive no response. The door with a handle swings open. I enter and approach. An elderly gentleman, white-haired with a black cap, is bent over his bench. His shoulders are broad and thick from years of labor. I stand to his right. He doesn't acknowledge my presence, his entire being devoted to his trade. He's a metalsmith. In his hand, a small hammer, tapping tiny rivets into brass. It appears he's completing work on a serving utensil. Looking around, I see tools of all kinds. Some from my time and some well before. There's a lathe, a grinding wheel, a bench vice, a metal press, and a forge - keeper of the orange fire. On the wall nearest him is a calendar. The month, October. In the year 1914. There are notations. Oct. 4—French & British fleets bombard Turkish forts. Oct. 9—German troops take Antwerp. Oct. 15— Battle of Warsaw begins. Oct. 21—Battle of Warsaw ends with German defeat. I understand. Europe is at war. Turning back to the gentleman, he looks up. There's a recognition as the light fades.

MONTH EIGHT

October 27
Seated on a bench in the fog, I'm approached. A burly man with a firm
handshake introduces himself as a psychiatrist from Switzerland. I'm to
know him as C.G. He's an acquaintance of Mr. Emerson and has been
sent as an escort. He knows of Thomas and Lao and has no intention of
appropriating their place in my life. His expertise is the twentieth
century until 1961, the year of his death. Emerson asked that he
accompany me on a tour of sorts, visiting people and places connected to
the present day. He explains that he was in the business of understanding
the unseen. The currents that influence the actions of individuals and
nations. He adds that he had a particular gift. The ability to derive
meaning from dreams. He knows of Anna, though he's never met her.
She studied at his Institute in Zurich and practices in his tradition. He
suggested I maintain contact with her, as the journey can be an arduous
one, taxing one's equilibrium at times. He took a similar journey once,
unaccompanied. Though a female colleague provided considerable
support, serving as a consultant while he was away. Without that support
to ground him, he might not have returned. I was taken aback by
Emerson's request of him. Though after reflection, I wasn't surprised.
Emerson had spoken of "the next phase." That there would be new
visitors. This Swiss psychiatrist seemed to be a competent chap. With
little time left, I could see no harm with entrusting my care to him.
Before I could speak, he assured me I would be in good hands. As a
Doctor of the Soul, he had years of experience in such matters. Patting
me on the back, he bid me tschüss.

October 28
At breakfast, Thomas commented that I'd seemed distant the past few
days. Apologizing, I offered assurance it had nothing to do with him. I
confided that I'd had a series of odd dreams. A Swiss psychiatrist made
his acquaintance in the most recent. Dead for nearly sixty years, he's an
acquaintance of Emerson and is to accompany me on a tour. I was
unsure of what to make of it. The fellow seemed harmless enough,

perhaps worth getting to know. Emerson convinced me that I should learn something of the twentieth century. This C.G. might be an appropriate mentor. Thomas smiled. That smile that conveys a knowledge not to be shared in the moment. When I commented that it might be good if I consult with Anna, he replied that he'd inquire of her availability. Perhaps I could meet with her "remotely" rather than travel to Maine. He then advised it would be best if I not dwell on that other world. Instead, I should go about my business in the usual manner - walking Molly, tending to the hens, working in the yard. "From time to time the unconscious erupts into our lives," he said, "spilling over into our waking hours. Such occurrences are to be taken seriously. But we should do our best to keep our feet on the ground and lean on those we trust." With that, he pulled out his iPhone and messaged Anna as promised.

October 29

Thomas introduced me to FaceTime today. Amazing. I still recall the excitement when the first telephone call was made. March of 1876, I think it was. From his laboratory in D.C., Alexander Bell spoke with a colleague in a building a thousand feet away. Once the news was out, everyone said the world would soon be shrinking. In this age, a person can't be without one of the handheld devices. Thomas has one, though he insists he uses it only when necessary. But I see him with it frequently, conversing with friends, sending messages, reading articles and books, even searching for recipes and the spelling of a word. Now I find it can be used to talk with someone across the country and see their face at the same time. I met with Anna that way this morning. She was sitting in her office. I was at the kitchen table, still in my pajamas. She said it's not uncommon for her to use the technology. Just a week ago, an analysand was on holiday in Europe. She'd had a falling out with her lover and needed immediate attention. An hour of FaceTime and the young woman was in a better place. Anna's account put me at ease, encouraging me to speak freely about my recent dreams. I appreciated her manner, questioning me just enough that I could recall the details. When I had nothing more, she commented that we should take the dreams seriously. "It's likely more will follow," she added. "Do your best to write them down." Anna suggested we meet again in a week or two. In the meantime, she encouraged me to enjoy the simple pleasures of life. And laugh whenever possible.

October 30

I woke in the dark, the air scented with a man's perfume. I wasn't alone.
Needing more sleep, I remained still, hoping the visitor would leave. It
wasn't to be. A light came on, revealing the Van Gogh and the hermit's
cabin. At the foot of the bed and to the right, there was a figure. It was
C.G., arms folded and leaning back in the chair. Apparently comfortable
in his surroundings. He gave me time to collect myself, then spoke.
"Walt. Our journey will soon begin. But first we'll go over the rules."
He went on. "You're to wear warm clothing every night. Shoes will be
necessary, and a cap. It may be possible to dress in period clothing upon
our arrival, but we won't know in advance. No matter who we meet, you
must remain silent unless spoken to. Should a question be posed, it's
imperative that you reveal nothing of the future. To speak of the next
day, or even the next hour, could alter history's course." With some
reluctance, I interrupted. "If I'm asked, who should I say I am? And
where should I say I've come from?" "Leave that to me," he said.
"Given the circumstances, it's not likely to come up. If there is such
curiosity, I'll handle it." I wasn't greatly concerned but did inquire about
the possibility of danger. "Your safety is of the utmost importance,
Walt. Should anything happen to you, the future could well be different.
Besides, Emerson would be very upset." Pausing to look me over, he
recognized that I was weary and needed additional rest before traveling.
"While there is some urgency in our mission given your limited time, I
think it best we get a fresh start tomorrow night." I agreed. With a hint
of kindness, he wished me a good night.

October 31

It was odd. Sleeping in my denims, shirt, jacket, and shoes. My cap
pulled tight. Assuming that C.G. isn't one to waste time, I resolved not
to delay him. No sooner had I fallen asleep than he was there, or so it
seemed. Smartly dressed in a white shirt and tweed jacket, with a hat to
match. Brown leather shoes. A cane in his hand. He offered a "good
morning" while scrutinizing me through wire spectacles. After the
longest time, he pronounced me fit for travel. I stood and out we walked,
pausing at the top of the stairs. He said a further explanation was in
order. "Journeys such as these are best made later in life. The early and
middle years of success and failure are necessary preparation." He
concluded by outlining the nightly routine. On every occasion, we
would begin in the same way. I would wake and he would be there.
We'd exit the room, descend the stairs, exit through the door at the
ground level, take the steps to the left, and walk along the house toward
the rear. Quietly, we would approach the old barn. "Everything will be

beyond the doors," he said, adding that he would lead the way and I should always be a step behind. And so we proceeded, pausing at the twin doors. Peering through the glass, the interior was noticeably different from a few days earlier. Absent was the old man and his shop. In their place was a large, flat expanse. A few hundred feet in the distance two men were maneuvering an odd contraption. "It will be a long day, Walt," C.G. observed. "We'll return tomorrow and get an early start. Don't forget your pen and notebook."

November 1

The day began as C.G. said it would. It was 10:30 on the morning of December 17, 1903. We were spectators on a sandy beach near Kitty Hawk, North Carolina, along with a handful of other gentlemen. Orville and Wilbur, the young men we'd seen the day before, were positioning a machine they'd designed and constructed in their Ohio bicycle shop. White, with parallel wings connected by vertical cables, it was equipped with what C.G. described as a 12-horse internal combustion engine. Gas-powered, it drove twin propellers. A moveable rudder was the centerpiece of the steering system. In a few minutes the brothers would attempt to fly their "heavier-than-air" aircraft. If successful, it would be the greatest feat of its kind. At 10:35 the engine was started. With Orville at the controls, the winged ship traveled down a monorail track, reaching a speed sufficient to lift it off the ground. Staying aloft over the next twelve seconds, it flew 120 feet. A marvelous sight. Three additional flights were attempted. Each a success. On the last, Wilbur piloted the craft over a distance of 852 feet for a duration of 59 seconds. I witnessed many inventions. The steamer on the rivers. The railroads. The tractor and the reaper. This flying machine may surpass them all and change the world.

November 2

It was a frigid day in 1905. We were in Room 86 on the Third Floor of the Office of Intellectual Property in Bern. A man was at a lectern, bent over, pen in hand, making a notation. C.G. identified him as Albert Einstein, a patent clerk. In their native tongue, the two engaged in conversation. I recognized a few words but understand little. C.G. explained later that Einstein was unknown at the time but would soon be world famous. 1905 was particularly noteworthy for him. In what Einstein called "that worldly cloister" of the patent office, he hatched five of his "most beautiful ideas." Each set forth in articles widely read by physicists. They would change how the world is viewed. The first, his "special theory of relativity," came to him on January 15, the day of our visit. He shared with C.G. that the speed of light is constant, the same for all observers, regardless of their motion relative to the light source. However, space and time are not absolutes. Instead, they are relative to the observer. Einstein's theory, according to C.G., created a link between space and time. "The universe," he said, "can be viewed as having three space dimensions—up/down, left/right, forward/backward— and one time dimension." Einstein referred to this four-dimensional space as the "space-time continuum." I'd head the term before. From Emerson. He'd told me months ago that the continuum allowed him to travel as he did. I would have liked to have learned more but the young clerk's superior approached.

November 3

"For three years blood has been shed across the face of Europe," C.G. said. "The war to end all wars." We were in the middle of it. Standing ankle deep in mud - a wall of dirt, sandbags, and wood planks in front of us. The same behind. A few feet separated the two. To the left and to the right were soldiers as far as we could see. Some upright, their firearms aimed in the direction of the enemy, a no man's land in-between. Some wounded. If fortunate, they were receiving medical attention. For some it was too late. Their deaths anticipated the day the trenches were dug. With no resting place for the bodies, a stench soon followed. The soldiers weren't alone. Rats were at home here. Their numbers often exceeding the combatants. The diseases they carried and passed were as deadly as the bullet, shell fragment, or mustard gas. Far smaller, but lethal as well, were the lice, the cause of a deadly fever. Our comrades were British and French, though I thought I heard an American chap yelling in pain some distance away. C.G. estimated that thousands of soldiers died in these ditches during what came to be known as World War I. Thousands more were killed at sea and in the air. I would have liked to have spoken to some of the men, but the chaos prevented it. Having witnessed similar bravery during the war of the states, I had a deep sympathy for these warriors. The causes of the horror were many and years in the making. Political, territorial, and economic conflicts were factors. The decline of the Ottoman Empire and growth of nationalism also contributed. Germany was defeated in the end. "The proud people suffered a monumental humiliation," C.G. said. "Even greater suffering will follow."

November 4

Within moments of waking, I was standing in a cavernous room. Later I learned we were in the cellar of a mansion in the town of Ekaterinburg. It was shortly after midnight on July 17, 1918. A husband, his wife, their five children, and four servants, were standing near the far wall as if posing for a portrait. It was the Romanovs. The father, Nicholas II, had been the Emperor of Russia until the revolution and his abdication in February of 1917. Three hundred years earlier, Michael Romanov had been elected tsar. His descendants would rule the empire for centuries. Now the monarchy was over and in a few years the Bolsheviks, led by Vladimir Lenin, would establish the Soviet Union. But Nicholas and his wife, Alexandra, would never see that day. Awoken by their captors and ordered to dress for a nighttime departure, they were led to the cellar. C.G. and I stood silently in the shadows. A dozen armed men arrived. Without warning, they opened fire, slaughtering the family and the servants. The massacre ended the Romanovs' political reign, though it would be a decade before the murders were fully acknowledged. In the meantime, the Bolsheviks defeated the counter-revolutionaries, various independence movements, and all other factions. Control over the new empire resided solely in the Community Party. "Communism," as C.G. called it, would assume many forms and spread around the world.

November 5
Waiting in line to enter, we stood out front, admiring the graceful structure that housed the state's elected representatives. Of all the days the body had convened, none had been of greater importance. The session would convene in an hour. At issue would be the question of ratification. Would there be sufficient votes to give women the right to vote? On May 21, 1919, the proposed amendment passed the House of Representatives. The Senate followed on June 4, 1919. Fourteen months and fourteen days later, the decision was in the hands of the Tennessee legislature. I supported the movement for years, following the Seneca Falls Convention in '48 and Elizabeth Cady Stanton's proposal. In 1850, more than a thousand attended the First National Woman's Rights Convention. Susan Anthony registered and voted in New York in 1872, only to be arrested a few days later. In 1890, Wyoming became the first state to allow women to vote. Thirty years later, it came down to this day. Thirty-five states had ratified. Tennessee could be the thirty-sixth. The line moved quickly, and we were seated in the spectator gallery. The gavel was struck, and order called for. The resolution was then read aloud, slowly and forcefully. One by one the votes were cast. There was a tie after the ninety-sixth. Twenty-four-year-old Henry T. Burn had to break it. Burn hesitated, remembering the letter his mother had written him a few days earlier. She'd directed him to "put the rat in ratification" by supporting suffrage. He did and the Nineteenth Amendment became the law of the land.

151

November 6

It was early autumn of 1928. Central London was bursting with visitors.
We exited the taxi in front of St. Mary's Hospital, C.G. and I wearing
white jackets and dark trousers. He wanted me to meet a Dr. Alexander
Fleming. We climbed the steps and passed through the main entrance,
making our way along the central corridor. After three flights of stairs
and a long hallway, we entered a small room at the end. A laboratory of
some kind. A gentleman wearing a jacket similar to ours was seated at a
cluttered table with his back to us. I could see that his left hand held a
small, circular dish. In his right was a thin metallic probe. He turned
and faced us, acknowledging to C.G. in a Scottish brogue that he'd been
expecting him. The two physicians had entered different fields after
medical school but were aware of each other's work. Introducing me,
C.G. suggested I might find interest in Dr. Fleming's recent discovery
and how it came about. Pleased, he asked that we take a seat. For the
past year he said he'd been investigating the properties of staphylococci.
After spending the month of August on holiday, he returned to the lab
and his cultures. Stacked on a bench in the corner, one had become
contaminated with a fungus. The staphylococci surrounding the fungus
had been destroyed. He thought it was odd and commenced to grow the
mold in a pure culture. To his surprise, he found it could kill a number
of disease-causing bacteria. He identified the mold as being from the
genus Penicillium. Calling it "mold juice," his intuition suggested it
might be effective against other bacteria as well. Returning to his work,
he thanked us for stopping by, apologizing that he had much to do. To
himself, mostly, he whispered "one sometimes finds what one is not
looking for." Waiting for a taxi, C.G. confided that Dr. Fleming's
discovery would not go far in the next decade. But another war would
break out, and a team of scientists would figure out how to mass produce
the drug penicillin.

November 7

It was high noon. We were two of thousands gathered on Wall Street.
Reality had sunk in. There would be no miracle recovery. The
Exchange would collapse before the closing bell. Fourteen billion
dollars gone in a day. Thirty billion in a week. More money than was
expended to finance World War I. Ten times the federal budget for the
year. Fortunes wiped out, including those of middle-class investors. The
selloff had begun the previous Thursday when the market lost ten percent

of its value at the opening bell. There was a slight rebound on Friday, but only temporary. According to C.G., unparalleled progress was at the root of the disaster. A few saw the Great Crash coming. Warning that the decade's prosperity couldn't continue, as stock prices far exceeded their actual worth. But the naysayers were ignored. Speculators argued that the clock couldn't be turned back. The unprecedented, newly created wealth was here to stay. But those who had become millionaires and more had ignored the financial despair of the American farmer. Increased efficiency, set in motion by Henry Ford and his assembly line production, had led to the overproduction of agricultural produce. The house of cards would fall. Fifteen years would pass before the economy would fully recover. I looked about. Grown men crying. Others walking speechless, their gaze communicating the depth of their despair. Lost not only their bank accounts but their vehicles, their homes, their jobs and, for some, their lives.

November 8

We were in Chicago, though C.G. said we could have been in any city in the country. The line, four or five men abreast, was blocks long. There was no hurry. No jostling for position. Everyone was the same, no matter their previous station in life. I was assured by a fellow next to me that by the time we reached the kitchen, there would still be soup. Bread and coffee, if we were fortunate. Marty was his name. The waiting has been part of his daily routine for nearly three years. He'd owned a grocery story in Nashville, but after the crash people didn't have money to buy necessities. He extended credit for a while, but few could pay him back. Within months he was out of business. Everything sold for pennies on the dollar. He owned an old truck at the time and he, his wife, and their three children took to the road. For a year they traveled throughout the Midwest. Marty and his oldest son, Joseph, did whatever they could to make a few dollars. At night the family slept in the back of the truck, eating seasonal fruits and vegetables and an occasional chicken. When nothing was in season they lived on canned meat and beans. Eventually they made their way to Chicago, sold the truck, and rented a one-room flat. Every morning he takes to the street with thousands of others. "But there's hope," he said. "President Roosevelt just announced the creation of the WPA, a federal work project." According to Marty, every unemployed adult male would get a job. He and his family would have to move, but he'd go anywhere for steady work. After an hour we were there, directed to a table where a dozen men were eating. Ham and bean soup was being served. With it, a slice of bread and cup of black coffee.

November 9

The "war to end all wars" wasn't the end after all. On June 28, 1919, Germany signed a peace treaty with the Allies. C.G. had told me another war would be coming. Today, we witnessed its first day. Twenty years after a humiliating defeat, the German military was at it again, determined to rectify its earlier mistakes. Striking swiftly and without mercy, those in the path of the German "blitzkrieg" were helpless. Sipping on beers at a cafe on the Danzig square, the street beneath our feet began to shake. Within minutes armored tanks were passing by. Soldiers on motorcycles, bicycles, and on foot soon followed. In the faces of the young men, we saw an unwavering confidence. There was nothing that could stop them. In the early going, they were right. The citizens offered no resistance. By the end of the day the "Nazis," as the world knew them, had abolished the city, incorporating it into the newly formed Danzig-West Prussian. Poland was next. Its young men fought bravely but were undermanned and ill-equipped. In five weeks, it was over. Poland had been crushed, divided and annexed by Germany and the Soviet Union. Within months Belgium, the Netherlands, France, Denmark, Norway, Luxembourg, and Romania were invaded. London was bombed night after night and Britain nearly fell. C.G. said the United States initially wanted no part of the war, declaring neutrality. But pressure mounted and its stance shifted to one of "nonbelligerency," so aid could be given to those in the fight. A year later, it would be forced to shift its stance again.

November 10

It was a beautiful Sunday morning. A few clouds here and there made little impression on the otherwise brilliant blue sky. Having finished breakfast, we made our way to the upper deck and fresh air. Just before eight, the ship's air defense siren sounded. I assumed it was a drill. But an explosion near the battleship *Nevada* suggested otherwise. One sailor and then another yelled that we were under attack. Machine gun fire commenced. Overhead, fighter planes as thick as geese approached. The first of two waves, an hour apart. According to C.G., later reports estimated that the Japanese Air Service had employed 350 aircraft in its attack on the base. By ten o'clock, it was over. 2,403 were killed. 1,143 wounded. 188 planes destroyed. 18 ships sunk or run aground. The debate as to whether the United Sates should side with England in its fight against the Nazis had ended. The surprise attack had silenced those who favored restraint. The next day, President Roosevelt addressed a joint session of Congress, describing the attack on Pearl Harbor as "a date which will live in infamy." Advocating for Congressional action, he predicted that "no matter how long it may take us to overcome this premeditated invasion, the American people, in their righteous might, will win through to absolute victory." Within the hour, a formal declaration of war against Japan was passed. Three days later, declarations were passed against Germany and Italy. C.G. said the war, far more devastating than the last, would be waged in Europe and the Pacific for nearly four years.

November 11
I woke and C.G. was waiting. Each of us dressed in British army fatigues. We proceeded in the usual manner. But as I grasped the handle of the barn door, he took hold of my arm. "You need to know, Walt, that what you'll see today is unlike anything I've shown you. You will be incredulous at first and then sickened. Whatever faith you have in the inherent good of man will be shaken." We then entered, finding ourselves with a platoon of soldiers who'd just arrived at Bergen-Belsen, a Nazi concentration camp. The conditions were ghastly. Surrounding us were prisoners, many near death. As we moved about the grounds, we came upon bodies of what had once been men and women. The camp, we discovered, was a place where people, Jews mostly, were brought for extermination. The "liquidation," as the Nazis termed it, took place in the form of slow starvation. C.G. spoke with one of the men. A bowl of turnip soup, he was told, was the daily ration, with a loaf of rye bread shared once a week among ten or twelve others. The bare minimum was given so death didn't come quickly. Instead, the inmates would waste away into living skeletons. In the afternoon we came upon a large pit at the rear of the camp, eighty feet deep. Thousands of corpses were piled in the bottom, partially covered with earth. Barely able to speak, I inquired of the madness that had brought it about. C.G. recounted the history. The first camps were erected in Germany shortly after Adolf Hitler became Chancellor. Initially they were used to hold and torture political opponents. The numbers and types of prisoners grew steadily until late 1939, when millions were enslaved, often tortured and killed. After the war it was estimated that the Nazis had operated 15,000 camps throughout occupied Europe, including hostage, labor, and extermination camps. Nearly 20 million died or were imprisoned from 1933 until the war's end. Most horrific was the systematic murder of six million Jews. I'll be haunted by the experience until the day I die.

November 12

After waking, we spent the hours before sunrise in a comfortable ryokan, halfway up the side of a valley stretching from the city into the mountains. Suddenly, the entire valley was filled with a garish light. Seconds later we experienced a wave of heat. C.G. and I jumped to the window to determine the cause but saw nothing more than the brilliant yellow light. We then heard a loud explosion some distance away. At the same time, the windows were broken in and we were sprayed by fragments of glass. A bomb had burst. Exiting into the hallway, we found everything to be in a state of confusion. All the windows were broken, and the doors forced inward. We made our way to the front of the house to see where the bomb had landed. There was no evidence of a crater, but the southeast section was severely damaged. Down in the valley houses were on fire. A storm came up and it started to rain. Over the city, clouds of smoke rose, and we could hear occasional explosions. An hour after the initial explosion, people began to stream up the valley from the city. A few stopped at the ryokan. We did our best to give aid, though some had wounds for which there was no response. A few of the wounded had seen and witnessed the collapse of their homes. Those that were in the open suffered instantaneous burns. Fires sprang up and soon consumed the entire district. We concluded that the epicenter was about three kilometers away. The procession of refugees continued into the afternoon and evening. News arrived that most of the city had been destroyed. C.G. then filled me in on the details. A single bomb had been dropped by an American aircraft. It was an "atomic bomb" weighing ten thousand pounds. When it exploded high over the city it had the destructive force of 20,000 tons of dynamite. 66,000 were killed as a direct result of the blast and just as many injured. Of the deaths, 20,000 were members of the Japanese Army. Three days later, a second bomb was dropped on the city of Nagasaki. 40,000 were killed instantly. Nearly the same died later from burns and radiation illness. On August 15, Emperor Hirohito announced the Japanese surrender. Two weeks later, World War II officially ended. I'd like to believe that this war was finally the war to end all wars.

November 13
It was rather odd, C.G. waking me in the middle of the night, announcing it was time for lunch. Not one to quarrel when it comes to food, I followed him to the barn. Soon enough, we were seated at a corner table of The Eagle Pub in Cambridge. It being mid-February and quite chilly, I ordered the soup of the day and a Guinness. The morning's *Boston Herald,* left behind by a previous patron, recounted news of the latest war. C.G. informed me that the U.S. is supporting South Korea in its

struggle with North Korea. I asked if we could talk about something else; anything but war. Pleased, he commenced to introduce me to genetics, an area of study he's greatly interested in. I knew something of Mendel's work but kept quiet, allowing him to continue. He said genetics identifies which traits are inherited and explains how those traits are passed from generation to generation. Some are inherited through genes, others come from interactions between our genes and the environment. Just then two men entered, greatly animated. The older of the two, a gentleman about forty, announced for all to hear that he and his partner "had found the secret of life." They were initially greeted with silence and then questioned. It turned out that the spokesman, Francis Crick, had been a physicist. His colleague, James Watson, a zoologist. Recently, however, the two had teamed up to determine the structure of DNA. The molecule had first been isolated in 1869, but it took Crick and Watson, working at the nearby Cavendish Laboratory, to make the breakthrough. C.G. called it the greatest discovery of the twentieth century. While the two bought a round for everyone, C.G. continued the lesson, explaining that genes are made from the long DNA molecule which is copied and inherited across generations. The molecule is made of simple units that line up in a particular order within the molecule. The order of the units carries genetic information, similar to how the order of letters on a page carries information. The language used by DNA, the genetic code, lets organisms read the information in the genes. That information is the instructions for constructing and operating a living organism. What Crick and Watson discovered was that the DNA structure is a "double helix" that can unzip and copy itself, its substance embodying the genetic code. I ordered a second Guinness, courtesy of the two scientists, and marveled at their genius.

November 14

I first heard of it in 1847. A newspaperman I was acquainted with had an eight-year-old son who suddenly lost the ability to move his legs. The boy's physician diagnosed him with "essential paralysis of children." Over the years I saw other instances, in both children and adults. But it wasn't until Thomas told me that Franklin Roosevelt had been stricken by the disease a decade before he became president, that I learned about "polio." Thomas said it's an ancient malady, but not until the outbreak of 1916 did scientists begin to take it seriously. That year 9,000 cases were reported in New York City alone. Polio continued to spread, peaking with the outbreak of 1952 and the debilitation of nearly 60,000 people, many of whom died. Americans were terrified, fearing polio as much as the atomic bomb. Today, C.G. took me to the University of

Pittsburgh Medical School and the laboratory of Jonas Salk. He'd been working on a vaccine from killed viruses. It was April 12, 1955, and Dr. Salk was about to meet reporters to tell of the vaccine proven effective in preventing the disease. Surrounded by colleagues, we didn't get to speak with him. But a short time later we stood in front of the hospital as the unassuming man in his white coat made the announcement. Word spread fast. By late morning, people were driving around honking their horns. Church bells were ringing, and schools were letting children out early to celebrate. Within a few years, the disease was under control and nearly every child in the country received the vaccine.

November 15

Waking at the usual hour, I knew immediately that something had changed. I was in the same room and in the same bed, at the foot of which sat C.G. No longer, however, was he the mature psychiatrist. He'd aged considerably and was now older than me. I felt a sadness, though I didn't share it. In fact, nothing was said at all as we commenced our routine. The door of the barn behind us, we stood before a stone tower, connected to a larger structure with a second story. He commenced to tell me its history. He'd bought the land after the death of his mother. A year later he built the tower. Over the next decade he added on, until there were four connected parts. A final addition was completed after his wife's death, signifying "an extension of consciousness achieved in old age." We approached a stone cube just west of the tower. On one side he'd chiseled an inscription in Latin, which he translated for my benefit: "Here stands the mean, uncomely stone, 'Tis very cheap in price. The more it is despised by fools, The more loved by the wise." Following him inside, he remarked that he has a family home elsewhere. "But here I am in the midst of my true life and am most deeply myself." He said he does without electricity and tends the fireplace and stove without assistance. He chops the wood, cooks the food, draws water from the well and, in the evening, lights an old lamp. He explained that such simple acts "make man simple," adding, "it is here that I live in modest harmony with nature." He then sat in one of two chairs near the fire, a small table between the two. On the table was a long-stemmed pipe cradled in a stand, a pouch and striker next to it. He filled the pipe, took it to his lips, lit the tobacco, and inhaled deeply. A gentle satisfaction filled his face. It was nice to see him relaxed, though he appeared tired. He acknowledged my observation and explained that the past two weeks had been particularly difficult for him. "Perhaps," he said, "it would be best if we end for the day. I'll not likely see you for a while, but we will meet again. In the meantime, reflect in your spare moments on the nature of good and evil, life and death. You've seen much. Now is the time to create your own impressions." Nothing more was said. An hour passed, maybe two. He drifted off, leaving me to tend the fire. I added a log, then another. All was consumed as sleep overtook me.

November 16

I woke in the night, no longer in the tower but in my own bed. I was awakened by a roar. A locomotive was approaching. With some struggle, the faculty of reason got the upper hand. No freight train had ever passed through the neighborhood, the necessary tracks miles away. I fell back to sleep, but the roar persisted, compelling me to peer within for its origin. Fully awake, I opened my eyes to the thin line of a coastal edge. A sliver of sunlight illuminating the treetops. Grays and blacks giving form to granite slabs holding back the encroaching sea. I was seated in the yogi's position. Lao was beside me, his gaze inward as mine had been. He spoke in a foreign tongue, chanting an ancient dialect. I was mesmerized by the central tone, rising and falling in unison with the crashing waves. Had the sun not given way to dusk, I would have thought time had stopped. Lao continued. His message always the same. If only I could discern its meaning. Hours passed. The song turned to the music of a harp and the wind moved through it. The sea suddenly calmed, becoming a place of constant beginning. I was nowhere and everywhere; in that home where the human heart never beats. Alone with the stars, I knew eternity.

November 17

For the first time in what seemed ages, I sat with Thomas at breakfast. I'd missed him more than I realized. I was changed too, having witnessed brutality and terror on a scale I didn't believe possible. Man's ability to fashion tools had created weapons of annihilation that would cause a God, if there is one, to turn away in disgust. Yet I also witnessed genius in the service of good - overcoming gravity, probing the mystery of inheritance, conquering disease, and preventing death. I shared my experiences with Thomas, though I was certain nothing I'd seen was new to him. I marveled, too, at my friend's capacity to live a life of meaning in the face of absurdity. A mystery in itself. I would have liked to have explored with Thomas his gift, but he informed me we'd be having visitors and there's much to do prior to their arrival. Ling is flying in from Boston, along with her grandfather. After Thomas' exile from the village and Ling's birth, she was raised in the home of the old man and his wife. While Ling's mother provided most of her care, her papa, or "gong gong," was always there with a warm lap and a gentle smile. After years of silence about her father, papa confided to Ling that he'd loved Thomas like a son, and still grieved the loss. Thomas loved him as well and is excited for the reunion. He's certain I'll enjoy Chuang's company, close as we are in age and temperament.

November 18

We met Ling and Chuang just as they stepped off the escalator. He has the appearance of an oriental St. Nick, though his thinning hair and scant goatee are black and he's about half the size. I immediately took a liking to him. Surprised by his English fluency, he informed me that for years he read and reread the books Thomas left behind. Secretly, Ling, her mother, and Chuang studied English vocabulary, then grammar, and eventually the spoken word. They took long walks in the foothills, repeating over and over expressions that might someday be useful. Over time, they were able to converse at length in the adopted language, quizzing each other on the correct pronunciation and meaning. By the time Ling left for America, Chuang had gained a mastery equal to hers. Had the situation been different, he would have accompanied her. But his beloved wife's health was poor and leaving her behind was out of the question. She's with the ancestors now, having died shortly after Ling's mother passed. Chuang said the grief was too much for her to bear. The remainder of the drive home was quiet. What can one say to a man who has lost both wife and child? Pulling up the drive and entering the house, the mood changed. Molly greeted us, licking Chuang's fingers and hands with great enthusiasm. In that moment, I wondered how I might be changed over the coming days.

November 19

I don't believe I've ever met a man who takes such delight in the world at hand as Chuang does. His curiosity appears insatiable. Nothing escapes his eye, or his touch for that matter. His fingers trace the contours of the most mundane objects, as if memorizing their lines in anticipation of a sudden blindness. There are those who carry libraries around in their heads. Chuang carries the material world, whether man-made or the result of a natural process. An oak leaf or the feather of a hen are no more or no less pleasing as a teacup or ladle. His interest is not in acquisition, but in experience. It's not the object he covets, but its essence. He wants to feel what it is to be the leaf or the feather. I need to inquire of Thomas what books he hid in that mountain cave. Was there a treatise on modern physics with a discussion on the subatomic world? Or does Chuang know intuitively that the sameness of all creation is to be found at the level where sight has no place? It's a joy to observe him. In doing so, my own fingers slide over the rim of a water glass or caress the face of my wristwatch. Plato had his theory of forms, asserting that the physical world is not as real as timeless, unchangeable ideas. He may have been right, but I prefer Chuang's way of embracing each thing for itself and not as a manifestation of the ideal.

November 20
Thomas took Ling shopping for a winter coat, leaving Chuang and me to walk the neighborhood. He was impressed with the modest brick homes and tidy lawns, commenting that suitable housing is a growing concern in China as millions are moving from the countryside to the cities. Put off by apartment living and crowded conditions, he's not inclined to relocate. Instead, he's intent on remaining in the wood and stone house he built for his bride a half-century ago. "It has been tested; surviving earthquakes, floods, and fires. Always it comes back, ready for the next blow." Chuang was a Confucian once, preoccupied with social status and civic responsibility. For years he contributed to village life, shouldering the burdens of the respectable man. Now he's a Daoist, following in the tradition of Lao Tzu and Chuang Tzu, his namesake. These days he gives little thought to the past or future, as neither are real. It's in the moment that he practices living a simple life. Having forgotten much of what he knew, Chuang prefers in advanced age to leave the world alone. "Men who interfere," he says, "are changed into something they are not. The wise man, when he must govern, knows how to do nothing. Letting things alone, he rests in his original nature." There's much to learn from this little man. It's a shame it takes a lifetime to arrive at the place he inhabits.

November 21
The temperature dropped below freezing during the night. Rather than bundle up, Chuang and I spent the morning before the fire. Knowing he chooses not to look back, I was curious at his adherence to an ancient philosophy. Years ago, I was told that when a man dies, his philosophy dies with him. That which survives is no more than commentary. Chuang smiled, intimating a truth to which I'm not privy. But I pressed on, truly curious. When I was young, I read the texts of the great religions, in search of the living truth. There was inspiration to be found, but rarely did I meet an adherent who embodied the spirit of the original teacher. Thomas comes close, but he lives his own truth and not that of another. Never has he suggested that he's a follower of anyone. Though

I've just met him, Chuang has a similar authenticity. So I asked, what is it about the old men who lived those thousands of years ago? He smiled again, then spoke of "the ancients." He said they were subtle. "Watchful as though crossing a winter stream. Alert like people aware of danger, yet courteous like visiting guests." If such men existed, I would have liked to have known them. Chuang went on. "They were yielding like melting ice. Simple, like a block of wood yet to be carved." My memory took me to chance meetings with a native of the woodlands and another of the prairies; similar as they were to Chuang's ancients. I then asked about the secret to such an existence. "It's simple Mr. Walt. Empty yourself of everything and let your mind be still."

November 22

In addition to his wisdom and gentle ways, Chuang is a funny man. In the face of absurdity, I'm inclined toward frustration, even short temperedness. Chuang prefers to see the humor in it. Actually, I don't believe it's a choice or conscious decision at all. He just does. Thomas says people are wired in a certain way. I assume he's referring to the mind an individual brings into the world. While events and circumstance may modify it, what we're born with is what we live with. I had a classmate in the second grade with the dourest disposition. At the end of the school year I never saw him again, until years later. He'd become highly successful, but his temperament hadn't changed a whit. Chuang, on the other hand, sees in the absurd the inner workings of the universe, its randomness and delight in chance. This tickles him, provoking a chuckle in response to the most serious of matters. I don't believe he ever loses a minute of sleep or frets over the loss of good fortune. On our morning walk, he talked about the tendency of humans to cling to a partial view of things, refusing to see its complementary opposite. He said Chinese call that "three in the morning." He then told about a trainer who one day approached his monkeys with a plan. "Concerning your chestnuts, from now on you are going to have three measures in the morning and four in the afternoon." They immediately became angry. The trainer responded by telling them that he would instead give them "four in the morning and three in the afternoon." The monkeys applauded. "The wise man," Chuang said, "considers both sides of a question without partiality. He sees them both in the light of the Tao." With that he grinned, commenting that both man and monkey are fickle creatures, easily tempted and prone to impetuousness.

November 23

Thomas has a favorite recipe for chicken soup. He's made it a half-dozen times since my arrival. It's delicious. One of those soups that's better the second or third time around. I like to help - scrubbing the carrots and potatoes, washing the celery and mushrooms, peeling the onions. Step one completed, I slice and dice in the manner Thomas has taught me. But when it comes to the chicken, Thomas takes over. Taught by Chuang, he's skilled with the knife. During the year Thomas lived with Chuang and his family, he learned to cook in the Chinese way, understanding for the first time that preparation is as important as recipe and ingredients. This morning Chuang cut up the chicken, the bright cleaver like a gentle wind. I inquired of his prowess. He said his grandfather was a butcher, renowned far and wide for his skill. For hours at a time Chuang would watch him, mesmerized. One day Chuang asked how his fame came to be. His grandfather told the boy his story. When he first began to cut up oxen, he saw it in one mass. After three years, he saw distinctions. After six he saw nothing, his spirit free to follow instinct. Guided by natural line, his cleaver found its own way, cutting through no joint and chopping no bone. He told the boy that a good cook needs a new chopper once a year. But that he had used the same cleaver for twenty. He explained that there are spaces in the joints, and the blade, thin and keen, finds that space. "In those secret openings, there is all the room you need." Watching Chuang separate legs and wings from thighs and back in the way of his grandfather, it struck me that this is how to live one's life.

November 24

Chuang asked me today about Mr. Trump. He said the Chinese don't understand him. They think he's crazy. Chuang has read Shakespeare and has wondered if there might be a method to the president's madness. I told him I considered that as well but have seen enough to conclude otherwise. Nevertheless, I'm as confused as the next man. "Trump does seem to have mastered the art of chaos," I said, "but to what end I don't know." Chuang responded that China has had its share of crazy emperors, some extremely dangerous. Most often they've believed that no one is smarter than them, behaving accordingly. "The truly great rulers," he said, "governed our country as if they were cooking a small fish. They knew that if they poked too much, more harm than good would come of it." We then talked about what makes a great emperor or great president, agreeing that restraint is the key, and allowing the people to govern themselves as much as possible. As wise as Chuang is, he doesn't have an opinion as to how America might extricate itself from the mess it's in. His only advice is that we step back, as the Chinese do, and look at the long view. "Mr. Trump will be gone in one year or five years. That is nothing. The problem is that Americans always want immediate results. We Chinese, on the other hand, think in terms of generations. We play the long game, as they say."

November 25
Molly woke an hour earlier than normal. She needed to be let outside. Wide awake, I walked about the dark house. Passing through the dining room, I saw a faint light coming from the office. The doors were shut, but through the panes I could see a flickering candle. Chuang was standing still, eyes closed, his arms at his side and legs bent slightly at the knees. I sat and waited, not wanting to disturb. Ten minutes passed, maybe fifteen. After what seemed the longest time, his eyes opened and caught mine. He motioned for me to come in. Though nothing was amiss, Chuang didn't seem his usual self. His presence appeared to extend beyond the boundaries of his skin. Odd as it may sound, his being had somehow merged with the candlelight, filling the room with a cloud-like calmness. Softly, he explained that he had been standing in the Wu Chi position - the position of primal energy. Every morning, after relieving himself, drinking a large glass of water, and "warming up," he stands that way before raising his arms as if holding a large balloon. A position he holds for as long as the Wu Chi. Other positions follow. He said he's practiced the Zhan Zhuang style of Chi Kung since he was a child. Sometimes with his grandfather, sometimes his parents, and sometimes in the village plaza, guided by the elders. To practice Zhan Zhuang is to "stand like a tree" Chuang said, "with its deep roots, powerful trunk, and great spreading branches reaching into the sky. Perhaps tomorrow morning you could rise at four and join me." Open to new things these days, I promised I would try.

November 26
I told myself I'd wake early. But old habits, including rising at a certain hour, are not easily altered. I would have slept beyond the agreed upon time had Chuang not approached in the dark. "Walt. It's after four." I apologized for my tardiness and followed him to the office and the waiting candle. Chuang said we first must breathe, instructing me to follow his lead. Standing with his feet shoulder-width apart, he placed his hands over his stomach, resting the left on top of the right. Slowly inhaling through his nose, his stomach expanded, pushing his hands out. He paused, then exhaled through his nose, just as slowly, drawing his belly in. Another breath, and then others, until he said we were ready. We then bent our knees, placing our hands on them and circling - thirty

times to the right and thirty to the left. Standing slightly more erect, we lifted our arms to the sky, paused, then lowered them to our sides. Slowly, inhaling with the rise, and exhaling with the fall. Over and over until we again reached thirty. "Now it's time to stand like a tree," he said. And we did, as he had done yesterday. Next we held the invisible balloon until my arms ached, though it was only five minutes. "That's enough Zhan Zhuang for today. Let's dance." Chuang told me that when he was a young man, he left the village to see the world - traveling by boat, bus, train, and walking a great deal. His journey took him through southern China, Bhutan, Tibet, Nepal and, finally, the Indian subcontinent. There he studied Hinduism, learning yoga postures and meditation techniques. But what he particularly enjoyed was the dance. "Even in my old age," he said, "I try to dance every morning. My favorite is the Gayatri Mantra from the Rig Veda. The yoga chant for gratitude, it's dedicated to Savitri, the deity of the five elements." Like the breathing, he started slowly, his body moving rhythmically to the ancient words: "Om Bhur Bhuvah Swah, Tat-savitur Varenyam. Bhargo Devasya Dhimahi, Dhiyo Yonah Prachodayat." I did my best to follow, and after a few minutes I'd caught on somewhat. Whatever the meaning, I was taken to a place of thankfulness. When the time seemed right, we stopped. Chuang place a hand on my shoulder, "Now we can start the day Walt."

MONTH NINE

November 27

Molly and Chuang have grown fond of each other. He has a gentle way with creatures and she responds. It's as though they know each other's thoughts. Horace once read an article to me by a Dr. Frederic Myers. It was about telepathy. I was excited, and not the least bit skeptical. There were occasions when I seemed to know the intellection of a friend before he spoke. Once on the train to Philadelphia I sat beside a woman, her eyes closed and hands in her lap. For a moment, it seemed that her musings had replaced mine. There was even an image of a gentleman waiting at the station. Soon the call was sounded for my stop. I exited, as did she. I followed her from a distance until she was approached by a handsome young man about her age. They reached for one another and embraced. At the time I didn't know what to make of what seemed to have been a premonition. But as the years passed, there were other instances. I eventually concluded that there are phenomena, the cause of which we will never know. So, when Horace informed me of the work of Dr. Myers, I wasn't surprised. I finally had a name for what I'd experienced. Observing Chuang with Molly, it seems reasonable that a man and a dog can communicate with each other without speech. It's Lao's way with me, and Emerson's too. Later, I spoke with Chuang about my observations and prior experiences. He smiled.

November 28

I've neglected my calendar recently. The time passing quickly now, I've not needed another reminder. The sun and moon have been enough, and the quiet voices in my bones whispering of the grave. And so, it was a surprise when Thomas bid me Happy Thanksgiving. Immediately I recalled the dinners mother prepared for us. They were the best eating of the year, even surpassing Christmas. My father, in spite of his faults, was always a good shot. Never once did he fail to provide a fat turkey to feed the family and any relatives who happened by. The feathered bird was his only contribution, mother doing the rest. It didn't seem to bother her though. Joy was in the serving. Her seat at the table always the last.

166

Her first bite well after the others. With just the four of us, there was no turkey today. Thomas and Ling fixed a simple meal of meatballs, baked sweet potatoes, whipped cauliflower, and a green salad. Candied pears for dessert. Chuang and I set the table before and cleaned up after. Saturday is the big day. A fat turkey will be served then. Friends will come and the house will be full. I look forward to that. In the meantime, I give thanks today in my old age. For health, the midday sun, the impalpable air. For precious ever-lingering memories of my dear mother, my brothers, sisters, and friends - and for my father. For gentle words, caresses, gifts from foreign lands. For all my days, of peace and war the same. For life, mere life.

November 29

I welcomed death the first time. There was little to live for, removed from the world and confined as I was. My writing days were long past. Morning walks and evenings out no longer possible. Conversations with friends provided little interest. Perhaps it could have been different. Having been robust once, I neglected my health prematurely. The doctors gave reasonable advice, which I failed to heed. I see now that movement is the elixir. Observing Chuang in his dancing, I regret my passivity. Had I known the ways of the Chinese, I might have booked passage to Hong Kong, embracing village life the last years. But I am where I am, grateful for Emerson's gift. Of the few remaining days, I know nothing of them but will embrace them just the same. There will be no time later. In Chuang's world, permanence is an illusion. No matter how wonderful a situation may be, it must end. "Death is the only certainty," he told me yesterday. "Face it honestly and do your best to prepare." I asked what I should do. "The first step is acceptance," he said. He then recited the Buddha's simple words: "Just as when weaving, one reaches the end with fine threads woven throughout, so is the life of humans." Tomorrow friends will come, some I've never met. I'll do my best to see them as they are and not as I think them to be. It's likely I'll never see them again.

November 30

I don't know when I've enjoyed myself as much. Past failures, the worries of the world, and the uncertain months ahead - all took the day off. Today was a time for fellowship. Though the meal was to be served at noon, the first guests arrived before nine. Others followed soon after. The morning activity centered on the kitchen, as everyone brought something to share. Thomas purchased the turkey earlier in the week. Chuang took over from there, marinating it overnight in a sauce his grandmother used for family feasts. It was first in the oven, an hour before sunrise. Chuang said a slow, steady heat is the secret. There were soups and casseroles. Salads and fresh bread. Vegetables on a platter and a dish called "Mac and Cheese." And there were pies - pecan, pumpkin, and blueberry - topped with whipped cream. We all crowded around a table for twelve - fathers and mothers, children, a newborn - squeezing in an additional four or five. The rubbing of elbows seemed to delight everyone. Reciting from the *Tao Te Ching*, Chuang offered a reminder of our common heritage: "There was something undefined and complete, coming into existence before Heaven and Earth. How still it was and formless, standing alone, and undergoing no change, reaching everywhere and in no danger of being exhausted. It may be regarded as the Mother of all things." There was a Jewish prayer of Thanksgiving and a Christian one, too. Stories were told and laughter exchanged. For those few hours, a single room was the center of the universe. In the evening there were card games, a Christmas jigsaw puzzle, and a college football game. Alabama lost when penalized at the end for having an extra player on the field. The highlight for me was holding baby Olivia.

December 1

We drove Chuang to the airport for his flight home. He'll stop in San Francisco and then continue to Shanghai. A long train ride and a bus will deliver him to the village. In the space of two weeks, I've come to know Chuang as a brother. Arriving unannounced, he left me with gifts of untold worth. I could mourn his departure, but for what purpose? Impermanence is the way of the universe, he would say. On one of our walks Chuang told me of Lao Tzu's wake, attended by his best friends and well-wishers of all rank. Chin Shih saw him in repose, let out three yells, and left. One of the disciples stopped him and inquired as to why he wasn't staying to mourn. Chin responded that the Master had come into the world at his right time; leaving when his time was up. "In this life," he told the disciple, "there is no room for sorrow for the man who awaits his time and submits when his work is done. It is as simple as God cutting the thread." We are visitors on this planet for seventy, perhaps eighty years. From the day of our first steps, we're in search of the wholeness we knew in our mothers' wombs. Once or twice, if we're fortunate, we meet another who comes close to assuaging that loss. But the cord must always be cut. I'll savor my time with Chuang as I would a perfect summer day. He would want it that way.

December 2

Just the three of us at dinner - Thomas, Ling, and me. We ate leftovers. There's a pleasure that comes from serving food shared earlier with friends. Every few bites I closed my eyes and recalled a snippet of the conversation. Those of the children the most vivid. I'm gaining an appreciation for living in the present - in the here and now, as they say. Though I believe it's just as good to savor memories of times past. Emerson says we take them with us. Perhaps if we recollect the best, they'll be the strongest. Often it is that old men gather youthful memories that youth could not. I wonder how it is with the sad ones. Should they be recalled too and, perhaps, reshaped? I fear carrying forward childhood slights laden with pain. Still, there's no good in forgetting, as the past never truly dies. Things have happened that I've done my best to bury. Yet, the skeletons linger on. When they rise up in the dark, terror overwhelms even the strongest. But if displayed as relics of an earlier time, they gain their rightful place.

December 3

We saw Ling off this morning. Boston was hit with a winter storm, but somehow she made it. It was touching to watch Thomas fret until her text that she was safely home. The parent-child biology remains a mystery to me. Though their days together have been few, their connection is as strong as if he'd raised her from birth. He dotes on her and would spoil her if she'd allow it. She appreciates his affection but respectfully asserts her independence. Thomas understands, skillfully maneuvering the boundaries of fatherhood. I had my moments as a young man, perhaps fathering a child or two. Rumor has it there were more. But none ever claimed me. I don't know what I would have done had I received a letter years after a broken engagement or a night of passion. Would I have responded, meeting my delayed obligations? I'm happy for Thomas, yet sad for what I've not had. Father taught me little, but mother made up for his shortcomings, providing a fine example. I wonder if I was given the necessary DNA to follow through. Thomas would declare that I'm exactly who I was meant to be. Pressed for specifics, he'd likely say my poems are my offspring. If that be the case, I wish them long and prosperous lives.

December 4

Behind on his work, Thomas spent the day in the office. I sat for hours, Molly my only company. Guests had filled the space, occupying my attention for days. I relished the conversations and the laughter, rarely dwelling on my mortality. Waking this morning, I felt stranded. Lost without the companionship of Chuang and the lightheartedness of Ling.

I'd come to rely upon them for a certain balance. By midafternoon, however, I'd reconciled with the silence. At first there was nothing. Then the sounds of emptiness creeped in. The wind against the shutters. The quiet whisper of the house. The sweet sound of the chimes. Molly's breathing. My own. It's easy to forget the secrecy of stillness. Yet, many nights I wandered, the stars overhead. My soul turning to the Dark Mother, her soft feet gliding just ahead, my body gratefully nestling close to hers. For hours I would ponder in silence, returning to my poems and lingering long. From time to time a Phantom would arise before me, terrible in beauty, age, and power. The genius of poets of old lands, pointing its finger to the immortal songs. Years have passed since its last visit. Now Emerson calls unannounced. Far different in character, his finger points forward rather than back.

December 5

Parks for dogs. Thomas had told me about them. The notion sounded silly at the time. Today Molly and I visited one near the river. Whoever came up with the idea must have cared deeply for our canine friends. The setup is a simple one. A large, grassy area, fenced in. Within it a second, smaller space. The former for big dogs, and the latter for little. When we arrived, there was a young man and his companion, Cam, about the size of Molly. After the initial getting acquainted, they got along famously. Chasing each other the length of the field. Engaging in tug-of-war with a ball that had been left behind. Resting together under the lone shade tree. For an hour, they knew only each other. I visited with Adam - handsome, bearded, and with long hair. He had the look of the Nazarene, and the gentility too. He's in town for the week, "catching up with a woman friend" he said. Adam lives on a small farm in the far north of California. He grows marijuana there, for sale to friends and acquaintances mostly. It provides a modest income, and a lifestyle he requires. There are forty acres of virgin woodland, three of which he cultivates. Everything is done by hand. The starting of seedlings in the greenhouse. The planting, one at a time. The tending of weeds, watering, and eventual harvesting. The separation of leaves from stems and the packaging. Adam said each day is a meditation on the wonders of nature. His life is mostly free of anxieties that burden others. He is concerned, though, about the takeover by big producers. They've made headway further south. He thinks he'll be okay for a while, isolated as he is. I considered inviting myself for a stay, offering to help in any way I could. But I knew it wouldn't happen with so little time left.

December 6

I couldn't sleep. Images of life on a California mountainside had me considering my life's path. Had I been raised with tenderness, I might have stayed on the farm. Though just a child, I enjoyed the chores. Gathering eggs. Weeding the garden. Helping mother in the kitchen. They were an escape from my father's indifference, and his meanness. He found little joy in caring for the livestock and crops, let alone the berries and flowers. I was sad for mother more than myself, knowing my life would be elsewhere when the time came. Chuang's prescription for insomnia is to stand like a tree. So, I crawled from my bed and assumed the posture. Hands loose and at my side, knees slightly bent, I followed my breath. Nothing at first. But then a deep warmth coursed through my body. I pictured the oak out back and crawled into it. My arms becoming its limbs. My torso its trunk. My legs its largest roots and my toes its smallest. Initially, I felt pity for my great friend, immobile as he is. Then, from somewhere in the back of my mind, emerged the sweet song of a sparrow, followed by a second and a third, and more. Faint at first but increasing as they approached. Soon they rested, clutching my branches with their tiny feet and sending a glorious chill throughout. My pity gave way to kindliness, realizing my friend is not alone. He has all he needs in the sun and the rain. The summer breeze and the cool winds of autumn. And the feathered ones who care for him dearly. I don't know how long I stood there, though it seemed as if seasons passed, even years. Ready for sleep, I returned to bed, grateful for the beings that will long outlive us.

December 7

I've given up coffee. My drink of choice these days is hot chocolate - morning and afternoon. Bedtime too, if I think about it. Thomas buys pure cacao powder. "Chocolate in the raw," he calls it. Nothing added. I measure a tablespoon into a mug, an equal measure of coconut milk, and a little stevia from the leaf of a Brazilian plant. Over it, I pour boiling water. In a few minutes I've concocted a beverage fit for the gods. Thomas says cacao has a compound called "theobromine." I believe it to be a miracle compound. It's a stimulant but relaxing, unlike caffeine. It lowers my blood pressure and elevates my mood, as well. Whatever its effects, I've found it to be a great pleasure. When Thomas was in China, he'd be invited on occasion to drink matcha with the elders. They were the old men who'd aged beyond the responsibilities of work and family. Most often, they would meet at sunrise in the smallest room of a house. Seated in a circle on woven mats, they'd drink the emerald green tea from a shared bowl. Specially grown and processed, the leaves had been ground into a fine powder. Water at just the right

temperature was poured over it and then agitated in a back and forth
motion with a bamboo whisk. They'd recite the words of the medieval
poet Lu Tong while sipping the tea one after the other. Thomas
describes the experience as a transcendent one, remaining with him for
hours. Following the ceremony, the men would tell stories of the old
masters who possessed little but had much. They didn't look back or
beyond, recognizing that the immediate, everyday experience, is it - the
entire and ultimate point of existence. Now, when I sip on hot chocolate,
I enter briefly into the minds of those ancient sages.

December 8
I took the bus today, just for the ride. It had been a while. The
automobile is a very seductive machine. Ever since I could drive on my
own, Thomas has allowed me free use of it when it's idle. Driving is a
unique experience. Nearly automatic. Although I've had more than one
close call. The day before Thanksgiving Chuang and I went grocery
shopping. Pointing out the sights, I neglected the roadway ahead and
nearly struck a bicyclist. I've vowed to pay better attention. The bus is
different. I can pay attention or not. Daydream, nap, visit with a
stranger. This morning I chatted with a delightful man. It took a few
minutes to decipher his English, his accent one with which I was
unfamiliar. But soon enough we were engaged in a most enjoyable give
and take. Faraji originates from Somalia, a country I'd not heard of.
"Our country is not yet sixty years old," he said, "but my people date
back 5,000 years." Situated on the Horn of Africa, its coastline is
bordered by the Gulf of Aden to the north and Indian Ocean to the east.
As a boy in Mogadishu, Faraji sailed small boats on the open sea,
dreaming of becoming a sailor like his grandfather and his father. But
the Civil War forced his family to flee to America. The early years were
a great struggle, but he finished school and eventually trained as an
electrician. He has a profitable business now, supporting his family of
seven. His passion, however, is poetry. He grew up reciting the great
Persians - Rumi, Hafiz, and Nizami, and has a box of notebooks with his
own verse. I told him I'd been a poet once, having filled many a
notebook myself. We exchanged information and promised to meet
again. Once more, chance had introduced me to a stranger I regret not
knowing sooner.

December 9
This morning, Thomas and I drove north about an hour to hike an
isolated stretch of the river trail. The broad, lazy tributary of the
Mississippi was open to us most of the way, as the trees were bare save a

few leaves clinging to their lifeline. Absent were the vessels that ply its waters well into September. In their place glided the fowl of late autumn and early winter. Brief visitors pausing a week or two before continuing their southward journey. Our best conversations are when we're walking. The further, the better. Most of what I've learned of Thomas has been on similar treks. Private by nature and preference, it's through observation that I often glean his ways. But when we amble without concern for time or destination, he gives voice to his inner world. Thomas cares deeply about the living, speaking of them, as did the Buddha, as sentient beings. He believes the primary, and perhaps only ethical principle we need abide by is that we have reverence for life. Though not a strict vegetarian, I notice the care he takes when preparing a chicken or fish for the oven. I remarked on that once. He told me our prehistoric ancestors would grieve for the soul of an animal after it separated from the body. Immediately after the taking, blood still fresh from the fatal wound, a prayer would be said for the safe passage of the departing spirit. Thomas has never been a hunter, but he experiences a similar sadness when he separates flesh from bone. The same in the garden when he removes a radish or carrot from the soil, or a spinach leaf from its roots. When he sits for dinner, there's no rush. Lowering his head and folding his hands in his lap, he offers silent thanks to the lives sacrificed so he might live. I've learned a great deal from Thomas. His erudition is considerable. Mostly, it's his attitude toward the world and to life I most admire.

December 10

The long walk with Thomas brought with it a sweet fatigue that accompanied me for the remainder of the day. Had we walked as far even a month ago, my limbs would have ached, contributing to a fitful sleep. The call for rest did come, but I was at ease and welcomed the other world as I would an old friend. I had little doubt the several hours before dawn would proceed uninterrupted. But as happens, I was visited midway through. There was no roar in the night, or C.G. waiting at the foot of the bed. No Emerson nudging me gently. Rather, it was a sublime stillness that wakened me to a white room where it seemed the walls and sun were one. The room was bare, but for two chairs in the center. I occupied one. A feminine presence the other. We sat at arm's length and the peace uttered its silence. She embraced my presence. I yearned to touch her but dared not. Her auburn hair and translucent skin spoke of youth and eternity. I felt young and ageless and spoke of my love for all things. Time passed without a word. To my later regret my eyelids grew heavy, closing for a brief moment. When next they opened,

I was seated on the edge of my bed. Alone, I wept for my loss. Looking inside, I searched, hoping for a last glimpse. Unable to find her, I roamed the house. After a while, a prayer arose in the form of a query. Was she a messenger or my own soul awakening me to something new?

December 11
I went to bed certain that the visitation of the previous night was of great importance. Restless at first, sleep did come, and with it the darkest of nights. At what hour I do not know, but in that dark a faint glow appeared, opening onto an unfamiliar scene. I was myself. Standing aside me was an unfamiliar friend. Dressed from head to toe in black, there were no obvious signs of gender. But upon closer inspection, the outward form suggested a feminine presence. As my vision widened, I could see the lights of a modern city in the distance, spreading across the horizon to the west. Outlines of buildings and towers were visible but little else, with the exception of faint threads reaching out in all directions. A single overhead thread approached. The nearer it came, the more definite its mass. Just above, it had the appearance of a cable, three or four inches in diameter. A few feet beyond, a tall, cylindrical object stood, at the top of which the cable terminated. My companion, silent as was the previous visitor, surveyed the structure as would a mountaineer before ascent. Strapped to her back was a tool of some kind, three feet in length. Broad handles on one end, a metal jaw on the other. Without a word, she leaped onto the pole, scaling it with ease. Arriving at its highest point, she sat on its flat surface, retrieved the tool with both hands and severed the cable from its junction. Instantly, the lights of the city disappeared. Descending quickly, she grasped my hand, leading me into the nearby woods. I followed willingly until realizing I was without my satchel. Without it I could not continue. Reluctantly, I retraced my steps. The scene narrowed to a pinpoint and I woke, seated on the edge of my bed.

December 12
It was late afternoon. Judging by the stubble of corn in the field, harvest was past. I could see the barn, the orchard, and the back side of the house. Mother stood in the doorway, the children behind her. Father was running about, in a panic I'd never witnessed. It seemed that an attack or invasion was underway. Emerging from the toolshed was a figure in black, quite like the one who'd turned the lights out on the city. She was holding a weapon that appeared to be from the future. Pointing it in the direction of the barn, a stream of light shot forth. Suddenly the barn was on fire, flames ascending to the roofline. She turned her

attention to the shed and it was reduced to burning rubble. She saw my father and depressed the trigger. The grass at his feet consumed immediately. Looking my mother's way, she lowered the weapon, suggesting she meant her no harm. Returning to father, she fired again, chasing him from the yard and toward the road. The scene shifted to the house on Mickle Street. With the weapon slung over her shoulder, she beckoned me to approach. Surprisingly, I felt no fear. In fact, there was a comfort in standing by her side. I asked how long it would go on. She smiled, "Don't worry, it will all be over in the spring." The scene vanished and I returned to the dark, sad not to be with her.

December 13

I woke into a cavernous space, well below a major city. Possibly New York. It may have been the underground subway, though no passengers or trains were in sight. My clothing was foreign to me - white, like that of a monk or Asian warrior. I was athletic and very skilled, able to leap stairwells in a single jump. In pursuit was something in black, nearly equal in prowess. Often, it was only a step or two behind, so close I could feel its body heat. On one occasion a hand rested on my shoulder. I evaded capture by hurdling a barrier at the last second. Throughout the chase I feared, despite my valiant efforts, that sooner or later I would be caught. Perhaps not then, but in the near future. But as menacing as my pursuer appeared, it occurred to me that it meant no harm. There was an instant, just before the end, when I weighed the risks of stopping rather than going on. Something within suggested that this shadow hound was the feminine presence I'd encountered the previous two nights. Before a decision could be made, a locomotive with a single railcar pulled in front of me. The doors opened and a stranger gestured for me to take a seat. I stepped over the threshold and the doors closed with no time to spare. I turned to look through the windows, detecting the slightest of smiles. Turning back, I was alone, and the lights went out.

December 14

It was early morning. I was sitting in a cathedral, near the back. It was an American church, though architecturally there were vestiges of the French medievals. The lighting was low, and the Mass had begun. Someone was seated next to me. So close we nearly touched. I did my best to attend to the priest at the altar, his intonations and gestures. Successful for a while, I resisted turning away. Nevertheless, I was curious as to the identity of the stranger to my left. Apprehensive as well. There was a lull following the homily and I gave in. Slowly turning, there was only black. I had little doubt it was my pursuer, though she took no interest in my presence. Her focus was on a red leather-bound manuscript, open and on her lap. Similar to the Book of Kells with its brilliant images, the text was in Latin and English, with a few Greek inscriptions. She seemed transfixed by what she held, as if some deep mystery was spread upon its pages. Closing the book and setting it aside, she shifted her weight and grasped my hands. Her eyes met mine. "I see deep within," she said. "There is much I can teach you if you will let me." She took hold of the book again, opening it at random. "There are truths here of which few are aware. I will introduce you to them, and other truths." Just then the fingers of her right hand intertwined with those of my left. They were warm and kindly. Ancient yet youthful. "She must be a healer," I thought. At that moment a bell rang as the priest lifted the bread for the benefit of the faithful. Bowing my head instinctively, I sought to grasp the stranger's hand, but it had been withdrawn and she was gone.

December 15
I took a late evening walk. Afterward, I bathed among warm silky bubbles, sipped on hot chocolate, then stood like a tree until drowsy. All in preparation for the night and her return. Sleep was long and deep until the touch on my shoulder. I took hold of the hand, but it was cold and not hers. Only Emerson's. I pulled back, disappointed, then ashamed. Emerson, the dear man, he's been so good to me. I would have died long ago but for him. I sought to reassure him. He reciprocated. "Walt, old fellow, I understand. I came into your life to give you time. You've needed others to give you life." I sat up and shared as best I could the recent days and nights. All of which he knew, though I believe he appreciated my telling of it. "You're at the threshold Walt. What has transpired has been necessary. But come the new year, the journey begins. You will continue to have companions. One, in particular, whom you've just met." He then suggested I make a short trip east. I could stroll in the woods. Sit at the water's edge. Visit with Anna, and perhaps C.G. Lao, too, if the weather permits. I told him I'd like that. "Wonderful. You'll travel tonight in the usual way. Thomas will stay behind, as he has matters to deal with. Besides, you're quite capable now of traveling on your own." I was taken by Emerson's generosity of spirit and embraced him, as I would a father.

December 16
Emerson's way of travel. It's like sleep. Solitary, dark, and silent. The difference is the movement. Like travel in a modern jet, you hurtle through space without the direct force of the elements. Time is

perceived differently as well. With sleep, no night is the same. Much depends on the state and nature of a given dream. A night's sleep can be over in an instant or go on for years. Emerson's way has an economy to it, depending on the place of origin and the destination. On this occasion, when it was over, I found myself midmorning in a room I didn't know. I was sitting in a straight-backed chair, my legs propped comfortably on a foot stool, my satchel in my lap. There was a log on the fire and a mug of hot chocolate in my hand. I was alone until the last drop. Just as I finished, there was a light knock on the door. I acknowledged it and the door opened. It was Anna. Greeting me warmly, she asked that I follow her. Down a short hallway and to the right was a room of similar size. There was a couch with a pleasant striped fabric and matching chair. Books shelved floor to ceiling along most of two walls. On a low table between the chair and couch was a red book, identical in shape and size to the one in my earlier dream. Imprinted on the cover in gold letters were the words - *Liber Novus*. Anna was cordial, but to the point. "Tell me about your dreams, Walt." Opening my satchel, I withdrew a notebook. The third since the first given to me by Emerson. Beginning with the sun-drenched room, I read about the silent meeting. The power cut off to the city. The burning of the barn and shed. The underground pursuit. The stranger in the cathedral with the red book. Every fact, every detail, was important to Anna. Colors, furnishings, time of day, light, or its absence. Most intriguing to her, though, was the feminine presence throughout. She offered no explanation, inquiring instead about the women in my life, past and present. My relationships with them and their impact on my psyche. I shared that I was often attracted to the gentleness of certain women, as well as their fierce devotion to a child or a cause. I admitted, however, that I never lasted long with any one of them. We returned to the dreams. Why, after the solitary white figure, were there four garbed in black? Anna said she had her suspicions but preferred to withhold judgment until later. In the meantime, I might want to seek out C.G. whose knowledge about such things runs deeper. On the way out, I inquired about the book on her table. "It is," she said, "a facsimile of a journal kept by C.G. over a century ago. It recounts what he called his *confrontation with the unconscious*."

December 17
It snowed all day, and into the evening. I napped in the afternoon, hoping to delay my usual bedtime. Nine o'clock came and I was wide awake, the fire burning yellow and hot until only embers remained. As the midnight hour approached, I laced up my winter boots - adding scarf,

coat and cap - and headed out. It was easy enough to find the trail that circles the pond. Choosing to proceed north, I made my way through the pines, kicking up white fluff as I strode. My breath hung in the air, small clouds always a step ahead. The silence was intoxicating. But after some time, I detected approaching footsteps, perhaps those of a man about my height and weight. At other times I might have been fearful, but what harm could come? I've learned that new encounters are rarely by chance. Approaching a bend in the trail I know well, I calculated that the stranger must be on the other side and near. Within the minute, we were face to face. It was C.G., donned in winter attire as if on an alpine hike. I surmised that he was expecting me and was sure of it when he asked that I follow. Proceeding north, we continued beyond the point of my previous explorations. Shortly after, we turned east, navigating the trail, suddenly free of snow but cluttered with roots and stones. C.G. encouraged me to watch my step, though he said it wasn't far to the end. Looking past him, I saw a clearing ahead and a structure set back from the shoreline. It was the Tower. Soon we were inside, coats and boots off, sitting by the fire and sipping on a dark beer. He lifted his pipe from its cradle, deftly filling and lighting in. Inhaling deeply, he passed it to me. The taste was mild, almost sweet, leaving a favorable impression on the tongue and palate. We continued the exchange in silence until all had been consumed. Returning the pipe to its cradle, he spoke. "Walt, tell me about your dreams." The most recent ones have remained vivid. Even without my notebook, I was able to speak of them as if they were right before my eyes. All the while, C.G. gazed at the fire, tapping his fingers lightly on his knees. "You've been visited by an archetypal presence, Walt. Do you know what I mean by that?" I told him I believed the stranger was a messenger, though I was at a loss as to what to call her. "It's late Walt. Perhaps you should turn in. I've prepared a bed for you. We'll talk again in the morning."

December 18

I slept without interruption. Perhaps it was the beer, or the late walk in the woods. More likely it was C.G. His manner invites trust. There's nothing he wants from me. I imagine it's that way with all healers. Thomas shares that quality. Chuang, too, in his own way. It's their fate, I suppose, to touch people deeply, expecting no reciprocity. After dressing I went looking for him. He was sitting by the fire; drawing sustenance from it, but his mind elsewhere. I took my place and waited. After a time, he directed his attention toward me. "Walt, I've given much thought to your dreams. Though not of the common sort, they're not unique to you. From what you've told me, it appears your visitor is a manifestation of the Black Madonna. You may know of shrines to her dating back to medieval Europe." He went on to educate me. While most think of her in the context of early Christian mythology, her roots go back deeper in time. The pagan goddesses Isis, Artemis of Ephesus, and Cybele are considered her precursors. "The Black Madonna," he said, "is the expression of one aspect of the Godhead, revealing its dark, unconscious, mysterious, and unpredictable side." I knew nothing of what C.G. was talking about, yet somehow it made sense of the past several nights. What concerned me was why she appeared, and at this time. He conjectured that there are two possibilities. One unique to me, and the second in response to humanity's present crisis. "As you know, Walt, you have just a few months to live. It may be that the Black Madonna is to be your guide through the last days. You'll know soon enough." He went on to explain that the Black Madonna has been appearing in recent years in the dreams of people around the world. Many believe she brings an energy absent in the male of the species and necessary for the planet's survival. "There is more I could tell you Walt, but there's much to do. Breakfast to prepare. Wood to chop. Water to haul. You'll be staying another night. I want you to be comfortable."

December 19
C.G has a routine. A morning walk. Quiet time by the fire. Breakfast faithfully at nine. Although he no longer sees patients, he continues to research and write. "There is never enough time in a life," he told me. "If we're fortunate, with age comes wisdom, and the recognition that we know so little." We talked more about the Black Madonna, her place in history, importance to modern man, and why she'd been sent at this late hour. After lunch I was left on my own to explore the library. "It's quite small," C.G. said, "in comparison to the library in my family home. But it's adequate for my days here." It appears C.G.'s mind ranges far and wide. There are ancient texts and modern treatises. Books on psychiatry, anthropology, the natural sciences, archaeology, alchemy, literature, philosophy, and religious studies. Reading enough for the most scholarly. I pulled several volumes off the shelf, intrigued by worlds I never imagined. After a while I tired and sought fresh air. I stretched my legs in the woods and then found a suitable place by the lake. So near as I was to the water, my musings turned toward Lao. I've met him but a few times yet miss him. I'd hoped to meet him on my trip east. Perhaps another time. As the sun was setting, C.G. approached to inform me of dinner. "You must keep your strength up, dear fellow. The journey ahead will require considerable stamina." He'd prepared a delicious mutton stew and a dark bread smothered with butter. Though

I'm not particularly fond of wine, the white Bordeaux was a perfect complement. After cleaning up, we sat by the fire and exchanged the pipe. When nothing was left, he said we must go. "There's a storm coming. You need to be back before its arrival. I'll accompany you to the bend." The return went quickly, too quickly for my heart. C.G. grasped my shoulders firmly, promising we'd meet again. "You need only follow the trail, Walt. I'll be waiting by the fire."

December 20

I slept uninterrupted, the sun overhead and snow covering the pond. Stepping out front to retrieve the newspapers from the past few day, yesterday's headline announced: "Trump Impeached: Leaders trade accusations of unfairness as Senate braces for impeachment trial." I read on for a while but then set it aside, saddened by the state of affairs in America. This country I've loved so dearly holds itself out to be a Christian nation but seems far from it. Wanting to come into the peace of wild things, I dressed warmly and sought my favorite place by the waterside. Not far from shore, a dozen geese waddled, discussing current events. To my surprise, one not of their own rose up, flew in my direction, and alighted next to me. It was Lao. He'd made the journey inland, he said, to assure me that I'm often in his thoughts. Seeing I was troubled, he inquired. I told him about the president, and the divide growing ever wider. I asked why it is that humans, of all species, can't leave each other alone. Lao responded with a story. "Long ago, one of our own was blown far off course by a storm. It came to earth in the inland capital of Lu and was escorted to the temple. The Marquis was delighted and made the seabird his special guest. Performers sang and danced day and night. Fine meats and sweet wines were lavished upon him. But our ancestor was terrified, refusing to eat or drink. After three days he died." Lao went on to explain the folly of it. "The Marquis wanted to treat our forefather the way the Marquis was accustomed to. Not the way our kind needs to be treated. Had the Marquis done so, he would have allowed it to roost in the forests, swim in the lakes, play among the islands, feed on the fish of the sea, and fly with its own. "Our young ones," Lao said, "are taught to treat their neighbors - whether bird or beast - as they would want to be treated. Stated simply, to be left alone." There is a wisdom in Lao, I believe, that comes from seeing things from a great height.

December 21

I had four, maybe five years of innocence before my older brother Jesse told me the truth about Christmas. In one fell blow he disabused me of two of the great pillars of my childhood. That the baby Jesus was born in a manger and that St. Nicholas delivered packages in a single evening to every child in the world. At the age of ten, Jesse knew more than any kid I'd ever met. When he told me something was so, I never doubted his veracity. The idea that three men on camels followed a star to a tiny hamlet to pay tribute to a homeless infant, did seem preposterous. Perhaps more so was the notion that a man with a little round belly could fit all those presents into a miniature sleigh pulled by eight tiny reindeer. Of the two, I wanted to believe in St. Nick more. Waking on Christmas to presents under the tree was the best morning of the year. No matter what the future might hold, I could always count on St. Nick, even when others failed me. When Jesse whispered the secret that the old fellow was no more than the subject of a poem meant to keep us from misbehaving, I vowed thereafter to reexamine everything I was told at school or church or in any book. However, things look different at the other end of life. Whether to believe or not seems to be less about the available facts and more about the soul's response to a given proposition. When I woke this morning, having returned from the east, I found the house decorated in my absence. Santas of various nationalities and ethnicities were to be found in every room. A freshly cut tree with a guiding star on top and presents beneath stood opposite the fireplace. A Nativity scene with visitors of all kinds was laid across the long table, capturing my attention and imagination. None of it insulted my soul as I saw the world again through the eyes of innocence. Truth be known, I recognized in Thomas' sentimentality that there must be a time in the mind of even the most skeptical when the learning of a lifetime is suspended, and a different wisdom is learned.

December 22

Thomas reminded me at dinner yesterday that the Winter Solstice was just a few hours away. The sun having set the hour before, I wasn't surprised it was the shortest day of the year. I'd forgotten, however, that on the Summer Solstice it was decided we'd meet with Emerson and Lao at midwinter. Emerson had explained that the solstices are the best days for space-time travel. From studying Hawking, I learned that both space and time can be curved or warped. Now I realize Emerson and others use warps to journey around and between galaxies and to travel through time. Certain the meeting would begin at 10:20, I curled up on the sofa hoping to nap until the last moment. Roused by voices soon after, I rubbed my eyes until my vision cleared. There was Emerson, Thomas, and Lao seated in a clearing surrounded by evergreens. I took my place as we shared in turn our recent comings and goings; though it seemed anything of which I spoke was already known. Next was an assessment of my progress. Each acknowledged that I'd done well. While not all expectations had been met, they agreed that, with three months remaining, I should proceed to Stage Four. Soon, I would have a new companion, a guide skilled in the art and history of dying. She would introduce me to stories of death and assist me in reconciling with those I'd neglected. I could expect her arrival any day. Until then I was encouraged to enjoy the holidays. Christmas comes only once a year, and this would be my last.

December 23
It's disturbing the extent to which America is held hostage by commercialism. Business influence has always been considerable, but I could usually escape the merchants and vendors. When I was in need of respite, I'd take the ferry to Brooklyn and walk the quiet streets. Now, buying and selling is everywhere. And the days leading up to Christmas are the worst. Our transactional society greatly troubles Thomas. Rarely does he go out to shop except for necessities. But this time of year, he likes to purchase small gifts for friends and neighbors. He says billions of dollars of merchandise is sold online. As a result, thousands of small shops have closed their doors for lack of customers. Refusing to buy through the computer, he's forced to drive to one of the retail malls; sprawling complexes housing stores marketing mostly national brands. This afternoon we went to Target, one of the major retailers. The experience was maddening. Hundreds of cars filled the parking area. Drivers competing for the available spots. One fellow, angry that he'd been cut off, nearly assaulted the offender. Inside, there was scarcely room to move as red pushcarts filled with merchandise took up nearly every inch of walking space. I didn't care to participate so I devoted my time to observation. There was little joy to be seen. It appeared that duty was the driving force, rather than a desire to please a loved one. Children were yanked along, forced to move at the frantic pace of a parent. Harsh words were common. Crying too. I wanted to take the little ones to a quiet corner and read them stories of simpler times. It took Thomas just a few minutes to find what he needed, but three times as long to pay the clerk. We finally made it to the car, taking the side streets home to escape the traffic. Thomas was visibly shaken. I'd never seen him quite that way. For once I took control, insisting he sit by the fire while I make hot chocolate for the two of us.

December 24

We went to Christmas Eve Mass. Every seat was taken. Late arrivals stood from beginning to end. Thomas says it's that way every year. Easter is the same. Some come from elsewhere to be with family. Many, however, are locals raised in the Church but who fell away after leaving home. Their faith lukewarm at best. But according to Thomas there is something, unnamable for most, that draws them to the celebration. He understands, having grown up Catholic himself. As a boy he attended Catholic schools and was an altar server when the time came. He knew little of the theology, but the mystery met a certain need. The lit candles, the bells, the incense, the ancient Latin, all designed to transcend the mundane; and they did. Thomas studied the Latin of the Mass so as to effortlessly read and speak it. It fell on his ear as would the chant of an exotic bird. There was no attempt to understand. He explains it was like swimming and knowing nothing of the atomic makeup of water. Things changed, though, when Latin was abandoned in favor of English. It happened just as he reached the age when boys begin to question. It wasn't long after that disbelief crept in. By the time he was at university, the overhaul was complete and there was no turning back. The teachings of Marx and Engels, and later social economists, came to inform his worldview. Salvation would not be found in ritual, but in revolution. Over the years he explored most of the great traditions, engaging in their many practices. "Now," he chuckles, "I belong to a religion of one, tinkering with it as I go." Still, every Christmas Eve he returns. Sitting in the back of the church he closes his eyes, returning to the faith of his boyhood, where he discovers once again that kernel of mystery nourished now with rituals of his own making.

December 25

I was like a little kid, tiptoeing up the stairs to peek at what had been left under the tree. Nothing was there when I went to bed. But someone had come in the night. Of course, it was Thomas. Still, there remained within me that tingle of excitement, dormant since my days as a true believer. Until Jesse's revelation, I could always see in my mind's eye the little man in red placing the packages so each could be identified by name. This morning, as I moved about quietly on hands and knees, I saw presents with names I didn't recognize, and two with mine. I dared not disturb them as Thomas would surely recognize my mischief. I would have to wait, as is the requirement of all boys and girls on the one special morning. To pass the time, I showered, put on my best clothes, and sat by the fire. Soon after, Thomas greeted me and proceeded to enumerate the events of the day. At the top of the list was the delivery of presents.

There were the loaves of banana bread he'd baked for residents of the care center down the street. A coloring book with crayons for the little girl next door. Socks for an elderly gentleman who'd recently lost his wife and a flowering plant for a woman recovering from surgery. There were seven or eight others that would keep us out until evening. It made me wish I'd been born at an earlier time. I would have traveled the countryside with the original St. Nicholas, comforting the sick and aiding the poor. At our last stop of the day, Thomas had a slim gift for the son of a friend, challenged with a rare disease. Thomas had been told the boy loved to read and write and wanted to be a poet someday. We were asked to stay for pie and ice cream, a request we couldn't refuse. Jonah, eight years old, but mature for his age, unwrapped his present in front of us. It was a book with a market scene on the cover that could have been my Brooklyn. Above the carts and carriages, peddlers and fruit vendors, there was the title: *Poetry for Kids – Walt Whitman.* The boy beamed, thanking Thomas with a hug. He then proceeded to find the first poem, reading aloud the first line: "There was a child went forth every day . . ." It was the best present I've ever received, surpassing the toy train I treasured for years.

December 26

We waited until this morning to exchange presents. Thomas first, a package wrapped in brown paper. Written was a single word in a beautiful script and penned with a rich, black ink betraying the benefactor. "Walt." I was touched, even before opening. Chuang had left me a gift, though he doesn't celebrate the holiday. Slowly I removed the tape, then the covering. Inside was a book on Chinese calligraphy, nearly every page with one or more notations. A white card bookmarked page 86, depicting three examples of the ideograph "to dance." On the card was a note: "Dear Walt. This masterpiece by one of the great calligraphers has given me much joy over the years. I no longer need it as my time is near. I know your time is as well, but perhaps a little practice each day will bring you peace as the end approaches. By the way, Walt, don't forget to dance! Your friend, Chuang." I could say nothing, choked with emotion as I was. When the time was right, Thomas handed me a second gift, complementing the first he said. Inside the wrapping was a box, and in the box a calligrapher's pen, a small bottle of black ink, and a tablet of Chinese paper on which to practice. On the outside of the tablet was a simple note from Thomas: "Merry Christmas Walt. Enjoy." I assured him I would. The last gift was mine for Thomas. Unwrapped, it was a small green notebook in which I'd rendered my epic, untitled in 1855. It was an emotional experience, putting it to paper after so many years. There were passages which I didn't recognize, and others in which I reclaimed myself after the long absence. As was I shortly before, so Thomas was without words as he silently mouthed the opening verse. I followed along, as certain as ever, that every atom belonging to me as good belongs to him.

MONTH TEN

December 27

I've been walking in the evening to best enjoy the lights and decorations. A block away is a street on which every house appears to be in competition with its neighbor. Normally, I'd think it a bit much. But I overlook the silliness in favor of pure delight. If I'm fortunate, there are children afoot, pointing out every detail to a parent or sibling. This morning, though, I returned to my routine, leaving the house for the park before sunrise. It was chilly, but the way one likes it when a good stretch of the legs is in order. As usual, Molly and I entered from the west, descended the first steep hill, crossed the stream, and headed up the other side in the direction of the bench. To my surprise, it was occupied. Sitting cross-legged with his eyes closed was Duc Lai in his monk's robe, apparently unconcerned with the world about him. I sat quietly so as not to disturb and followed my breath. Sensing that he'd returned, I looked up. He smiled. "Good morning Walt. It's been a while." Though just our second meeting, it was easy to be with the little man. In a most unobtrusive way, he inquired of my life. I shared what I thought might be relevant, then paused to let him do the same. Rather than speak of himself, he observed that I was looking well, adding, "Your time is nearly here, isn't it, Walt?" I was taken aback, but answered honestly, "Yes, it is. How did you know?" He responded matter-of-factly, "You may remember that I spend much of my time with the dying. Depending on the state of their soul, I can discern a faint aura. I see yours. It's healthy and suggests you have but a few months left." With little hesitation, I told him my story, beginning with my deathbed visit from Emerson. He said nothing, looking upon me with great compassion. Then, "I've been with others, fortunate to have been given a year to prepare. To be chosen is a great honor." I told him that, of late, I'd been thinking the same. "I want you to consider something," he said. "I would be honored to assist you at the end. There's no need to make a decision now. One month from today, on the 27th, I will be here at sunrise. You can let me know your decision then. In the meantime, enjoy your life." With that, he left me to imagine my future.

186

December 28
I find it difficult these days to know what is dream and what is not.
There seems little difference between day and night, conscious and
unconscious. Even between black and white. All seems relative, as the
physicists now tell us. Last night I had a dream that was as real as a walk
in the park. In fact, I was walking, on a beach somewhere miles away.
On the edge of Chile, perhaps, or Argentina. A cool breeze from the
south relentlessly pushed the waves ashore, suggesting colder
temperatures beyond the horizon. I was alone but for footprints in the
sand. The impressions were of a three-pronged leaf, alternating side to
side. It was evident that they were to be followed, and so I did for a mile
or more. Abruptly, they terminated at the mouth of a cave a short
distance from shore. Crouching low so as not to be seen, I approached
under cover of shadow. There, just inside the overhang, was a great bird,
likely an albatross. In its beak a slender stick, nearly the length and
width of the pencil I use with my daily journal. The creature was
scratching in the sand, but not haphazardly as one would expect. Instead,
it progressed from right to left, as if laying down ideas in the manner of
traditional Chinese. From top to bottom there were eight or more,
unrecognizable to me but imbued with thought. I held my breath as best
I could. The writing continued until a dozen lines were complete.
Setting the instrument aside, the great bird turned in my direction. It
was, unmistakably, Lao. I waited. "Thank you for allowing me to finish
Walt. I write every day, having agreed with my muse that morning is
best. It's a habit of mine to record my impressions - distinguishing, in
particular, the sun from the moon, the stars from the darkness, and the
sea from the dry land." It was good to see Lao, but I was curious.
"Aren't your efforts destroyed by the flooding of the cave at high tide."
Lao's eyes appeared to twinkle, like those of a grandfather delighted by a
young one. "Oh Walt. Nothing is ever destroyed. And for me, I think
best when I write. Once I've committed my thoughts to characters, they
exist forever." I knew exactly what he meant, for no poem of mine ever
existed until captured in my notebook. And so I woke, at my desk with
pencil in hand.

December 29
It was bone-chilling cold today. Meant to put an end to Christmas
celebration and usher in the bitter months of winter. I dreaded this time
of year and its dark isolation. The nights in bed shortly after dinner,
shivering under blankets, thin and frayed, until sleep prevailed. Modern
Americans are remarkably blessed to have light and heat at their

fingertips. I wonder if they consider their good fortune. It seems nothing ever quite satisfies them. De Tocqueville found my countrymen to be a restless lot as well. Tireless in their pursuit of comfort. Little has changed except the appetite for more is even greater. Thomas spoke today of the ancient Masters. The contentment they found in having little. "For them," he said, "simplicity in all things was the Way." I have to admit that as a young man I desired success. When it did come, I was rarely satisfied. And what did it gain me? A fame scarcely rewarded. So little I had to rely on others to help purchase my modest home on Mickle Street. And near the end, though I could afford food aplenty, there was no satisfaction in it. But that's behind me now as I see the wisdom in embracing the minimal, as Chuang and Thomas do. "You can't take it with you." A great truth.

December 30
Over breakfast, Thomas and I continued our conversation about the ancient Masters. "They looked like everyone else," he said, "but their wisdom was profound." Never deviating from the truth, the wealthy couldn't corrupt them, and politicians couldn't persuade them. They passed their days performing mundane tasks, finding pleasure in whatever touched their hands. "They're still around," Thomas said, "often hidden in plain sight." It took him a while, but he can easily identify them now. It may be the blind man, shut off from the world, carving a songbird with his pocketknife. Or the panhandler at the intersection, grateful for the quarter pressed in his palm. Or the elderly woman, cleaning tables at McDonald's while humming a tune to herself. They might appear simple, but behind each smile is a mind that soars to the edge of the universe. And when they gaze into your eyes you sense they know you as a brother or sister. According to Thomas, common to every one of them is generosity, no matter how meager their income or minimal their savings. There's no reason for their giving, nor an expectation of response. I asked Thomas how it is that such people are alive today. "It's quite understandable," he explained, "they see no difference between self and other."

December 31
We attended a wedding today. On New Year's Eve of all days. The service was at a Catholic Church, presided over by an aging priest. His homily left me wanting, as he said nothing about the couple standing before him. I believe he'd given the same many times before, removing it from its dusty resting place and brushing it off for the occasion. This evening there was a meal and dance, which I enjoyed greatly. Before the

music, friends of the bride and groom offered toasts, recounting silly and sometimes embarrassing anecdotes from the couple's younger days. The last to speak was the groom, a handsome young man and an engineer by training. He explained why the last day of the year had been chosen for the ceremony. Shortly after he proposed, a friend of the family suggested New Year's Eve as a fitting wedding day. "People are always looking for a place to go to bring in the new year," he said. After reflection, he realized there were other good reasons as well. At the top of his list was the fact that, years in the future, he would always remember their anniversary date. And, the next day being a holiday, he would never have to work. With that, the partying began. I drank a beer or two and danced a little. But mostly I observed and listened to others. There was a gentleman at my table. A few years older than me. After the pleasantries, he confided that he has cancer and only a few months to live. He told me he'd often imagined death would come on the freeway. It would all be over in seconds. There would be no sorting it out. But with the diagnosis he'd been given time to think and listen to others. "It's been a blessing," he said, "I've been allowed to grow up. Being told you're going to be dead soon opens your eyes. Now I see the light of eternity shining through every flower and leaf. And an ant walking across the floor moves me to tears." I've taken the man's story to heart. The new year looks different to me now.

January 1
I lay in bed this morning, in no hurry to start the day. I wasn't apprehensive, or fearful. There were no obligations awaiting my attention. I was just in a mood, having woken from a full night. Staring at the ceiling, it occurred to me that someday there will be a great awakening. I'll realize this was all a dream. The ups and downs, the successes and reversals of fortune, had been imagined. What I had called my life was merely an endless cycle of dreaming and dreamlessness. I replayed the previous hours. I was riding on a bus, in search of an ancient Master, someone like Thomas had spoken of. Seated in the back, pressed against the window, I considered every passenger a possibility. Each had the potentiality, no matter their age or gender, height or weight, belief or skin color. A boy was seated in front of me, his little sister by his side. He read to her about another boy by the name of Harry Potter. I was impressed by his kindness and attention to her questions, answering each with the utmost patience. A large gruff man sat two rows up, a lunch pail in his lap and phone at his ear. He was speaking with his mother, promising he'd visit after work. His voice was gentle, seemingly out of place. At the end he whispered, "I love you mom." As

the bus progressed, we passed through an affluent neighborhood, a business district, and a neighborhood with modest homes. Another mile and we were in the heart of what some call "the inner city." The houses were from early in the last century - several boarded up, many more in need of repair. There were few whites on the street, mostly blacks, Latinos, and Asians. It's the kind of neighborhood I would prefer to live in. At the second stop, an elderly black woman came aboard, a bag in each hand. Making her way to the back, she spotted the vacant seat next to me. "May I sit down young man?" I was delighted to have her company and made as much room as I could. I recognized her as a gentle soul, the kind that's known a life of hardship and carried it with grace. She dug through one of the bags, withdrawing a plastic container with cookies. "They're ginger," she said. "Would you care for one?" I accepted, eating it far too quickly. Recognizing my delight, she offered another. She then told me she was on the way to the hospital to visit a friend. The stop was just ahead. Preparing to exit, she withdrew from the second bag a small notebook. Removing the first page, she handed it to me and walked away. Confused at first, I then realized it was addressed to my attention: "Dear Walt. I will attend the noon Mass at the Basilica tomorrow. I hope you will join me. I'll be seated in the back." Reading the note a second time, I realized I must be in a dream.

January 2

All day yesterday I puzzled over the dream, sharing it with Thomas at breakfast this morning. He was puzzled as well, but certain it should be taken seriously. "It might be entirely symbolic," he said, "though it's difficult to say. My opinion is to consider it an actual visitation. You've nothing to lose by attending the Mass." The Basilica was Thomas' home church as a boy, and he offered to drive me. Entering together through the side door, Thomas left me on my own to find my way. He believed it best that, if she did show up, I meet her alone. Walking toward the back, I was struck by the similarity of the interior with that of the cathedral in my dream of two weeks ago. The altar, the icons, the stained-glass windows, each appeared the same. The last pew was vacant so, as in the dream, I sat near the pillar, hopeful she'd come but half expecting she wouldn't. The choir sang as the priest with his servers began their procession down the center aisle. A step behind was a woman who approached from the left and asked if she could sit down. It was not the woman from the bus, though she carried in each hand similar bags. Settling in, she removed a red book, opening it in her lap. The age-old rite played out in front of us, concluding as it always does, with the priest directing the faithful to go in peace. Ten minutes passed and I was alone, but for the woman. I summoned the courage to turn in her direction. She was beautiful. As beautiful as the woman I sat with in silence in the room without walls. Had I only felt her presence, but not seen her, I would have thought her the same. The only difference was one of color. Dressed in a multihued garment, her face and hands were a rich chocolate brown. Her hair, falling softly upon her shoulders, was shimmering black. Taking my hand, she introduced herself as Isis, sent to prepare me for the final days. Cautioning that it would be difficult at times, she promised to never leave my side. I told her I wasn't sure I was up to it. She smiled, a smile I'd seen before, and assured me that it was my decision alone. She then encouraged me to talk it over with my friend. "I will return in two days," she said. "We can talk again if you like. I'll answer any question. In the meantime, Walt, pay attention to the voice within."

January 3

"I have little doubt," Thomas said, "that Emerson chose well. Any one of several could have been sent. Each gifted in the art. But if the woman is truly Isis, she has experience surpassing all others." I told Thomas I had no way of knowing, but it did seem she could be trusted. "My worry is that I'll be taken to places from which I'll be unable to return." Thomas shared my concern. "Many of sound mind have lost their way on the final journey. No one is so grounded that safety can be assured." Thomas explained that, as odd as it may seem, the early years are critical. Those who had it difficult have the greatest chance to succeed. "Resilience is the reward for having suffered and survived." He then cautioned that, though I might want to place complete trust in Isis, I shouldn't. "She's strong-willed, and her way is not necessarily yours. It's critical you exercise discernment and take periodic leave." Thomas warned that my chances of returning diminish the longer I'm away. "Regular contact with routine and loved ones is essential. You must summon the strength to bargain with her, and insist you be allowed to return when you feel the ground giving way." Suggesting a week at a time is enough, he reminded me that there are delights still to be had in the world of sea and sky. "Sleep on it tonight, Walt. You need not decide until your meeting tomorrow."

January 4

My sleep was fitful. Images I'd never encountered populated the landscape. Though not of my making, they seemed to recognize me as a fellow traveler. I woke, struggling with the question before me. Should I journey with the woman, knowing little of her intentions? It's true that I have nothing to lose. I'll be dead soon enough. Yet, I'd prefer to be of sane mind my remaining days. I recalled her introduction, that she'd been sent to prepare me. I have no reason to believe Emerson would place me in harm's way. If he chose for me an emissary of great renown, I must believe that I'll profit from her guidance. Shortly before noon, we arrived at the Basilica. Isis was alone in the back where we'd sat two days earlier. I followed the Mass as best I could, but my attention was weak, anxious as I was for our meeting. The church was soon vacant, and I turned toward her. All fear vanished. The decision had been made. I would trust her, but not entirely. Heeding Thomas' warning, I told her my stamina isn't what it used to be. She smiled. "You are right to be hesitant, Walt. I assure you, nothing will be asked that you are not capable of. But should you need to rest, it will be allowed." I responded that I was prepared to go forward but would likely need a break after a few days. "What I suggest, Walt, is that you prepare for yourself a private space in your dwelling. Go there in the evening, and dance in the manner Chuang taught you. When you're finished, follow your breath. I will arrive once you are far enough along. Any evening you choose not to engage in the practice, I will stay away." This seemed a reasonable compromise, and I told Isis as much. She smiled again. "We can begin tomorrow or the next day, Walt. It's up to you."

January 5
Thomas joined us on our morning walk, talking at length about what lay ahead. Though he's never been on such a journey, he's read accounts. At the university, he studied *The Divine Comedy*, *The Cloud of Unknowing*, written by a 14th century mystic, and *Dark Night of the Soul*, by St. John of the Cross. Most recently, *The Red Book*, C.G.'s personal account of his journey while a young psychiatrist. Thomas said there's much to learn from each, but he advised I not study them. "As your departure with Isis is near, it's best to have a clear mind without preconceived notions. One man's journey might be seen as another's nightmare. Your best preparation is the life you've lived." Following our walk, we prepared my room, pushing the bed against the far wall to provide an open space. On the table, we placed a candle with matches and a teapot with cup. Thomas loaned me his iPod and a small speaker so I can play appropriate music. "There's nothing more to be done, Walt. Enjoy the day tomorrow. If you're ready, summon Isis in the evening."

January 6
To ease my anxiety, Thomas suggested we attend a matinee film. It was the story of Fred Rogers who entertained children through his daily

television program. If Mr. Rogers was as portrayed by actor Tom Hanks, he was an uncommonly sweet and gifted man. Like Thomas in many ways, but more endearing. I was in a better place afterward, enjoying dinner more than usual. At the stroke of nine, I went to my room and dressed for bed. After lighting the incense and candle, I poured boiling water over a leaf favored by the indigenous of Ecuador. As it brewed, I danced to "Mother Night" and "Persephone's Song," then followed my breath, sipping the tea slowly. Not long after, I sensed that she'd arrived. Patiently, she waited for me to turn. In the candlelight, she was the loveliest creature I've ever seen. Though of flesh and blood, and likely possessing many humans traits, she was more than that. I hoped to come to know her. "I'm pleased, Walt, that you followed my instructions and prepared yourself appropriately." She explained that we'd travel for many nights, first visiting the earliest days of mankind when the idea of an afterlife was in its infancy. From there, we'd move forward, exploring other traditions and cultural practices. "The duration will depend on the degree of your attentiveness. It's likely you'll want to rest after that. We'll see." Suggesting it was time to leave, she promised to return tomorrow if summoned. Placing a delicate hand on my shoulder, she leaned over and blew out the candle. I slept like a baby.

January 7

I began at nine, commencing the practice as prescribed. Midway through, I sat with my tea and waited. A breeze passed through the room, interrupting my thoughts. "It's time to go, Walt. Watch your step." She took my hand as we navigated the smooth stones of a mountain stream. Just ahead, twin rocks rose up, a gap of several inches between. She entered first, encouraging me to follow. We descended slowly, the rocks becoming steps evenly spaced. The going was difficult at times, as the passage was apparently designed for those considerably smaller. Soon, we reached the bottom and paused. I could see nothing at first, the sunlight unable to penetrate. But as I adjusted to the dark, it became obvious that we were in a cavern, its height and breadth far greater than any cathedral. In the distance was a faint light that grew as we moved toward it. Isis whispered that we must tread quietly so as not to disturb. After a time, I was able to make out human forms, illuminated by torches. Two males, naked but for loincloths tight around their waists, were carrying a litter or stretcher upon which a much older man lay motionless. Behind were males and females, carrying baskets with native fruits and meats. Moments later, the old man was lowered to the cave floor. What followed was most astounding. Those without baskets began to beat on drums covered with animal skins. As they did a male, wearing a long robe and taller than any other, began to chant. The entire entourage swayed in time. This went on for an hour or more, bare shoulders and arms glistening with perspiration. Then, as suddenly as it started, it stopped. Two women approached with baskets of flowers. Others stepped forward, spreading the flowers over the length of the man's body. A prayer of some kind was recited by the man in the robe while the others turned and walked away. The priest, if that's what he was, followed from a distance as the torches grew fainter and were finally extinguished. Alone in my room, I was left to wonder.

January 8

The night began where the previous ended. Standing in the dark beneath the dome of the great cavern, the stream from above flowed between and around our feet. In the distance was a light, but different from that of the torches. Isis nudged me forward. After several minutes we were at the cave opening, beyond which was a vast plain. Stepping out of the stream, we followed a path parallel to the bank. Spring was in the air, the long grasses green as was the foliage on an occasional bush or tree. The walking was easy, and we covered a great distance over several hours. I neither tired nor wanted food or drink. As the sky darkened hundreds, perhaps thousands of stars made their appearance. Without warning, a structure appeared directly ahead. Soon we could make out its shape and dimensions. It was a dome made of natural material, with lines similar to the interior of the cavern. Thirty or more feet high, it was equally wide. Drawing nearer, we could hear drums accompanied by chanting. There were four openings, equally spaced. Choosing one at random, we quietly entered, taking a place behind a large circle of natives seated before an open fire. Polished, white skulls of large mammals ringed the slightly sunken pit from which warmth and light spread in all directions. Nearby, a woven mat was spread, upon it the corpse of a child – a girl, possibly eight or nine years old. A man with long black hair and braided hovered over her, repeating a sound without words. While doing so, he washed her limbs with a damp cloth dipped into a clay vessel. After a time, I found myself looking at the faces of the bystanders. Surprisingly, there were no tears, signs of anguish, or even loss. It was as though they had gathered to wish the girl well; to see her off, knowing they would see her again. Four women approached. Lifting the girl from the mat, they placed her on an animal skin, and wrapped it around her. Then they lifted her on their shoulders and walked toward the opposite opening. The man with the braided hair extinguished the fire and led the others into the night.

January 9

We continued our journey at sunrise, following the trail from the day before. By noon, what had been a pleasant stream had grown to a wide, lazy river. No longer were we on the plains. The open grassland had given way to a dark forest. From time to time there were clearings. Villages sprung up, their inhabitants supported by crops from the adjacent fields. Pressing on, the villages grew larger and more numerous. The trail widened into a path and then a road. Increasingly we shared it with other travelers, on foot, riding in carts pulled by oxen, even atop massive elephants that owned the right-of-way when coming through. Frequently a beggar would approach, rewarded by Isis with a coin from a small purse that was seemingly bottomless. The river, too, had become a highway. Long, open crafts ferried passengers from one side to the other. Occasionally a larger, more ornate vessel floated by, carrying royal travelers to unknown destinations. With sunset came light from open cooking pits and small dwellings. On the bank of the river, however, fire was used for another purpose. There were pads, eight to ten feet square, constructed of numerous flat stones. Upon them were wood supports. Funeral pyres, I soon discovered. We passed a few as yet unoccupied. But it wasn't long before we saw a large crowd gathered around one, flames licking it from its base to its highest timber and beyond. At the top was a body, wrapped in white cloth but nearly consumed by flames. Most observers were in deep mourning. As the fire died down, we could see that the flesh was no longer, leaving only charred, skeletal remains. Late in the night, when the bones had cooled but were still burning, a priestly figure pierced the skull with a bamboo poker, creating a hole to allow the release of the spirit. Soon, the pyre was reduced to embers. We reclined on the ground nearby, warmed by the remains as sleep overtook us.

January 10

The miles of travel caught up with me. I slept deep and undisturbed, not waking until the touch of Isis, the sun nearly overhead. "Walt, today will be easier. Nevertheless, we must be on our way. We'll be visiting my home." Gathering myself, there was no option but to follow, having realized that her agenda was mine. We were no longer on foot but on the deck of a sleek, wooden vessel, a warm breeze filling the solitary sail, rectangular and white. The river, a brilliant blue, provided easy passage for similar vessels in either direction. The shoreline was a summer-green with rows of crops extending to the base of sand-colored hills stretching the length of the horizons east and west. "This is a prosperous land," I marveled. "It knows what it's about." I can't recall a time when my soul was as light. All burden had been lifted. Every concern vanquished. Isis left me to my thoughts, and I drifted in and out of sleep, enjoying the brilliant sky one moment and a rising moon the next. When I last woke, we were standing in a great room full of activity. "Walt, we are in the Hall of Maat. The deceased are brought here to have their hearts weighed on the Great Balance." I looked around and saw that to which she referred. It was a scale. Taller than a man, and wider too. Below it a creature, its body that of a lion with the head of a crocodile. "She is Ammit, Devourer of the Dead, Eater of Hearts." As with any scale, there were two circular pans. Each made of gold. A human heart had been placed on one. A feather on the other. Isis explained that it was the feather of truth, belonging to Maat, the goddess of justice. "Should the heart outweigh the feather, it has been found to be unjust and eaten by Ammit. Hearts that pass judgment are taken by my son, Horus, and delivered to Osiris, my husband and God of the afterlife. He rules the Underworld and tends to souls in his care with great compassion and tenderness." One after the other we witnessed the passing of judgment. Sadly, more hearts were devoured than spared. Eventually I tired, my own heart weary.

January 11

I had hoped to travel with Isis this evening, having grown accustomed to her manner. In fact, I enjoy her company. The feminine perspective is not one I'm accustomed to. It's a pleasant departure from the masculine way of being in the world. Though she's insistent on an agenda of her own design, it's not meant to satisfy any self-interest. Emerson entrusted her with the task of providing me with a peculiar education. Like mother, she's dogged in following through. I don't know what Isis thinks of me. Perhaps as a wayward child in need of correction. Or as a soul not quite worthy of being judged fit. She seems to care enough to want it in the hands of Osiris rather than the stomach of Ammit. But I'll learn nothing more tonight. Thomas received a call from Ling shortly before dinner. Chuang is gravely ill. His physician has given him a month to live. The responsibility is on Ling to make final arrangements. Thomas must travel east to help and asked if I'd like to accompany him. I could stay on the pond for a few days while he's in Boston. Of course I said yes, knowing how much Ling and Chuang mean to him. Rather than prepare for Isis, I'll forego the practice and try to sleep an hour or two before Emerson arrives.

January 12

I woke at midnight on a pebbly beach to the first wave of the rising tide. Rushing inward, it brought with it a voice out of the deep. A mysterious sound, as that of a cataract from a mountainside, yet interior in origin. As I listened, it appeared to be the sea-tide rush of my soul, both inspiration and divine foreshadowing. Beyond reason and not of my own control, it could only be one thing. Lao must be nearby. Standing silent, I heard the crush of pebbles underfoot. Soon enough he was at my side, a pleasant sight for a road-weary sojourner. He greeted me, as always, in his gentle way. I love to hear his "Walt" echo in my mind. He said he'd been in conversation with Emerson and learned that I'd be traveling east. It so happened that his travels would intersect with mine. As with Emerson, he's always aware of my recent adventures so it was no surprise that he inquired of my time with Isis. I told him that it's been quite an experience. Otherworldly in some respects. He smiled. It's interesting how a smile can be seen with the inner eye. Then he shared that he'd also traveled with her. In the days before love and family. "She's well respected among our people. Encouraged to experience all we can while tethered to this world, a trip with Isis is recommended to round out one's education. I was fortunate to spend most of a summer with her. My knowledge of humans would have been lacking without it." Lao then asked if I might want to better know his kind. "In two months, we'll be together for our annual reunion. You're welcome to join us. You might find it relaxing after everything that's gone before." I accepted his invitation without hesitation. "I'd be honored Lao. I can think of no better way to spend my time in the days before my last days." As we parted, I promised to prepare as best I could so I might be worthy of his hospitality.

January 13

I spent much of the day on the enclosed porch overlooking the pond. I didn't read, or watch the television, or even listen to music. I just sat, counting the birds come and go, the only life for miles it seemed. Alone, and without distractions, one wonders about things not associated with daily life. How is that ducks stay warm, covered with feathers no thicker than my shirt? Why does ice freeze on the water's surface, but fish live not far below? What allows the naked tree to withstand the bitter cold until the miracle of spring? And those plants and creatures that don't survive the winter. What is death to them? Does it come as easily as a summer rain or the setting of the sun? Chuang told me once that the ancient Masters were more like the hawk and the deer than their fellow man. Life was not serious for them, nor was death. Even if the world should collapse, the Masters would not be disturbed. They recognized that a current flows through all living things, carrying each along whether they want it or not. "Suffering," he said, "only comes with resistance." There's a big game on the television tonight according to Thomas. The two best teams in college football will play for a championship. I told him, though I've always enjoyed games of strength and prowess, that I have no interest in it. Sport in this America is much like war. The young and the poor play so the rich get richer. No, I will forego the spectacle in favor of a good night's sleep and the chance that I might be touched by the current that flows through me.

January 14
I drifted off to sleep, a gentle snow falling just beyond reach. Wrapped in a cocoon of sheet and down cover, I entered the dark world without expectation. I had no need to speak with Emerson, travel with Isis, or even be with Lao, though he brings me a peace no other can. I'm learning that there is a time for experience, for sensation - and a time for nothingness. If it is as the *Tao Te Ching* and modern physicists would have us believe, that all things came from nothingness, then that timeless womb of nonexistence must have had the potential for sublime qualities present to this day. The creation of being by non-being. The empty giving birth to infinite worlds. It was the first miracle, I suppose. There is no understanding what was or might have been before the big moment. Nor is intuition of help. Nevertheless, there's something in our flesh and bones that recognizes that first mother. She, and I can only imagine her as female, carried to term all there is, ever has been, and ever will be. What a burden, and yet she bore it in silence; no midwife at her side or partner to hold her hand. I've never been present at the birth of a child, but the event must be earth-shattering. In that cataclysmic eyeblink, the one becomes two. Thomas says the original separation occurred billions of years ago in some murky pool of possibility. The cosmic dance, with its fits and starts, has been going on ever since. Eons have passed and here we are. Yet there are times, like last night, when I believe I hear the Great Mother whispering ever so softly, "It won't be long my son."

January 15
In the years before electricity and the light bulb, we rarely stayed up late. When the days were shortest, my siblings and I were often in bed by seven. Mother, too, if her chores were done. Though they rarely were. And if they weren't, and she was tired, she would lay down with us, tell us a story from her own childhood, and sleep for a while. But when I would wake in the middle of the night, I would find her sewing, or in the

kitchen preparing for the day. More than once she told me that we are meant to rise in the dark. That our bodies have an internal clock, with an alarm that beckons us midway between midnight and sunrise. When I'm alone on the pond I find myself abiding by that timepiece, often wide awake at the darkest hour. And so, very early this morning, the moon having begun her ascent, I was up and out the door to walk the shoreline path. I know it well now, able to navigate by starlight. This morning, however, the moon shone a bright beacon the length of the trail and I moved quickly, as if in pursuit of game. In little time, I reached the great bend where I'd met C.G a month ago. There was no meeting on this occasion. Nevertheless, I continued on. As before, I arrived at the clearing and the Tower, illuminated from overhead. Hesitant at first, I sounded my presence with a rap on the door and was greeted with a gravelly response. "Come in Walt, I've been expecting you." I made my way with the aid of shadows cast on the walls by the fire burning continuously. As expected, I found him seated, a wool blanket covering his legs, his pipe between his lips. "Walt. You've had some adventures since we last talked. I'm particularly pleased you and Isis have hit it off. I'd like to talk with you about her. But that can wait. For now, I want to recount a story." He proceeded to tell me about an evening, a few years past. He was sitting in the very chair, the fire dancing just as now. In preparation for bed, he'd put a kettle on the fire for washing. The kettle began to sing with a sound like voices or musical instruments. Before long, an entire orchestra was at play. A second orchestra began, beyond the walls of the Tower and near the lake. One dominated and then the other, as though responding to each other. "My life has been blessed with such happenings, Walt. They've accompanied me on my journey. They are available to all, if only there is faith in their existence." C.G. spoke no more as we shared his pipe until first light. When I dozed off, I don't know, not waking until the call for breakfast.

January 16

We spent the morning at the kitchen table. Few words were exchanged, enchanted as we were by the falling snow. It fell in clumps, heavy and wet. I imagined Hoder, the Norse god of winter, heaving fistfuls from some lofty perch. Slowly disintegrating on their downward descent, their mass still great enough to make deep impressions in the inches that had fallen. Like miniature craters formed by detached walnuts. From time to time I observed C.G., mesmerized by nature's display. What had slowly been growing in me since our first meeting, had emerged into a love for this man, though he's of a different time and culture. He'd introduced himself as a psychiatrist, but I believe the heart of a poet or sage beats within. At lunchtime he served a delicious soup from a large pot simmering on the stove. "Basler Mehlsuppe, a favorite of mine. The red wine and garlic make all the difference." He sipped each spoonful as though his last. When he finished, he rose and left without a word. Returning a few minutes later, he was clutching a pair of alpine snowshoes in either hand. "It's time we stretched our legs. You must see the lake in all its glory." Through the afternoon we tromped, leaving our mark six to eight inches deep with every step. Though nearly eighty, I marveled at his vigor. We had soup again for dinner, and a traditional pudding he'd made from scratch. After cleaning up, I could have gone to bed then and there. But he insisted we stoke the fire and share the pipe for a while. Again, few words were spoken, though I longed to know his deepest thoughts. Treading lightly, I asked if he considered himself wise. He declined to answer. Instead, he told of a man who dipped a hatful of water from a stream. "I am that man," he said. "Others are at the same stream and must do something with it. I do nothing but stand and admire what nature can do." He went on. "Few are willing to stoop a little to fetch water from the stream. But that is what a man must do to perceive the processes going on in the background."

January 17

Waking early, I went out alone to greet the morning. Four inches had fallen since yesterday afternoon. Relieved to not have to keep up with C.G., I was content to be on my own. As much as my health has improved since Camden, my sedentary life those last years has led to an atrophy from which I'll never fully recover. Nevertheless, joy comes with making the effort. Skirting the lake's edge, I wondered how a man like C.G. comes to be. Medical training, and years of listening to the troubles of others, seems insufficient. No doctor I ever met "stooped a little" to perceive what goes on behind the curtain. I, too, reveled in nature's innumerable manifestations. But my attention stopped there. Further inquiry never crossed my mind. Returning to the Tower, I found C.G. bent over his porridge. I spoke first. "Tell me, why do you dip water from a stream and yet do nothing with it?" He set his spoon down, clasped his hands, and rested his chin on them. "I led a solitary life as a child. The woods and all they contained were my friends. Hours I'd spend, considering their place in the world." He told me that at the university he studied natural history. Then the human body in medical school. When time came to specialize, he turned his attention to the human mind. "I was fascinated by the images it produces, especially in those others considered insane. As a young psychiatrist working in the asylum, I came to see that dreams often suggest the cure." He went on to tell me of a pivotal time. He had a falling out from his mentor, leaving him adrift. His dream life accelerated, prompting him to study himself as he'd studied his patients. Approaching the inquiry as a scientist, he commenced on a journey that occupied many nights for several years. There he discovered living images, autonomous and free of his control. What he learned in his confrontation with the unconscious informed the rest of his life. "Walt, you've embarked on such a journey. But, unlike me, you approach it with the sensitivity of a poet rather than the discipline of a scientist. I encourage you to take note of all you encounter. You have little time left. What you discover you'll take with you." After finishing our porridge, C.G. encouraged me to enjoy the day. "My home is yours Walt."

January 18
I had a fitful sleep, never descending into that place of dark comfort. I'm not sure of the time, but well before dawn I abandoned the effort. Dressing for the day, I thought I might rest by the fire. In a few hours, C.G. would join me. To my surprise he was waiting, pipe pressed between his lips. Then, the oddest thing. He withdrew it, passing it to his left as if I was seated next to him. What followed nearly caused me to jump from my slippers. C.G. let go of the pipe, leaving it to float a good three feet, where it stopped. At first it was motionless. Then it moved slightly, in the direction of the back of the chair. It occurred to me that the Tower is haunted. That C.G. shares his home with ghosts or spirits. But as quickly as the notion came, it fled, replaced by the familiar voice. "Walt. So good to see you." Of course, it was Emerson. Arriving unannounced, as always. Leaving me to stand, odd man out. "It was not my intention to startle you. I'd merely hoped to spend some time with my dear friend before you woke. Please join us. We've been talking about you, and about Isis." Each, in turn, then told stories of their time with her. How she'd introduced them to death in a way not otherwise possible. No amount of study or research could equal the firsthand experience she provides those under her tutelage. Though death has never been more than a passing interest to me, I had to agree. Already privy to my initial days with her, they pressed me for an account. C.G., in particular, was truly curious. "The images of our collective psychic past are available to all. Yet they are filtered through our individual histories. As a poet, Walt, your perspective is a unique one." I did my best to recount the journey from the beginning, including the dreams that apparently set the stage for my meeting with her at the Basilica. C.G. seemed to hang on every word, as if my narrative held some importance. "You must continue with her, Walt. Understand that

what you learn is not for your edification alone. It will be added to the evolving consciousness of the cosmos." Not understanding what he was talking about, I remained silent except to say that I would endeavor to do my part. Emerson then spoke. "We need to be on our way, Walt. Thomas will be home soon. There's much for the two of you to talk about."

January 19

Thomas was home when I arrived, sitting in his favorite chair and stroking Molly absentmindedly. He didn't notice me at first, his attention elsewhere. I realized I hadn't called once to check on him and see how Chuang was doing. I felt ashamed. Thomas is always present when I need him, and yet I'd spent the time away self-absorbed. He must have read my mind. "Walt, it's alright. We were busy with preparations and sharing stories of Chuang. You were busy, too, from what I've heard." I apologized. "I should have called, Thomas. I'm sorry." He looked up with the eyes of one who has never had an unkind thought. There was sorrow as well. "Chuang has cancer of the pancreas. It's spreading quickly and there's nothing to be done. I'll be putting my affairs in order and leave for China within the week." He then spoke of his love for Chuang, and how he'd been treated like a son. "He was the father I never had. He taught me much. But more than anything, he taught me character." Thomas spoke of the ancient Masters, and that Chuang was a present-day embodiment. "He delighted in sickness and in health. In an early death and in old age. I learned from him that our bodies are constantly changing, and that change is an opportunity to rejoice." He said Chuang wandered at ease. Nothing was unwelcome to him. Once Chuang inquired of Thomas whether it's the same "you" after the body dies. Thomas had no answer. To which Chuang responded, "It doesn't matter my boy. The way in and the way out are one and the same." We spoke of the days ahead. Thomas has much to do before leaving and asked that I take care of the house. "Most important, Walt, enjoy each day. Learn something new. Delight in the body that's been given you. It won't be yours for long."

January 20

I slept until nine, with no interest in getting out of bed. Though I never played rugby, I understand how a player must feel after a particularly contested match. My body ached in every imaginable place; my arms and legs of no use. Add to the beating a sore throat, inflamed twice its size, and the pounding in my head. When I didn't appear for breakfast, Thomas came looking. Initially, he could find nothing but blankets in a large pile. Noticing their rise and fall, he gently pulled them back, exposing a flushed forehead and cheeks. "You're a sick man, Walt. No doubt you've contracted influenza. It's going around so much the hospitals can't keep up." Responding meekly, I told him I felt fine the evening before, just weary. And besides, I'd only been around C.G. and Emerson. Neither appeared ill when I was with them. "You never know," Thomas said. "Did you share C.G.'s pipe? He has a strong constitution, as does Emerson. Either one could have been harboring a nasty virus with no noticeable symptoms. It's well known that those who visit from the other side are frequently sought after by infectious agents. As celestial hosts, they're immune, while the earthbound who come into contact with them are not." He said no matter the virus, the symptoms must be treated the same. "Water, tea, saltine crackers, soup, a pain reliever, and bedrest. They're the best we can do." I objected at first, having promised I'd take care of the house for the week. Of course, it was useless to attempt to convince him otherwise. "As I said, Walt, you're a sick man. You have no choice but to play the part of the patient." And so I did for the remainder of the day and evening, leaving my bed only to relieve myself.

January 21
I did everything as Thomas said I must. Nevertheless, the fever hadn't broken by the end of the day. "If you're not better in the morning, Walt, you'll need to be seen." Through the early hours of the night my temperature fluctuated wildly. Hot flashes gave way to chills, which melted into sweat. My nightgown was soaked, as were the bed linens. I could do nothing to remedy the situation. Dante and his descent into the abyss captured my attention. What if his journey through hell had a basis in fact? Flat on my back, I traced the circles and sub-circles upon which he traveled, concluding that man is the maker of his own hell. Virgil came into view, as vividly as if he was seated at my side. I then felt a hand resting on my forehead. So cool, it drew the fever from my flesh. It was Emerson, my own ghost, resolute and wise. "I apologize, Walt. I'm afraid I'm the cause of your infirmity. Before arriving at C.G.'s I had spent the afternoon with schoolchildren. Several had the sniffles. No doubt some of their bugs hopped aboard. Unaware that they were along for the ride, I delivered them to you." I told him apologies weren't necessary and that I was suddenly feeling my old self. "Tell me Ralph, if you don't mind me calling you that. Why is it I can't see you, but C.G. appears every bit as real as Thomas?" Emerson cleared his throat. "That

is one of the mysteries. It's never been explained to us. Yet we've come to recognize that, just as on earth, there is a hierarchy on the other side. Not one of wealth, power, beauty, or even intelligence. Instead, the more we shed the vestiges of our prior lives, the more we become spirit. C.G. is in the early stages. I can't say for sure, but I believe I'm halfway along. My teacher is pure thought. She has a teacher as well. It all seems quite natural." I thanked Emerson for the explanation, promising to reflect on it. "Walt, when you wake in the morning, it will be as if you were never ill. As you go about the day, give honor to Chuang in some way. He's very fond of you." From that moment on, I slept like a baby.

January 22
Feeling much better, I inquired of Thomas over breakfast about the Trump impeachment trial. What did he think would be the outcome? "It's not likely, Walt, that a complete picture will emerge. The Republicans are opposed to allowing much evidence in. As they control the Senate, the president is likely to be acquitted." He went on to say that, no matter a person's political affiliation, it's a sad day for all Americans. "The polarization in this country is as great as that of the Civil War or Vietnam era." I asked how a reasonable person should look at these times. Whether optimism is a possibility. He excused himself, returning with a book that he handed me. "This is a copy of the *I Ching*. I left it behind when I fled the village. Chuang returned it to me during his visit. It was helpful to him in learning English. You might find it useful in other ways." Opening it, I found notations on nearly every page. Some in English, but most in Chinese. It had ideographs similar to those in the book on calligraphy. "Spend some time with it, Walt. Perhaps it can answer your question." I got a glimpse of the *I Ching* years ago. As a reporter for the *Daily Eagle* I was fascinated by the city's diversity. One autumn day I met an old man at a back-alley restaurant in Chinatown. He was seated at a table with a large red book, a tablet and pencil, and three coins. When I asked what he was doing, he offered to give me a lesson. If I recall correctly, the question I posed was answered in a most profound way. I sat down with Thomas' book, paper and pen, and three one cent pieces. Recalling the instructions of the old man, I posed a simple question, seeking advice rather than prediction: "How do I approach life with optimism in the face of uncertainty?" I tossed the coins six times. Two backs and one face, a divided line. Three backs, a single line with a circle in the middle. Two backs and one face. Two backs and one face. Three backs. Two backs and one face. I then consulted the last page of the book to determine which number of the 62 hexagrams. "29 . . . Darkness." I felt sick but knew I must read

on. I discovered that the central theme of the "gua" - the six lines – is "falling but not drowned; in danger but not lost." The advice given was that I maintain confidence and soothe my mind. If I did, I was assured that "with faith, caution, and trust" I could pass through any difficult situation. I closed the book and retreated to my easy chair to soothe my mind.

January 23

Thomas leaves for China in three days. It's a long journey. Nearly twenty-four hours by air, with layovers in Chicago and Hong Kong before arriving in Shanghai. Then a domestic flight to Chengdu, capital city of Sichuan province. From there, buses and cars to the village. Thomas says he'll be fortunate to arrive by midday on Tuesday. He doesn't mind, as he enjoys the vagaries of travel. His only concern is that he'll be too late to spend time with Chuang. I rarely do such a thing, but I asked how he was feeling. "How heavy is your heart, Thomas, knowing that when you return your world will have been turned upside down?" He looked at me, sorry for my lack of understanding. "Walt, if everyone was to live indefinitely, even a decade or two beyond their hundredth year, we would overcrowd ourselves far beyond what we've already done. It's honorable for one person to die to make way for another." It was obvious that Thomas had given considerable thought to death. "It is the passing of a torch. There comes a point when you hand it to others to do the work. Nature prefers to continue the process of life through different individuals rather than the same." What Thomas said made sense, though I thought there must be exceptions. Certainly, some individuals give more than they receive. They have a value that outweighs the cost of their upkeep. "That's not nature's way, Walt. Life is renewed with each birth. Children see the ordinary as marvelous and new. Profit and survival are not a concern of theirs." I knew what he was saying to be true. Despite my early hardships, I saw magic all around. Delight became the source of my early poetry. Only later did survival and profit dim my vision. "Nature wants to be aware of itself Walt. When we die, another is born who is given the opportunity to view the world anew. Chuang's passing makes that possible. As will yours." My sadness for Thomas, and for Chuang, had been lifted. I looked forward to the remainder of the day.

January 24

Nearly every morning, I find Thomas sitting near the fire, doing nothing it appears. I've assumed he's doing more than planning his day. Praying perhaps. We've talked in the past about meditation, and he's given me advice on the technique of following one's breath. But when I observe him, it doesn't seem quite like that. When he concluded this morning, I asked. Forthcoming, as always, he said it's a simple form of meditation he learned from a Zen master. "There's nothing complicated about it," he explained. "The easiest way to get into the meditative state is by listening. It took me a while, but every day, preferably in the morning, I listen." I asked if he would teach me, as it might help soothe my mind. And so, he coached me. "Simply close your eyes and allow yourself to hear all the sounds going on around you. Listen to the hum of the world as if listening to music. Don't identify the sounds or put names on them. Just allow them to play with your eardrums. Let your ears hear whatever they want to hear. Don't repress thoughts by forcing them out. Listen to them as part of the general noise going on. As you would listen to the sound of cars going by, or birds outside the window. Look at thoughts as just noises. Soon, you'll find that the outside world, and the inside world, come together. Your thoughts are happening like the sounds going on outside. Everything is simply happening and all you're doing is watching. Your breathing is happening too. Allow it to run as it will. Watch it breathe the way it wants to breathe. As you become aware of your breath, you'll realize that the hard and fast division you make between what you do and what happens to you is arbitrary. As you watch your breathing, you'll become aware that the voluntary and involuntary aspects of experience are all one happening. Let your breathing happen naturally, without forcing it. You'll discover you can breathe more and more deeply, and that your breathing gets naturally easier, and slower, and more powerful. You begin to listen to sound, interior thoughts, and feelings as if they're just happenings. As you watch your breathing as a happening, that's neither voluntary nor involuntary, you enter the state of meditation. Don't hurry anything. Don't worry what progress you're making. Don't be selective in any way. Just watch what is happening and be content with what is." When Thomas finished, I continued on, finding every sound precious and something to behold.

January 25

We had guests for dinner. Many of the same who came for Thanksgiving. Thomas had invited them to share a meal that Chuang would have enjoyed, each of the dishes originating from his region. I accepted the task of preparing the stir-fried beef, served over steamed rice. The combination of chili bean paste, ginger, and rice wine transformed ordinary beef into something delectable. Thomas made complementary dishes of shrimp with sugar snaps and stir-fried green beans. The young parents of Olivia brought a delightful desert called "laughing donut holes." I enjoyed them too much, I'm afraid, eating more than my share. The first topic of conversation was the spread in China of what's being called the "coronavirus." Nearly sixty have died, with a travel ban in effect for several cities in Hubei Province. Authorities believe the outbreak started in an animal market in Wuhan. Everyone at the table, me included, expressed concern about Thomas' departure in the morning. He assured us that he would take every possible precaution. Besides, he'd spoken with Ling, who arrived in the village on Thursday. She said there were, as of yet, no reports of illness in the southern half of Sichuan. Someone brought up the impeachment trial and the superb presentation made by Adam Schiff in laying out the Democrats' case against President Trump. I'd watched several hours and weighed in when appropriate, offering how much it pleased me that Rep. Schiff spoke so highly of President Lincoln. One of the men spoke of the baseball scandal which I'd not heard about. Apparently, an elaborate scheme to steal signals from catchers had been concocted by the team from Houston. The stratagem was then taken to the Red Sox by a coach. The discussion got quite lively, particularly among the men. Olivia became agitated, so I offered to try to soothe her. Drawing on what Chuang and Thomas have taught me, I took her to the fireplace room, closed the doors, lit a candle, and danced with her while humming the Gayantri Mantra. It worked! For nearly an hour we moved about as if on a ballroom floor. All the while, I breathed in her sweet fragrance and felt her innocent warmth against my cheek. In those moments I knew the truth of Thomas' words - "Life is renewed with each birth."

January 26

I drove Thomas to the airport, saying little, worried as I was for his well-being. He read my thoughts as usual, assuring me there was no need for concern. It's likely he also knew that I'd be lonely in the house with only Molly as company. He promised to stay in contact, though the phone signal in the village is intermittent. He then suggested I continue my work with Isis. "It's been several days, Walt. Isis is like a muse. You must make a date with her. Unlike Emerson, she's not one to arrive unannounced. With your health returned, take advantage of it." Arriving at the terminal I offered to help, though he carried only a large knapsack. "All I need, Walt, is a big hug. It will serve me well." I willingly obliged, a few tears welling up which I attempted to hide. Returning home, I decided to make the best of it - showering, trimming my beard, and putting on my Sunday clothes. Standing in front of the mirror, I had the oddest sensation. It was as if someone, or something, else was present. I looked around, and there was no one of course. Then a voice spoke in the way Lao and Emerson do, greeting me with a smile. "Welcome Walt. It's been a long time. I am the stranger you've ignored. Who's loved you all your life." I knew who it was. It was my friend, from when I was a boy. My companion when no others were around. The one always there when I called upon him. "I never left you Walt. Others came into your life. Pursuits and distractions as well. But I was there. Do you recall instances of the inexplicable? When a fatal accident was only a step away? It was I who alerted you in the nick of time." I did recall and felt shame for my neglect. "Don't feel bad, Walt. You are human, set down here to know the world. With your days numbered, I ask only that you love again the stranger who is yourself." The tears that began with Thomas began to flow uncontrollably. With them came a peace, unknown to me for the longest time. I embraced by friend and promised to be faithful until the last moment.

MONTH ELEVEN

January 27

Every evening I cross off the day. Yesterday it was 60. This evening it will be 59. Tomorrow, 58. Last March, day one seemed so far away. I asked myself, "How will I fill the year?" I recognize now that it's filled itself. One by one, sunrise and sunset, strung together as they say, like pearls. We don't create the days, they're given to us. Each life allocated its share from the beginning. Some die at birth. Others a century later. Most after a reasonably long life. Many say it's an injustice when a life is cut short. Even more so when the span is measured in hours or days rather than years. It's Chuang's belief that, just as the calendar has its predetermined start and end, so does a life. The contract is irrevocable. As agreed, I met Duc Lai at the park this morning. He appears to never change. Yet, I detected the faint emergence of a wrinkle not present a month ago. I sat patiently, in no hurry for attention, knowing that when it arrived it would be complete. In the meantime, I gazed upon his face, imagining the Buddha reincarnated. He stirred. "I knew you would come, Walt. This is a time of deep reflection for you. As it should be. Politics, injustice, poverty, global warming, even poetry, are of little importance now. What matters is the attitude you are cultivating." I acknowledged the truth of it. Duc spoke of the Dalai Lama. That he was asked on his fifty-ninth birthday what he hoped to do in the year to follow. He replied that he wanted to make a greater effort in his preparation for death. "You've started a little late, Walt. But that's alright. You're working at it." I asked Duc if he's still willing to be with me the last few days. "Of course, Walt. Let's meet here in a month to discuss the details. Bring your friend Thomas if he's available."

January 28

Soon after sunset I retired to prepare for Isis. She arrived just as I finished. "Hello, Walt. I have missed your company. I hope you're ready to continue. There are many faces of death, as you know. I think it best we resume our journey by visiting those who approached it with

courage. You've heard the story of Socrates, of course. His conviction
at trial for impiety against the gods and corruption of the city's youth.
The subsequent sentence of death by execution. Come, let's be with him
in his last hour." No sooner had she taken my hand and we were in a
large, low-lit room with walls of stone; a single torch burning near a
vacant cot. Around it men were standing, dressed in robes of various
colors. A few held their heads in their hands, weeping. Others waited
anxiously. After a short time, a well-built man, in his sixties perhaps,
entered the room. Partially clad in white, he walked toward the cot and
sat down. A servant approached and stood beside him: "Socrates, you
know the message I bring. Try to bear what you must as easily as you
can." Socrates responded, "I will do as you say." He then turned to the
others, "Let someone bring the poison." An objection was made: "But
Socrates, the sun has not yet set. There is still time." Socrates replied,
"Crito, I would gain nothing by taking the poison a little later, making
myself ridiculous in my own eyes if I clung to life when there is no more
profit in it." Crito then nodded to a boy standing near, who left then
returned with a man carrying a cup. Socrates asked, "Well, my good
man, what must I do?" "Nothing, except drink the poison then lie down.
It will take effect of itself." The man held the cup out to Socrates, who
accepted it without expression. "I must pray to the gods that my
departure be a fortunate one." He raised the cup to his lips and
cheerfully drained it. Having completed the task, he walked about until
his legs were heavy. He then reclined, fully extended and on his back.
The man who'd administered the poison examined his feet and legs, then
pinched his foot hard and asked if he felt it. Socrates said "No." Moving
upwards, he demonstrated that Socrates was growing cold and rigid,
remarking that when the poison reached the heart he would be gone.
Before that, however, Socrates addressed Crito: "We owe a cock to
Aesculapius. Pay it and do not neglect it." Shortly after, his eyes were
fixed. The attendant reached down and closed them, thus ending our
visit.

January 29
All day I considered Socrates' response to Crito, that life shouldn't be
clung to when there's no more profit in it. It occurred to me that there's
as much courage in acknowledging that as in draining the cup. Therein,
it seems, is the secret to taking the poison with good cheer. For then it is
not poison at all, but the final act of an intentional life. Come evening, I
wondered who would be next. The answer came soon enough. "Walt,
do you recall the madman, Nero, and the plot to remove him after the
burning of Rome?" I did, bringing to mind an image of the tyrant

fiddling while the city burned. "And do you recall that Seneca, his adviser, was implicated in the plot?" I did as well, having read that Nero's paranoia had cost Seneca dearly. As with Socrates, he'd been ordered to take his own life for alleged deeds against the state. As Isis took my hand, we stepped back nearly two millennia, into the bathing room of the Roman noble. Like Socrates, he was surrounded by friends. Prohibited by the attending centurion from memorializing his will, he bequeathed to his companions his greatest possession. "I have only the pattern of my life to give you. Learn from it and it will serve you well." He turned and embraced his wife, asking that she not grieve too much. In response, she said she was resolved to die with him. In the next moment, they cut the veins on their arms. Bleeding, Seneca dictated his last words as he stepped into the bath filled with warm water. Taking a cupful into his hands, he sprinkled it about as a sacrifice to Jupiter. Shortly after, he expired, and his friends removed him for cremation.

January 30
When Isis arrived, I asked if we might talk. I told her I was curious about courage in the face of death. Whether the noble man acting upon principle is a common theme. She sat beside me and explained that courage, like death, has many forms and is not the sole province of gender, age, or station in life. "In fact," she said, "an example I'm particularly fond of is that of a peasant girl who had visions that compelled her to action." Not yet twenty when her life was taken, Isis said the girl already had a following with the poor and dispossessed. "It's not a pleasant sight, Walt, but let's honor her as she is about to meet her God." A moment later, we were standing with others in the center of a medieval village. All eyes were upon a young woman, tied to a wooden pillar. She was clutching a crucifix as flames engulfed her, burning her long, white garment and then her flesh. Never once did she cry out or curse her executioner. In the crowd of hundreds, there was barely a one not overwhelmed. Had there not been sufficient English soldiers, the peasants would surely have stormed the platform and freed her. But it was her time, apparently, and she accepted it with a faith in something that negated all doubt. As Isis suggested, it was an honor to witness her last breath and the departure of her spirit. Though many left, many remained as the body was consumed and the ashes cast into the river Seine. Preparing to leave, we noticed the executioner, off to the side and sobbing, repeating over and over that he'd burned a holy woman.
January 31

I ate little today, the vision of the French girl etched in my mind. Her torture within arms' reach, yet I remained incredulous that one so young could bear the unbearable with such equanimity. I found it difficult to begin the routine, my concentration inadequate for the task. Nevertheless, Isis responded to my meager call. Intention alone apparently enough. "I see that you are troubled, Walt. Consider the certainty with which she left this world. Faith is a mysterious and powerful tonic. Let's move on to a different time and the story of one Thomas More. Though a friend and confidant of King Henry VIII, he refused to compromise his beliefs and was arrested for treason. His case was pled before a compromised jury that found him guilty in a matter of minutes. Let's attend his execution." As with the girl, a large crowd had gathered, forming a circle around an elevated stand. A man in black stood waiting. At the stroke of nine the convicted traitor was led from the London Tower. His beard was long and his face pale and thin. In his hands he carried a red cross. Led to the scaffold, he remarked to the Lieutenant, "Pray, sir, see me safe up. As to my coming down, let me shift for myself." Erect and self-assured, he asked the crowd to pray for him, "and bear witness that I will die a faithful servant both to God and the King." He then knelt, asking for mercy. "Wash me from my guilt, O God, and cleanse me from my sin." Visibly moved, the executioner asked for forgiveness. More, in turn, kissed the man and said, "Pick up thy spirits and be not afraid to do thine office. My neck is short. Take heed therefore thou strike not awry." Laying his head upon the block, he requested that he be allowed to set his beard aside, "for it has committed no treason." With a great cheerfulness to the final moment, his head was removed with a single blow.

February 1
I read this morning about the vote on the Democrats' motion to call witnesses in the impeachment trial. Only two Republicans were in favor. As I understand it, the vote was not to decide the president's guilt or innocence, but merely to allow testimony that might shed further light on the truth. The party in power did not want to hear it. Absent, apparently, were sufficient men and women with the courage to go against their king. I worry about this thing we call Democracy. In my day, I looked to a future in which it would be perfected. With Trump, Democracy is on shaky ground. I spoke with Isis this evening about my concerns. Her suggestion was that we visit a fellow countryman who gave his life in the furtherance of the American ideal. She then related a series of events of which I'm somewhat familiar. Early in the fall of 1776, after the Continental Army suffered a terrible defeat near my home on Long

Island, General Washington needed to know the British intentions.
Nathan Hale, along with other officers, was asked to volunteer for a
mission behind enemy lines. Only Hale stepped forward. Setting out
from Norwalk, Connecticut, he was ferried across the Sound to
Huntington, where he evaded the British guards. From there, he
proceeded to New York, getting by every guard but the last. Stopped
and searched, drawings were found on his person that declared his
mission. He immediately gave his name, rank, and objective. Without a
trial, orders were given for his execution. At daybreak, I accompanied
Isis to the site where stood an oak tree, a rope with a noose hanging from
its largest limb. Present were but a few British troops. Captain Hale
entered the scene, dressed in brown clothes and wearing a round, broad-
brimmed hat. Much like that of a Dutch schoolmaster. He was calm and
bore himself with dignity. With death but a few moments away, he
asked for a clergyman. His request was refused. He asked for a Bible
but was denied one. A final request for writing materials was granted, as
well as a brief time to compose two letters. Upon completion, he was
summoned to the gallows, where the noose was placed around his neck
and tightened. As he was hoisted off the ground by two stout Brits, he
proclaimed, "I only regret, that I have but one life to lose for my
country."

February 2
I vacillate between hope and despair. Not for myself, but for those to be
born into this strange new world. Thomas has spoken of how difficult
it's become to discern the truth. That the internet is both hero and
villain. With the creation and promulgation of "alternative facts," the
waters of reality are muddied. Thomas says President Trump has taken
the art of distortion to new levels, sowing seeds of authoritarianism. I'm
not immune to the seduction of the internet, "surfing" it from time to
time. Today I learned of PEN America, an organization which draws
attention to attacks on free expression. Journalists from around the world
regularly contribute exposés on state-sponsored disinformation
campaigns. When Isis arrived this evening, she spoke of how the Nazis
in Germany rose to power with the aid of such disinformation. "It would
be good to meet someone who gave his life to stop the madness." I
agreed. She then told me about Dietrich Bonhoeffer, a German
theologian. Two days after Hitler became German chancellor,
Bonhoeffer took to the radio and denounced the Nazis. The broadcast
was cut off before he could finish. He continued to object to Nazi
policies, eventually losing his freedom to lecture or publish. In response,
he joined the German resistance, participating in a plot to assassinate

Hitler. In April of 1943, he was arrested by the state police, court-martialed, and sentenced to death. We arrived at a concentration camp in Flossenburg just as Bonhoeffer was taken from his cell and led to an enclosed courtyard. Stripped of his clothing, he was left wearing only his spectacles. A guard approached and asked if he was afraid. Bonhoeffer replied simply, "I'm cold." We then watched as he stepped onto the executioner's stage. There were no mourners in attendance. No last cigarette or opportunity for prayer. Like Nathan Hale, the noose was applied quickly and with certainty. Without delay, the lever was pushed forward, exposing the ground below. His feet free of foundation, he spoke his last words: "This is the end for me, the beginning of life."

February 3

I've been humbled these past few days by the courage of those we visited. I would not have it in me to act similarly. Surely a lesson is to be learned from witnessing such valor. Why else would Isis have chosen each as an exemplar? Yet they are rare among our kind. What of the rest of us? Is there a courage attainable by the common man or woman that can be summoned in the last hour? Slow to muster an answer, I waited for Isis to provide assistance. Appearing at the appointed time, she anticipated my question and said she had a surprise for me. In the next instant we were in a strange land, high in the mountains and amongst a people I had no acquaintance with. Brown-skinned and black-haired without exception, they wore costumes as if for a grand celebration. Handsome boys and beautiful girls danced. Older men played on stringed instruments unfamiliar to me. My spirits were lifted by the shared playfulness. Suddenly, a large gong sounded and an elder called for attention. "It is nearly time. Let us be with our friend and brother." Silence followed as the community came together in a single line and walked a path to the lakeside. There they knelt around a raised bed, upon which was the one they called Papa. To my astonishment it was Chuang, a surprise indeed. The man I'd grown so fond of, though much frailer than when he departed Thomas' home. Yet his demeanor was the same. That big smile. Eyes alive to the world. Arms embracing one after another, as if each was a son or daughter, grandson or granddaughter. Thomas and Ling were at his side, basking in the warmth of his spirit. A rabbit sat on his lap, which he stroked when not hugging a well-wisher. He took Thomas by the arm and pulled him closer, whispering in his ear. Thomas spoke to the crowd: "Papa has something to say before he leaves." Ling propped him up so he could see everyone. Chuang cleared his voice, then spoke softly, all strength nearly gone. "My dear ones. I thank each of you for bringing joy to my life. I will take it with me and spread it wherever I go. Now is my time. I bid you farewell." The light went out as he fell into Ling's arms. With great tenderness, she stroked his head and laid him down.

February 4

I lay in bed unable to move. Worse than influenza, grief had taken hold of me. And remorse. I should have gone with Thomas. The nights with Isis could have been delayed. Chuang had given me so much, yet I didn't make the effort to acknowledge his generosity. Just steps from his deathbed, I watched others step forward. Yet I failed to do the same. I've long struggled with demonstrations of affection, even to those most deserving. Midday came and passed. No interest strong enough to move me. Then, on the edge of consciousness, I saw Chuang, walking at my side, telling the story of Lao Tzu's wake. How Chin Shih, his dear friend, saw him in repose, let out three yells and left. At that moment some force took hold of me, flung me from my bed, opened my mouth, and yelled three times. I ran up the stairs and into the bathroom. Relieving myself, I showered, dressed, and stood before the mirror, hoping. In the time it took to pass a comb through my hair, he arrived. My friend, who I'd treated as a stranger for so long. He embraced me with an affection as real as if he was before me. "Walt. Be kind to yourself. I assure you, Chuang knows what's in your heart. Live fully the days remaining. Eat bread. Drink wine. Feast on your life." I recalled another story of Chuang's. His namesake, Chuang-tzu, was fishing when an official arrived, sent by the king. "Sir, his majesty requests that you come to the capital and serve as prime minister." Chuang-tzu responded, "I've heard of a sacred tortoise that died thousands of years ago. Its shell kept by the king, wrapped in silk and hidden in a golden box. If you were the tortoise, would you prefer to be venerated in such a way, or be alive, crawling in the mud? Please, give my regards to the king, and tell him I'm happy right here, crawling in the mud." When Chuang was with us, he and Thomas would often play a game late into the night. It was an ancient game, revered by Chuang's people for longer than was known. I knew what I must do. I would find the game. Acquaint myself with its rules. And play it as if Chuang sat across from me.

February 5

I searched Thomas' library in vain. Unable to find the game, I was at a loss until I recalled how, months ago, he told me that anything of his was mine to use. Though I'd never been in his bedroom, I knew he kept many of his prized possessions there. And there it was, on the top shelf opposite his bed, along with several books on China, a flute, an exquisite tea set, and miniature statues of Lao Tzu, Confucius, and the Buddha. I lowered it gently, respectful of its importance to Thomas. Next to it were two square tins with small black and white stones, and a manual of instruction. After dinner, I prepared a cup of tea and sat at the kitchen table with the game board, a wood square with 19 lines drawn east-west and 19 north-south. Where the lines intersect there are points, and on the points each player places a stone. I recalled that the rules are simple, but the possibilities innumerable. Unlike any western game, the object is not to defeat another but to preserve and extend one's own land. The Chinese have long believed that if you possess land, you have an area to base life on. You have liberty and freedom. I was ready to begin, but realized I had no opponent. It occurred to me that, somehow, I might be able to summon Chuang. Holding the cup to my lips, I sipped slowly. Perhaps the Chinese tea could work some magic. The room suddenly dropped in temperature and the lights dimmed. It was working. Seconds passed and someone took the seat opposite me. I waited. "I'm so pleased, Walt, that you've chosen to have some fun. May I join you?" The voice was not Chuang's but Emerson's. I did my best to disguise my disappointment. "Of course you can, Ralph. It will be a pleasure. I'm curious, though. Why did you respond rather than Chuang?" Emerson chuckled in a way that's slightly irritating. But I'm accustomed to it. "It's far too early in Chuang's new life to be able to move about as many of us do. Years will pass before he will join our ranks. But I came so you wouldn't be disappointed." I said nothing but had to wonder how a New Englander from a century-and-a-half ago would know anything about the game. Of course, no thoughts I have are mine alone when Emerson is present. "It's quite understandable, Walt, that you would be skeptical. I learned the game from Chuang's great-grandfather, and we play regularly. You have the black stones. It's your move." One stone at a time, we played well into the night. Territory expanding and contracting and expanding again. We ended before there was a clear winner. The enjoyment was in the fellowship. "Well done, Walt. I'm impressed. We will play again I'm sure. By the way, get to know your friend. No one knows you better."

February 6
"Eat bread. Drink wine. Feast on your life." What did he mean? Is it an expression? A figure of speech authored by the unconscious? Or did he intend for me to take it literally? I recalled how, in my youth, he would speak both concretely and in the abstract. Often, I would follow his whispers as if commands. Other times they seemed the stuff of

dreams, and I would ponder them for days. Perhaps there's a message within the message. I've never baked a loaf of bread, though I watched mother on countless occasions sift flour, combine ingredients, add warm water, and knead. Neither her recipe nor her method ever failed. This morning I went to Thomas' cookbooks and found one specific to breads and muffins. Wanting to start simply, I chose one with just three ingredients. Heating three cups of water to 100 degrees, I poured it into a large bowl, stirring in 1 1/2 tablespoons of yeast and the same of kosher salt. I then added 6 cups of unbleached flour and mixed it all until there were no dry patches. Covering it with a thin towel, I let it rise unattended for two hours. In the interim I went shopping for sherry, always my favorite wine. At the shop Thomas visits occasionally, I was helped by a young man who was quite knowledgeable. "Most of our sherries are for cooking," he said, "although it's not uncommon for customers to purchase a bottle for an inexpensive drink." I knew all too well, my own resources nearly always inadequate to buy the best. "But of course," he said, "there's Harvey's Bristol Cream. It's both fragrant and elegant." I knew of it, having had it once. Though it wasn't available in the states, an admirer from Europe visited over Christmas, gifting me with a bottle. Over a long evening, we imbibed until the last drop. I still recall the experience of its velvety finish. Knowing Thomas would understand, I handed the clerk a twenty, receiving little in the way of change. On the way out, the young man suggested I pour it over ice and a slice of orange. I tipped my cap and thanked him. Returning home, I again consulted the recipe, following each step exactly. Finally, I placed the loaves on a heated stone for twenty minutes, then baked them until browned. I never knew bread could be so good. Smothered in butter with the sherry over ice and orange, I had quite a meal. Sitting by the fire afterward, I opened at random the slim volume of *Leaves* Thomas had given me the first day. So many years ago, I wrote: "Stop this day and night with me and you shall possess the origin of all poems. You shall possess the good of the earth and sun…" There's wisdom in my friend's encouragement to feast on my life. I've had but one and will take it with me.

February 7

Thomas called this morning. The connection was poor, but I understood most of what he said. Due to the spread of the coronavirus, his flight home had been cancelled. Having spoken with Emerson, he was assured other arrangements would be made. "There's much to talk about, Walt. The final week with Chuang, his last hours, the days since. It was a beautiful death. I wish you could have been here." He then asked if I've had an opportunity to look at the calligraphy book Chuang had given me. Chuang had wondered as well. I felt terrible but had to be honest, promising I would do so today. After a simple dinner, I sat at the desk, nervous as a schoolboy about to be tested. Paging through the book, were examples from the six periods dating back to classical antiquity. Similar, but each distinct in the length of line and width of stroke. I familiarized myself with the paper, ink, and brush. I studied the basic movements - horizontal from left to right, and vertical from up to down. Next, I worked the bristles until they were pliant, soaking them in water and removing just enough so there wasn't a drip. I placed a sheet of white paper on top of brown wrapping paper and poured the rich black ink into a cup. Dipping the bristles, I rolled them round and round until the ink and bristles were one. Drawing the black tip over the edge of the cup, I held the shaft of the brush between my middle and ring finger as my hand hovered over the paper. My throat tightened but I pushed forward, gently lowering the brush to the white expanse, the point touching down and then swishing. I couldn't believe the pleasure in such a simple act. The silent laying down of ink, so different than writing in my journal. I continued, stroke after stroke. The outcome wasn't important. That would come later. For now, the mere pleasure of practicing the ancient art was enough. I could think of no better way to honor Chuang.

February 8

I considered preparing for Isis, but didn't have it in me, what with Chuang's passing and the uncertainty around Thomas' return. Instead, I fell back on the old habit of walking with Molly to the park. I needed a good stretch, but with it came a sadness. I've grown quite fond of the little dog, an attachment I never anticipated. There's never a time that she doesn't greet me as if I'm her one and only friend. I know it sounds silly, but I need to ask Emerson about dogs. Where do they go, having only love in their hearts? I would choose Molly to accompany me over many who called me friend but left me for another. Yet it wouldn't be fair to Thomas, as he cares for her as much as I do. Returning home, Molly and I sat by the fire. She with her bone and me with my sherry. If only I could know her thoughts as I do Lao's. Tiring of her bone, she hopped up on my lap, licked my face twice, and fell asleep. After a few minutes I did the same, waking in an open field somewhere in the north of France. Long grasses provided a lush green cover. In the center was a lone tree, its trunk rising to a great height until giving way to branches as green as the grass. After a minute or so, the leaves turned yellow, then golden, then brown, before falling to the field below, leaving the tree bare as if in winter. Soon though, buds appeared, birthing newborn leaves. Seconds passed and the tree was fully mature, the branches lost to the midsummer green. The leaves turned yellow again and the cycle continued. Years passed it seemed; centuries even. Life begat death which begat life. The cycle repeating itself over and over, well beyond the lifespan of humankind on the planet. I felt a kinship with the tree, believing it to be the source from which all life flows. Had Molly not awakened me, licking my face, I would have stood before it for eons.

February 9

There's a statuette on Thomas' shelf seemingly inappropriate for its surroundings. Amid the fine pieces of pottery, stone and metal artifacts, it sits in a place of prominence suggesting a value beyond its appearance. Inside is a music box, activated by a turnkey on the bottom. The tune is a simple one, but seductive. Encasing the box is a figure, dressed in a well-worn and frequently patched overcoat, wearing a hat of the same vintage. Its footwear has seen many miles, the toe caps so worn they no longer protect the occupants. Its face is a kindly one - red nose, red lips, eyebrows attentive, eyes weathered and wise. Its left hand holds an open book with indecipherable lines. The index finger of its right points slightly upward, suggesting a noteworthy thought. The longer I consider it, the more I recognize it to be part clown, part hobo, and part sage. I've never asked Thomas about it, though I believe it tells a story with which he identifies. He places great stock in the simple wisdom of the storyteller. My experience was the same, having learned much from itinerant philosophers who deftly evaded the railroad bulls to traverse the country in the open air, free of charge. My heart was lightest when I possessed little and roamed freely. The world is the great teacher, and the wanderer its best student. I remember the day I bid goodbye to indoor complaints and querulous criticisms. Traveling the open road, I was strong and content, the earth beneath my feet sufficient. Slowing down these final days, I pray that in the next life I'm free to travel at will.

February 10

There was a knock on the door just as I turned in. "Walt, are you up?" It was Thomas! I jumped from bed, greeting him with a big hug, then told him how worried I'd been. He didn't downplay it. "Many have died. Many more are gravely ill. Fortunately, it hasn't spread to the village or the surrounding area. They're safe for now." I asked about Ling. Is she safely in Boston? "Ling stayed behind, Walt. She wants to practice medicine there and live with her people." He told me the story, going years back. When Ling was growing up, her best friend was Zhang, a boy about her age. He was eight when his parents died in a fire. Ling's family took him in. Her mother tutored him with the books Thomas had left behind, just as she tutored Ling. All through school they excelled, earning top honors. When Ling came to America, Zhang stayed behind, attending the university in Chengdu and obtaining a degree in public health. A year ago he returned to the village. After years apart, Ling and Zhang have fallen in love. They plan to marry soon and raise a family. "It's their destiny, Walt." I asked Thomas how he felt about it. Rarely seeing his daughter and future grandchildren. "It's the right thing, Walt. Ling and Zhang believe in giving back and the Yi need their help. Besides, I've exacted a promise. Once their first child is born, they'll travel every Christmas to be with me. I couldn't be happier." Thomas then acknowledged the late hour and said it's best I get to bed. "There's something I want to show you in the morning, Walt. It's a gift from Chuang."

February 11
I woke feeling like a little kid. More than curious, I couldn't wait to see the gift Thomas had returned with. I imagined it would be a cherished book of wisdom. Or an heirloom generations' old. As saddened as I am by Thomas' loss, and mine, I'm pleased he had a father figure who cared for him so deeply. I found Thomas seated by the fire, deep in thought. Approaching from behind, it appeared that Molly was on his lap. But it wasn't her, it was a rabbit. And not the rabbit I've seen from the office window racing across the lawn. Longer than usual ears, with a golden brown coat and a white belly, the hair about its eyes a silver gray. Thomas sensed my presence and looked up. "Here he is, Walt. Chuang's longtime friend, entrusted to me to provide a new home." My initial response was one of concern. Would Molly and this newcomer get along. "This is no ordinary rabbit, Walt. He's older than anyone knows, and wiser than most men your age or mine." I knew there was a story and asked Thomas if this rabbit has a name and a history. "Almost from the beginning, Chuang knew him as Kicus. When Chuang was five, the rabbit arrived in the village. Chuang's father found him in the family garden and gave him to Chuang as a pet. Shortly after, the name Kicus came to mind and the rabbit has responded to it ever since." I've never known a rabbit up close, having been told at an early age that they're a nuisance. My father had no tolerance. Shooting them on sight for dinner. Though I enjoyed the occasional story about rabbits outwitting the fox, I always knew them to be fiction. But there was something about this rabbit that suggested a truth in the old fairy tales. Then I recalled my journey with Isis. "Thomas, you may not be aware,

but Isis and I were amongst the villagers as Chuang bid them farewell. Am I correct that the rabbit he was holding was Kicus?" "Of course you are, Walt. The two were nearly inseparable. When Chuang visited us, it pained him to leave his dear friend behind. Fortunately, Zhang is a gentle man who knows the ways of creatures and looked after Kicus until Chuang's return. Now, let's get about, and find a suitable place in the house for Kicus to call his own."

February 12

I rarely know what a day will bring, who will knock on the door or appear in the dark. I've heard it said that when one's productive life is over, there's an opportunity to construct a new life. Others insist that it's best to take each day as it comes. I had neither in mind when I first woke in my new bed in this new world. What was it, then, that prompted me to accept Emerson's radical offer? Perhaps it was curiosity that tipped the scale in favor of another year. With the approach of that final hour in Camden, I did not rage against the dying of the light. Nor did I fear it. I believed I had nothing more to live for; the looming silence to be preferred over the monotony of infirmity. And then Emerson arrived. How could I know at the time how unprepared I was? Though I admired him in my early days, I never appreciated his essence. It's clear that Emerson and the others, as he calls them, did not choose me for my journalistic skills. Nor did they need a report on the state of the nation. Nothing I might share would be new to them. I'm humbled that there are beings who care for a poor soul not yet ready. That may well be the task of those on the other side. I'll learn soon enough, I suppose. For now, I favor taking each day as it comes. I'm enjoying getting to know Kicus. There's more to the little fellow than just a rabbit. And I look forward to continuing my journey with Isis. If I've learned anything these past several months, it's that everything is of consequence.

February 13

I sat at my table with renewed interest. Having danced to "Mother Night" and sipped on the special tea, I was in that liminal space into which Isis enters. She arrived, not with a cool hand as does Emerson, but with a warm breeze befitting her origin and temperament. Seated beside me, she spoke of her intentions. "Walt, these next few nights may be difficult. But I assure you they are necessary for your education. Recall that, in your lifetime, you lost loved ones before their full flowering. Grief is often greatest when this happens. No earthly reason can be given for the loss and one's faith can be shaken to a degree that it never recovers. Nevertheless, the taking is of the natural order. Let's first travel to a destination you knew well." It was after ten when we found ourselves standing behind patrons on the upper level of a theater. From the laughter, it was apparent that a comedy was unfolding. I soon realized it was a performance of *Our American Cousin*. As my vision adjusted, I recognized President Lincoln seated just ahead, his wife to his right. My heart raced and my stomach tightened, for I knew what would transpire. Just behind and to my left, a young man entered the vestibule, stood silently in the shadows, and waited. As the audience roared following a particularly witty line, the assassin stepped forward and fired a single bullet into the back of Mr. Lincoln's head. The president immediately lost consciousness and history was forever altered. My grief, in that moment and for many days afterward, was beyond measure. I knew only emptiness and dread for the future. Grabbing Isis by the hand, I pleaded that she spare me the minutes to follow. My only consolation these many years later is that my president would be regarded as the greatest president in our nation's history.

February 14
It's one thing to have a memory painful in the recall. I learned of President Lincoln's death the morning after. Piece by piece, and over several days, a tragic portrait emerged. But to visit the source and witness it for the first time is much more difficult, even devastating. I had no appetite today, nor energy for the simplest of tasks. What little enjoyment I had was in watching Kicus and Molly. How they played as if brother and sister. Kicus, by far the wiser, deferring to Molly's proclivities. By evening I was better and resolved to continue with Isis. It meant a lot that she understood my sadness, remarking that she's witnessed others, uncommonly good, who died far too young. "This evening Walt, we will visit another man, as great in his day as Mr. Lincoln. Like your president, he lived and died in pursuit of freedom for the black man." Moments later we were in a room with matching beds, a desk, and a toilet to the side. It was a late afternoon in early spring. Isis suggested we move to the balcony for fresh air. Exiting, we observed a black man step from his room two doors down. His bearing was that of intelligence and strength, yet he appeared to carry a heavy burden. There were voices coming from behind, but he stood alone, his attention elsewhere. In the next instant, a shot rang out. A lone bullet struck the man in the face, ripping his necktie off and forcing him to the balcony floor. Three men emerged and attempted to provide aid. Medical personnel arrived within minutes and an ambulance rushed the man away. Later in the evening, we learned on the television that the civil rights leader, Martin Luther King, had been shot at a local motel. He

died an hour later. A special report was broadcast, during which was played an excerpt from a speech Dr. King had given the night before: "We've got some difficult days ahead. But it doesn't matter with me now. Because I've been to the mountaintop. And I don't mind. Like anybody, I would like to live a long life. Longevity has its place. But I'm not concerned about that now. I just want to do God's will. He's allowed me to go up to the mountain. And I've looked over. And I've seen the promised land. I may not get there with you. But I want you to know tonight, that we, as a people, will get to the promised land."

February 15
Thomas and I walked this morning, talking only of Dr. King. He remembers the assassination as if yesterday, and the speech given the night before. Every year on the 4th of April, he reads it to honor the slain leader's legacy and to remind himself that the work is never done. Returning from the park, Thomas recited word for word a passage that still haunts him: "If something isn't done, and in a hurry, to bring the colored peoples of the world out of their long years of poverty, their long years of hurt and neglect, the whole world is doomed." Thomas said politicians give lip service to progress, but little has been made. Most blacks earn significantly less than whites and are murdered disproportionately. This evening, Isis took me to a community in Florida to witness something she said is all too common in America. We arrived as a black teenager was walking on the sidewalk across from us. He'd been visiting relatives and was returning to their home from a neighborhood store. A vehicle slowed down and stopped. A male, in his late twenties or early thirties, exited and approached the young man. A physical altercation ensued. Abruptly, the man displayed a handgun and fired. The unarmed boy fell to the ground, just a few hundred feet from the door of his relative's residence. Isis said the death of Trayvon, the boy, received national attention. The man with the gun was eventually charged with murder. Following a trial with nearly all-white jurors, he was acquitted.

February 16
Another day of grief. For President Lincoln, Dr. King, the innocent boy; for all the innocents slain out of hate or fear. With Isis soon to arrive, I wasn't sure I could stomach more bloodshed. I thought back to the thousands of young men who gave their lives to end slavery. It was a heavy price, but I assumed at the time it would end the racism that had infected the nation for two centuries. I was often accused of naivety, and rightly so. Isis sat next to me. I sensed that her agenda could wait. In

that moment I recalled how mother always brought understanding to our childhood concerns, never placing her needs before ours. I looked up and told her I was ready. "You've seen much, Walt. More than most. Let's visit a scene from yesterday, to remind you that some bring about their own demise." We were soon on another sidewalk in another city. Isis took me by the arm, encouraging me to walk carefully, as ice was just below the falling snow. We paused in front of a large home, occupied by a wealthy businessman and his wife. Nearly seventy, he continues to work long days, believing that one can never have enough. He loves his children and grandchildren but spends little time with them. "That will come later," he tells himself. "When I've saved enough to meet their needs and more." The front door opens, and the man rushes out, late for a meeting. His feet fly up and his body strikes the pavement with full force. His head bounces then rests. The snow turns red, and the circle around his lifeless body grows larger.

February 17

I'll never have the heart Thomas has. When I told him of the man, dead in the snow, he wept. I asked why. "Every death brings with it loss Walt. The man, unlike you, lost the opportunity to do it right. His children grieve for the loss of a father they never knew. His grandchildren lost a companion to delight in their innocence." I understood and felt selfish for the gift Emerson had given me. Late in the evening, I stood with Isis in the home of a friend. We held back tears as Emerson and Lidia kissed their beloved Waldo, taken without warning by scarlet fever. Though Emerson never acknowledged it, Waldo was the favorite child. Sensitive and inquisitive, he was wise beyond his years at the age of five. Father and son spent hours together - in the library, studying nature, enjoying each other's company. Emerson stood before us in disbelief, his faith on shaky ground. I never spoke with him about the loss, but I heard from close friends that his life was changed that evening. He never again knew pure joy. Though his fame continued to grow, the wound never healed. I still recall the lines he wrote, not as poet or scholar, but as grieving father: "But over the dead he has no power. The lost, the lost he cannot restore. And, looking over the hills, I mourn the darling who shall not return."

February 18

One never knows what another carries. Observing Emerson in his sorrow, I felt a tenderness for him I didn't think possible. The great man of letters revealed without pretense a heart equal to his mind. Though I've missed much not being a parent, I don't know that I could have carried the loss of a child. In the dark of my room, with only the candle to illuminate her face, I saw Isis shed a tear. It was a mother's tear, having suffered the great loss as well. "They arrive a gift from the gods, Walt. From that day forward, joy and fear walk hand in hand. My second born was taken at an early age, a piece of my heart buried with her. Though I bore two more, I never fully recovered." Even the gods weep, they say. I felt inadequate in that moment, incapable of consolation equal to the pain. "Walt, I need to leave you for a while. But let's make a last visit so you might know a place for the first time." There was little time to consider her meaning, as we were soon witnesses again to the death of a child. I looked upon mother with new eyes, revisiting what I'd first seen as a boy. Jesse was there, as were Mary Elizabeth and Hannah Louisa. Father was absent, perhaps making arrangements. In the cradle was our baby sister, taken at six months by influenza. Mother never again spoke of her, though I realize now a piece of her died that autumn morning. Andrew, George, Thomas, and Edward all came after. But her last girl was laid to rest that afternoon in an unmarked grave. I ache for my dear mother and regret my inability to comfort her.

February 19
We spent the evening with Willie. Just six weeks old and already he has a personality. His parents live nearby and are friends of Thomas. Today being their anniversary, Thomas volunteered to sit with him so they could have the night out. It's fascinating, watching Thomas with children. Not having raised Ling, I imagined he had little experience in such matters. But I've observed enough lately to see that he has a deft hand and a gentle way with children. Willie is a delightful chap. Eyes big and dark. Little fat balls for cheeks. A chin, round and firm, supporting a tiny mouth that mirrors his infant mind. When he's awake, it changes every few seconds, revealing pleasure, curiosity, hunger, a wet diaper. I held him while Thomas prepared dinner. Willie easily found a home in the crook of my arm, stretching and yawning, unconcerned that I was a stranger. He reminds me of George. Mother's seventh. I was ten when he arrived. As Jesse and I were the oldest, we helped a lot. I never tired of entertaining him. Perhaps my poetry has roots in the stories I fabricated. Whether he understood or not, he hung on every word. And once he learned to navigate the world, on hands and knees at first and then upright, he followed me everywhere. It saddened me to quit school in his first year, entering the world when he still needed a big brother. Andrew was just three at the time, too young to teach George much of anything. Thomas and I alternated eating and parenting. After dinner

and the dishes, I held Willie again, my heart opening to his tiny universe. Long after I'm gone, Willie will be making his way. Judging from what I've seen of his parents, he will have had a good start. I do hope that Thomas can stay in his life.

February 20

Thomas spoke with Ling late yesterday. She certain she won't be returning from China, except for the promised Christmas visits. Good father that he is, he's taking it upon himself to vacate her apartment, separating what she needs from what can be given away. There's a gap in his schedule, so we flew to Boston this morning. I told him I'd like to help. He appreciated my offer but declined, explaining that the task will be a personal one. I understood. Rather than stay in the city, Thomas suggested I spend a few days at the Pond. "It will likely be your last visit, Walt. With little more than a month, it's best you spend some time with yourself. Feast on your life, as your friend suggested, and continue preparing for the journey ahead. He was right of course, so I boarded the 1:30 Concord at Logan, arriving in Portland by 4:00. Thomas had made arrangements for a driver and within an hour I was at that tiny sanctuary overlooking the water. Little had changed from my last visit, with the exception of the snow cover. Sunny days having reduced it by several inches. The cupboards were well stocked and in the freezer were frozen dinners I've grown fond of. After much debate, I chose the chicken fajitas. Thanks to the microwave, I was at the table within minutes, a hot meal and a bottle of Dos Equis before me. After cleaning up, I took to the easy chair and counted my blessings. A second bottle of DE ushering in the night.

February 21

I woke in a sweat, a dream having occupied my sleep for hours. Though I recalled few of the specifics, there lingered a sense of urgency. Questions had been posed for which I had no answer. It was as if I'd been sitting for an exam. Success meant I'd move on. Failure, and I would be left behind. I dressed quickly, intent on traversing the shoreline trail to the far side. The early light was sufficient, and I made easy work of it. Still, I feared I would be too late. Arriving at the Tower, I was heartened by the smoke curling upward from the chimney. "C.G. is alive," I told myself. "He will surely have the answers." I entered without introduction. As expected, he was resting in his easy chair, the fire a comfort as always. Turning slightly, he spoke. "Walt, you have questions. Please sit down." He reached slowly for the pipe, struck the match, and inhaled. Passing it, I could see there'd been a change. C.G had aged a decade since our last meeting. "Speak, my friend. My days are numbered. Fewer than yours, I fear." I couldn't help myself and blurted out, "Does something of us live on?" Retrieving the pipe, he drew in the smoke as if for the last time. "Dear Walt. The closer we are to the finish, the less it seems we know. What I can say is there is no proof, in the scientific sense, that anything of us is preserved. At most, there is a probability that some aspect of our psyche continues beyond death." I slumped in my chair, deflated for the moment. But something inside pressed on. "If consciousness did survive upon death, what might it look like?" Again he inhaled, the vapor offering sustenance. "It's my belief that the maximum awareness realized on earth constitutes the upper limit of knowledge to which the dead can attain. That's why man's time here is of such importance." Panic took hold of me. What had I accomplished over seven decades? Have my poems contributed in any way? C.G reached for my hand, grasping it with a warmth I sorely needed. "Walt, much of what I know at this time of my life means little. What I hold onto, though, is that the purpose of our existence is to kindle a light in the darkness of mere being. Rest assured, my friend, you have done much. Let's enjoy the day and talk again this evening."

February 22

It was a vigorous day. I gathered firewood much of the morning, splitting it when necessary, then bundled and stacked it beneath the overhang. Inside work occupied the afternoon. Baking bread, preparing a stew for the week, cleaning up in the kitchen and elsewhere. Dinner was leisurely. C.G. spoke of his advanced age and the recent emergence of early memories. He recounted at length his childhood, his university days, and the many hours spent with the mentally ill at the Burgholzi hospital. He learned much from the dreams and fantasies of those under his care. "Looking back over my long life, Walt, it's been the inner life that has brought the greatest meaning. Awards, honors, recognition, all seem inconsequential now." He inquired of my inner world; the images and figures residing there. "My mother, father, and my siblings live in me," I confided. "Alongside them are others I've never met, known only by their words. They were most active during the creative years. The stretch of time when my muse visited nearly every day." C.G. seemed pleased by my account. "You should call upon them again. I'm certain they miss your attention." He then said there's a process by which unconscious contents can be brought forth. "The object is to give voice to that which is not normally heard." He explained that the first stage is like dreaming with open eyes. "You should endeavor to choose a figure and concentrate on it by catching hold of it and looking at it. The second stage is participation with it." He stressed that I enter into the process as though I was one of the figures. As if the drama being enacted is real. "If you do that - if you can integrate the unconscious with your consciousness - your remaining days will have greater meaning." I was humbled by C.G.'s concern for the unseen within me. "Walt, my home is yours for the next few days. Enjoy it and come to know yourself better."

February 23

I walked the shoreline much of the day, returning to the Tower just in time for dinner. I ate in silence as C.G. told of his middle years and the onset of the second half of life. Afterward we shared the pipe until the fire burned low and I excused myself. Anxious to attempt what he had suggested, I retired to my room, hoping to summon the original "good gray poet." Long before I read Homer, I listened to his tales. The exploits of Odysseus and his men sparked within me a love for the epic. Seated at the small desk, I concentrated my full attention on the inner image that has remained unchanged for decades. Perhaps because of my experience with Isis, it wasn't long before I was standing on the edge of a distant land, Homer at my side. An approaching ship soon landed, and the crew came ashore with two sheep in tow. "It is Odysseus, having been sent by Circē to the dark realm of Perséphonē and of grim Hades. He's here to consult Tirésias, the blind prophet from Thebes." Setting foot on the sand, the small band made its way to the place Circē had spoken of. Waiting for them was the blind prophet. Wielding his sword, Odysseus dug a pit, pouring into it a mixture of milk, honey, wine, and water. He offered a prayer for the dead then cut the throats of the sheep, allowing the blood to fill the shallow pit. Ghosts swarmed up, crowding around the pit. Among them was the ghost of Odysseus' mother. Speechless, she couldn't look him in the face. "Tirésias," Odysseus pleaded, "what can I do to make her see me?" The prophet answered without hesitation, "Whichever ghost you allow to drink the blood will speak to you." Odysseus waited until his mother came forward and drank. She immediately recognized him, crying out, "My child, how did you come to the land of darkness while still alive? Have you not gone home to Ithaca and seen your wife in your palace?" Odysseus replied, "Mother, necessity brought me to Hades to consult the prophet. I've yet to set foot on my own land, wandering these many years from one misery to another. Please tell me, what happened to you? How did you die? Do you have news of my father? And what of my dear wife and son? Is she at home with the boy or has she married?" His mother answered, "Your father yet lives on his farm, sleeping with the servants in clothes wretched and threadbare. There he lies, mourning your death. I died of that same sorrow. But your wife is alive and still faithful, though she weeps day and night." Odysseus stepped forward to embrace her. Three times he tried and three times she slipped through his arms like a shadow. He cried out, "If only we could hold each other. Or are you a phantom sent by Perséphonē to load more sorrow upon me?" She responded, "My child, I am not a phantom. It is what happens to mortals after they die. When fire consumes the body, the spirit slips out and flutters away like a dream. Please make haste and return to the light. When you reach Ithaca, tell your dear wife everything."

February 24
At breakfast, I spoke with C.G. about my meeting with Homer, and of my dismay. I'd hoped the poet and I would talk of our craft, and the pleasure that comes from its exercise. Instead, I was witness to a most heartbreaking scene. C.G. explained that it doesn't work the way I imagined. "You may summon an inner figure, but you have no control of what accompanies it. The figures residing in your unconscious live independent of you." It's difficult to grasp the world C.G. is so familiar with. Nevertheless, I trust he knows what he's talking about. "I'd like to continue this exploration. What advice do you have?" "Walt, If it's the poets who most interest you, I suggest you summon those with a lighter spirit." After dinner I returned to my room, intent on proceeding as C. G. suggested. Again, concentrating with all my being, I called forth Li Po, that Chinese poet I took great pleasure in and whom Chuang was particularly fond of. With little hesitation, the old man emerged. Standing among yellow flowers as far as I could see, his long, thin beard, slanted brows, and black cap were as I had imagined. Alone but for a cup and a pot of wine, he beckoned me to partake, which I did. He then lifted the cup to the moon and asked that it drink with us. Receiving no response, he sighed, sad that the moon was incapable. "I have no other friends here. Only my wine for company. My shadow goes emptily along, and I never say a word." Li said he was happy once and to be happy again he must sing and dance and imagine that the moon accompanies him. "If I dance, my shadow dances with me. And if I'm not yet drunk, the moon and my shadow are friends." I politely asked what happens if he has drunk too much. "Then we part, and I'm alone again." I told him I know his poetry well and enjoy it very much. "It would be an honor if you would delight me with your favorites." His

eyes twinkled and a broad smile spread across his face. Deep into the evening he recited one poem after another until his pot was empty and the moon danced with the stars. "Mr. Walt, you are a true companion. I hope we meet again, deep in the Milky Way."

February 25

I felt a kinship with Li Po and would like to have stayed longer, but in two days I'm to meet Duc Lai. With only a night and a day remaining with C.G., I had time for just one more visit. Completing the preparation, I scanned the horizon of my inner landscape, on the lookout for the Persian upon whom all seek inspiration. It wasn't an easy task, as the land of mystery flanked by the Mediterranean, Black, and Caspian Seas has given birth and nurtured many great ones. But finally he showed himself, seated alone on a stone bench, observing the play of the village children. He looked up, catching my gaze as he would a butterfly. His eyes a deep dark brown, twin sanctuaries of the sublime. Before I could introduce myself, he spoke. "Walt, old fellow, we finally meet. I've looked forward to this day, as we have much in common. Sit my friend, let us talk before Shams returns. He's likely to monopolize the conversation." I nearly blushed at the attention. "I'm honest when I tell you that I'm not jealous that in the age from which I've traveled, your poetry is more popular than mine." He appreciated the compliment but said his poems were written for God and for lovers, and no others. "That said, my friend, I do hope those of your time find something of value in my verse." I then asked if he would share his thoughts on aging, as I'm still learning its true purpose. "There are many questions once one begins the inquiry. Why does the date palm lose its leaves in autumn? Why does a beautiful face grow old and the head of hair become bald? Why does the young man, straight as a spear, bend over double late in life?" I responded that I've asked similar questions but received no response. "Have you inquired of God, my friend? The answers are his, and his alone." I admitted I had not, believing I could rely on those wiser than me. "I have posed the questions, Walt, and listened. This is what I have learned. We put on borrowed robes and pretend they are ours. God takes them back, so we learn that the robe of appearance is only on loan. Likewise, our lamp is lit from another lamp. In the end, God asks only for our gratitude."

February 26

At breakfast, C.G. ate in silence, allowing me to speak freely. Though he's shared much, I find him to be an attentive listener. He's like Thomas in that way. Each has an allegiance to something inside himself.

Their loyalty is to the internal. Their need for external validation having long passed. To be in their presence is to be in a space that's safe and secure. Sitting with either of them, I find myself imagining I'm in mother's womb as she listens intently to the beat of my heart, the nuances of each thump and pause. I can't recall anyone in my lifetime, other than mother, who attended to my thoughts as well as Thomas and C.G. Even Emerson, kind as he was in those days, seemed to place opinion above attention. I have to say, though, that since passing over he's improved a good deal. It was midmorning before I realized how long I'd gone on. I apologized to C.G., though he didn't seem to mind. Then it struck me. This is likely the last day I'll ever be with him. I asked, almost pleaded for him to speak of his life as he prepares to move on. "I have no complaints, life having given me much. Everything developed by destiny. It was as it had to be." He then surprised me by saying that, in advanced age, he has no definite convictions. "I know only that I was born and exist and have been carried along on the foundation of something unknown." He spoke of Lao Tzu, offering the sage as an example of the old man with superior insight who desires to return into the eternal and unknowable meaning. "Old age has its limitations. Nevertheless, the eternal in man and the mysteries of nature fill my days. I want for nothing more." Just then, there was a knock on the door. "Walt, it's Emerson. You need to be on your way."

LAST MONTH

February 27

I was with Emerson at the edge of the park. "I'll be leaving you here, Walt. Duc is waiting. You understand that the morning you first met him was not by chance?" I did not know. But I wondered, Thomas having told me anything is possible. "It doesn't surprise me now. Very little surprises me these days. Nevertheless, I'm amazed." "Good, Walt. Isn't that the way it should be, right up to the end?" Such a comforting thought. Perhaps I will be amazed, if I expect to be. "Let's meet here in three days, at the same time. There are matters we need to discuss. You should be going. Don't want to keep the good man waiting." Emerson vanished and Duc was there, on the bench, as promised. "Good to see you, Walt. Time does fly, doesn't it?" He reached for my hand and asked that I sit. "I believe this is your last month." "I'm counting the days," I told him. "They'll pass quickly. Let's do our best to make certain you are ready. There is a meditation technique known as Phowa. Do you know of it?" I said I didn't, as my experience with meditation is recent and very rudimentary. "That's okay, Walt. You'll learn. For now, just be aware that we Buddhists, no matter our lineage, practice it in preparation for death. Over the four days we're together, you will gain certainty that the self doesn't die with the body." I said that I have misgivings. "Do your best, Walt, not to be preoccupied by the possibilities. Sleep well and return tomorrow with Thomas. There are plans to be made."

February 28

Thomas was pleased to meet Duc, though introductions weren't necessary as Emerson had spoken to each of the other. After an exchange of greetings, Duc directed his attention to me. "Walt, have you given thought to your last days? Who do you want with you? Where would you like to be?" I admitted the specifics hadn't entered my mind. That when I consider that hour and minute, I fixate on the notion that one moment I'll be alive and the next not. "It will be like the switch on the wall of my room. Death will come as easily as turning off the light."

232

Duc smiled. "In one respect it's like that. Yet it is not. Annihilation is perceived only by the observer. But before we get to that, it's important that your final days be passed with great intention. No one but you should decide how they will be spent." A warm feeling passed over me, and with it a realization that the universe is benign, even kind. I said I'd like to take a train ride, stopping in Chicago and New York City before taking a bus to the sea. "Along the way, I would see many people, holding their faces and committing them to memory." Thomas asked, "And what of your arrival, Walt?" I responded that I hoped there would be a cabin. That the sun and the wind would be just outside, and I could walk if I was able. "Of course, I want the two of you with me. No one else, as I would have already said my goodbyes." They promised that, if at all possible, it would be that way. Duc spoke softly. "Each of your remaining days is precious. I have no doubt you will honor their sanctity." Standing to leave, he reached under his robe and retrieved a small, yellow book. "Walt, this is *The Tibetan Book of Living and Dying*. It has benefited many. I ask that you spend time with it so when we're together again, you will know how to proceed." I took hold of it, expressing my gratitude. He bowed in return and left.

February 29

C.G. says some dreams are compensatory. A message is sent in hope that one's attitude might be corrected. Others are prophetic, and tell the story of one's future, perhaps years in the making. A few affirm a decision under consideration. Of the compensatory, I've had many. Some ignored and others received for the advice they offer. Likewise, I've been visited by a prophet who foretold what I might become. As a boy on the streets, laboring for pennies, I would dream at night that I was old, with white hair and a beard, sitting at my desk with a single book that revealed a poet's life. But last night's was unlike any I've ever had. I was in a house, built long before my time. A bed was waiting by the window, a deathbed, just the right size for my heft and frame. A voice within whispered that I should lie down. That I would be safe to finish what must be finished. I accepted the invitation and took my resting place. After some time, when all thoughts of before had vanished, I heard a sound, rather like music. A spirit, waiting patiently, thumped its staff and called: "Come, Walt. Come. It is time." I woke from my dream free of all care and concern.

March 1

I had another dream. As vivid as the night before. Walking beside me was someone I could not see. It wasn't Emerson, nor C.G., nor Isis. It was someone I visit on occasion, but more often forget. I had the oddest sensation that the I that is Walt, is not me. Instead, the one beside me is who I truly am. The one who remains silent when I speak. Who forgives when I need forgiveness. It occurred to me that the benevolent I, the I who goes where Walt cannot, will be with me at death and will continue on after my last breath. Perhaps the I in my dream was my childhood friend. Neglected for so many years, but present when I turn to him in these latter days. In my dream, we walked the city streets until nearing the intersection of a major thoroughfare. Waiting at the red light was Emerson. I approached, but my companion did not. "He's not left, Walt. He's merely stepped aside so we can talk." At another time, I would have been irritated with Emerson, showing up unannounced as he often does. But nothing happens by chance, and in my dream I welcomed him with sincerity. "Ralph, you said we'd meet again in three days. Thank you for keeping your word." He seemed touched by my greeting. And when he took my hand there was a warmth I'd never recognized. "I want to suggest something to you Walt. It might be good if you made a visit to Long Island. It's been years since you last saw your family. There might be something you would like to say or a gesture you would like to make. The decision is yours, Walt." The light turned green and I was left alone to ponder.

March 2

All day I reflected on Emerson's suggestion, realizing I've thought little of my family since coming here. There's been much to experience and learn. Growing pains, too. Perhaps, however, my neglect was by design. Not by me, Walt, but by my unconscious. It could be I wasn't ready. That it would have to come down to the end before returning to those days. My friend may have had a hand in it. Steering me away from the painful times until I'd developed sufficient strength. With Thomas out late, I had a light dinner, prepared a sherry with ice and orange, and retired by the fire. For some minutes I remained in the present day, occupied with the virus and the growing fear of it. Local authorities have reported nothing about its presence but warn that it's inevitable. I have no worry for myself. Instead, I fret for those I consider friends, out in the world and at risk of exposure. One of them could be among the two percent who perish. Imagining the interment, I found myself seated on an old grave on the Whitman burial hill. Fifty or more markers plainly traceable, and just as many decayed. There's always the deepest eloquence in these Long Island graveyards. Sadness, too. Though two and three centuries have passed, the sight of them grieves me, especially those of the Whitmans and the Van Velsors. Nearby is my grandfather Cornelius; Grandmother Naomi at his side. Many of my generation, brothers and sisters included, are within walking distance. The scene, the delicate odor of the woods, the slight rain, the emotional atmosphere of the place, summoned reminiscences long forgotten. I'll return tomorrow to remember.

March 3

A man's family is the people who love him, who comprehend him. For the most part I was isolated from my people. In a certain sense they were strangers to me, or I was a stranger to them. They always missed my intentions and didn't know me for who I became. Nevertheless, they were family and I loved them. George, Jeff, and Mary, they were the normal ones; though Mary suffered greatly from rheumatism. Yet returning to Whitman hill, my thoughts were with the others, the damaged ones. My siblings dealt blows so great they were rendered incapable of success in life. I grieve for them and regret not doing all I could to ease their pain. Jesse, who lost his mind and died in the asylum. Andrew, the alcoholic, who died still a young man. My beloved Hannah, neurotic, quite likely psychotic near the end. But my tears flow heaviest for Eddy, partly crippled and retarded from birth. A poor, stunted boy, he had the convulsions, the damnable fits, that left him not half himself. I promised mother just before she died that I'd look after him. I stinted, spared, saved, cherished, and watched poor, helpless Eddy. In my last decade we visited, though mostly in silence. Eddy was inarticulate, and I sadly ruminative. When we did talk, we spoke in monosyllables. Mostly, though, I would take his hand and hold it, saying nothing. Eddy lived in a darkness. He appealed to my heart, my two arms, but I could never reach him. This afternoon, as the sun waned, I walked the adjacent meadow, gathering the early wildflowers - red trillium, blood root, trout lily, and spring beauty. When I could hold no more, I divided them equally among several markers, spreading the delicate perfume around the graves of those I loved.

March 4

I'd forgotten that father wasn't buried with the Whitmans. Strolling today among the generations, it saddened me that he'd been hastily laid to rest in Brooklyn. I don't recall the reason other than that George, Jeff, and I were too busy with our lives to make proper arrangements. I recall the day of his passing, just a week after *Leaves* first went on sale. The three of us had barely made it to his bedside. Hannah did not, and Mary didn't learn of his death 'til much later. Though my relationship with father was a complicated one, I felt a deep, unspoken kinship with him. Moody and taciturn, as those of English stock often are, his temper was terrible to behold when aroused. Most severe during the periods of heavy drinking. Yet he loved children and cattle. I recall riding with him on trips to town. He'd load the wagon with children from the road and give them a lift. And despite his failures in business, he was handy as a carpenter. More than once he would say, "Oh what a comfort it is to lie down on a floor laid with your own hands, in a house of your own handiwork - cellar and walls and roof." Sitting on Whitman hill and looking back, I could see that the unhappiness of my childhood had less to do with him than with our family's precarious circumstances. Two years before father died, he and I took a week's jaunt to the place where I was born. Riding around the familiar spots, viewing and pondering and dwelling long upon them, everything came back to me. We went to the old Whitman homestead on the upland and took a view eastward over the broad and beautiful farmlands that had been my father's and his father's. There was the new house, the big oak, the well, the sloping kitchen-garden. Nearby, the grove of stately black walnuts. On the other side of the road spread the apple orchard, the trees planted by hands long moldering in the grave. We both became teary, reminded of what was once but no longer. Returning to that moment, I embrace him and forgive him much.

March 5
Lingering this morning amongst the Van Velsor tombstones, I considered my Dutch heritage and how much I was one of them - grandson of Cornelius and Naomi, great-grandson of Garrett and Mary. Recalling each face and pair of hands as best I could, I descended from the ancient grave place and walked the eighty or ninety rods to the site of the Van Velsor homestead. Mother was born there, and every spot was familiar to me as a child. The rambling, dark gray, shingle-sided house, with sheds, pens, and the great barn. I have little doubt that not a vestige is left, all pulled down, erased, and the plough and harrow passed over the foundations. Yet I imagine mother, carefree girl that she was, still wandering those wooded surroundings. The Van Velsors were noted for fine horses and mother, it was said, was a daring rider. Years later, asleep on her deathbed in Camden, I didn't see her as elderly and wasting away. Always, she had been next to me. Always, she was and will be my great chum. Mother thought I was a wonderful thing. No matter the difficulty or circumstance, she would put her hand in mine, press it, and look at me, as if to say everything was all right. Though she never

understood *Leaves,* and inquired little of it, I do believe my poet's traits came from her womb, and from her birth out of her mother's. I long thought of myself as her only child. In complexion, features, gait, and voice I took after her, favored her, and attributed to her every creative impulse in myself. *Leaves* was the flower of her temperament active in me, a reflection of her reality and transparency, of her mingled Dutch strain of the practical and the transcendental. Her death was the great shadow of my life.

March 6

C.G. once said that the past is never past. Returning to the ancestral burial ground, I know that to be true. Painful though it was at times, I recognized the value in it. I needed to be reminded of my family lines, however tenuous they became in later years. I needed to touch my blood and kin before departing. But sitting with Molly and Kicus this evening I was ready to put that past behind me, certain in the thought that it was all meant to be. I have no desire to sever the ties, for they will always be the first. I believe now, however, that I am part of a stream of life - human and other - that for eons has been flowing into the present and will flow on for eons into the future. I am one with all people, and all species. Molly and Kicus have convinced me of that, as has the great oak out back, the hens, and the red buds out front heralding the spring season. Relaxing in the presence of my faithful sidekick and my new long-eared friend, the chair opposite us was quietly taken. Emerson had joined us, content to rest and say nothing. After a while, I glimpsed that our minds were interconnected. Or perhaps not connected at all, but a single mind. Thoughts traveled seamlessly from one to the next. None more or less important than another. I once mused while under the influence of an intoxicant that such was the reality of nature. This evening I experienced the truth of it. A fifth voice joined the conversation from a distance. It was Lao, coming on board as if he'd been with us all along. The pleasure he brings to my psyche is unsurpassed. I've wondered who I would be if I'd grown up with him. But regrets are no longer a part of my life. It's enough that Lao entered it when he did. As the fire died down so did our chatter, and silence ensued. Then, quite gently, Lao inquired if I was still interested in meeting his family. I'd forgotten the invitation but immediately said yes. "I'm delighted, Walt. But the timing has changed as the month of storms will soon be upon my people. It's best you avoid it." He asked if I could depart at midnight, as Emerson would be free to accompany me. "You will arrive on the eastern shore, Walt. Everyone will be there to greet you." I could barely contain my excitement.

March 7

The eastern horizon at dawn was ablaze with orange and yellow. I was greeted by Lao and his family. But there were more, many more. A thousand at least, on the beach and clinging to sheer cliffs rising high above the sea. I'd never seen anything like it, or even imagined it. This was a city, as densely populated as my Brooklyn. Everywhere, pure white heads with coal black eyes were fixed on me. There wasn't a hint of hostility, or fear. Only curiosity. Soon, I understood. Lao emerged from a nearby gathering and approached. Trailing behind were six or seven younger ones, children to adolescents, and their mother I assumed. "I'm so pleased you made the trip, Walt. As you can see, my people have a considerable interest in you. Quite understandably, as few humans have ever set foot on these shores. Legend has it that a wise one once stopped here, though we have no record of it. An occasional poet has visited as well. I want you to meet my mate and our children. I've told them about our special relationship." One by one, they waddled toward me, the littlest first then the next in size until the last, nearly as large as Lao. Each bowed, referring to me as "Uncle Walt." Their mother then graciously extended a welcome, addressing me the same. His family accounted for, Lao whispered that it would be a busy day. "It's custom that every member of the community come forward, no matter the species of the newcomer." Looking about, I wondered how it would be possible. The remainder of the morning Lao and I walked the length of the beach in either direction. By midday I'd met everyone. But there were the others, completely inaccessible. Sensing my weariness, Lao sat me in the shade, spread his wings a full ten feet, and let out a screech originating from deep inside. Within seconds, every resting bird rose up, adjusted the angle of its wings, and glided down the cliffsides, alighting as close as possible to Lao and me. Introductions continued until all had made their acquaintance. The sun about to set, Lao and his eldest led me to a shelter where I would have privacy. Settling in, I inquired of Lao why every one of his people referred to me as "Uncle Walt." He smiled, promising to enlighten me in the morning.

March 8

There was no sleeping in. The squawk of hungry young ones over the sound of pounding waves made it impossible. I resisted at first, but finally opened my eyes fully, only to find Lao within an arm's length, eyes closed and following his breath. Sensing my restlessness, he suggested we take a walk. "There is a narrow canyon a short distance from here. It offers a silence found nowhere else on the island." Making our way through the underbrush, we arrived at the entrance. From there, a narrow path led deep into a nave as awe-inspiring as that of a medieval cathedral. Far overhead was a streak of blue sky. Below, only the sound of our footsteps on loose rock. "This is where we bring the young to have first contact with the ineffable. Only later, when they've taken flight, do they know it again." I thought back to my early education and its lack of substance. "Walt, I know you have questions. Let me answer them for you." I wasn't sure where to start, there were so many. So, I started at the beginning. "Lao, do your people believe time had an origin?" "Excellent question, Walt. Yes, we do. And we believe there was a time before its origin. And a time before the time before the beginning of time." Unable to grasp where Lao was taking me, I thought it best to return to earth. "Lao, you seem ageless. Do you know how old you are?" He smiled. "The truth is, Walt, I don't. I'm the oldest of our people and have had several mates and many more children. But we don't mark time in human years. I can say that I've seen and learned much." I then asked the question that had been nagging me since yesterday. "Why does everyone call me Uncle Walt?" Lao smiled again. "To be an uncle is to be revered. While we often have long lives, it's not uncommon to die young. Hurricanes take us. The nets of fishermen. The garbage and pollutants that poison our seas. Widows are left to raise the young. Fortunately, our kind is wired to parent. Brothers of the lost ones are the first to come forward, adopting nieces and nephews as if their own. There is a second reason we call you uncle. Tomorrow you will know why. Let's be content now to simply listen so we can be touched by the hand of God."

March 9
Free this morning to go wherever I liked, I learned that age is no limitation among these gentle creatures. The longer the lifespan, the greater the respect shown. Lao's people are wonderful storytellers. When not feeding their young or tending to the needs of a partner, they're seated in small circles reveling in a tale told and retold by one who has seen the world. Even the youngest sit spellbound as a yarn is spun of an adventure on the high seas or in a far-off land. These albatross value two seemingly incompatible ways of being. They're equally at home with family and communal life as they are aloft, solitary and for months on end. Near the place where the sand meets the cliff, several had gathered. There was an opening and I took my place in the circle. Bits of raw fish and tropical fruit were passed as a wise one recounted the story of a voyage and the hunt for a great whale. I was delighted to learn that the cast of characters is among my favorites:

Captain Ahab, Ishmael, Queequeg, Starbuck, Stubb. My companions knew the story too, mouthing the words in synchrony with the narrator. Anxious to speak with Lao, I quietly withdrew, making my way in the direction of the family nest. Halfway there, he came alongside. "Good morning, Walt. It was nice to see you enjoying yourself. Qui is revered by everyone and is happiest when breathing new life into the great myths." I wanted to tell Lao that I wish I'd been born one of his kind. Instead, I inquired of their wisdom; their secret. "There is no secret, Walt. We merely adhere to that which the ancients taught. In dwelling, be close to the land and sea. In meditation, be true to the heart. In speech, be honest. When dealing with others, be kind." I then asked of governance. Lao responded that, in all things, simplicity is the key. "The ruler must be just and say little. Example is always the best teacher." Approaching his brood, I asked a final question. "What is the second reason they call me Uncle Walt?" Again, the smile. "I'm glad you reminded me, Walt. In our language, there are two meanings for the word uncle. As with the first, the second is a term of respect. We honor the storytellers, as you know. Likewise, the poets, for they were the first. As the brother sustains his nieces and nephews, the poet offers sustenance to each of us. In good times and in bad, we are elevated by the language of image. My people have long known of you Walt. Many of your lines are memorized at an early age. I need to be with my family now, but please consider sharing your verse before leaving us."

March 10

Lao spoke with Emerson in the night and shared their conversation. "The human virus is spreading, Walt. Emerson and Thomas agree that it's best you return home. If conditions are right, you will depart at midnight." I didn't know what to say, except that I wasn't ready. For the first time since leaving Camden, I prayed that time might stand still. Never have I been treated with such unconditional care, nor witnessed the intelligence of nature manifest at such a high level. Lao assured me I would not be forgotten. "You are beloved, Walt. We see the eternal within you." He then made a request. "There is a cave on the far side of the island. The interior space reaches high into the mountain. Both sun and moon find their way into it through ancient fissures. We call the place "The Great Hall," meeting there only on special occasions. As the moon will be nearly full tonight, we would be honored if you would join us and share your poetry." I didn't hesitate, asking only that I be allowed time to prepare. "Of course. My eldest will come for you at sunset. Everyone will be waiting." I spent the remainder of the day at my desk in Brooklyn, in the months before the first edition of *Leaves*. Line by line I read what had yet to be given to the world. An energy coursed through my veins that had long abandoned me. Sunset came and I was summoned. Following my guide step for step, I was hopeful I wouldn't disappoint. When we arrived, every seat was taken from floor to ceiling. In the center was Lao, standing on a rock at least six feet square. He beckoned me to join him. Wasting no time, I was introduced. "This is the moment we have long waited for. The greatest poet of his people is now with us. Please honor him with your silence." With that, I was left alone but for my muse who stood with me for the duration. The words tumbled without effort or pretense: "Stop this day and night and you shall possess the origin of all poems . . . Clear and sweet is my soul and clear and sweet is all that is not my soul . . . As God comes a loving bedfellow and sleeps at my side all night . . . Loafe with me on the grass, loose the stop on your throat . . . Has anyone supposed it lucky to be born, it is just as lucky to die." On and on, propelled by a volition not my own. As if in a trance, controlled by some unseen hypnotist. In a moment of sanity, I looked up and beheld that every word of mine was theirs as well. I finally stopped, exhausted. Time had stood still for an evening. Rising as one, the clamor was deafening. I sobbed with joy.

March 11

Detached from my body, I dreamt. From that vantage, I could see that my soul was not asleep, but wide awake. For the first time, I realized it never sleeps. Instead, with eyes wide open, it watches for far-off things and listens at the shores of the great silence. When morning came, I was in my own bed, reunited with my body. Seated in the chair next to me was Thomas. "You're home, Walt. I'm sorry your return was premature. Were it in my power, you would have remained with Lao until the last day." I told him I understood and appreciated his concern. "I'm carrying a sweet sadness Thomas. The time was brief, but my life would have been incomplete without it. Now I know it's possible for sentient beings to live in peace. It's given me hope." Thomas responded that we have much to learn from the higher species, if only we would make the effort. He then expanded on what Lao said about the spread of the virus. It appears a majority of the population will be infected. Many will die. Services will be compromised, including public transit. "Walt, you chose to spend your final days by the sea. For that to be a reality, I believe we should travel by car. To do otherwise is to risk being stranded en route." Though disappointed with Thomas' assessment, I didn't allow myself to dwell on it. Instead, I assured him a cross-country drive suited me fine and that I would look forward to it. "I suggest we leave the second Sunday from now. In the meantime, Walt, spend time with the book given to you by Duc. The attitude you bring to your last hours is critical."

March 12

Molly grew quite shaggy over the winter. I like her that way but, with spring coming, Thomas insisted she get a trim. So off they went to the dog groomer, leaving me home alone with Kicus. He's a mystery to me. Youthful in demeanor, yet ancient in attitude. Thomas says he's quite old, having lived far longer than any of his generation. This morning Kicus followed me about as I did my chores. It was as if he had something to say. After a time I rested, and he did the same, first at my feet and then on my lap. I patted him on the head then stroked his ears in the manner he likes. As I did, an odd thought appeared, then a question: "You have two weeks, Walt. Are you prepared?" Responding out loud, and to no one in particular, I said, "Of course I am." In a tone of incredulity, another thought, more urgent, "You are not. Duc Lai left you with the guide. You would be wise to consult it." I couldn't deny it. I've been neglectful, wishfully thinking that the end determined by Emerson is not as imminent as it actually is. Retrieving the Tibetan book, I discovered that Duc had placed a marker at the midpoint. There, I opened it to chapter fourteen, "The Practices for Dying." I was confronted with the "Moment of Death" and the imperative to "Let Go of Attachment." Thanking Kicus for his insistence, I began. By the time Thomas and Molly returned, I had three times completed the Phowa meditation "Transference of Consciousness." The author encourages the adherent to adopt it as a daily practice. "It is the most essential practice we can do to prepare for our own death."

March 13

Following the Tibetan way, I assumed the posture, relaxing completely. Having brought my mind home, I imagined before me a golden light in the sky. It was the embodiment of truth, wisdom, and compassion. Focusing all my being upon it, I began to pray: "Through the power of the light that streams from you, may all my negative karma, destructive emotions, obscurations, and blockages be purified and removed." Softly, a voice I recognized followed mine, word for word. It was that of Isis, seated across from me, cross-legged and eyes closed. We continued, "May I know myself forgiven for all the harm I may have thought and done." She then spoke directly: "I apologize for intruding, Walt. There is a final teaching I must impart. Together we've observed many faces of death. What you have yet to see are faces of those in ordinary times who have loosed the bonds of attachment. I would like to introduce you to some of them." Accepting her invitation, we stood in the corner of a small bedroom. Candles were lit, incense as well. The sound of a harp played from a small device. In the center of the room was a bed where a woman, about sixty, held her husband of many years. Isis whispered that he has long suffered with cancer, the pain unbearable at times. His physicians had subjected him to treatments that exacerbated his condition. Finally, the couple said no more. Shortly before we arrived, the woman had administered to her beloved a potion, designed to take away all pain and then release him. As we looked on, they prayed the Phowa prayer: "May I accomplish this profound practice of Phowa and die a good and peaceful death. And through the triumph of my death, may I benefit all other beings, living or dead." There was a moment of silence, and then the welcome sound of his last breath. At that moment, the candles flared up and then died out.

March 14

This evening, I practiced a variation of the Phowa meditation. As before, I began by resting quietly and then invoking the presence of light. I imagined my consciousness as a sphere of light, flashing out like a shooting star and piercing the heart of the presence in front of me. After some time, the light before me took on a form. It was that of Isis. I understood, without an exchange of words, that we'd be visiting the bedside of an English intellectual and writer. Late in life he experimented with psychedelic drugs as an aid in the expansion of his own consciousness. While on his deathbed, he asked his wife to inject him with a drug called LSD. Isis and I arrived as she finished. The dying man was at home and in a hospital bed, his wife beside him. Standing respectfully at a distance were two longtime friends. We took our positions behind them as the man's wife began to speak: "You can let go, darling. Forward and up. You are going forward and up, towards the light. Willing and consciously you are going, and you are doing this beautifully. You are going towards a greater love. You are going forward and up. It is so easy, so beautiful. Light and free. You are going towards a love greater than any you have ever known. You are going towards the greatest love. It is so easy, and you are doing it beautifully." She paused, then asked, "Do you hear me, darling?" He squeezed her hand. A short time later she asked the question again, but his hand didn't move. A minute or so after, his lower lip began to quiver, as if struggling for air. She spoke forcefully. "You are doing this beautifully and willingly and consciously, in full awareness. Darling, you are going towards the light." She repeated the words over and over again. The twitching lasted only a short time, seemingly responding to what she was saying. "Darling, you are doing this willingly and beautifully. Going forward and up, light and free, forward and up towards the light, into the light, into complete love." The twitching stopped as his breathing became slower and slower. There wasn't the slightest struggle. Finally, the breathing stopped, ceasing like the coda of a wonderful piece of music. A serene and beautiful death, it didn't feel as if his spirit left his body with the last breath. Instead, it had been gently leaving since he was given permission to let go.

March 15
Thomas and I talked at breakfast about the spread of the virus. Health experts are calling it a pandemic. The president minimized the crisis for weeks, insisting it would miraculously go away. He finally declared a national emergency after scientists and others convinced him of the gravity of the situation. All the while, he spoke of the "foreign virus." Thomas has read that people who look Asian and wear masks have been physically threatened and verbally assaulted. "It's sad," he said, "how humans often react out of fear. A person with the illness is not the infection. The enemy is the disease, not people." I shared my feelings, that those who shun strangers aren't just unmannerly, they're uncivilized. Thomas agreed. "Everyone infected needs our compassion, Walt. The elderly and uninsured the most." I obsessed about the virus all day but found a place of ease midway through the Phowa practice. As I recited "my mind and the mind of the Buddha are one," Isis arrived. "Humans are flawed, Walt. As you well know. Fear is the greatest obstacle to them seeing the best in others." She then told me of a virus that emerged near the end of the last century. Scientists called it AIDS. The disease took millions of lives, most in communities of homosexual lovers. She said millions around the world live with it today, but medical advances have greatly reduced the death rate. "Walt, I'd like us to visit a man who was spared. Yet, for most of his life he was forced to hide his true self. In his last his years, however, many came to see the Buddha within him." In a moment, we were two among several, gathered around the bed of a large man, a gentle giant. One by one, he was approached. Some kissed his hands. Some his cheeks. Others hugged his bear like frame, not wanting to let go. We stayed the day, and into the evening. Not until late did the crowd thin, leaving his most cherished friends to send him off. As if on cue, the eight of them drew close and sang a hymn the man learned as a child. The concluding words brought tears to his eyes, as they closed for the last time.

March 16

I thought about mother today. How she held the family together during the epidemic of the 1820s. I was too young to remember the devastation, but over the years it was a topic of conversation whenever the seasonal influenza was severe. "The fever," as it was called, spread across the country. Many families were decimated. Few were spared. This evening's practice focused on "right attitude" and the development of deep compassion. I learned that the Tibetans believe that what is intoned over and over with sincerity becomes reality: "I have arrived at the time of death, so now, by means of this death, I will adopt the attitude of loving kindness and compassion." Isis sat with me, reciting from memory. At the conclusion, she asked if I would accompany her to a nearby hospital. An elderly woman had been transported from a care facility where she'd been infected with the virus. She was clinging to the hope that her beloved son would arrive in time. In a matter of seconds, I was seated in the chair next to her bed. A mask over her face fed oxygen. A needle fed pain relief into her arm. There was no one present but Isis and me to witness her suffering. I thought of mother, of her last hour when I could do nothing but hold her hand. As the woman labored, my hand found hers, nearly lifeless. I held it tight, as if it was mother's, and prayed that she might see her son one last time. Some hours later, the door opened. A tall, slender man entered, holding a vase with flowers. Approaching the bed, he spoke softly. "Mom, it's me." Her eyes opened and her face exploded with joy as she held out her arms. "My dear boy. I could have died tonight, but chose not to, knowing you would come." She reached up as best she could and held him with all her might. Finally, unable to hold any longer, she fell back into the bed. Her eyes closed and she stepped into the long night.

March 17

It rained all day, as it does in the last days of autumn when winter is at the door. I was moody, the way I get when my bones feel a change coming. I never tolerated change, preferring old habits over the unknown. But scientists tell us that the universe is nothing but change, that even the subatomic world is a continual dance of creation and annihilation, of mass changing to energy and energy to mass. Even the Buddha taught that what is born will die; what has been gathered will be dispersed; and what has been accumulated will be exhausted. Isis arrived this evening, for the last time she said. "I will miss our travels, Walt. You have been a model student. I appreciate how you look at the world. Your poet's eye sees what others do not." I thanked her for the care she'd taken with me. "I don't know that anyone is ever ready, but I would be far less prepared without you." She then suggested we make a last visit. I expected to witness a death brought on by the virus, or another modern-day assassin. So, I was surprised to be standing in a crowd of brown-skinned natives, mostly men and boys, and most dressed in white. Not a word was being spoken, their undivided attention on an elderly man lying between two large trees. Isis said it was the Buddha, critically ill as a result of tainted food he'd eaten a few days before. Despite his grave condition, he spoke with gentle concern to his disciples. "The teachings which I have given you, I gained by following the path myself. You should follow them and conform to their spirit on every occasion." Then, with but a moment remaining, he uttered his last words. "Make of yourself a light. Rely upon yourself. Do not depend on anyone else. Make my teachings your light." And so, he left them to go their own way. On our return home, I inquired of Isis, "What kind of man is it that, even at the very end, cares more about others than himself?"

March 18

I dreamt that I was dying. That my time on earth was ending and there would be no more thoughts. No more past or future. My body was disintegrating into the basic elements and merging with the universe. Suddenly I was surrounded by a ball of fire, and the warmth inside me merged with it. The air in my body merged with the atmosphere, and the water with an infinite ocean. Whatever space my body had occupied merged with infinite space. Everything that had constituted me - body, mind, emotions, and thoughts - was gone. Yet something remained. It was the witness to the death of my mind and body. My true identity. The self that silently watches everything that comes and goes and remains after all is gone. When I woke, Emerson was waiting. He knew of my dream and what it foretold. "Walt, treat as sacred your remaining days. Sing and pray. Dance until you can no longer. Know that your life is in the hands of others. Reach out with your words while you can still speak. When speech abandons you, reach out with compassion to all who are visible and invisible." He then commented on my visit with the dying woman; how my compassion enabled her to live long enough for her son to arrive. "You must know, however, that you were infected. It makes little difference to you of course. But please keep your distance from Thomas and others and wash your hands." He then reached for mine and held them tightly. "I won't see you again, Walt, until it's time. Until then, love this world for better or worse, in sickness and in health, until your last breath."

March 19

I woke with a fever. The infection had taken hold. "So, this is how it ends," I thought. "Whether it's the virus that takes me or something else, it makes little difference. I'll be dead in a week no matter the cause." In a strange way, there's something right about it. To succumb to the unseen; to an alien life form that kills without knowing. The fact that I'll suffer the fate of thousands offers a certain solace. We're victims of an enemy that respects neither race, nor color, nor creed. I didn't want to get out of bed but needed to tell Thomas so he could plan accordingly. "We'll adjust, Walt. You realize we won't be able to travel east. I'm truly sorry for that." I told him there's nothing to apologize for. "I brought it on myself, and don't regret for a second having comforted the dear woman. I'll always treasure the look on her face when her son arrived." I then asked Thomas what needed to be done so he's not at risk. He described the protocol and said it would be best if my room was put in order. "The disease will move quickly, Walt. I'll meet with Duc today. By the end of the weekend we'll need him. By Monday it's likely you'll be confined to your bed. In the meantime, let's make the most of the next few days." I was struck by Thomas' calm and told him so. He said his year in the village had changed his life. "Chuang would frequently say that the Master treads lightly. Life is not serious for him, nor is death. He realizes what is essential and what is not. Even if the world collapsed, he would not be disturbed."

March 20

I was in my home in Camden, in the room where every day was spent. It was a week before I was to die, although I didn't know it. Seated at the table across from my bed, a bowl of chicken soup was in front of me. I studied it with curiosity and amazement. Quite suddenly, I was drawn to it, almost in a sexual way. It was no longer enough to observe and contemplate. Life must be experienced. I plunged my spoon deep into the broth, retrieving plump noodles and bits of scrumptious chicken, carrots, and celery. I beheld and then devoured them, my mind responding in great appreciation, as if it had been bathed in a warm liquid of good feeling. Each bite thereafter was the same, the fifth and sixth as savory as the first. Sadly, I discovered I had eaten all but one. For a moment I was paralyzed, unable to extend my hand and spoon. I looked down upon the one, as if it had life, and asked, "When you are gone, what is left?" The reply was immediate, but sincere and kind, "I don't know, Walt. No one does." I woke in a start, coughing, almost choking. I first thought there must be something stuck in my throat. Then I remembered what Thomas had told me about the symptoms and the order in which each would occur. For several minutes I tried to suppress them, but without success. I tried to ignore them, but my ability to control had fled. I relented, choosing to just observe them, leaving me to enjoy the remainder of the day. Thomas helped with my room, setting up a teapot with cup and saucer on the table. He brought down a heater, as I might be chilled at night. Then a small refrigerator and his phonograph player. He asked what I might like to listen to in the remaining days. I told him I've always wanted to hear Beethoven's symphonies, all nine of them. He smiled, "Anything is possible, Walt," then left me to my thoughts. I was surprised to find there to be few, and unimportant in the world of ideas. Thomas had left me a jar of M&M candies, equally red and green in number. I wondered if they'd been prepared for Christmas. I then looked closely at a red one. It had a thin white "M" imprinted on its face. Drawing back, I saw that they all did. "How was it done?" I wondered. "How could any number of fingers, or futuristic machines, accomplish such a task?" I imagined the assembly line, candies fifty abreast and extending infinitely in either direction. "Everything is a miracle," I mused.

March 21

Another dream. I was alone, seated at the bow of a small sailer, tethered to a dock by a single line. Friends and neighbors had gathered on shore. Thomas, Molly, Lao, Anna, Ling, Kicus, Duc Lai, and others. There was an urgency in the air. Gulls circled overhead, beating their wings and screeching at a high pitch. Harbor seals barked nearby. Suddenly a fierce wind blew, billowing the sail beyond its limits. The strain on the cleat too great, the line broke, pushing craft and passenger toward the open sea. I tried to wave to my dear ones, but in the rolling fog they had lost their faces. For a brief moment the tiller bounced wildly, but then an invisible hand wrested control. I was certain it was that of my friend. Deftly we navigated the maze of occupied moorings and lobster pots until all but the horizon was behind us. My friend at the helm, I was content to lie down with the family ghosts. Rocked by the infinite, I was free of life's burdens and at peace, forgetting that I'd wanted to stay forever. With the sun's rise I woke to the smell of spring, intent on living the day fully. Soon enough, though, I discovered that my legs weren't up to the task. Though rested, they were weary; my arms, too. With great effort I ascended the steps, arriving at the top short of breath. Thomas greeted me from the far side of the table and inquired about my night. I told him I'd slept well, keeping the dream to myself. He asked if I had plans. I responded that I hoped to visit the park one last time. But lacking the strength, I put it off. Somehow, though, my energy

returned in the late afternoon and Molly, Kicus, and I headed out. It was
slow going. By the time we reached the park, I was nearly spent. But
the bench was ahead, beckoning the three of us. With an effort I didn't
think I possessed, we made it, resting an hour or more high on the hill.
There was satisfaction in the accomplishment, as if we'd summitted Mt.
Everest. Surprisingly, the return home wasn't nearly as taxing. Thomas
called for us as we neared the kitchen. "Dinner is ready, Walt. I hope
you like it." Exhausted, but hungry, I dived into a most delicious
chicken noodle soup.

March 22
Again, I dreamed. I was riding on a blue ox. Lao Tzu, the great sage,
was seated in front with me behind. We were in a valley, surrounded by
a purple mist that dissipated just as we reached the frontier. There, a
guard approached and asked that we dismount. Recognizing Lao, he
bowed. Turning to me, he made a request: "Since you are going away,
Mr. Walt, would you write what you know to be the art of living for me
to share with later generations?" I agreed, promising to do my best. He
then sat me at a small table, providing a pen with ink and parchment. I
began, the words flowing effortlessly onto the paper:

*This is what you shall do. Love the earth and sun and the animals,
despise riches, give alms to everyone that asks, stand up for the stupid
and crazy, devote your income and labor to others, hate tyrants, argue
not concerning God, have patience and indulgence toward the people,
take off your hat to nothing known or unknown or to any man or number
of men, go freely with powerful uneducated persons and with the young
and with the mothers of families, read these in the open air every season
of every year of your life, re examine all you have been told at school or
church or in any book, dismiss whatever insults your own soul, and your
very flesh shall be a great poem and have the richest fluency not only in
its words but in the silent lines of its lips and face and between the lashes
of your eyes and in every motion and joint of your body.*

After I finished, I handed it to the guard to do with it what he liked. Lao
and I then mounted the ox and rode to the west, never to be heard from
again.

I woke with pain in my chest, my breathing more labored than yesterday.
With difficulty, I made it to the bathroom, having to rest on the toilet for
several minutes. Thomas must have heard me, knocking on the door
with concern, "Walt, are you alright? Can I help?" Unashamed, I

responded that I would appreciate any assistance. Wearing a hospital gown, mask, and surgical gloves, he helped me stand and then walked me back. "It's progressing rapidly, Walt. More than I anticipated. I had hoped to take you for a drive, but I don't think you can make it up the stairs." I had to agree, although I would have enjoyed a final excursion. He then asked if I was hungry. I replied that my appetite was gone, but a cup of hot cocoa might be nice. Leaving the room, Molly and Kicus entered, jumping up on the bed to keep me company. Thomas returned soon after with a tray, the cocoa, my pen and journal, and a small bell. "Normally, Walt, I'd insist you eat to maintain your strength. Instead, just let me know if your hunger returns. I'll prepare whatever you like." I slept off and on most of the day, never caring to eat. Duc arrived in the evening and helped Thomas settle me in for the night.

March 23
8:22 It was a restless night. About midnight, Duc straightened my bedclothes. It felt as if every bone in my body was being shaken up. I do appreciate that he's made a place for himself in the adjacent room.
9:12 Needed pain relief. Rang for Duc. He returned with ice water and two pills. I told him my bladder was full. He brought a bed pan and urinal. It's clear, now, that I'll pass the days never leaving this room.
10:47 Duc straightened my sheets and fluffed the pillows.
10:57 Thomas came in with a cup of black tea, then opened the phonograph. "Beethoven's Symphony No. 1," he said. "From the *Bicentennial Collection*." For a while, my spirits were lifted.
12:28 I napped for a good hour before Duc inquired about lunch. I said I had no desire to eat. He returned with a hot cup of broth from Thomas' soup. It was heavenly. I sipped it slowly and took two of the pills.
2:45 I napped until needing to relieve myself. Duc helped and then turned me to the right. Not long after, I rang and asked that he turn me back.
3:45 Duc turned me to the right. I told him I would not stop there long and asked that he come back soon. It distressed me to run him around so much. This sorrowful unrest is leaving its trace on him.
5:40 Thomas asked if I might want a meal. I requested toast and canned peaches. It went down relatively well.
6:10 A few minutes after Thomas left, I called for Duc to turn me again.
6:12 Called for Duc again. I needed the pills. He asked if I wished for anything else. "I have everything," I told him. "Nothing is wanting. You and Thomas are kind and loving. No man could have more than that. Bless you always."

7:33 Thomas sat with me. We listened to Beethoven's 2nd and 3rd. I drifted off.

10:19 Duc brought ice water and two pills, then tucked me in. Pulling the chair up beside me, he read from the book, "Through your blessing, grace, and guidance, through the power of the light that streams from you, may all my negative karma, destructive emotions, obscurations, and blockages be purified and removed . . ."

11:35 Called for Duc. No request for water or sherry. I remarked, "I don't like death - it is so white; so still."

March 24

8:18 The night was bad. About the worst of any. Duc said it was time to better address my pain. "I have a tincture. We will start with a few drops under your tongue. You'll let me know if it works." He then began Symphony No. 4 and asked if there was anything I needed. "Not for now, Duc, but tell me, what do you believe to be the essence of wisdom?" He parted the curtains slightly, then responded, "When spring comes, the grass grows by itself."

8:28 Drowsy. Looked at the watch Emerson gave me. I've never paid attention to the sweeping hand. It moves so quickly - accelerating, it seems, before my eyes.

11:17 Woke to a knock. It was Thomas. "Just checking in, Walt. Was the tincture effective?" I told him it's much better than the pills. "Excellent! There is no need for you to suffer. By the way, if you're up to it, let's have a conversation this evening." I said I'd like that, as dying can be very boring. On his way out, he replaced discs and started No. 5.

12:07 A light knock. It was Duc. "How is your pain, Walt?" I told him the tincture was wearing off. He removed the bottle from under his robe. "Let's increase the amount a little. I'll return in twenty minutes with lunch."

12:28 Broth again. I still had an appetite for it. Duc cleaned my tray, replacing bowl and spoon with scissors and a mirror. "It's time to clean you up, Walt. You hold the mirror to keep me honest." Duc is a master. His hands and scissors drifting over my beard like a mist. I would have thought he was accomplishing nothing but for the residue accumulating on my bib. His skill is reminiscent of the butcher in Chuang's tale of his grandfather. Setting the scissors aside, Duc took up a brush and combed my hair and remaining whiskers vigorously. He then washed my face and hands with a scented soap before leaving me to nap.

5:19 I slept. Too long, probably. I don't believe I turned once, judging by the crick in my neck. In considerable pain, I rang for Duc. The tincture is a godsend. Thousands would have been spared an agonizing death had it been available during the War.

6:00 Coughing uncontrollably. Duc came right away, adjusting bedclothes, sheets, pillows. It helped. He has a knack for doing the right thing at the right time. I asked if I might have toast and canned peaches for dinner. He was back in a minute.

7:14 Thomas knocked. "Is it a good time to visit, Walt?" "Always," I replied. He entered with hands full. Two glasses with ice and orange, and a bottle of Harveys. I was tickled by his thoughtfulness. For minutes we sat in silence, listening to No. 6 and reflecting on our time together. I believe the year has been as important for Thomas as it's been for me. Seeing that my glass was empty he replenished it, and then posed an end-of-life question: "What do you want to remember, Walt?" "For later?" I asked. "Certainly. The better you remember with intention, the better those memories will follow you. The exception, of course, are memories of regret. They follow no matter what." He suggested I write, and so I began: The sky. The sun's birth at dawn. The moon and stars. Mother Earth. Her animals, plants, and trees, and their histories. My mother and how she gave me life. My father and siblings, as well. Thomas, Molly, Kicus, Emerson, Isis, and Lao. All who have influenced me. Having finished, I read the list over and over, treasuring each word and accompanying image.

11:25 Called for Duc. Apologized for waiting so long. I lifted my tongue as he retrieved the bottle. We then rehearsed the Phowa until I drifted off.

March 25

1:10 Turned to right.

1:15 Turned to left.

2:15 To right.

2:30 Much pain. Left again, then the tincture.

3:25 Took bread and milk. It was good. Duc remarked that I was "afloat." I responded, "Like a ship or duck?"

7:52 Considerable pain. Rang for Duc. Tincture increased.

8:20 Drowsy. Thomas in and took my hand, but I had no remarks. Sipped on milk punch.

9:27 Duc asked if I would have breakfast. I declined. He tidied the room and found an envelope to my attention. Almost a year ago, Thomas wrote, ". . . I look forward to making your acquaintance."

9:34 Rang for Duc to be turned. He then read from the book, "Now when the bardo of dying dawns upon me, I will abandon all grasping, yearning, and attachment . . ." Drifted off.

10:03 Woke to a vision. I was with old man Wordsworth. Old, but not as feeble as me. He was in a chair, his arm resting on a book. The open window looked upon a mountain valley in autumn. I felt a presence that disturbed me with the joy of elevated thoughts. A sense of something sublime and deeply interfused. It's dwelling was the light of setting suns, and the round ocean and the living air, and the blue sky, and in the mind of man. I discerned a motion and a spirit that impels all thinking things, all objects of thought, and rolls through all things. The sun set and I slept peacefully for a time.

11:22 Restless. Thomas in. I told him, "I am sapped, nothing is left, only a last flickering spark, somewhere." He took my hand and calmed me, then asked if I'd like Symphony No. 7. I said yes and thanked him.

12:17 Feeling very poorly. Needed relief and called for Duc.

5:12 Awoke from nothingness. Much pain, but no fear. Lifted my tongue for Duc.

5:30 Duc urged me to take some broth. I rejected the idea, telling him, "I cannot eat." The processes of decay go on.

6:10 Woke to a thick rattling in my throat, my breathing quick and labored. Thomas was beside me and touched my head. I slept, recalling solemn moments.

8:19 Called for Duc. "Over" was all I could manage. He turned and covered me, then lifted me a little higher. I thanked him, "Any change is good."

9:20 Pain. Called for Duc. Tincture again.

9:45 Thomas in. "How can I help, Walt?" I asked him to play the 8th. Midway, I wondered if he might find the passage from Leaves, about the time after Lincoln's passing. Holding the volume so I might follow along, he read slowly, "When lilacs last in the dooryard bloom'd, and the great star early droop'd in the western sky in the night, I mourn'd, and yet shall mourn with ever-returning spring. Ever-returning spring, trinity sure to me you bring, lilac blooming perennial and drooping star in the west, and thought of him I love . . ."

11:59 Called to be turned. "Duc, please put me a little higher. I don't rest any way I am put, but a change now and then relieves the terrible pressure." Sipped on the brandy punch. Pushed the bedclothes back. They're so heavy, and I'm so very weak. No power to clear my throat. It grows worse and worse. Duc administered the drops, then washed my face with a warm cloth.

March 26

1:26 Pain. Too much. Duc and Thomas with me. Took the tincture and two pills. Duc washed my face. Thomas my feet and hands.

1:58 Much better. Quiet in the house. I believe there will be a certain freedom when it's over.

4:42 Can't sleep. No sadness - just the uncertainty.

4:45 Rang for Duc. Needing the tincture.

5:07 Thomas in. Thanked him for everything. I was very teary. Thomas as well.

5:15 Drowsy. Fragments of what's to come float by.

7:36 Cloudy. Rain this afternoon. It's a good day to die. More tincture.

8:12 Black tea and an egg for breakfast. I'll miss the hens. Thomas asked if I was ready for the 9th. I told him not yet. Duc opened the window a crack. I listened.

11:00 Duc asked to wash me. I said "no," but he gently insisted.

11:56 Lunch. Tea and tincture. Thomas read from *Leaves*. Symphony No. 9 playing.

12:27 Thomas back. Just off the phone with Ling. "Walt, Ling is pregnant with twins. She's fine." Teary again. It's fascinating how nature continues the process of life through different individuals. Life is renewed in that way, I suppose.

1:19 A vision. Standing again in the field with long grasses; in the center, the lone tree. I was the tree, a vessel for the great cycles. Summer, a distant memory. Autumn nearly over. Winter soon to begin.

4:25 Rang but could say no more - totally exhausted. Wished to be lifted.

4:45. Called to have pillows changed. Motioned to be lifted higher and have my feet put out of bed.

5:06 Sweating dreadfully. Asked Thomas to wipe my face, adding "please" after he commenced. Wanted to say more but too weak.

6:00 Heard Duc tell Thomas, "This is the last. Walt is dying." Duc put a hot water bag on my feet. Breathing faster and weaker. I could say nothing.

6:07 Duc and Thomas just beyond the door. "Thomas, it is nearly over." I looked toward the window and closed my eyes. Thomas took my hand and held it, as if it was his last touch of my life. I breathed on, more lightly, more quickly - my mouth now and then twitching.

6:17 Duc and Thomas on the bed. Molly and Kicus, too. Duc spoke softly, "May you know yourself forgiven for all the harm you may have thought and done. May you die a good and peaceful death. And through the triumph of your death, benefit all other beings, living or dead."

6:23 Duc lighted a candle. "This light will guide you on your journey, Walt." Thomas leaned down and kissed me hand and head, "Remember, Walt. Remember everything."
6:24 Knock at the door. "Walt, it's Ralph. Ralph Emerson. It's time to go."

At 6:25 he emitted a marked "Oh!" and seemed to stop breathing. Harned exclaiming, "It is all over." McAlister announced, "No, his heart still beats." After a struggle again there was a flutter of life. At 6:28 came a long gasp—we all took it to be the last. The Doctor cried, "A candle—let me have a candle." And by its light peered at W. For a minute breath was suspended. At 6:29 another slight heave of the chest, a twist of the mouth and a labored breath. Here his eyes opened but gave no sign of recognitions and languorously closed again. These were the final flickerings of life—a breath again at 6:30, 6:31 (three here overlapping each other), at 6:32 and at 6:34—and this was the last. Harned turned his head away—I heard a choked sob from Mrs. Davis— and nearby was Warrie, still eagerly observant, but with a mixed sigh and cry in his throat. "Is he gone?" I looked at McAlister, who had his head low over W.'s breast. "The heart still beats." But there seemed no pulse. "Put your fingers here," he counselled; and I did so, and caught the feathery beat, as a gentle breeze on silk. (When I first took W.'s hand the palm was warm and its back cold—and I touched his head, which was cold.) And so Warrie felt—and so Harned—and still the life seemed to stay. "He is dead!" said McAlister, "practically dead—see," and he lifted the fallen eyelid and touched the ball of the eye, which was fixed and showed no sense of impact. But at 6:43 came the last. The heart was still! No contortion, no struggle, no physical regret—and the eyes closed of themselves and the body made none of the usual motions towards stiffening out—towards rigidity. By and by McAlister and I together laid him decently and reverently straight. I laid his hand quietly down—something in my heart seemed to snap and that moment commenced my new life—a luminous conviction lifting me with him into the eternal. Harned murmured, "It is done," and I could not but exclaim, "It is triumph and escape." The life had gone out at sunset— the light of day not yet utterly gone—the last rays floating with timid salutation into the gloom. The Doctor had said to me, "He's likely to stretch out," but there was no effort—not the first trace. One time when the breath got slow there came a sigh and almost sob, perhaps only the reflex pressure of the air—all was peaceful, beautiful, calm, fitting. The day clouded—a light drip of rain now descending. I leaned down and kissed him, hand and head—and then I went out, shadowed, into the penetrating night.

26th of March 1892 - Horace Traubel

THE FINAL JOURNEY

I'd heard stories of the soul looking down on its body. Of long, dark
tunnels with a brilliant light at the end. Of hurtling through space toward
some unknown destination. I experienced none of that. No sooner did
my heart beat its last than I was in the Hall of Maat. The line was long
but moving efficiently. Far ahead was the Great Balance. One by one
hearts were weighed. Those too heavy were determined unjust and
devoured immediately by Ammit. A frightening scene. I endeavored to
divert my attention to those around me. Most were of my generation, but
every age and land was represented. Despite the multitude of languages,
I understood every word. There was a common sentiment that the end
had come too soon – without warning and the opportunity to prepare.
Many had died of the virus, on the street or in overcrowded hospitals. I
felt a great sadness and was again humbled by the gift given me by
Emerson. Sooner than I would have liked, I was next. Isis, just a few
feet away, looked upon me with compassion but betrayed not a hint of
the outcome. My heart, scarcely different than any other, was placed on
one of two scales. On the second, an ostrich feather. Immediately, my
heart and its scale dropped toward the floor. In the next instance,
however, it rebounded, and the feather dropped. Back and forth the
scales danced as I stood mute and trembling. Finally, they stopped, the
scales in equal balance. Were it not in poor taste, I would have jumped
for joy. Instead, I was directed toward a short line under the purview of
Horus, son of Isis. He explained that we'd depart once there were twenty
and two of us. After a while, the last joined our ranks and we arrived at
Sekhet Hetepet, the Happy Fields. Osiris, God of the afterlife, greeted
us. He held a tablet on which were listed our names alphabetically.
When announced, a man or woman, elder or child, would approach and
he would whisper in their ear. They would walk on, traveling alone on
one of many possible roads. Then it was just the two of us. With a voice
as deep and firm as any I'd ever heard, he called, "Walt Whitman, Poet."
I approached. "Sir, look beyond me and to the right. Do you see the
twin peaks?" Though far in the distance, I did see them, at an elevation
significantly greater than our present location. "You will take the path

257

leading toward them. At the pass that separates the two, you will be given further instructions." I said nothing but fretted that I would not be up to the task. Recognizing my concern, Osiris placed a hand on my shoulder. "Dear fellow, you must know as well as anyone, that the path to heaven does not lie down in flat miles, it is in the imagination with which we perceive the world, and the gestures with which we honor it." I was buoyed by his counsel, yet still hesitant, harboring a concern that I might lose my way. He responded to my thoughts, "It is not possible. There is only one path for you. It has always been that way. And you must know by now that your friend will be at your side. The one who has loved you all your life, who knows you by heart. Trust him and you will not stray." I thanked this most benevolent of gods and bid him farewell. Time passed quickly, as there was much to see and talk about. The sun had traveled mid-way in its daily journey when we were stopped at the pass by a lone sentry. "Welcome, you are nearly there." Politely, I inquired as to where "there" was. "You are now beyond all ideas of wrongdoing and rightdoing." He then turned and pointed to a patch of green not far off. "Do you see the field? You will be met there where your soul can lie down in the long grass." We continued on and soon could see the outlines of a broad meadow. By late afternoon it was apparent that a gathering was taking place, a celebration perhaps. As we drew closer, I could make out the figures. Mother and Father. Jesse, Mary Elizabeth, Hannah Louisa, Andrew, George, Thomas and Edward. Grandpa Cornelius and Grandma Naomi. Harned, Warrie, Mary, Mrs. Davies were there too. And Horace, dear friend Horace. Off to the side was Isis, and many she had introduced me to. Socrates, Seneca, the young French girl, the young boy Trayvon, Dr. King and Mr. Lincoln. The woman from the hospital was seated with her soul mate. He holding her hand as I did. Suddenly there was a murmur among the guests, as they made room for three figures approaching from the rear. It was C.G. and Chuang - and Emerson. Taking center stage, Emerson asked that everyone be seated. Out of nowhere, a chair and small table appeared. "Sit here, Walt." He then turned to the crowd. As if on cue, they each raised a glass of wine, and raised their voices as well.

"Welcome Home Walt!"

ABOUT THE AUTHOR

Fred Van Liew is the author of two works of non-fiction, *The Justice Diary* and *A Third Half Journal*. He makes his home in Des Moines, Iowa, with his wife and two dogs, Wilma and Molly. Fred and Jen have five children and four grandchildren. A retired lawyer, Fred is active as a mediator and facilitator of peacemaking circles and travels to Portland, Maine, on a regular basis to work with the Portland Center for Restorative Justice.

Made in the USA
Middletown, DE
23 January 2022

59382354R00149